Lying on Sunday

A NOVEL

SHARON K. SOUZA

Mary ~
Follow Truth! Blessings,
Sharon

NAVPRESS

NAVPRESS⬤

NavPress is the publishing ministry of The Navigators, an international Christian organization and leader in personal spiritual development. NavPress is committed to helping people grow spiritually and enjoy lives of meaning and hope through personal and group resources that are biblically rooted, culturally relevant, and highly practical.

For a free catalog go to www.NavPress.com
or call 1.800.366.7788 in the United States or 1.800.839.4769 in Canada.

© 2008 by Sharon K. Souza

ISBN-13: 978-1-60006-176-9
ISBN-10: 1-60006-176-1

Cover design by The DesignWorks Group, David Uttley, www.thedesignworksgroup.com
Cover image by Steve Gardner, PixelWorks Studios
Author photo by Lisa Lesch
Creative Team: Rachelle Gardner, Darla Hightower, Kathy Mosier, Arvid Wallen, Kathy Guist

Published in association with the Books and Such Literary Agency, 52 Mission Circle, Suite 122, PMB 170, Santa Rosa, CA 95409-5370, www.booksandsuch.biz.

This novel is a work of fiction. Names, characters, places, and incidents are either the product of the author's imagination or are used fictitiously. Any resemblance to actual events, locales, organizations, or persons, living or dead, is entirely coincidental and beyond the intent of either the author or publisher.

Most Scripture quotations in this publication are taken from the HOLY BIBLE: NEW INTERNATIONAL VERSION® (NIV®). Copyright © 1973, 1978, 1984 by International Bible Society. Used by permission of Zondervan Publishing House. All rights reserved. The other version used is the King James Version (KJV).

Library of Congress Cataloging-in-Publication Data

Souza, Sharon K.
  Lying on Sunday : a novel / Sharon K. Souza.
     p. cm.
  ISBN-13: 978-1-60006-176-9
  ISBN-10: 1-60006-176-1
  1. Widows--Fiction. 2. Adultery--Fiction. 3. Forgiveness--Fiction.
I. Title.
  PS3619.O94L95 2008
  813'.6--dc22

                              2008010257

Printed in the United States of America

1 2 3 4 5 6 7 8 9 10 / 12 11 10 09 08

"A moving drama in the tradition of *The Pilot's Wife*. Sharon K. Souza is a talented author who never fails to impress."

— KATHRYN CUSHMAN, author of *A Promise to Remember* and
Waiting for Daybreak

"*Lying on Sunday* is the sensitive portrait of a woman's transformation and healing after a devastating loss. Funny, poignant, real to the bone. You won't want to put it down."

— DEBRA FULLER THOMAS, author of
Tuesday Night at the Blue Moon

"How do you get your life back when you've lost the joy of living so slowly you never noticed it was gone? Main character Abbie Torrington will lead you on an insightful, funny, heartbreaking path of self-discovery that will leave you eager to read more, much more from Sharon K. Souza. You're going to love *Lying on Sunday*!"

— KATHLEEN POPA, author of *To Dance in the Desert*

For Deanne and Mindy, *my* girls

Acknowledgments

Rick, again I want to say that your enthusiasm and encouragement for my writing mean everything. It's why you're holding this book in your hand. We've been through much since that day in November so long ago. I'm just glad we've been through it together.

Mindy and Deanne, you are the joys of my life. (Don't tell Brian.) I feel like I'm skipping down the yellow brick road, and you two and Dad are with me. We'll all have to figure out who we are, but, Deanne, you are *not* the cowardly lion!

Wendy Lawton, thank you for all you do and for your high praise, which blows me away. You're so much more than an agent. You're a friend, and I'm thankful for you.

Rachelle Gardner and Kathy Mosier, as my editors you make it too easy, but thank you. Kris Wallen and everyone at NavPress, thank you for making my publishing experience so positive. It's a pleasure to work with all of you.

Katy Popa, here we are again. Do you believe it?

"For it is God who works in you to will and to act according to his good purpose" (Philippians 2:13). Thank you, Lord.

One

The Chiffons were singing "One Fine Day" on the golden oldies XM Radio station. And it was. One of those rare August days when a front moves into the valley, knocking the temperature down a good twenty degrees with a chime-rattling breeze, a gift from the ocean two hours west. This blustery hullabaloo in the heavens offered a respite from the hundred-plus days so typical of August in Granite Bay, a town on Folsom Lake, northeast of Sacramento at the base of the Sierra foothills. It was summer without the sizzle. The colors all primary.

The windows and doors were open throughout the house, the air conditioner off for the first time in two months, and I was baking a chocolate cheesecake for Becca's birthday. Our baby was eighteen and leaving for college. But I put that thought right out of my mind every chance I got. I still had ten glorious days in which to enjoy my full quiver, small though it was.

Bailey, our firstborn, had made the same trek a year before, paving the way for her sister. The more adventurous of our girls hands down, Bailey left without a single backward glance, though she did call home for money and advice on a regular basis. Money from me, the easy touch; advice from her father, the wise one. And she came home every holiday and vacation. That had more to do with Tim McGuire than anything, but I liked to think the tie that binds hadn't completely unraveled yet.

Becca was more timid about that first real independent step. College she faced with excitement, but leaving home brought trepidation. If Cal Poly hadn't been nearly six hours away, she'd have forgone dorm life and commuted, a fact that left Bailey absolutely speechless. A mama's girl, she'd taunt, but that wasn't the truth. Becca was and always had been the wink in her daddy's eye—well, once Trey got over the shock that I was pregnant a second time in a year. But by her first birthday she'd charmed her way into his heart. I mean, who could resist those dimples and a face the shape of a perfect valentine?

Our girls are as different as oranges and figs. Both sweet in their own way, but Bailey definitely has a tartness to her that Becca doesn't have. And a boldness that terrifies me. From the time she could talk, I've never known what would come out of her mouth, only that it would probably embarrass or stupefy. Like the time years ago when Trey's best friend, Adam, came for a Saturday barbecue with the latest pearl in a long string of purely sensual date choices. Trey barely had the burgers flipped when Bailey, three, looked at the young woman in her Daisy Mae shorts and kerchief halter and said, "What's a bimbo?" I thought it humorous myself, but Trey, out of whose mouth the original quote had come, turned pomegranate red while Adam went chasing after his date.

We had plenty of leftovers that night.

My girls amaze me, and for the longest time all I could think was that they were fortunate to have dipped in Trey's gene pool a bit longer than mine.

I've had cause to reconsider.

Anyway, Trey had been in Dallas for the week, like he was for five days every six weeks, and, as always, I felt as liberated as a size-eight foot slipping out of a size-seven shoe. But I can handle only so much freedom before I crave routine, so I was ready for the normalcy his return always brought. Besides, it was Becca's birthday and I couldn't wait to show him the laptop we'd gotten her.

Mother and Dad were coming at five, right when the girls got in from their summer jobs as baristas at Starbucks. That would give Trey and me a few minutes alone before everyone arrived, assuming his plane was on time and traffic from the airport wasn't too heavy. But this was Friday, and that was a lot to hope for.

Mother and Dad, now in their late sixties, still live in the house I grew up in on the *established* side of Fair Oaks, a Sacramento suburb. The houses there are ranch style, which popped up all over town in the sixties, and have on average a half-acre of back-yard sprawling under trees as old as me.

In contrast, our home on Wexford Circle sits on one acre and is chock-full of all the latest amenities. Granite kitchen, marble bathrooms with the finest in Jacuzzi tubs, six bedrooms, seven baths, four fireplaces, media room with wall-to-wall screen and eight theater seats, continuous heat flow underneath the floors, central vac. Extravagant built-in barbecue and nature pool. And from the upstairs sitting room, a perfect view of the lake. Believe me, that upped the price of the lot.

Mother has talked for a decade about selling their rancher to downsize, particularly the yard. Lately Dad has begun to do some repairs and I know it's only a matter of time. A swell of panic starts in the pit of my stomach whenever I think about someone else's pictures hanging on our walls. So I do my best not to think about it. All that borrowing trouble and stuff. But if I had my way I'd snatch it up in a minute and leave the high life to those more suited to it.

I'm lucky to still have Mother and Dad, no matter where they live. Shawlie Bryson, my best friend since second grade, was ten when her father left and thirty-something when her mother died. A late-life child, Shawlie has no siblings. That she knows of.

Shawlie and I have been on the wrong side of forty for a year and a half now. She's been married twice, and as Shawlie would say, "You'd think there was a fifty-fifty chance that one of the lechers would not have graduated from the same school of morals and ethics as my father. But no." And so she enjoys her single-ness and swears she'll not marry again until she needs someone to pluck her chin hairs.

Like that would ever happen.

Shawlie is not just beautiful. She's Michelle Pfeiffer, one-in-a-million beautiful, where every right gene fell into place, like the tumblers of a combination lock. Click. Click. Click. And the real beauty is that she doesn't flaunt it. I've always thought she could have been my daughters' mother because they're beauties too. Except that Shawlie dislikes—and that's shining a positive light on the picture—my husband. Robert Andrew Torrington the Third. Trey to everyone. RAT to Shawlie—always in caps—but only in my presence. To his face she calls him Rob, the word marvelously extended and spoken like an indictment. They make it a rule to avoid one another whenever possible. Hence, Shawlie dropped Becca's present off the night before. She wasn't coming for dinner.

I planned taco salad for Becca's birthday, her request, along with fresh cantaloupe from the fruit stand on the south edge of town. And, of course, a bowl of strawberries because they would only be in season a few more days. But I didn't have to start any of that until the afternoon. I reached over and turned up the volume on the radio. I love The Chiffons. And The Supremes, The Shirelles, The Dixie Cups, all those girl bands from way back when. It doesn't matter that most of them had hits before I was even born. I grew up listening to them on the oldies station with my dad while he worked in the garage or when he'd drive me to school. We were karaoke before karaoke was cool, Dad and me.

I like the newer oldies too. The ones from my own generation: U2, Phil Collins, Bon Jovi. And I like how satellite radio lets me choose which decade I want to listen to. Today it was the sixties. And, yes, it was one fine day. Right up to the time the phone rang.

"Abigail Torrington?"

"Yes, that's me." Inwardly I groaned. It sounded like one of those survey calls that takes half a day. When would I learn to check caller ID before I picked up? I could hear Bailey saying those very words in my mind. "But I'm sorry, I don't have time—"

"This is the nursing supervisor at Sharp Memorial Hospital in San Diego, California."

"Nurs— Hosp— San Di—" I sputtered like a hot steam iron, all the while trying to figure out what this call had to do with me.

"Is this Mrs. Torrington?" The voice was rife with authority and brought me to attention.

"Yes," I said, then said it again because the first yes came out a whisper.

"Mrs. Robert Torrington?" The emphasis was on Robert.

I dropped onto the bar stool where I conduct much of my casual phone conversations with Shawlie and others, flipping through recipe books and jotting down grocery lists as we chat.

All the mundane things that I love so well. But this was no casual call.

"Yes," I said again. Now my heart was beating like those bass tones you hear coming from vehicles with windows too dark to see through.

"Mrs. Torrington, your husband was brought into our emergency room early this morning. In cardiac arrest. We were unable to revive him. I'm very sorry."

I cocked my head like a sparrow, trying to think who would find this type of joke funny. Trey? Cardiac arrest? *San Diego?* "I really think you might have the wrong Mrs. Torrington. My husband, *Trey*, is in Dallas. Well"—I glanced at the clock on the microwave—"on his way home from. Before long."

There was a pause on the other end of the line and I could hear the shuffling of papers. "Robert Andrew Torrington, date of birth 5-11-58? Social Security 563—"

A little whimper worked its way out of my throat as fear began to constrict my torso. "You . . . you're sure?"

"Mrs. Torrington, I'm very, very sorry." There was a pause. "There are several mortuaries we work with in your county. If you would select one from the list someone will contact you to make arrangements to bring Mr. Torrington home."

"Mortu—" The timer went off on my cheesecake. "It's Becca's birthday."

"Mrs. Torrington, I'll call back in a few minutes. Give you some time to . . . I'm very sorry."

The continuous beeping sounded through a fog and I rose from the bar stool. Without recall after the fact, I went through the motions, quieting the timer, placing the cheesecake on a cooling rack, turning off the oven. Then returned to my position on the stool. Looked at the notes I'd jotted: *Rob And Torr. 5-11-58. Card arr.*

That's when the uppercut came, knocking the wind right out of me. I gasped, but the most sickening feeling I'd ever had kept my lungs from opening to receive the breath. My vision began to recede as sparklers crackled inside my head. I was going down, not with a thud, but sinking, as if I were melting from the feet up. I didn't faint but came as close to an out-of-body experience a soul can undergo without actually achieving that phenomenon. I was a spectator, watching myself come unglued. My mouth worked like a guppy. I needed to breathe, breathe, bre—

My lungs opened up, reviving me with oxygen, sending a sharp pain to my brain. And my heart, "Trey." It's all I could say. All I could think. Trey. He wasn't coming home.

And it was Becca's birthday.

Was this some kind of cosmic *Candid Camera*? I looked around suddenly, as if everyone would jump out of hiding and yell, "Surprise!" "Gotcha." "Gotcha good."

I climbed back up to my stool, a furious trembling in my arms and legs. Caller ID gave me the number and I dialed it.

"Sharp Memorial Hospital. How may I direct your call?"

It wasn't a joke. I blinked away more firecrackers, forced myself not to hyperventilate, and squeaked into the phone, "I . . . I need . . . someone from . . . they said my husband died."

Perkiness gave way to professionalism. "Let me connect you with our nursing supervisor. One moment."

"Ms. Waters," she announced. It was the same official voice I'd heard before. "Hello?"

"It's Abigail Torrington."

"Oh. Yes. Mrs. Torrington."

"I just wanted— Then it's— He's really—" Sputter,

sputter, sputter.

"Would you like to discuss the" — her pause was practiced — "arrangements?"

"Can you tell me? What happened?"

"Certainly." I heard the shuffle of papers again. "He was brought into emergency at 5:18 this morning. In cardiac arrest."

"That means his heart wasn't beating?"

"Correct."

"But, but, he's in Dallas."

The silence on the other end of the line said otherwise.

"He is. Supposed to be." I felt myself turn gray. Felt all the blood drop to my toes. "Who brought? Was anyone — ?"

"He came by ambulance. Let me see. Unattended."

"Alone?"

"It would seem."

"From where?"

"The ambulance company would have that information. Dr. Stillman was the attending ER physician. I assure you he did everything he could."

Stillman. Everything. I wrote every major word she spoke in my own form of shorthand. I would need it. To tell the others.

"I see there was one inquiry made by a person who arrived shortly after the ambulance, but — " Ms. Waters paused a little too long. "She didn't leave a name. We assumed, well, she wasn't there when Dr. Stillman went out to speak with her."

I swallowed a sob. "She?"

"Mrs. Torrington, is there someone you can call? A friend, a minister?"

"Call?" Of course! I said good-bye, then went to the numbers stored in my phone, starting from the bottom and working up. When I came to Trey I engaged the number for his cell phone, my heart pounding out a savage beat. The call went immediately to voice mail.

"Well, of course. He's on an airplane. All phones off." Right? *Right?*

She has his date of birth. And his Social Security number.

But he's on a plane. Coming home.

A millennium might have passed in the moments that followed. As if time and tide had come to a screeching halt at last. For Trey. My Trey. I couldn't stop the tears. I soaked everything in sight, then soaked it all again. But a niggling thought kept poking itself into my consciousness, like a prairie dog popping up in the desert, here, there, everywhere. *San Diego. San Diego. San Diego.*

I knew he had no business dealings there, and that fact generated the tiniest bit of hope in my heart. Impossible though it seemed, this had to be a mistake. I calmed myself, blew my nose, and reached for the phone. It took only a minute or so until I was connected to American Airlines.

"No, I don't have the flight number." His travel had become so routine over the years he no longer worried about giving me an itinerary. He left on Monday, spent the week at corporate headquarters, came home on Friday. Every six weeks. "He's a passenger on the flight from Dallas that arrives in Sacramento somewhere around three this afternoon." I gripped a pencil, waiting to write down the information that would make this nightmare go away. "Robert A. Torrington. Double-r-i-n— Yes. Torrington."

Suddenly it wasn't so cool. I flipped on the ceiling fan and waited for the man on the other end of the phone to put an end to the madness. "Yes, from Dallas. He's a reg— Are you sure?" I was trembling again and trying not to let it sound in my voice.

"Is . . . is there another flight?"

He said it would take only a few moments to run Trey's name through their computer. And he was right. It didn't take long to confirm that Robert A. Torrington was a passenger on American Airlines flight number 1282. From San Diego. Direct to Sacramento. At one that afternoon.

Two

Feeble. I knew exactly what it meant in that moment. Altogether inadequate. I stared at the phone in my ice-cold hand as if that would somehow change the information I'd received. With hope fading like a winter sun I dialed the local number for Washington Mutual Insurance, Trey's home office.

Trey was not just an insurance salesman. He was an award-winning insurance salesman. He conducted seminars for the company, earned extravagant trips, was the top in his field. A salesman's salesman. His success put us in the top 5 percent of U.S. wage earners. Admittedly, at the lowest level of that top, but with room to grow. Trey thrived on the challenge.

He had three years in with Washington Mutual when we married. A degree in business and a mind that turned numbers like a computer, he was well on his way. We purchased our first home a month before the wedding, bought "up" eight years later when the housing market was soft, and sold house number one five years after that when the prices soared. Those funds went into the girls' already burgeoning college funds. Then, just because we could, Trey purchased a lot in the best development in Granite Bay, hired an architect, and went to work on our dream house. The dream was mostly his, but I didn't mind going along for the ride. And here we'd been for the last six of our twenty years together.

I'd wondered what Trey would do with both girls going off to school now, if he'd think about another move. But, happily, he'd not so much as hinted at the idea. We were so very settled. And the valley oak in the front yard was a century-old work of art.

I pressed the extension for Trey's secretary, Theo. She answered on the second ring. "Abbie, nice to hear your voice. Hey, tell Becca happy birthday, will you? Eighteen and college bound. Oh, those were the days, huh?" The normalcy of her voice, rich as velvet cake, soothed me. I took heart.

"Theo, would there be any reason for Trey to be in San Diego this week? You know, for . . . for work? Instead of Dallas?" There was a frightening little pause and my pulse quickened.

"Well, Abbie, he hasn't been to Dallas in months. Not since he passed the training sessions on to Wilson. That was back in January." Now her voice was faltering as badly as mine.

"January?"

"I believe."

"And . . . and San Diego?"

"Gee, I don't know anything about San Diego. He's been in the central valley this week. Like usual."

My mind was not getting around this information.

"Abbie? Hello?"

The phone was heavy in my hand. I turned it off and laid it on the counter, all the while trying to sort information I had no ready place for. I wanted to dial Trey's cell phone again, but I needed a minute to summon the energy. Altogether inadequate. That was me.

Suddenly the handset began to ring, its little screen throwing off a pale green light. Incoming call, it said, as if a verbal grenade had been launched my way. Lord, I couldn't take another hit. An instant later it revealed Shawlie's name and number.

"Shawlie?" The panic that had been building was unleashed in that simple utterance.

"Hey, girl, I— Abbie? What's wrong?"

"Shawlie." I was unraveling like a knitted sock, with no way to pick up the stitch.

"Are you hurt? Sick? Should I call an—"

I choked out a no.

"I'll be there in five minutes. Five minutes, Abbie."

Relief came like a trade wind. I could hold on that long. And then Shawlie would know just what to do.

She let herself in, calling my name as she hurried through the front of the house toward the kitchen. She took me and the room in with one quick glance, ecstatic, I could tell, not to find blood everywhere. "What on earth?"

"It's Trey." My face scrunched, my chin quivered. "They say he's—" I just couldn't finish it.

"What, sweetie, what do they say?" Suddenly, both hands covered her heart. "Oh my. A crash? A plane crash? Oh, Abbie—"

I shook my head fiercely. "No. No. Not a crash. A heart attack." My voice fell to a whisper. "Shawlie, he's dead."

She crumpled onto a stool and exhaled all in one motion, her mouth a gaping cavern. "Dead?"

"I don't know what to do." A sob escaped. "How do I tell Becca?"

"Where is he? I mean, who called?"

"San Diego." I picked up the telephone and read back the name of the hospital.

"San Diego? I thought he was in Dallas."

I gave an empty shrug. "They have his Social Security number." As if that explained it.

"I don't know, Abbie. Are you sure there isn't a mistake?"

"Oh, Shawlie, do you think? I asked, but . . ." I shrugged again. "They have his number. And his birth date. It sounded so official."

"Who did you talk to?"

I showed her the number. "I don't remember her name. The nursing supervisor. Ask for her."

Shawlie did just that and was connected to the same woman who made the initial call. "I'm calling in regard to my brother-in-law, Robert Torrington." She turned and gave me a wink as she stretched the truth. "There seems to be some question about your Mr. Torrington's identity. Our Mr. Torrington has been in— Yes, I believe we have that number. Five-six-three—"

She jotted down the rest of the number and slid the paper in my direction. It was Trey's Social Security number, no question.

"Uh-huh, and— Yes, that's his birth date. But— Uh-huh. I see. Mortuary? Well what if, I mean, we get him up here and, well, you know, it isn't our Mr. Torrington?" She squinted as she listened, clicking the pen off and on. "You know, I'll just get back to you on that. Right. Thanks."

She turned a defeated gaze on me. "What's RAT's—Rob's— cell number?"

I dialed it, and together we listened as the call went right through to voice mail.

"Well, sweetie"—she looked at her watch—"he is on a plane. Supposedly."

I nodded, my heart filling with hope again.

"Did you call the office?"

Hope hit an invisible wall and tinkled to the ground in bits and pieces. My chin began to quiver again. "He wasn't in Dallas."

Shawlie's skin took on the color of paste. "What do you mean? Where was he?"

"The central valley," Theo said. "He hasn't been in Dallas"—I gulped—"all year."

She sat up and straightened her blazer. "What?"

"Theo said."

"You mean he's been lying to you? Abbie?"

"I don't know." I was unable to keep the tears from spilling. "I don't know what to think."

"Oh, honey, I'm sorry." Slight though she was she pulled me into a strong embrace. "We'll get to the bottom of this. We will."

The doorbell chimed "Ode to Joy," and we both turned. "I'll get it," Shawlie said.

I pulled a paper towel off the roll, wiped my eyes, and blew my nose. But the tears continued to come. I felt like I had a school of fish in the pit of my stomach. Mean fish engaged in a turf war. *Trey? Lying? To me?*

"Abbie." Shawlie nodded toward the front door and whispered, "Someone in a suit. Probably from the funeral home. "

"Funeral home? But we didn't call one."

Her shoulders lifted slightly. "He looks official."

I wiped my eyes again and followed her to the door.

"Mrs. Abigail Torrington?"

Well, that was the second time in less than an hour I'd been addressed by my official name. I motioned behind me, toward the phone in the kitchen. "I know. They called."

"Excuse me?"

"The hospital." I took a brave breath. "They already called. But I don't know if—"

"You are Mrs. Abigail Torrington?"

"Yes."

He extended a manila envelope toward me, which I accepted. Then he touched his brow in a little salute and nodded. "Have a good day, ma'am."

"A good day?" Shawlie and I said it in unison. I wondered if my face looked as bewildered as hers. "A good day?"

I clicked the front door shut and turned the deadbolt out of habit.

"What on earth?" Shawlie said.

I shrugged and crept back to the kitchen. Shunning the stool, I opted instead for a chair, unclasped the envelope, and tore open the sealed flap. I pulled out the pages and scanned the first paragraph of the cover letter. My heart skidded to a stop. Absolute and complete.

"I've been served divorce papers."

Three

Shawlie coaxed the letter out of my hand, studied it, then pulled out the chair next to me. "Of all people, I should have known."

"Okay, now I know this whole thing is a joke. And, I might add, not a funny one."

"Abbie, I don't know. It looks awfully official."

"Divorce?" I stood to pace, letter in hand. "You really think Trey would file for divorce? Everything's been so"—I swallowed the word *good*—"normal. And on Becca's birthday? No, this is someone's sick joke."

The letter was from J. Davis Balfour, attorney-at-law. I dialed the number on the letterhead. A sweet voice that could have belonged to either of my daughters said, "You have reached the law offices of J. Davis Balfour. If you know your party's extension you may enter it at any time. If you would like to hear this message in English, please press one. To hear it in—"

I pressed one.

"Please select from the following main menu. If you are a client of J. Davis Balfour, please press one."

"I'm not a client," I said into the phone, knowing full well there was no one to hear my sorrowful voice. "Give me another option."

"If you know your party's extension, you may enter it at any time. To return to the main menu, please press one."

"This *is* the main menu. I want option two."

"To return to the—"

I pressed one.

"You have reached the law offices of J. Davis Balfour. If you know your party's extension, you may enter it at any time."

"I don't!"

". . . hear this message in English, please—"

I pressed one again.

"Please select from the following main menu. If you are a client of J. Davis Balfour, please press one."

I quickly pressed one.

"Please enter your account number, followed by the pound sign."

"I don't have an account number. I just want to talk to J. Davis." Hysteria was setting in.

"If you know your party's extension, you may enter it at any time."

I punched the off button, breaking the tip of my index nail in the process.

"What?" Shawlie said.

The tears began to flow again. "They want an account number."

She took the phone from me and dialed the number. She listened, pressed one, one again, then zero. "Yes," she said, giving me a thumbs-up, "I have a question regarding a letter I received—Yes, from your office— No, I'm not a client. It appears my husband is— Mr. Balfour's voice mail would be fine." When she was connected to it, she left the following message: "This is Mrs. Robert Torrington. I received a letter from your office this morning along with"—she gave a sarcastic chuckle—"divorce papers. I believe this is a huge error on your part. I'd like you to call me at the earliest possible opportunity." She left my number and a curt thank you.

Our eyes locked in the crazy silence that followed. "Zero?" I asked.

She shrugged. "It usually gets you where you want to go."

"Oh," I said. "Shawlie, do you think—? Is this for real? I mean, what if he's really . . . dead?"

She brought a flat hand down on the manila envelope in front of me. "Well, if he's not, I'll kill him."

The phone rang, showing Balfour's name and number on the screen. I let Shawlie answer.

"Mr. Balfour, thank you for getting back so quickly. I received a letter today along with— Well, that's exactly what I thought." Her body relaxed as she mouthed the word *mistake* to me. "How could such an err— Yes, a gentleman— Just a few minutes ago— Excuse me? Ex*cuse* me?" She picked up the letter. "August 27— Yes, that's Monday. But— I see." The color drained completely from her face, and her lips got tight. "Well, then, you might like to know that"—she shifted her body away from me—"your client *won't* be keeping his next appointment." With that she hung up the phone.

"Shawlie, tell me. It can't possibly get any worse." I didn't believe that for one second, but I couldn't stand another moment of this.

She turned back to me and put a hand over mine, looking as pathetic as I'd ever seen her. "You weren't meant to get this . . . today. It was supposed to be served on Monday."

"Well, of course." I felt the earth drop out from under me. "Trey would never intentionally have done this on Becca's birthday."

Shawlie's eyes flashed with who knows what kind of comeback, but she kept it to herself. I had to give her that. She picked up the phone again. "I'm going to call your dad."

"Mother will answer."

"Then I'm going to call your mother."

"Wait. If you call Mother from my phone she'll think something's wrong."

Shawlie's forehead crinkled in the middle. "Abbie, something *is* wrong."

"I mean—" I was too dazed to explain. "Right. But wait! Shawlie, not a word about this." Meaning, of course, the divorce papers. "To anyone. Swear."

"Well, of course I swear." She made a locking-her-lips motion as if we were ten, then found my parents' number in the phone's directory.

I crammed everything back into the envelope. "You have to help me hide this. At least until— Oh, Lord. I have to choose a mortuary."

"Gebhardt, of course."

"Of course, Gebhardt. I just mean—"

"We'll let them figure it out. I'll call and explain. They must deal with this kind of thing all the time." She shrugged weakly. "Well, on occa— Mrs. Woodruff? Um, hi, it's Shawlie."

❧

Mother calls me Tippy. When I was less than two, she would sit me on my potty chair and leave me to my business. According to Mother, I would fold myself in half, with my little tush positioned over the bowl, my tummy flat against my thighs. And I'd push and strain, eager to produce. And then my eyes would light on something lovely, say the pearl polish Mother would dab on my teensy toenails. My fingers would reach to touch, and off I'd go. Literally. Tip right off the potty chair. She'd laugh, she said, until she cried.

I would like to have seen that. But that was in the days before Aunt Lizzy died, before Mother packed away the fun-loving version of herself, leaving Dad and me to deal with the one-dimensional woman who remained.

Trey calls — called — me Ab. At least in the last few years. That should have been a clue. Who calls the woman they love by a body part?

When we first started dating, he called me Abigail. Three lovely syllables pouring off his tongue as if it were new wine and he was savoring its bouquet. Just hearing him say it sent feelings through me I didn't know how to deal with, but then, everything about Trey did that. Like the way his lips pursed when he smiled. Or the way he'd send me a slow wink when no one else could see. Or run his finger over the palm of my hand, light as a whisper.

I was nineteen and a freshman at Sac State, having worked a year between high school and college. He was twenty-five and taking the express elevator to the pinnacle of the insurance world. I had no idea what I'd do with my degree once I earned it, but it would have everything to do with English. But sophomore year is as far as I got.

Trey and I were married in the fall of what would have been my sophomore year. In grand style, I might add. Trey had his eye on things aristocratic right from the start. He chose the church, a Sacramento crown jewel near the capitol, and paid for it too—an exorbitant fee, if you ask me, for the three hours we were there. It was neither of our denominations, not that we practiced religion. But I had always thought to marry in the church my parents dedicated me in.

The stained-glass "jewel" was ornate and cavernous, and I was certain my beating heart could be heard reverberating throughout its vacuous heights as I wedding-marched my way down the long aisle. *Ka-thump. Ka-thump.*

Trey had ideas about everything. Especially the family structure. He would bring home the dough. I would bake it and be only too happy to do so. And in five years, once Trey had earned a key to that express elevator, we'd have a son. Three years later, a daughter. They should be born in late summer so their ages would properly coincide with the beginning of the school year. Not too young to keep up with their classmates, nor too old to look as if they'd been held back.

Trey honestly thought this was doable. But my estrogen-rich body hadn't gotten the memo. I missed my first period exactly three months after our wedding. I cried all day. How could I possibly tell Trey that I'd already messed up his timeline? And on top of that, I was carrying a girl, which of course we didn't know at the time. At least she was born in September. I cooperated in that little regard.

Well, need I say that another pregnancy ten weeks after Bailey's birth was not cause to celebrate? And yet I did. Secretly. Not sharing my news with anyone until I could no longer hide it.

Trey brought out the "A" word as soon as he caught his breath. It was the basis for the worst fight we ever had. I defied him then and only then. Unless maintaining my friendship with Shawlie counts. And to see how Becca fought for and won the rightful place in her daddy's heart was my greatest triumph. He adored her.

And now he was gone. And it was her birthday.

"Tippy?" My mother rushed through the kitchen to where I sat and dropped her handbag onto the table. "Oh, Tippy. This is too cruel. How will we ever tell Becca?" Mother wept into a paper towel pulled from the roll hanging under my cabinets. "She'll never get over it. She just won't. And Bailey. Trey is everything to her."

Ah. Well, then.

"This is just too cruel."

Shawlie opened her mouth to speak, but I shot her down with a look. We both knew I was used to this.

"Baby." My father opened his arms to me. I stood and leaned into him, burying my sobs in his strong embrace, all the while thinking this could still be a mistake. Trey could walk through that door in time to witness our foolishness. And then he'd chide me for believing such a ridiculous story. And this time I'd deserve it.

Only it wasn't a mistake. And by eleven thirty that morning what we presumed to be his body was on its way home. To Granite Bay anyway. He would never see home again. And pragmatic though she was, Mother was right. How on earth would I tell my girls?

"Maybe I should go bring them home," Dad said.

Mother looked up from her paper towel. "Well, Edward, of course you should. We can't just let them waltz in here at five o'clock expecting a birthday party." She swept her hand over the room as if the balloons had already been hung.

Dad looked to me, but what did I know about such things?

"I'll go," Shawlie said.

And of course, that was best. Dad would take one look at his grandgirls, and his heart would fracture like thin ice in winter. He'd never get them back here without going to pieces himself. And I so needed him whole.

"Have you called his father?" Mother asked.

Oh, gosh.

Robert Andrew Torrington the Second sold burial plots and funeral plans in the greater Sacramento area. He wore white shirts, black suits, and a gray fedora. Always. He was long past the age of retirement but had no intention of turning in his spade, an occupational idiom he liked to use for its shock value. No, he was born to tend to the dead.

His mouth was a grim three-inch line of demarcation that separated his nose from his chin. To my personal knowledge it never curved one way or the other. Just opened to receive his daily bread and to effuse his superordinate opinions.

Shawlie called him The Undertaker, though technically he was not. I called him "your dad" when speaking to Trey and "Trey's dad" when speaking to anyone else. Except the girls. Then he was "your dad's dad."

I had a healthy fear of Robert Andrew Torrington the Second, and it stole my good sense whenever I was around him. I could hardly put a sentence together in his presence, so I know full well why he considered me the village idiot. And not at all what his son deserved.

But Winnie Torrington, now there was a woman. I never laughed more than when I was in her presence, a bubbling brook of a laugh that sprung from the pit of my gut and flowed out of me like pure joy. She sparkled with fairy dust and blew it my way every chance she got.

She was mischievous. And when her crystal blue eyes began to crinkle at the edges, I knew she was devising one plan or another. A slumber party at our house when Trey was away. "I'll bring the brownies." A trip to a day spa, just the three of us: "You, me, and that wonderful Shawlie Bryson." And, oh, the lunches we'd have.

She loved having a daughter at last, she'd say. And that was me. Me. And granddaughters. If she loved me before I supplied her with two, she adored me after.

Winnie loved to cook. With wine. Not in the recipe. In a glass. Two servings, to be exact, of glistening chablis, with just a blush of pink that matched her hair most of the time, which she took care of herself using a wash-in rinse. She'd put on her favorite Don Ho record at precisely four o'clock, then flutter her way to the kitchen, wearing one of her trademark muumuus imported from Maui and the variegated knitted socks her sister sent every Christmas. She'd place a gardenia in her hair when she had one, a camellia when she didn't. Then she'd pour the wine, prop up her *Joy of Cooking*, and proceed with her dinner preparations. By the second glass of chablis she'd be dancing the hula and hardly remember what recipe she was working from. But then, "working from" was a loose term to Winnie.

All that was before she wandered into that little spiraled church around the corner from their house. Winnie loved to walk, to take in the magic and mystery of nature. Before breakfast, after dinner. Faithfully. One Sunday morning she stopped outside the church whose denomination was of no concern and listened, transported, to the sounds of "Rock of Ages." She went in after the final chorus, underdressed though she was, and, well, every Sunday after that her walk coincided with the morning service.

Her joy was fueled by a new Source after that.

We talked for years about going to Oahu, she and I "and that wonderful Shawlie Bryson." For a whole week we'd go, dig our red-toenailed feet into the warm tropical sand by day and dine with Don Ho by night. Every night. She'd get her fill of "Tiny Bubbles" and then some, if I had my say.

But I didn't.

"Of course you can't leave the girls, Ab. They need their mother." Trey would give me that *what-were-you-thinking?* look. The one that made me wonder what I *was* thinking. There would be time for that later, I'd agree.

So Winnie and I would talk about next year or the year after that.

I cried for days when she died.

Robert the Second moved into an assisted-living home after that. Not that he needed the assistance. Oh no. But he liked his dinner served promptly at six, and that made it simple. I often wondered if he missed the Hawaiian flare Winnie put into her meals. Or if he'd even noticed.

I looked at the clock for the gazillionth time that morning. It was almost noon. And promptly at twelve Trey's dad would pull into whatever Denny's was closest for lunch. But it would be impossible to reach him. He didn't believe in cell phones. Or computers or fax machines. No, for business he believed in "making calls." By a telephone with a cord, rotary preferred, or in person. He'd conducted business that way for fifty-plus years. Why on earth would he change? His question, not mine.

His son would be halfway to Sacramento before he knew the worst.

And speaking of worst, the front door opened and I heard my girls whispering their way to the kitchen. Bailey led with timid steps, uncharacteristic but indicative of the trepidation she had to be feeling. One wasn't hauled home from work with one's sister for just any old reason. Something must be more than wrong. Their wide eyes were filled with questions. Shawlie passed them off to me with a glance erupting with sympathy.

"Mom? What?" It was Bailey, of course, getting right to the point.

I motioned to the chairs that Dad and I had just vacated. "Girls, here, why don't you sit down."

Becca lowered her body into a chair next to Mother in slow motion. But Bailey took a defiant step backward and planted herself for what was to come. "What?" she said again, her unflinching eyes demanding that I speak the words that in all of this world she would least want to hear.

I didn't know which daughter to look at, where to aim my pitiful announcement. A little sob caught in my throat. "It's your father," I said, dividing my look between them.

Becca stood. "Is . . . is he okay?"

"No," I said. "He's not."

I told them only what I had to, but they weren't in the frame of mind for details anyway. Becca wailed in her grandfather's arms. Bailey refused to be touched.

❧

Details of the funeral came in bits and pieces. Even now I can't remember how all the plans were made. I just know that for five long days I functioned like a disembodied soul. There but not. Making decisions I was ill-equipped to make, comforting those who called to comfort us, finding strength on loan from I know not where.

At least there were no technical arrangements to fret over. Trey and I already had our burial plots, et cetera, bought and paid for. Trey's dad had seen to that long ago. But I put my sneaker-covered foot down when they tried to include the girls in the family plan. No child of mine was going to pick out her casket while I was alive. Score one for Abbie.

Dad was the rock he always was. There when I needed him, which was pretty much all day every day, till after the funeral. He even broke the news to Trey's dad for me. No parent wants to bury their child, but in this case Robert the Second couldn't have been more helpful, though the line of his mouth was more grim than ever.

Not surprisingly, my girls gravitated to Dad. He'd stay until late in the night, letting them talk and cry and whatever else they needed, an emotional lifeline for both, but especially for Bailey. She had no words for me in the early days. And that was okay. She could barely manage her own pain. She had no way to deal with mine.

But Becca. She would come as I lay in my half-empty bed, fall asleep on her father's pillow, and dispel the tormenting thoughts that came in the dark. My lifeline.

The cool spell was gone by the day of Trey's funeral. Ninety-eight was the forecasted high, and it was getting an early start. By nine thirty when we left for the funeral home it was already eighty-two. And by eleven forty when we gathered at the cemetery for the interment, a merciless sun hovered in a cloudless sky.

Trends have changed, yes, but when your father-in-law is "in the business," you still wear black to a funeral. And the only black I had was a wool-blend winter dress, long-sleeved and high-necked. Shawlie did her best to find something else at the mall. But in August? Even for the trendy, a cocktail dress is hardly apropos.

I changed the instant I got home, standing under my bedroom ceiling fan in just my underwear until the rash began to dissipate. But I couldn't hide out forever. I eventually dressed and made my way downstairs, where clusters of well-wishers spoke in whispers about "how young he was" and ate sliced ham and fluffy Jell-O salads provided by the women's group of Mother's church. Then this person or that one would see me and their voices would rise ever so slightly as they offered a kind sentiment.

It was a sizeable group that came to bury Trey. I wasn't surprised. He was as personable as a man could be. Winnie's touch was on his life in the best way, but it was tempered by the no-nonsense work ethic of his dad. That meant Trey could work and play with the best of them, though I'd seen far less of his fun side in recent years. Which led to the unthinkable. And every unfamiliar female face I saw that day drew me. Was she the one?

"I know what you're doing." Shawlie pulled me toward the powder room. I followed her inside. She locked the door. "You don't really think she'd come, do you?"

"Pardon me for stating the obvious, but there's been a huge disconnect between what I thought and what I know." My eyes looked upward, where just above us divorce papers lay hidden in my hope chest — the only thing I had that I could lock.

"Abbie, there is no way that woman would show her face in this house. Presuming there is another woman. You don't actually know."

"I know."

Her eyes went wide. "You know? What haven't you told me?"

I twirled my wedding band. "I just know." I'd had five days to consider the signs. And not even counting the woman at the hospital, there were plenty. But I'd lulled myself into a nice state of denial. I'd forgotten how positively amorous Trey was in the early days when he returned from his week-long trips, how he'd try to get home—no, be sure to get home—an hour before school got out. These days I'd been lucky to get a kiss on the cheek—with three hours to burn.

And how long had it been since Trey had taken me away for a weekend just because it *wasn't* our anniversary? So we could spend the weekend naked and make all the noise we wanted. Five, six years at least. Six years? Okay, things had cooled down, but that wasn't uncommon. It didn't have to mean another woman, a divorce. It didn't have to. But it did. How stupid could I be not to have seen this for what it was? Every thought of Trey's betrayal took a little more out of me, like a rag doll losing her stuffing. My raw, mascara-less eyes filled once again.

"Oh, sweetie, I know your life has been charmed, but after all, Trey was just a man." She rolled her perfectly lined eyes. "Need I say more?"

Charmed?

"Here." She pulled a tissue out of the woven-straw holder and handed it to me.

I wiped and blew. "So you really don't think she's here?"

Shawlie waved the thought away like a pesky gnat. "No way. The other woman never has the guts to show her face."

If anyone should know, it was Shawlie. Still, I took care to stay an arm's length away from any woman I didn't know personally by name.

Four

"I don't want to go." Becca sat at the foot of her bed, flanked by her favorite jeans and shirts, suitcase open but empty. Her laptop, still wrapped in purple birthday paper, lay atop the clutter of her desk. A week later, and her eyes were still moist and puffy. "It just isn't right to leave you."

"Honey, I know things are nothing like we thought they'd be right now. But your dad would want you to go forward with your plans." I tucked a strand of chin-length hair behind her ear. "Your dreams."

Of the girls, Becca was more like Trey in appearance. She had the same fair skin, with a splattering of freckles across her nose. The same green eyes. The same sweet face that came to a soft point with her chin. Her hair was darker than Trey's, but it held the same cinnamon highlights as his.

Bailey was just like Trey in temperament. "You have to go," she told her sister. "It's already paid for."

Becca turned a narrow-eyed glance toward Bailey. "I don't

have to do anything."

"Of course you don't." I threw Bailey a look of my own. "The money has nothing to do with it. There's just no reason for you not to go. Your classes will help keep your mind occupied, and I have so many things to think about and take care of that I'll hardly have time to miss you."

Now there was a lie, and it didn't get by Bailey for one second. A half-hearted snort escaped through her nose and she raised her left eyebrow just the way Trey would do.

I gave her a pleading look.

Her jaws clenched for a moment. "And you can stay in my dorm room anytime you want."

Becca looked up, hope in her burdened eyes. "Really?"

Bailey shrugged. "The first semester."

Well, that was something.

Becca reached for a stack of jeans. "Mom, are you sure?"

"Absolutely." I scooted the suitcase closer to her. What I really wanted was to clutch their shattered hearts to mine, lock out the world, and not let go till the pain was gone. But Bailey knew, if Becca and I didn't, that wasn't the answer. "I'm sure."

❧

We left for San Luis Obispo Sunday morning as planned. Well, not quite as planned. There were three of us instead of four, and not once did we engage in Slug Bug. We took shifts driving Bailey's overpacked 4Runner, barely finding room for feet or elbows.

We stopped at Harris Ranch for an early lunch, one of our favorite places along I-5, and ate our French dips with feigned pleasure. I even skipped the gift shop. No jam or tea towels on this trip. *How long*, I wondered, *before the sharps and flats of our emotions get back in tune?*

With impeccable timing, we arrived at the dorm promptly at four and unloaded the car. One-third to Becca's room, two-thirds to Bailey's. The girls were in the same building, but on different floors, much to Bailey's delight. She was already friends with her roommate, but Becca had yet to meet the girl she'd live with the next nine months.

Nine months. I hoped joy would be reborn in my daughters' hearts in those months. And more. Much more.

I made up Becca's narrow bed with sheets we'd bought at Target the day before, along with a bulging cart of items for both girls, while she transferred the contents of two huge suitcases into one small chest of drawers and emptied the few boxes she'd filled at home. I slipped her CDs into the spiral holder purchased on our shopping spree. It was significantly smaller than the one she left behind in her bedroom, but she brought only her favorite music. Good thing. They weren't kidding when they said space was limited in the dorm room.

"Here." I handed her the laptop once Bailey rejoined us. "Open it."

Becca took it reluctantly and eased off the card I'd taped on top, placing it in a dresser drawer. I knew it would be weeks, maybe months, before she'd break the seal. Then she slid one finger under the flap of paper on the bottom of the package.

"Thanks," she said but didn't remove the laptop from the box. She stood and kissed my cheek. "Really."

A swell of sadness went through me. Birthdays were going to be a problem now.

They drove me to the airport for my eight o'clock flight. Trey and I had originally planned to drive down to Santa Barbara for the rest of the weekend. But that was before. Our table at Emilio's had been cancelled, along with the luxurious room Trey had booked for the two of us at Villa Rosa, one of the finest inns in Santa Barbara. With only eighteen rooms, reservations were made months in advance. Oh, I had looked forward to that night with Trey, to a walk on the beach under a star-glittered sky, getting cozy before a crackling fire back in our room—salve for the pain of going back without my girls.

Now I just wanted to be home.

I drew my daughters to me, kissed them, and breathed in the fruity scent of their hair. "Call and tell me about orientation. And next week after classes. I want to hear all about your first day." The request was wasted on Bailey, I knew, but Becca would call. And she'd share all the details. I waved from the escalator and turned before the tears began to flow.

How would we ever get through this?

❧

When I got home that night I went straight to my bedroom, plopped down on my side of the bed, and did what I'd waited nine days to do. I screamed. And screamed. And swore. And stomped. Letting the anguish and anger that had churned to a full boil simply erupt. I pounded Trey's pillow and dumped his underwear drawer. "How could you? How could you!?" I demanded. But there was no one to give an answer. That was really the worst of it. A woman in San Diego had shared, among other things, my husband's last heartbeat. And I would never know who or why.

I moved out of the master suite that night. Took all my clothes and moved them into the guest room at the far end of the hall. Emptied my dressers, gathered my jewelry and everything in my bathroom. I'd have to find my own groove in the barely used bed and break in a new pillow with my tears, but there would be no trace of another woman between these sheets. Not that she'd ever been in my bed, but some of her DNA had to have clung to my husband, who had.

I'd need a shoe rack—okay, two or three—for my new closet. There's usually something we women find hard to resist. For some, it's another woman's husband. For me, it's shoes. I'm the Imelda Marcos of the New World. I simply can't resist a sweet pair of pumps in a store window. I love the smell and feel of the leather as I lift the shoe out of the box, love the subtle cracks, like fine wrinkles that tell the story of a life. Smooth and shiny is not for me. And fabric only when necessary. If there's one thing I don't like about shoes, it's worn heels, scuffs, and a color that's not quite right. Okay, that's three.

"Ab." Trey tapped the table with what I called his lecture finger, sometime around our ninth year of marriage. I obeyed his call to sit. Before either of my babes were out of diapers I'd become well acquainted with the way he used that index digit. Sometimes he'd point with it or draw little circles on the tabletop or press the tip against his lips. Whatever he did with it, it always preceded a lecture.

"We're going to have to put you on an allowance."

"Allowance?" Envision overflowing treasure troves of shiny gold dou-bloons because a few hundred years ago that's how our bank account would have looked. I thought I managed the household exceptionally well.

"A shoe allowance." Trey brought out a color-coded chart with four col-umns and twelve rows. The columns were designated by seasons, the rows by months. "Each quarter, indicated here by the seasons, you will be allowed to purchase two"—he made a V with the first and middle fingers of his left hand—"primary pairs of shoes."

"Primary?"

Up went the lecture finger, an indication that I should not interrupt.

"That's two pairs of shoes" — he made the V again — "for each three-month period. That means you have to decide which one of the months each quarter you will not buy a pair of shoes."

I gave this a moment of thought. "What if I bought both pairs in one month?" Assuming that were even allowed.

"In that case, there would be two months in that quarter with no shoes." Out came the V again.

"But wouldn't it be simpler just to say three pairs of shoes each quarter?"

"Ah, sweetheart, it's all about discipline."

I tilted my head and gave him a smile that said the game's up. "This is a joke, right?"

He slid the chart over to me, the nail on his lecture finger buffed to a high shine. "There's no limit on the price of the shoes, just the number you purchase. And for each two pairs you buy" — I closed my eyes before he could give me the V again — "you have to give one pair away."

I was squinting by now. "Away?" Away?

He nodded.

"You said something about primary."

He winked and pointed to three little asterisks at the bottom of the chart. "I realize things come up beyond our control. If you need a pair of shoes for something unexpected" — he used his fingers to put the word in quotation marks — "you can use these like Get-Out-of-Jail-Free cards. Simply mark the asterisk in the appropriate cell up here, but don't forget to cross it off down here. And remember, you only get three for every" — we said it together — "four quarters."

"This seems like a lot of work just for shoes."

He gave me a patient smile. "You want to be a good example for the girls, don't you?"

I admit it, I was puzzled. "Example?"

"Well, Abbie, what if Bailey and Becca bought shoes the way you do?

We'd need another house just to store them."

At the time, we lived in a four-bedroom, five-thousand-square-foot house that still had empty closets. Bailey, eight, wore nothing but flip-flops unless she was playing ice hockey, and Becca, seven, well, she wore what her friends wore. My influence, when it came to shoes, was wasted on them. But I could see Trey was trying to be generous. I took the chart, pinned it up in my closet, and replaced it with a new one every January. For eleven years.

I stacked the last of the shoe boxes in my new closet. Tomorrow I would buy those shoe racks. And towels, new towels. I found a notepad and started a list.

&⊂∞⊃

Grief was tainted with the horror of my secret. My failure. I needed to mourn like the widow I was, but with those divorce papers calling out like the telltale heart, every tear seemed fraudulent. When Shawlie stopped by for coffee the next morning on her way to a closing, it was obvious the wellspring had yet to be capped.

"I'd think your anger would trump your grief to Cancun and back." She cupped a hand over her red lips. "Sorry."

Cancun is where Trey and I spent our honeymoon. But in all fairness, that was Shawlie's favorite home-grown phrase.

"I was a widow first," I said. "I know it doesn't make sense, but there you are."

"A widow only," she corrected. "You were served. That's just the first step in a very long process. RA— Rob may not have even gone through with it. People do change their minds, you know?"

Well, that was something to hold onto, especially coming from Shawlie. I squeezed her hand. "More coffee?"

"Nope. Gotta go. Just wanted to make sure you got home

okay." She stopped short of the front door and turned back to me. "Did you?"

My eyes began to swim. When I thought I could trust my voice, I said, "I'm going to buy a new pair of shoes today. Something with a polka-dot bow." Lord, help me, but I still had an asterisk.

She winked. "Good girl."

Five

We made it through a simple Thanksgiving. Mother, Dad, the girls, and me. Mother prepared a small turkey with all the trimmings and two pies: pecan and pumpkin. She wouldn't let me bring a thing, not the sweet potato casserole I always made, not even the brown-and-serve rolls.

"Next year," she said, "when you're back on your feet."

She was more optimistic than I was.

We invited Trey's dad, and I honestly hoped he'd accept, but in twenty years of marriage, our families had not conjoined like other couples I knew. Trey's schedule was the cause. He devised it shortly after the honeymoon.

"We'll work it out like this." Trey brought me his chart. *"Thanksgiving with your parents this year."* He smiled, and I thought, What a nice concession. *"Christmas with mine."*

Ah.

"You know, Trey, since we all live so close, we could actually spend part of the day with one set of parents and part of the day with the oth —"

Trey was making circles on his chart with his lecture finger.

"At — at least Christmas?"

"Abbie, sweetheart, when we have our own family that would never work."

"Well, but that won't be for years, right? Five anyway?" That was before the hormones kicked in.

He turned back to the chart. "Since this is an even year, this will be the schedule for every even year. We'll reverse the order on odd years. Thanksgiving with my parents, Christmas with yours. At their house or ours, it doesn't matter." He paused a moment. "Once you've learned to roast a turkey, of course."

I'd watched my mother countless times. How hard could it be? As long as you didn't forget to empty the orifices.

"And on Mother's and Father's Day we'll have brunch with one set of parents and an afternoon visit with the other set of parents, alternated of course, even years belonging to my parents." He shrugged. "Just to keep it simple. That means" — he gave me another smile — "since we're just three months from an odd year, your parents will be first."

Odd. Right.

"What about Easter?"

He showed me Easter on the chart. "We'll stay at home and hide colored eggs for the kids. In the meantime, we'll spend it with our parents —"

I said it with him. "Even years, your parents. Odd years, mine."

"Right."

"What about church?"

"Odd years we'll go with yours."

Because that was ages before Winnie found her way into the fold.

"And Fourth of July week we'll set aside for our family vacation — you, me, and eventually the kids."

I was leaning into the table and squinting, a habit Trey was trying to break me of. It made me look like a dolt, he said, like thinking didn't come easy to me. *"What if one set of parents has other plans on their year?"*

He held up the chart. "I've made them copies."

Oh, well, then.

So that was our life. Neatly arranged. With my family on the odd side of the equation.

Birthday parties and graduations were about the only times we all got together. Winnie in her muumuus, Trey's dad in his fedora. My parents, the odd couple, looked dull in comparison. But everyone got along, especially Dad and Winnie. They both had the same fun spark that crinkled their eyes.

And a partner only too willing to snuff it out.

⟨⟩

I had six days with my girls over Thanksgiving, and I was going to savor every moment. In twelve weeks' time Becca had turned into a bona fide college student. No longer a girl, she had blossomed to something beyond, and I knew our lives had entered a new phase. I was proud, so proud. But I had to hide out in the powder room more than once when a fleeting glimpse of the old Becca would surface. I wasn't ready to let the child in her go, but I'd never let her see the tears.

"You have to meet my roommate, Mom." Becca gave Bailey a conspirator's smile.

"Ellie? You like her, don't you?" I'd heard all about her that first Monday, the day classes began.

"Oh, I love her. But I saved the best part to tell you in person. Her last name is Rigby."

"Rigby?" I squinted and chewed the inside of my lip. Was the name supposed to mean something to me? I thought back to high school and my one year of college. I hadn't known a Rigby, so this wasn't the daughter of an old friend. Maybe the gymnast? I held up empty hands.

"Rigby, Mom!" Becca was bouncing and giggling. "Ellie Rigby."

"Ellie Rigby." I shook my head.

"As in Eleanor," Bailey said, not so enthusiastic as her sister.

"Eleanor? Rigby? Oh!" And then we laughed. Becca and I, and Bailey a little.

"So her mom was an even bigger Beatles fan than you."

The Beatles hadn't been a group for nearly a decade when I discovered them, but what did that matter?

"Imagine!" she said. Then she caught herself and laughed again. "Imagine! Get it?"

Oh, this was fun. And fun is something I'd sorely missed over the past thirteen weeks. Eleanor Rigby. That would bring a smile all year long.

As did having my girls with me. It was healing just to breathe the same air.

"Mom?" Bailey stopped at the top of the stairs, where the landing led into what was formerly the main guest room. It was Wednesday night, their first night home, and we were finally turning in. She looked at the door that led into the master suite, the door that had not been opened since my first night alone. And then into the guest room, where the bedside light cast a golden glow over all my belongings. "What's this?"

I was surprised at the flutter in my stomach. "I moved." I really hoped I could leave it at that.

"Out of your— your and Dad's room?"

Becca took in the scene, then put an arm around me. "Well, Bailey." She gave her sister a little glare. "Think about how hard it would be."

Bailey glared back, then turned to me. "Does Gramma know?"

"Gramma? What does this have to do with Gramma?"

"She said you'd do something like this."

"Like this?"

"Something desperate. She said you'd do something desperate."

I stiffened. "And when did she say this?"

Bailey turned defensive for the first time all night. "We talk."

"About me?"

"About things, Mom. About Dad, and things."

Becca touched the arm I'd planted firmly on my hip. "She said we should watch out for you, that's all. That this would be a difficult time. I mean, we"—she motioned between herself and Bailey—"have school and each other. You don't have anyone."

"I have Grampa and . . . and Gramma." I sounded pathetic. "And I have Shawlie."

Bailey took over again. "Practically the first thing they teach you in Psych I is the stages of grief. The first is denial."

"Psych I? Bailey, you're a computer science major."

"Mom, everyone takes Psych I."

I thought back to my freshman year at Sac State. She was right.

All of a sudden, she walked to my closet and flung open the door. Oh my—" She cupped her head in her hand. "There are six new pairs of shoes in this closet. Six."

And I hadn't worn any of them yet.

Even Becca looked as if they'd unearthed a stack of bones.

"Becca, grab your pillow," Bailey said.

"My pill—"

"You too, Mom. We're all sleeping in your room." She turned and looked down the hallway. "Your real room."

"Oh, Bailey, I don't know—"

"Mom, without help these stages can last forever. Remember"— she held up — oh, Lord — a lecture finger — "even the longest journey begins with the first step." She went for her pillow. "This is the first step."

Before I knew it, the three of us were lying in the dark. In the king-sized bed I swore I'd never go back to.

It was going to be a long six nights.

Six

Christmas was another matter altogether. I could hardly bear to think of all the traditions that would be broken. For twenty years Trey and I and then the girls had driven to the mountains to cut a noble fir *"because, Abbie, sweetheart, noble firs have the most agreeable branches for decorating. The bulbs hang perfectly and don't get lost in all the needles."*

I'd never heard of a noble fir before marrying Trey, nor had I cut down my own Christmas tree. We'd always purchased our pre-cut Douglas fir from Hank's Tree Lot because, well, Doug fir is what he carried. I had to admit Trey was right. Noble firs had a much more regal look than the thick, cone-shaped Doug fir, on which the Christmas bulbs would lie rather than hang. Still, I did miss its more pungent, long-lasting scent.

One tradition I didn't mind breaking was the annual Christmas newsletter we sent out instead of Christmas cards, which I much preferred. I dislike Christmas newsletters. Most of the information belongs in a phone conversation to one's mother or maybe one's sister, if she lives across the country. But a running account of a year in the life of, using eight-point font, well, that isn't my idea of holiday greetings. I want snowmen and elves, all the fun things of the season.

Our Christmas newsletter commenced the year Bailey learned to ride her two wheeler without the training wheels. Which just happened to coincide with the year Trey received the top sales award for the entire state of California. But in all fairness, I was as proud as he was.

We typed it up — and I was adamant about this: one page, no more, ten-point Arial, no smaller — and sent it out on Christmas paper that Trey found at Staples. Every year it was the same. Our very own trademark. Trey selected it, he said, because it had four sparkling bulbs bound by red ribbon and holly in the upper left-hand corner, one bulb for each of us Torringtons. I fancied myself the red bulb, Trey the green one, Bailey the silver one, and Becca the gold. We never veered from that pattern. Thinking about it now, I'm sure much could be made of the psychology of that in either of the girls' Psych I classes. I was smart to keep that information to myself over the years.

So I was more than disappointed when Bailey brought up the Christmas newsletter the day before going back to school after Thanksgiving.

"You're sending one out, right?" Bailey's voice added the question mark to the end of the sentence, but we both knew it was a declarative statement. I waited a second too long to respond. Bailey turned on her heel. "I'll do it," she said.

"Bailey, honey —"

She turned back with a glare. "Mother, we can't not send our Christmas newsletter, this year of all years."

"But, honey, there isn't anyone on our list who doesn't know

about . . . things. What on earth would we have to say that would
be news?"

"We have to do this in honor of Daddy."

I couldn't formulate my objection, though it was there inside
my head.

"I'll do it," Bailey said again with a roll of her eyes. And I said
okay because whatever Bailey wrote would be far more suitable
than anything I'd come up with.

She emerged from Trey's office an hour later, eyes and nose
as red as the bulb that was me. "Here." She handed me the sheet
she'd printed out. The opening line read, "As most of you already
know, the shiniest bulb of our cluster is no longer with us . . ."

"This'll be fine," I said, without reading further.

"I'm going to get the stationery," Bailey said. There were only
six sheets left from last year. We'd need six packs of fifty to cover
everyone on the list. Trey's list.

"Can I go?" Becca asked.

It was only a trip to Staples, but in that question I saw how
important this newsletter was to Becca too.

Bailey shrugged a shoulder and nodded toward the garage.

Becca hurried for her jacket. "I'll do the envelopes for you,
Mom, as soon as we get back."

"Then you can mail them December first as always." Bailey
gave me one more glare, then snatched up her purse and disappeared into the darkness of the laundry room. A moment later I
heard the garage door slam.

Well, wasn't I just the ghost of Christmas present?

❧

When Bailey was three, Trey began to hire a Santa to come to our house every Christmas Eve. Usually it was a college student out to earn some extra money for the holidays. Becca hid behind me during the entire visit and wouldn't even come out to accept the gift he pulled out of his fur-lined bag. It was the one gift the girls could open on Christmas Eve, and it was always the same. New pj's.

But Bailey was enthralled. She never hesitated to tell him exactly what she expected to find under the tree the next morning. That year and every year right up through the fourth grade. That's when she found our Hire-a-Santa card in the Rolodex.

"What's this?" She held the little square of cardstock as if it were a report card without a single passing grade. *My* report card. Her body language left no room for a creative answer.

"Well, um, you see, we—"

"And the Easter Bunny and Tooth Fairy? Is there a card for them too?"

Ah. What a tangled web we weave. This came much sooner than I anticipated, and in true Bailey fashion. When Santa came that year, she sat on the sofa with her arms crossed and her eyebrow raised. She rolled her sharp blue eyes when Becca recited her list to him and bit the heads off both gingerbread men from Santa's special plate.

Well, Santa may have gone by the wayside, but the pj's remained a tradition. Every Christmas Eve a new pair. The cutest I could find. I fought back tears as I searched the mall that first year without Trey.

"Maybe it's time for new traditions," Shawlie said. "How about a book, a mug, and a canister of chai tea?"

I found myself squinting.

"Just to be different," she pressed.

"That would be different."

She led me to the New Fiction shelf at Barnes and Noble. "You and the girls could spend Christmas Eve reading the latest in great fiction and drinking spiced tea. How cool is that?"

I ran my hand over the cover of the book she handed me. "But what would they wear?"

She squinted back. "Would it matter?"

I put the book back on the shelf with a sigh.

"Okay." She handed me the book again, plus another. "We can take it slow. In with the new doesn't always have to mean out with the old. Get the books, the mug, the tea, and the pj's. Next year, the books, the mug, and the tea."

So the girls and I spent Christmas Eve, they in their new pj's, sipping chai tea in the king-sized bed with Kidd, Grisham, and Grafton.

What was noticeably absent downstairs was the noble fir. We just couldn't bring ourselves to drive to the mountains as a trio instead of a quartet or to visit Hank's Tree Lot for a pre-cut Douglas. So the few gifts we'd had the heart to purchase we placed on the living room hearth, where we assembled the next morning with our spiced cider and blueberry muffins.

Because that's what we always did.

Traditions die hard.

❧

Winter lingered, as if unwilling to let go of its own gray mood. Mine lingered right along with it. I thought the sun would never shine again, the trees would never bloom. I was stuck in a no-man's-land between death and life. Shawlie did her best to pull me from its clutches, but in all honesty I wasn't ready to be sprung.

"Work with me," she'd say whenever I turned down her invitation to dinner or a movie. "There's nothing like a good flick and Milk Duds to put the mind on hold. And if there's a mind that needs a break, Abbie, it's yours."

She was right. My thoughts never shut down. Day or night, it was Trey, first and last. Like it had been for twenty years. I saw it now for what it was, the frog-in-the-kettle syndrome. Trey's control started out lukewarm, and without me ever realizing it, it had boiled away every trace of my own essence until all I could do was croak his tune. What Shawlie could not understand was that my grief was intensified, not lessened, by Trey's other life. I had yet to call it what it really was, this aberrant lapse of judgment. Instead, I sought to trick myself with words like *fling*, *dalliance*, and *mid-life madness.*

But divorce papers don't lie. This was more than indulgence. I couldn't stop wondering, *why, who? Who else?* And the tears would flow. *How could a relatively enlightened individual be so deceived?* I would ask myself.

"Do you think there were others?"

Shawlie picked a speck of lint from her blazer, then looked away. "What does it matter? Betrayal is betrayal."

"It matters. So darn much."

She looked at me with rare intensity. Then she blinked. "Romance or comedy?"

Seven

When spring finally tapped on my back door I had to admit it presented a vista filled with promise. Every new bud, every baby-bird chirp nudged me to look forward, forward, and only forward. I worked the crick out of my neck from constantly looking over my shoulder at the ghosts that shadowed me, though I had yet to lay to rest the two haunting specters: Why? and Who?

Combined with savings and investments, the insurance money left me a woman of independent means. Regardless of his intentions, Trey had not yet disenfranchised me. Another six months, and the story might have been altogether different. But then, Trey always had impeccable timing.

And to his credit, he'd made Bailey and Becca the beneficiaries of separate life insurance policies that would cover their college expenses and get them off to a good start in life. Like his father before him, Trey maximized his profession to the benefit of his family. God rest his soul.

"I've made a decision."

Shawlie and I sat on my patio one late April morning, sipping freshly brewed coffee and taking in the goose bump–inspiring view of the lake far below. "I'm going to sell the house."

Shawlie sipped her coffee without the slightest sign that she stood to make $150,000 on the sale, minus broker fees, assuming she were both the listing and selling agent. And I had no doubt she would be. "They say not to make major decisions for a year."

"If it weren't for that manila envelope locked away in my hope chest, they'd have to haul me out of here in a hearse. I love—*loved*—this house," I said. I gave her what I know was a pathetic look. "Selling it is the only way I'll ever get out of that bedroom."

Now she gasped. "You're not still sleeping in there, are you?"

"Only when the girls are home. And in five weeks they'll be home for the whole summer." I shuddered.

Shawlie leaned forward in her chair. "Well, Abbie, just put your foot down."

"So Bailey can stomp on it? No, thank you."

"I've always said you've given her way too much free rein."

"No. What you've always said—with that rollicking look in your eye—is, 'She's the spitting image of me at that age.' She is and always has been so much more you than me. And, of course, Trey. Through and through."

She leveled a look at me. "Abigail Torrington, do not compare me to that man."

"Why do—did—you hate him?"

She looked down toward the lake, and I thought at first she wouldn't answer. Then she said, "Hate's a strong word."

"Which leads me back to my question."

"He wasn't the right man for you."

"Not the right—? Shawlie, we had twenty good years together. Well, twenty years anyway. Some of them were good. Look around you. He gave me this. Not to mention Bailey and Becca."

"Bailey and Becca? If Trey'd had his way neither of them would even be here."

Though no one was around, I held a finger to my lips and shushed her.

"And your mother."

I squinted. "My mother?"

"She called this a marriage made in heaven, yes?"

I nodded. "Yes."

"Well, there you are." She stood and collected her things. "Abbie, we are never going to agree on this, but the bottom line is, in the end Rob broke your heart. It just took longer than I expected."

I tried to formulate a comeback, but all I could muster was a sigh. She was right. In the end he did exactly that. "I don't want a sign."

"Sign?"

"In the yard. No sign. This will be hard enough on the girls."

"You're sure you're ready for this?"

My stomach sank like a weighted corpse at sea. "I'm sure."

"Okay then. I'm on it. And, Abbie." She looked up toward the master bedroom. "Get a safe deposit box."

When she left I picked up the phone and dialed my parents' number. "Mother? Hi, it's—"

"Tippy. How are you?"

As if anyone else would address her as Mother.

"Are you and Dad free for dinner tonight? I thought we could go—"

"Nonsense. You'll come over here. I already have a roast in the Crock-Pot."

—*out for Italian.* I unclamped my lips and silently counted to five. "Pot roast sounds great. What time?"

"Well, Tippy, six o'clock, of course."

Of course. Robert the Second wasn't the only one whose schedule was lord. From my earliest memory, we lived by the clock. Up at seven, lunch at noon, and dinner always, *always* at six. To give the stomach plenty of time for digestion before bed. Mother and Trey had long, friendly conversations about the merits of this, in which he would complain that I never quite hit the mark. Five till, twelve after. But never, *never* at six. From behind his newspaper, Dad would send me a wink and a nod, sometimes even a thumbs-up when no one was looking. "I'll see you then," I said to Mother. "Oh, can I—?" *Bring dessert?* I was going to say. She'd already hung up. But if I knew her—and, trust me, I did—she already had a cobbler baking to perfection at this very moment. And it wasn't even ten.

There was a time when Mother wasn't so obsessive/compulsive. I just can't remember back that far. By the time memory clicked into motion for me, Mother's ironing always hung the same direction, mugs were placed in the cupboard top down with handles aligned to the right, toilet paper rolled over the top, and shoes were arranged in the closet by season and color. And you never, ever, wanted to play canasta with Mother. Her stack straightening would drive you to distraction.

꧁꧂

I rang their doorbell at five forty-five. The table would be set just so, with four ice cubes in each glass, but maybe I could open a slab of butter. Or something.

Mother kissed the cheek I offered, which I changed from time to time, just because.

"The biscuits are in the oven. Everything else is ready."

Well, naturally.

"But you could pour the tea—"

I reached for the pitcher.

"—as soon as the timer goes off. We wouldn't want it to dilute." We said this last part in unison.

"There's my girl." Dad wrapped an arm around me and squeezed.

Oh, how I missed a man's shoulder to lean into.

"Was the traffic bad?"

At five forty-five, traffic in the Sacramento valley was bad no matter where you were going. "Nah," I said. "Oh, there's the timer."

We joined hands for grace just as the clock on the mantle began its first of six chimes.

Mother served our plates, clockwise of course, starting with me, the guest. "So, Tippy, what did you want to talk about?"

"Oh, well, I just, um—"

"Nonsense. You have something on your mind. That *is* why you called, correct?"

I toyed with my fork. "Can't I invite my parents to dinner without an ulterior motive?"

"You could, but usually you don't."

"Oh, Alice, leave the girl alone. At least let her eat her dinner. We can talk over coffee."

I patted Dad's knee under the table.

"The girls, they're fine?" Mother pressed.

"They're good. Gearing up for finals."

"They're brilliant girls, those two. Brilliant. It's all the more tragic that Trey isn't here to see his handiwork."

My stomach rose and fell like a buoy in a swell at the mention of his name.

"Alice, really."

"Edward, women who have lost a husband the caliber of Trey Torrington are only too willing to keep his memory alive." She looked at me for confirmation. "Am I right?"

I filled my mouth with pot roast and smiled.

"See there?" *Touché*, she might have added.

There was a time when she actually called my dad Eddie. But that, too, was before I was old enough for my memory to kick in. "Mmm. I never can get my gravy to turn out like yours."

"That, Tippy, is because you use corn starch."

I wasn't looking forward to coffee.

But with the dishwasher loaded and set to delay-start as soon as the ten o'clock news was over, as always, and with the cobbler heated to just the right temperature, I'd run out of time. We three marched to the family room with our coffee and dessert and each took our appropriate spot. *Wheel of Fortune* was spinning through its half hour on the muted television.

Mother placed her mug on a coaster. "Now, Tippy, what's on your mind?"

I drew in a breath and let it out slowly. "Well. Actually." I looked from one to the other, then at my icy hands clutched in my lap. "I'm thinking about, I'm *going* to, sell the house." When I looked up again, Dad was nodding thoughtfully, but Mother? Mother looked as if I'd thrown up my pot roast on her newly shampooed carpet.

"Sell? You said sell?"

"I'm thinking—"

"Abigail—"

Uh oh.

"—you cannot sell that house."

"And why not?" Dad said.

"Well, because. Because that's completely unfair to Bailey and Becca. Of course. That's their home."

"It's Abbie's home first. And I keep telling you, Alice, it's a seller's market. Trey would consider it good business sense." Dad tugged on the lower edge of his sweater. "If he were here."

Mother sniffed. "Trey did not work himself to death to have her throw it all away."

"Throw it— She's not—"

"Mother. I live in an eight-thousand-square-foot, six-bedroom house. By myself mostly. I think I could downsize."

She squared her shoulders and looked away. "Well, there's one bedroom it seems you don't need."

"Mother!" I blushed to the bottom of my hair follicles. *Bailey!*

"It's your responsibility to keep Trey's memory alive, if not for yourself then at least for your daughters. If you sell their home out from under them, what kind of message does that send?"

"The girls have their own memories. And I'm not selling the house out from under them. They're away at school nine months of the year. I doubt Bailey will ever live at home again once she graduates."

"And why should she with no home to come home to?"

"Alice, this is Abbie's decision. She didn't come here to ask permission, she came here to share her decision with us. Honey, I support whatever you decide."

I could have kissed his argyle-stockinged, slippered feet.

"Well, I know what Bailey will say about this. And then we'll see."

I stood, leaving my untouched cobbler on the end table. "I sign the listing papers tomorrow."

Dad brought my jacket and kissed my forehead. But Mother raised an eyebrow and smirked. "We'll see," she said again.

I looked over my shoulder at the television on my way out, and with only four letters exposed I solved the puzzle: Throw Momma from the Train.

Well, then.

Eight

To say that Bailey pitched a fit would be to say the South Pole is nippy in winter. It was Mother's Day weekend, and the girls were home one last time before the end of the semester. When I told them — and I knew I had to — Bailey's glacier-blue eyes went wide and the spots just below her cheekbones glowed cherry-Popsicle red. Just exactly like when she was two and I'd make her give Becca her bottle back. "You can't do this! YOU CAN'T DO THIS! YOU! CAN'T! DO! THIS!" Those were her exact words. The only thing missing was the stomp of her little foot. "Dad's essence is here. If we move, he'll be gone forever! Is that what you want? Is it, Mother?"

Ah me, there it was. *Mother.*

I remember the day my mom became Mother. I was fourteen and secretly going steady with Tom something-or-other from my freshman class. I wanted desperately to ask him to the Sadie Hawkins dance. It was my own version of coming out, dancing the Hustle with Tom for all the world to see. But Mother insisted

I ask Robert Parker, the son of her new best friend—Cookie, I think was her name—who not long after had her breasts enlarged and moved to Las Vegas to become a showgirl.

That humbled Mother for a month or so.

Anyway, I begged and I pleaded. Dad went to bat for me too, to no avail. It didn't matter that Robert was three inches shorter than me or that his favorite movie was *National Lampoon's Animal House*; it somehow fell to me to make him feel welcome at John F. Kennedy High. So with great reluctance I bought the tickets, praying he'd come down with mono. But no.

Every morning the week of the dance, Tom—I really should look up his name in my yearbook—met my bus to walk me to my first period class, Earth Science, I think it was. By Wednesday, his hints about the dance had gone from subtle to overt, no mistaking the desperation in his tone either, and by Thursday I was praying that *he* would come down with mono.

Shawlie said to just tell him the truth, for crying out loud. But I couldn't.

So Friday afternoon I told Mom that *I* had mono and that if I showed up at the dance, I'd be expelled for exposing the whole school and would flunk my freshman year.

She didn't buy it for one minute.

When Tom, who went to the dance with Jill Houghton, saw me there with Robert Parker, he asked for his 8-track of Shaun Cassidy's greatest hits back. If I could have produced it, he'd have given it to Jill—his new steady girl—right there on the spot.

I spent most of the evening in the bathroom tending to my broken heart.

"How was the dance?" Mother asked afterward, with an expectant smile, as if beholding the zygote of the next great romance.

"Fine, Mother," I said. And she never realized that everything had changed between us.

Like it had just changed between Bailey and me. "That isn't what I want, honey. And Dad will always be in our hearts, no matter where we go." Of course, her recall was not tainted like mine. She could rest forever in the fact that her father loved her. That the man who wrapped her in his arms was genuine to the marrow. But the man who'd brushed my cheek with his lips on Monday and died in another woman's bed on Friday, well, let's just say I didn't mind leaving Trey's essence behind.

"Mom, are you sure?" Becca's voice was soft with emotion.

Oh, Lord. *Did I ask for this? For any of it? Did I?* "The papers are signed," I said.

"Well, then." Bailey stomped her way upstairs to her room. To call Mother, no doubt.

I withered into a kitchen chair, feeling doomed to live a life of wrong choices.

"Mom, it's okay." Becca lay her head on my shoulder. "We'll get used to the idea."

I touched her baby-fine hair, promising myself one heck of a lecture if I let a single tear fall in her presence. When I could finally inhale, I drew in a life-giving breath of her presence. She smelled of little girl and vanilla body wash. I could have died happy at that moment.

❧

"I have a client who wants to see the house." Shawlie's call came Saturday morning before I'd even put the coffee on. "At ten."

"Oh, Shawlie, I don't know." I paused at every word.

"Oh, come on. Your house is always spotless. It'll show like a model."

"It's not that. It's, well, the girls are here. I'd rather wait till Monday." I'd not seen Bailey since the night before when she'd huffed her way upstairs, but I knew this wouldn't go over well.

"Abbie, this is a serious buyer. And he's only here for the weekend."

In the pause that followed, I couldn't think of what to say. It would be hard enough showing the house when it was just me. But to show the house—and to another man—with the girls there seemed, I don't know, sordid.

"They didn't take it well, did they?"

Sitting there in the kitchen all alone, I shrugged. "Bailey didn't take it well."

"Now, there's a surprise. But there has to be some way to work this out. Hey, you could take them to breakfast and I could show it while you're out. Or they could take you. It is, after all, Mother's Day weekend."

"Yes, and I don't want to ruin it."

She was quiet for a moment. "What time do the girls leave to go back to San Luis tomorrow?"

"We're having brunch with Mother and Dad." And on an even year. "After that, I guess."

"Then how about tomorrow afternoon? My client doesn't fly out—in his private plane, I might add—until evening."

I knew I should say yes. I really did. But on Mother's Day? "Shawlie, please, I'd really rather wait."

She sighed. "One year. That's what they say, Abbie."

"Next time. I promise."

But next time I was running the self-cleaning feature of my double ovens. I certainly couldn't show the house with that acrid smell soiling the air.

The time after that I was having another shoe rack installed.

"Abbie." Shawlie sat across the table from me at Olive Garden, picking at a breadstick. "The house has been listed nearly a month and except for the realtors' tour we haven't shown it once. If you think this is hard now, just wait until Bailey and Becca are home for the summer. We might as well kiss the peak selling season good-bye. Plus" — she leaned into the table and whispered — "do you want to be stuck in that bedroom for three long months?"

I squeezed my eyes tight at the idea. "I just didn't think I'd feel like this."

"And how exactly do you feel?"

"Like a tree being yanked up by the roots."

She took another pinch of the breadstick. "What kind of tree?"

"I don't know. A birch?"

"Good choice. Now, let me tell you how you'll feel when you sign on the dotted line. Like a new woman, Abbie. Like a brand-new woman. Trust me on this."

I didn't want to point out that Shawlie doesn't have children, and therein lay the difference. "If it were just me . . ."

She waved a finger side to side. "You can't think like that, Abbie. Those chicks of yours are about to leave the nest. They are, in fact, balanced on the rim, wings flapping up a storm. The choices you make will affect you more than anyone now. You gotta keep that in mind."

Absently, I stirred my iced tea. "Remember last year, I told you about the finches that nested on our patio?"

"Up on the light fixture, yeah. There were two babies, right?"

"Three. One morning they were just like you said. Perched on the rim of the nest, flapping their wings. Peeping or cheeping or whatever they do." I shrugged. "Making lots more noise than usual. So I stood at the window and watched and, Shawlie, it was the neatest thing. The daddy bird was sitting on one of the blades of the ceiling fan above the patio table, and he was calling out to them. And baby number one inched its way to the edge, flapping like crazy while the daddy called and called."

"How do you know it was the dad?"

"The males have all the color."

"And all the fun," she said drolly.

"Anyway, all of a sudden, that baby bird just took off and fell in line behind her dad—or his," I said, before she asked. "They were gone about twenty minutes, and then—and this is the neat part—when they flew back to the patio the baby landed on the window ledge. And that daddy nudged that baby all the way back to the nest. Just nudged and nudged. Then he flew to the fan and did the very same thing with the second baby bird, and then the third. And then"—my eyes began to blur—"the mama joined them and that whole little family flew off together. And that was that."

"Abbie." Shawlie pushed her plate away and rested her chin on a fist. "You have way too much time on your hands."

I tried to keep my tone even. "There's a message in that, don't you think?"

"A message?"

"Shawlie, honestly."

"Look." She opened her arms as if presenting herself. "I didn't have a dad to coax and nudge and look how I turned out."

If she was trying to make me feel better, well . . . I sighed. "I just think my girls need Trey now more than ever." I shrugged and looked away. "And all they have is me."

"You can say that, knowing what you know?"

"He was a good father."

She closed her eyes, probably counting to ten. "He lived a

double life, Abbie. He cheated. He lied. And only God knows what else." I knew she wouldn't get it. But her tone softened a bit. "Bailey and Becca are lucky to have you, my friend. You can coax and nudge as well as any robin."

I gave her a half-hearted smile. "Finch," I said, but she was already digging in her purse for a credit card.

Nine

Of all the firsts we'd experienced since Trey's death — Thanksgiving, Christmas, Valentine's Day (which I slept fitfully through, with gratefulness, thanks to the flu) — Father's Day was the worst for Bailey and Becca. Yes, they were home. No, I hadn't sold the house. Not even close. I bravely decided I owed them one more summer at home. Shawlie took it off multiple listings, with this warning: "Beware September."

We planned brunch with my parents for Father's Day — again, an even year — then an afternoon visit with Robert the Second, but the morning was pure agony for the girls. Ever since they'd been old enough to pad around in their footed pj's, they'd helped me prepare The Father's Day Tray, for Trey, which we'd carry to his bed, where he'd pretend to wake up and be surprised. It was years before they caught on that he had already brushed, shaved, and coiffed, because, you see, we took photos.

By the time Bailey was seven, she was in charge. I got to make and pour the coffee for another three years, but that was all. She did everything else, with Becca, ever her sister's shadow, fetching the newspaper.

The Tray, which wasn't really a tray at all but a doily-covered cookie sheet, consisted always of a new mug filled to the brim with caffeinated French Roast and one heaping teaspoon of creamer. Beside the mug lay a saucer-sized, heart-shaped sugar cookie we'd secretly baked the day before. Never mind the heady scent of butter and vanilla filling every crown-molded corner of the house, driving us crazier than Pavlov's dogs. We all pretended not to notice. After it cooled we'd scrawl "We Love You" across it in blue frosting, then hide it till Sunday. But this mother of all cookies wasn't just for Trey. We'd share it in a holy ritual, breaking, biting, savoring, all at the same time, not caring one bit about the crumbs peppering the sheets. Next to the cookie lay *The Wall Street Journal*, unbanded, ready to read, and beside the paper, the cards. My card, Bailey's card, Becca's card. Mine, Hallmark. Theirs, handmade in the early years. Then Shoebox. Always Shoebox.

That Father's Day I crept down the stairs at first light and turned the burner on under the teapot. I didn't dare unleash the aroma of coffee. Spiced orange pekoe would suffice today. I pulled a mug out of the plain side of the cupboard, bypassing anything with "Dad" or "T" or baseball. Just white ceramic, the one without the chip.

Of course, there was no cookie, no *Wall Street Journal*, no Shoebox.

Bailey was the first downstairs, after me. She took one look at the teapot and went straight to the freezer. In minutes, the smell of French Roast filled the kitchen. When it finished brewing, she poured a mug full, added a heaping teaspoon of creamer, and joined me at the table. Without a word she drank her father's coffee from her father's favorite mug, a tsunami of emotion surging behind her determined eyes. I knew from experience the storm wall would hold until she was alone.

"Morning." Becca bent to kiss my cheek. She was freshly showered and smelled of tropical sea breeze. She noted the empty coffee
mug and gave her sister a wordless hug.

My peace child.

"Let's take balloons instead of flowers." She caught the question
in my eye. "To the cemetery."

Of course. The girls would want to go.

"Between brunch with Grampa and our visit to Grampa
Torrington."

Well, that only made sense since the cemetery was on the way
to Robert the Second's new abode.

"Maybe he'd like to go," Bailey said. "To the cemetery."

"You think?"

"It's his son, idi—"

"Bailey." I lifted an eyebrow for emphasis.

She rolled her eyes.

"You want me to call?" Becca said.

"You don't make a date to go to the cemetery."

"We are."

Bailey's voice lost some of its edge. "That's different."

"Then what?"

"We'll wait till we get there. Mention we're going and then . . ."
She ended with a shrug, a sigh, and another eye roll, weary, no
doubt, of having to think for the plebes.

"Well, that sounds like a plan." I took my cup to the sink, eager
to get this portion of our day behind us, ready for the calm my dad
infused into every situation. But then there was Mother. My sigh
sounded exactly like Bailey's. "I'm off to the shower."

❧

The obsession struck like a toothache as I stood under the tepid flow, and there was no Novocain to numb the montage of feelings that came with it. Who was she, this woman who'd made a mockery of my widowhood? Suddenly I had to know. I wanted a name—other than the ones I used for her. A face. A reason.

I know. Trey was as much to blame as she, scads more in fact, but I wasn't ready to accept that. My mind needed someone to hang in effigy. Someone besides my husband.

Balloons? Egads, I did not want to go to the cemetery.

But I put on my best face. Studied it in the mirror. And wondered, *Why wasn't I enough?*

"This way." Trey turned my chin toward the camera and held it steady. *"That's your best side."*

"Really?"

"Trust me."

I sat on the sofa, holding my pose, with three-year-old Becca on my lap. Bailey stood at my side, waiting for her daddy, who was setting the timer. This was to be our Christmas photo for the cards we'd send. To everyone in the world we knew. We wanted it just right.

"Teeth, everyone," Trey said. And then came the flash.

"I think I blinked." I didn't move my head, barely moved my lips.

"You're sure?"

"We'd better do one more."

"Up we go," Trey said to Bailey. He walked the six feet to the tripod, turned, and looked through the camera lens, raised his head and then his lecture finger. He tapped the air twice, and I raised my chin. Then once more. I honestly thought I hadn't moved.

But we wanted it right.

So I held my eyes wide, chin just so, showing teeth in a fixed smile.

Trey picked up the photos a week later. I was right, I'd blinked the first time. But that photo was far preferable to the one we sent out. The one where I looked like the "after" pose of a facelift gone bad. And I was only twenty-five. More than one of Trey's associates showed surprise when they actually met me, probably thinking he was wise to have ditched his first wife, you know, the woman in the picture.

"So, Trey, why wasn't I enough? Will you tell me that?"

∽

It did not escape my notice that Bailey and Becca flanked their Grampa Woodruff from the moment we met up with them at Mimi's Cafe, taking possession of him body and soul. Nor did it escape Dad's. The girls kissed both sides of his balding head, leaving lip prints in flecked gloss, which caught the light from time to time, making me smile. He refused to offer his head to Mother when she pulled out a tissue, and he winked at me, his coconspirator in all things of which Mother disapproved.

It was clear my girls missed their dad. I pushed back a swell of emotion, thankful I still had mine, for them as much as me.

"Now, this is the definition of blessed, it is," he said. "An old man surrounded by the best and brightest women in all the world."

I noticed he didn't commit himself to a number.

"I want to hear all about school. Becca first." He patted Bailey's leg, knowing she'd understand.

Becca's dimples engaged. "I can't wait to go back." Then she threw a look my way. "I mean . . . it's not that . . ."

"It's all right, sweetie. I know exactly what you mean."

"I'm glad to be home too."

"And your favorite class was . . .?" Dad asked.

"Biology."

"Biology?" Mother and I said it as one.

Becca breathed a little laugh and held up empty hands. "I know, who'd have thought?"

"Of course, it had nothing to do with Will Hunter." Bailey whipped her napkin and draped it over her lap.

"Will Hunter?" Mother and me again.

Becca leaned back and gave her sister a tight-lipped glare. "As a matter of fact, it didn't."

But Bailey's smile was downright devious. "What was your final grade?"

"Honestly, Bailey, I didn't say I was going to major in biology. I just said I liked it."

"Final grade?"

"Morning." Our waitress passed the menus around. "Can I get you all started with some coffee? And happy Father's Day," she said to Dad.

"Well, thank you"—he lowered his head to see over the top of his glasses—"Tiffany."

She patted her name tag and smiled.

Becca opened her menu and gave it her full concentration.

That's what you call timing.

❧

Our visit with Trey's dad wasn't quite as engaging, and, no, he thought he'd pass on the cemetery. But he loved the cards.

The girls and I stood arm in arm at Trey's grave. The bold-colored balloons, weighted with . . . something . . . sparred in the breeze. Bailey looked off toward the blue gray mountains while Becca sniffed and worked to keep her tears from hitting the granite. I felt as cold as the slab.

"Why?" Becca's whisper barely reached my ear.

I squeezed a little harder, my jaws tight. *Indeed. Why?*

When we arrived home I made deviled egg sandwiches. And waited for night. I had something to do.

Bailey wadded her napkin. "I'm going to Tim's." She tossed her paper plate and mine as well and reached for her strappy purse. Then something softened her face. She turned to Becca. "Want to go?"

My vision suddenly blurred, and I made myself busy with something.

Becca's eyes went wide. "To Tim's?" She thought for a moment, then smiled and shook her head. "But thanks."

"I won't be late."

"Wow," Becca said when the door closed behind her sister.

Yeah. Wow.

⌘

I'm not 100 percent sure, but I don't think Bailey caught onto the fact that before the girls came home from San Luis I switched beds. The one I'd shared with my unfaithful husband was now in the guest room, and vice versa. Believe me, it was not easy to do alone. But I could keep my girls happy, lay my head on the pillow at night, and sleep. Without thinking of her. And Trey. Together.

Funny. You'd think a person would know the moment infidelity occurred, that the weaving—begun from the first magical touch and improved on with a span of common living—had begun to unravel. Because your soul would tell you. Like a mother knowing her child was in danger, or twins with the funny things they do. You'd know. You just would.

It shook me that I didn't. That as I lay beside Trey that last

Sunday night, sharing mundane chatter and the breeze of the ceiling fan, I had no idea how broken we were. Or how long we'd been that way. That shook me too. That I couldn't place the line between before and after. Or that there maybe never was a before and that's why I couldn't find it. That he'd never loved just me alone.

I reached for the handle of Trey's closet door, for the first time in over nine months, as if it would open to *The Twilight Zone*. Before I could even reach for the light switch, I was overcome with the scent of him. I stepped back and leaned against the wall, holding my breath.

Why was he the one I wanted for comfort at times like this?

"Shallow breaths," I said and tried again. I felt in the dark for the switch plate and pressed. The closet, substantially larger than the average bedroom, glowed with soft light. And then one of the bulbs under the hand-cut lead-crystal flush-mount globe flickered and went out. I reached for the next switch and turned on the fluorescents. They buzzed and came to life.

I entered the cavern and closed the door behind me. The far wall was lined with cedar, and soon the rich smell began to over-power the lingering cologne.

The shoulders of Trey's suits and sport coats were veiled in a thin layer of dust, as were his Doc Martens and Bruno Maglis lined up on the shoe rack. Like achromatic laser beams guarding the booty, an occasional cobweb, stretched from hanger to ceil-ing, caught the light and drew my eye. Trey would be appalled.

Where to begin? My heart thumped, my palms perspired. This felt so tawdry, as if I were desecrating his memory. Then I considered the memory he left me with. I crossed to the dresser and slid open the top drawer, afraid of what I'd find—and what I wouldn't.

Trey's linen handkerchiefs were folded into neat squares, the silver *T* on top as always. I ran my finger over the raised monogram on all three stacks, paused, noted the disconnect between my finger and my heart. The action generated nothing. Not a whimper, a sniffle, a catch in my breath. Nothing. The woman scorned, I'd become the Shrew, Becky Sharp, and the White Witch rolled into one. I closed the drawer.

And opened the next. Ah, yes. The one I'd dumped. Mounds of underwear still lay in unfolded piles. And so they would stay.

I went through T-shirts, walking shorts, designer jeans, and—yuck!—magazines. The ones he "kept for the articles." Right. The trash came Tuesday. I'd wrap them up in a black lawn and garden bag that no one could see through and smuggle them out while the girls were at work on Monday.

Eight drawers yielded nothing toward my search, but the ninth drawer, the sweater drawer, made my mouth go dry. On the very bottom, underneath the sweaters I or the girls had bought for him and the two or three he'd bought for himself, was a sweater I'd never seen. It was moss green, a color I loved on Trey because it made his eyes come alive.

I lifted it out of the drawer and held it up. It was a golf sweater, 100 percent cotton, just right for the weather in, say, San Diego. The label was one I didn't recognize.

I shifted my weight from one leg to the other. Okay. This didn't have to mean anything. Trey went lots of places, bought things for himself all the time. But, and here was the stickler, for the last ten years at least, Trey had worn nothing but Ralph Lauren's Polo cologne. I sniffed the sweater. This was not Polo.

So Trey had reinvented himself in all kinds of ways.

A faint tapping on the bedroom door startled me and threw my heart in a dither.

"Mom?"

Becca. Oh, Lord. She was supposed to be in bed.

"Mom? Can I come in?"

I wadded up the sweater and shoved it in the drawer. "Ah, ah, be right there. Hold on." I surely had to sound, like Becca, as if I were in another county. I reached for the closet door to say it again, where she might actually be able to hear me. I stepped out.

As she stepped in. "Mom, where's my—? Oh, Mom." Becca took in the scene and moved toward me with arms extended, forehead crinkled, lips turned down. "I know. It's been a hard day." She wrapped me in thin arms and patted, then stepped back and peeked inside the closet. "You come here often?"

As if it were a shrine. I gave a weak smile.

"That is just so sweet."

Sweet. Right. My heart plummeted. *Fraud!* it screamed. *Phoney, phoney fraud!*

Ten

Fall had yet to tease us with even a slight appearance. Even so, the girls would leave for school again soon. First we had one enormous hurdle to get past. Becca's birthday.

It was impossible to believe a year had passed. The morning of Trey's death was still so vivid in my mind. My insides did a loopty-loo whenever I thought of that call, and my heart took a tumble each and every time I heard the doorbell ring. But one thing had changed, besides the obvious. I could no longer cry for Trey. Not so much as a tear. It's not that my allotment for Trey had been exhausted, oh no. It's that the well had been filled with contaminates, until all that remained was a mucky mess stopping the flow of anything pure. My heart needed a hosing, a filter change, but the way of it eluded me.

"Mom, I don't want a party." Becca was adamant, her green eyes wide and calling for a nod at least.

"It'll just be dinner with Gramma and Grampa, and maybe Grampa Torrington."

"Okay." She shrugged. "And Shawlie, but that's all."

"And Tim," Bailey said. "Now let's go."

She and Becca were working their last shift at Starbucks. Next week we'd get them ready for school, then they'd be on their way to participate as mentors in freshmen orientation. I'd have to get used to life alone all over again. The thought caused my stomach to take a dip, but not so deep as last September.

Bailey and Tim had spent a good deal of time together over the summer. I was partly okay with that. I just didn't want either of my daughters to do what I had done, to trade their own dreams for someone else's only to find the sacrifice had not been valued.

Tim was in his last year at Sac State, majoring in criminal justice. He didn't yet know what he'd do with his degree, but he had a year to figure it out. He treated Bailey well, at least in front of me, and neither seemed to be pushing for a serious commitment. I looked for any sign of Trey in the boy. So far I hadn't seen one.

I picked up the phone and dialed Shawlie's cell phone.

"I was just going to call you," she said. "I found the cutest purse made out of—you won't believe this—old jeans. There's a red bandana around the waist and pockets on the backside. It's just so cute. I think Becca would love it."

I smiled all alone in my kitchen. "Sounds like her."

"Meet me at the mall."

"Now? I'm getting things ready for—"

"The party. I'll help. I don't have any showings today."

"Oh, please, don't say the p-word in front of Becca. This is dinner, not a party."

"Of course. Poor darling. Now, come have one of those blended caramel thingies you love, then we'll look at the purses. They're at a kiosk in front of Bath and Body Works. I'll meet you at the coffee counter in Barnes and Noble."

Any effort at hesitation was wasted. Shawlie had hung up. She knows exactly how to get around me.

She sat at a tall round table, holding it for us because the place was packed. Malls and Sundays is a combination I'm not fond of. I prefer to do my shopping on, say, Tuesday mornings between ten and eleven forty-five, when the shoe department is all mine.

She hopped down and gave me a friendly hug. "Wait here. I'll go order. You want— What's it called?"

"Frappucino. Caramel."

"That's it! Me too."

My eyes grew large as Shawlie approached the table with our drinks. She ordered venti with whipped cream. When had coffee shops become such decadent places? I drew on the straw. "Pure heaven." Then drew again. "This is breakfast *and* lunch."

"And for dinner?"

"Anything but taco salad." Which I'd not made in the whole year since Trey died. "I'm thinking about barbecuing burgers."

"Oh, well, Abbie, burgers aren't your, you know, strong point."

I stirred the drink with my straw. "What's wrong with my burgers?"

"It's the whole barbecue thing. You've just never gotten the knack of it. Charbroiled takes on a whole new meaning in your backyard."

"Well, then, what if I ask my dad to do the burgers?"

"And you stick to the potato salad?"

I nodded.

"Good. I'll bring my famous baked beans."

I raised an eyebrow. "*Your* famous baked beans?"

"I add the dry mustard and onions. That makes them mine."

"That would not hold up in a court of law."

She gave me the smile she really was famous for and went back to her drink.

"Shawlie? I found a sweater."

"Oh, Abbie, it's way too hot to think about sweaters. Give it a few weeks."

"In Trey's drawer."

She stopped midpull on her straw and frowned. "RA— Rob wore sweaters all the time. Anything special about this particular sweater?"

"I'd never seen it before, but he'd worn it. It came from a shop in Imperial Beach. That's near—"

"San Diego." I had her attention. "How do you know it came from there?"

"The tag said."

She sat back and waited for the rest.

"It smelled of some sexy cosmopolitan cologne. Which didn't happen to be Polo. It was hidden under all his other sweaters."

"Hidden? You really think he'd hide something in such an obvious place? I mean"—she shrugged—"a sweater in his sweater drawer?"

"I never got into his things. I only found it because—"

Her eyebrow shot up. "Because?"

I took a long drink of my Frappuccino.

"Because?"

"Shawlie, I have to know who she is."

She dropped her forehead into the palm of her hand. "No, no, no, no, no. Abbie, you are asking for heartache."

"Heartache? It couldn't possibly get worse than it already is."

Her eyes were intense. "Trust me, Abbie, it can. Phil—you remember Phil?"

Husband number two, who was out of her life before the first

MasterCard bill for their honeymoon arrived in her mailbox. "Of course."

"And Darla?"

"Only the little bit you told me about her, which"—I looked around the small café—"isn't repeatable in public."

"Think Pamela Anderson. Only more"—she pulled back her shoulders—"enhanced."

"Yuck."

"Exactly."

My shoulders caved. "You really think Trey would leave me . . . us . . . for boobs and lips full of silicone?"

"Abbie—"

"He was a man," I said along with her.

"And I don't think they use silicone for the lips. I think it's collagen or some—" She caught my look and stopped.

"I don't know, Shawlie. That's not the kind of woman you divorce for. Not if you're Trey."

She slurped the last of her drink. "Let it go, Abbie. Get on with your life. Now"—she hopped down from her chair again—"wait till you see these purses. I might as well get Bailey one too. Her birthday isn't far away." She noticed my look. "Different, of course. I'll get hers with chaps."

"Chaps?" I laughed in spite of myself. "You do know my girls."

◈

Mother and Dad arrived at five forty-five, just in time for Dad to start the grill. Mother carried an understated gift bag and not one balloon. Bless her. We were all anxious to make this a good day for Becca. Ease her back into the idea of celebrating the day.

She put on a good front, but I knew my daughter too. Behind the smile was a heart full of broken shards, behind the eyes, a look that said, *Nothing is quite right anymore.*

"I have the patties all ready," I told Dad. "The girls will be home any minute, so crank up the barbecue."

"Be sure to brush it first," Mother called after him. As if he wouldn't. "Now, what can I do?"

"Toss the salad and crumble the bleu cheese?"

She made a face as she went to wash her hands.

"Or just the salad. I'll do the bleu cheese."

"Oh, I don't mind," she said, with the same conviction she'd use if I'd asked her to plunge the toilet.

"No, really, I was just going to set the table."

"I'll do that," Shawlie said. She'd come from the computer room, where she'd spent the past half hour.

"Oh. Shawlie."

"Evening, Mrs. Woodruff." Shawlie gave me a sideways glance. "Paper plates?"

"For a bir—" Mother bit off her sentence, shook her hands into the sink, and reached for a towel. Her back was ramrod straight.

"Since it's too hot to eat outside, I guess we'll do"—I took a breath—"china."

Shawlie gave me another look. *For burgers?* she mouthed.

"Don't be silly." Mother turned back to us. "Your everyday will do. Since we're not having anything formal."

Formal. Ah. "You know kids and burgers," I said.

"At nineteen and twenty, they're hardly children."

"Nineteen and nineteen, for three more weeks anyway," Shawlie corrected. Then she saw Mother's face. "Time sure flies," she stammered.

You had to give her an A for effort.

Dad opened the patio door. "I'm about ready for the cheese."

I glanced at the clock. Almost six. Why weren't the girls home? They should be home. My heart did a little dance, something downright tribal from the feel of it. I reached for the phone just as the door between the garage and kitchen opened. Relief was so sharp it hurt.

I mean, it's not like the day were cursed. Like there could ever be a repeat of last year's sorrow. The girls were just late.

"Hey." Becca gave a half-hearted smile to everyone in the room.

"Happy birthday," we all said at once.

Bailey passed through without comment.

"Thanks. We're, we're just going to change. We'll be right down." Becca hurried after her sister.

I exchanged a blank look with Shawlie. Everything about those brief seconds was wrong. I should go up and find out what.

"Abbie, sweetie? You have the cheese?"

Cheese. Yeah. "Coming, Dad."

True to her word, the girls did come right down. They'd both changed clothes, and Bailey was a little more herself, at least not so sullen. She poured herself a soda and carried it to the table, along with the mayonnaise and ketchup clutched in her arms. She came back for the mustard and the plate of fixin's: tomatoes, lettuce, and sliced red onions.

"Rough day at work?" I kept my voice low, my question between the two of us.

She shrugged. "Later."

I nodded.

"Now that's what I call a hamburger." Shawlie took the platter from my dad, who headed to the sink to wash up. He smiled and winked.

She was right. There wasn't a charred edge anywhere.

We found our places around the table. I opened the package of buns and handed it to Mother, on my left. "Oh, hey, Bailey, shouldn't we wait for Tim?"

Becca cleared her throat and gave a quick shake of her head just as Bailey said, "No."

Ah. "Dad, would you like to say grace?"

It was a lovely prayer he offered, mostly for Becca, but his thank-you list included "all those we cherish." Present or not. He meant Trey, of course. I opened one eye as Becca shifted in her chair. Bailey shifted too, her mouth a tight, thin line.

Becca smoothed a napkin across her lap. "What about Grampa Torrington?"

"He sends his regrets, sweetie. He doesn't like to drive after dark."

Mother speared a patty from the platter and passed it on. "Now there's a man who knows his limitations."

Dad snapped to on my right. "I happen to be ten, no, eleven years younger than Robert Torrington, and my night vision is as sharp as ever."

"That's not what Dr. Sutter said at your last exam."

"Last I heard, he wasn't using my eyes to drive at night."

Mother made that sound through her nose that drives me nuts.

"Beans?" Shawlie offered them, counterclockwise, to my dad.

"Love some." He scooped a ladle full onto his plate while Shawlie held the dish.

"Mrs. Woodruff?"

Mother lifted her glasses and scowled at the bowl. "They have onions?"

Shawlie smiled and nodded.

"I'll pass."

"You love onions," Dad said.

"Not in pork and beans."

Shawlie held her smile. "Baked."

"Well. I don't know what on earth I'll do with myself after next week," I said. "I'm going to miss you girls."

"Mom, I've been thinking." Becca spread mayonnaise on her hamburger bun, then gave me that studious look that makes my heart melt. "Why don't *you* go back to school?"

"Me? School?"

"Now there's a dumb idea," Bailey said. Trey's words in a higher pitch, and like his, aimed and tossed like so many darts, each one hitting its mark in a tight pattern, moving ever toward the center, until . . .

"What's dumb about it?"

"Well"—Bailey turned to me—"no offense, Mother, but aren't you a little old for that?"

. . . bull's-eye.

"Lots of people go back to school." I tried not to sound as defensive as I felt. I did not succeed.

"That's right, Bailey. Mom's only in her early forties."

Bailey held up empty hands. "I rest my case."

"Life isn't exactly over once you reach forty."

I could have kissed Becca.

Mother dabbed her mouth. "No, but reality should have set in by then."

"Reality?"

"Mother, honestly," Bailey said. "Say you did go back to school. It would take four, maybe five years to get your degree. You'd be almost fifty."

"Forty-five."

"Or forty-six," Mother said.

"I mean, who starts a new career at fifty?"

"Ronald Reagan," Dad said.

"Well, there you are." I patted his leg. Chalk up a point for our team.

Shawlie shot me that look she got whenever she hatched a plan. "You could always get your real estate license and come to work for me."

"Oh, Shawlie, I don't know about that. But really, Bailey, why shouldn't I take a class or two at American River?"

She wound a strand of hair around her finger. "American River?"

"Well, it's not like I'm going to tag along with you girls to Cal Poly."

"Oh."

Becca laughed. "Is that what you thought?"

Bailey rolled her eyes. "No."

"Sure sounded like it."

"One or two morning classes at ARC." I brushed my napkin across my lips. "That's really not a bad idea."

"You always said you'd like to go back to school once Bailey and I were on our own."

"Well, you're not exactly on—"

"So I don't see what the big deal is." This she said to Bailey.

"Who said it was a big deal?"

"Just because you're—" Becca stopped, went white.

Bailey's cheeks turned crimson. She wadded her napkin,

dropped it on her plate, and left the room. Twenty seconds later her bedroom door slammed.

Becca looked as remorseful as I'd ever seen her.

"Excuse me." I pushed back my chair, dreading every step that took me upstairs to my daughter's room. I knocked once, then opened the door, surprised the knob actually turned in my hand. "Bailey?"

She stood at her window, looking down toward the lake, arms wrapped around her thin waist.

"Honey?"

She turned, her cheeks still red. "In case you'd like to know, Tim is going to be a father."

My knees went weak. I reached for the corner of her bed and sat before I fell. "A fath—" My voice failed. I swallowed hard. I admit it, my eyes dropped to her middle, where pelvic bones jutted out just above the top of her low-rise crops. Her yellow T-shirt ended three inches above, exposing a flat tummy and skin smooth and gold as summer honey. A silver ring protruded from her navel.

"The problem is"—her eyes flashed—"I'm not the mother."

I loosened the grip I had on her comforter and breathed again. "Oh, sweetheart."

She looked up sharply and fanned her eyes. I know beyond all doubt she was thinking to herself, *Do not let one tear fall, Bailey Rianne Torrington.* I wanted to go to her, to put my arms around her, to whisper, "I'm sorry," and "It'll be okay," but that would have sabotaged the gallant effort she was putting into not falling apart.

"Oh, but it gets better. He doesn't think it should affect our relationship. After all, he doesn't love her. She was just there and I wasn't." She dripped of sarcasm. "As if this is my fault"—she slapped her chest—"because I was at school. Because I wouldn't—" She turned away.

Well, heartbroken as I was for my daughter, I could have cheered at that.

"Guys are so stupid."

Oh, yeah. "How did you find this out?" Ordinarily we would have laughed out loud at the double entendre.

"He came to my work!"

"And told you? Just like that?" Well, he had more guts than Trey.

"She had just called him, I mean not an hour before, with the results of one of those pregnancy-test-in-a-box thingies. The stick was—well, whatever color it turns when you get caught."

Royal blue. How well I knew it.

"And somehow he thought I'd feel sorry for *him*!"

"For him?" Stupid didn't begin to cover it.

"I mean, I hope the test is wrong, for her sake at least. But Tim McGuire can take a dive off the dam, headfirst. Well, you know what I mean."

"Do you know the girl?"

She gave me her best *you're-not-going-to-believe-this* look. "Amy Brennan."

"Amy Brennan?" Well, that did it. If Tim didn't take the dive, I'd be only too happy to push him. She'd had a crush on Tim as long as Bailey had known either of them. But Amy wasn't the kind of girl Tim would "take to a dog fight." She didn't have the right face, the right figure, the right pedigree.

Evidently he didn't mind taking her to bed.

"If he calls here"—Bailey's eyes narrowed—"I do not want to talk to him."

"Of course not, honey. I understand."

"Mother, you're sweet and all that, but how could you possibly understand? You were married to Daddy."

Eleven

"**S**he and Tim broke up." No point in saying more.

Becca and I exchanged a quick glance, one that Shawlie didn't miss. But then, she doesn't miss much.

Mother closed the door to the dishwasher she'd just finished loading. They'd taken care of everything while I was upstairs. "Maybe I'll just go up and—"

"Um, Mother. Let's give her some time. She'll come down when she's ready." Mother's nod was curt, but I was sticking to my guns. "How about cake?"

"And presents." Shawlie winked at Becca, whose smile was half-hearted at best.

Why did the worst things happen on her birthday? That's what she had to be thinking. And so was I. I raised my head to the ceiling. *So if you're up there, do you have an answer?*

"I made coffee," Mother said. "Shall we move to the family room?"

❧

Dishes were done for the second time, and Becca was upstairs transferring things to her new purse. It was as big a hit as the diamond studs I gave her, chosen because they wouldn't take up precious space in her dorm room. Mother and Dad were finally gone, after Mother spent half an hour upstairs with Bailey—at Bailey's request, I have to add. I took the opportunity to fill Dad and Shawlie in on the news. Now I was ready for Shawlie to finish her tea and leave me to a cool shower and the book upstairs by my bed. The one whose title I couldn't remember, but that didn't matter. I used it mostly to put me to sleep.

"I talked to the owner." Shawlie held her mug with both hands and smirked at me.

"The owner?" It was the end of a long and trying day. I wasn't up for a guessing game.

"Of the sweater shop."

My eyes went wide and she smirked again. "In Imperial Beach?"

"I found it online."

"And you . . . you called him?"

"Her. Parker Davis. A really delightful woman."

"Parker?"

"Not everyone's as good at picking names as you are, Abbie. But, I don't know, I think it sounds wonderfully entrepreneurial."

"What on earth did you say to her?"

"I had a client—I couldn't bring myself to say friend—who owned a couple sweaters from her shop. By the way, it's called— Oh, but you know. It was on the—"

"Label," I said along with her. "The Turtle's Neck."

"Now, there's a great name."

Under any other circumstances I might have agreed. "A couple sweaters? Why a couple?"

She shrugged. "I didn't want to say just one. Anyway, I said I lost contact with the client but remembered the name of the shop—who wouldn't?—and wondered if by chance she still carried one of the sweaters he used to wear. Then I described it."

"The green one?"

"Of course the green one."

"Why?"

"Well, how else would she know which one I was talking about?"

"No, I mean, why ask about it at all? You certainly weren't going to ask if she remembered who besides your client bought that same sweater, were you? Were you?"

She took a long drink of her tea.

"Shawlie?"

She leaned in, my conspirator, pulling me in with her. "What if she remembered? What if she could tell us the name?"

I leaned back. "Oh, Shawlie, I don't know."

"You said you wanted to know."

"And you said to let it go. I think you were right. I'm not ready for this." I chewed the polish off my thumbnail, and then the thumbnail too. "What did she say about the sweater?"

"It was quite a popular style. She sold all three dozen but probably won't order any more, at least for a while. She likes to provide variety for her customers."

"Three dozen." Oddly, my heart took a dive. "So then, she couldn't really tell us the name of the woman who bought it."

"Maybe if she saw a photo of Rob."

"That would assume he was there at the time of purchase." Our eyes locked. "And we both know that sweater was a gift. So that's that."

We sighed in unison.

"Well, we're one step closer than we were. If you want to pursue this, you know I'm here for you."

I squeezed her hand and nodded. "But now I need to concentrate on Bailey."

She came around to my side of the table and hugged me. "So tell me something new."

❦

Classes had begun at American River the week before Becca's suggestion that I go back to school. I still could have made it in with late enrollment, but there were things I needed to settle if I was really going to do this. The next semester started in January. That would do just fine.

I decided not to sell the house as long as the girls were in school and/or living at home. It was only fair they had a home that belonged to them, that held their DNA. But in fairness to me, keeping all things equal, some changes had to be made. I needed to eliminate as much of Trey's DNA as I possibly could without coming across like the Ice Queen, to maintain a balance between what was normal and what appeared ruthless.

I started with the master bedroom.

Sage green had been Trey's call, and though I melded into its soothing touch for six years, all I saw now was that sweater. The walls, the valances, the duvet. All sweater. It didn't matter that one was sage and the other moss. The green had to go.

It was Monday morning, the second week of September, the day after the girls left for Cal Poly. I dialed Shawlie's cell phone. "You busy?"

"You know how it is after summer."

"How near are you to a Starbucks?"

"Three blocks is as far away as you can get these days. What's up?"

"Bring the mochas and your imagination. We're doing a makeover."

"Oh, girl, you are singing my song."

Thirty minutes later she pulled into the driveway. The mochas were nice and hot and chocolaty.

"Now, Abbie, you know I love you, but I've wanted to do this for so long." She reached for my hair, touched her fingers to the tops of my shoulders, then slid them inward toward my chin. "Take off six inches. That will show off your neck. Do you know how many women would kill for this neck, Abbie? And bangs. You haven't had bangs in years." She pulled a magazine out of her satchel, flipped it open, and jabbed a fingernail at one of the models. "Sassy. Like this. And highlights. Summer's over, so gold, not blonde, and, oh yes. *Yes.* Look here. Red. Just a few."

"Shawlie. What in the world are you talking about? And that's plum!"

She pulled the magazine closer. "Not really plum. It's more — what do you mean, what am I talking about? The makeover."

Droll isn't my forte, but I did the best I could. "Not me, Shawlie. The house."

"The house?"

"You can't have the mocha back, but I'm — "

"Not selling." She sat down on a stool and closed her eyes like shutters against bad news.

"And I know you love me. I was banking on that."

"Oh, Abbie. I had lined up the cutest places for you to look at."

I almost chuckled at her sigh. She could be so melodramatic.

"So you're just going to let your mother win?"

"That part's hard, I know, but it's only till the girls are on their own."

"You're in denial, my friend. They are on their own."

"Only in part. When they aren't coming home anymore, then I'll sell."

She slapped her magazine closed. "I certainly hope you don't tell them that. I can see Bailey making her pilgrimage one weekend a year for*ever*, just to keep you here. If you're not careful, that girl will control your life."

I choked, coughed, and said nothing about the color that pots and kettles call one another. "Don't you want to hear my idea?"

"I like mine better."

She wasn't ready to give up her pout just yet. I sipped my mocha and indulged her.

"You're really going to clunk around this mausoleum for the next decade?"

"Mausoleum? That's not how you listed it, I hope. And I'm thinking three years at the most."

She finished her drink in one long gulp. "All right, show me what you're thinking."

"Come on. Upstairs."

"Well, naturally."

∝∨

We spent the morning at Sherwin-Williams looking at paint chips. Every color of the spectrum, minus the wedge that represented any shade of green. It was my new least favorite color.

Shawlie shuffled through a chained deck of color strips. "Bold is in. But then, we are talking about you."

I looked up from my own deck. "I can do bold."

"Cranberry?"

"On . . . how many walls?"

"See." She went back to her colors.

"This is nice." I singled out a strip.

"Mauve. Now there's bold."

"Well, it won't keep me up at night."

She dropped her deck and reached for her purse. "Come on. I want to show you something."

"But—"

"Now."

We drove in her car through the heart of Granite Bay to a brand-new, high-end development on the eastern edge of town. I bolstered my defenses right away. "Is this one of those cute places you wanted to show me?"

"Does it look cute?"

"It looks expensive."

"It is, though you could easily afford it. And no, this is not one of the houses I wanted to show you. But"—she stooped down with a key to open the lock box—"you have to see this master suite."

Shawlie led me through a house I could only gape at. It was gorgeous, stupendous, with a view of the Sierras out one set of arched windows and the lake out another.

"Up here," she called from the second-floor landing. She led me through double doors into, well, heaven's a bit extreme, but this came close.

"Oh." It's really all I could say.

"And not one speck of bold." She turned and gave me a half smile. "Say the word and it's yours."

Bolster. Bolster. Bolster. That was my mantra of the day.

"The owners are relocating to Martha's Vineyard. They're eager to sell." The last five syllables went up the scale: *do, re, mi, fa, so.*

"No." I shook my head. "No. I'm staying where I am." I'm not sure who I was trying to convince more.

"Well, that's what I figured, but I know the decorator. She's a local. I wanted you to see what she can do."

"You got my attention."

"Good. I'll get you her card. Oh, and there'll be a waiting list."

There was, ordinarily, six to eight months, but oddly enough Portia had a cancellation that very week. A couple deciding to divorce rather than redecorate. Trouble, trouble everywhere. If I knew exactly what I wanted, she could work me in.

Well, thanks to Shawlie, I did, didn't I?

❦

I made the most of my time waiting for Portia. I took down the valances, rolled up the duvet, and put them all aside for Goodwill. And good riddance. Portia was arranging to have the wing chair in the sitting room recovered. In the meantime, I hauled it downstairs and out to the garage. The lamps went, the wall art, everything down to the polished wood. Then on a whim out went the polished wood too. No more dark, heavy furniture. I wanted light, and I started with an armoire that took my breath away.

The guest bed went back to the guest room, and I went in search of the perfect replacement for what had been the bed I'd shared with Trey. Of course, Portia knew the best places to shop, and together we found a sleigh bed that perfectly matched the wood of the armoire.

A sleigh bed. For me. Oh my heavens, this was fun.

Now that I had a bed and a color scheme—taupe, charcoal, and ivory—I began to search for sheets and a comforter. Comforter. What a perfect name for what I needed. And I found the perfect one in San Francisco.

Everything came out so the suite could be painted, but when the reconstruction began, only my things went back in. The bathroom was decked out in new towels and throw rugs, a new gilt-framed mirror had been hung, and every drawer and inch of counter space was mine. By November, Trey had been eradicated from the master suite. There wasn't a trace of him anywhere.

Almost.

"It doesn't count if you stockpile all his stuff in here, Abbie." Shawlie came up for the grand unveiling, and before I could stop her, she opened the door to Trey's closet. With one glance from her I felt like a puppy who'd piddled on the new carpet.

I confessed. "I don't know what to do with it all."

"You get rid of it, plain and simple. Phillip was easy since he'd barely moved in before I threw him out, but when Donald left, what didn't fit in his suitcase ended up in a Dumpster before he got back for a second load."

I gave a little shake of my head. "This is so different, Shawlie."

She gave me one of those looks so rare in Shawlie's repertoire and closed the closet door. "You, of all people, don't deserve this."

I blinked, swallowed, turned, and blotted my eyes. "Aside from the closet, what do you think?"

She made a full sweep of the rooms, emerging from the bathroom with an approving smile. "Divine. Absolutely divine. This will show beautifully." She held up a hand to stop the words about to tumble off my tongue. "When it's time." She took another turn about the room. "What's next?"

"Oh, well, I think I'd better get used to this first."

"You mean Bailey and Becca need to get used to this first?" She turned to me with an arched eyebrow. "And Mother."

A shiver worked its way up what would have been my backbone if I had one. "They'll be able to see it all next week." I feigned delight.

"Oh, goodie."

I looked toward the closet on the way out of the room. "After Christmas. I'll do something about the closet then."

Twelve

The thing I missed was Trey coming home at night, especially when he'd been gone all week. I feel contaminated now, thinking about what he came home from. But back then, when I didn't know, I loved the anticipation of his homecoming. If I was in the kitchen, I'd hear the garage door begin to rise, and I'd smile. My pulse would escalate like a school girl with a crush. He had that effect on me till the day he died. Trey had so many charming ways. Deceitfully charming, yes. I see that now. But honestly, he could sweet-talk a bone away from a pit bull—as long as that pit bull's name wasn't Shawlie.

In the early years he'd come home hungry for love, and I was happy to oblige because I was hungry too. Not for physical love so much but for the closeness that filled my reservoir with joy and contentment, peace and pleasure.

I meant to reciprocate. I know now how miserably I failed.

There was an indescribable allure about Trey that had nothing to do with physical appearance. Yes, he was nice to look at, but not in a movie star way. In a word, his looks were . . . sweet. But it wasn't his looks that first attracted me. It was that *je na sais quoi* that reeled me in like a fish on the line, that kept my eyes focused on Trey and no one else for twenty years. Really, he could have looked like any plain old fellow and still captured my heart.

Except he wasn't any plain old fellow. There was magic in Trey. Magic in the way his lips puckered when he smiled, the way his smile engaged his whole face, crinkling the outer edges of his eyes. And his laugh . . . his laugh? My stomach lurched. I couldn't hear it in my head anymore. Couldn't summon it at all. "Oh, Trey." He was leaving me in yet another way, dissipating like fog in the sunshine.

When I was in danger of giving way to sentiment, and I fought that battle more than once, I brought out the sweater. I'd finger its softness, breathe its unfamiliar scent, and remind myself what this was all about. It brought the arcane parts of my life into focus, reminding me that at midnight the carriage turns back into a pumpkin. End of story.

I spent a good deal of the days leading up to Thanksgiving in Trey's closet, arranging and straightening what I'd tossed in during the makeover. My heart thumped every time I thought about Bailey and Becca getting their first look at Portia's handiwork. I had to at least make the closet look like I'd taken care of their father's things, that they mattered as much to me now as they once had.

While I missed the life I thought I'd had with Trey, I sorely missed the physical presence of his mother. Winnie had been such an instigator of fun. Her laugh—which I still recall without any effort at all—was pure mischief, and the sparkle in her eye a golden key to any number of secrets. Like how to stick a feather in the band of Robert the Second's fedora just as he walked out the door in the morning. She could laugh all day wondering how long it had taken him to discover and remove it. And if it came back home in the evening still in its hiding place, well, it wasn't hard to imagine that mirth could be hazardous, for Winnie could just about laugh herself into the grave. But what a way to go.

A bit different from Trey's exit.

Winnie was always there when I needed her, from the beginning of our relationship.

Trey kissed the back of my neck, startling the breath right out of me. I hadn't heard him come in.

"What are we reading?"

I pressed the book, facedown, onto my burgeoning lap. I was just into maternity clothes with my first pregnancy and was reading Naming Your Baby, *which I'd checked out on a whim from the library. I blushed a coral pink, feeling the heat in my cheeks. "Oh, well . . . I just . . ."*

He lifted the book and the hand that held it. "Ah," he said. He came around and joined me on the sofa.

"I'm making a list." I smiled, sure he'd be pleased at that, and held my breath as he scanned it.

"I added a couple of girl names, you know, just in case."

"Ah," he said again.

"I really like Grant. It goes so well with Torrington."

His eyebrow arched. "For a girl?"

I breathed a little chuckle. "Of course not. Grant's a boy's name."

He took the book from my hand, closed it, and laid it on the coffee table. "Oh, but, Abbie"—he'd not yet shortened me to Ab—"he'll be Robert Andrew Torrington the Fourth. Of course." He wrapped an arm around the back of the sofa, letting his fingers play on my shoulder. "And if by some strange turn of events it's a girl . . ." He laughed a bit at the absurdity of it.

But I held my breath.

"I kind of like Roberta."

It's a bad enough testament to the vanity of men that they name their sons after themselves, generation after generation. Henry the Eighth, Louis the Sixteenth, Robert the Third. But too many of them want to claim their daughters as well. Think of all the Glendas, Frankies, and Geraldines in the world. They aren't named for their mothers, that's for sure, for the ones who surrendered their bodies to stretch marks, swaybacks, and varicose veins. Oh no. Whoever started the practice should be made to write his name a hundred times on every chalkboard ever made. Maybe then men would appreciate originality.

Roberta? My heart sank. "I was thinking of Gail." *I wasn't. Not for one minute. But this would surely show him how silly the tradition was.*

"Gail?" *He clearly didn't get it.*

"For" — *I pointed to myself* — "Abigail."

I'd never seen Trey's face such a blank page. Every tiny muscle went slack, and for two or three seconds his mouth hung open. Then he closed it and licked his lips. "Gail. Aha." *He began to draw circles with his lecture finger on my list of names.* "Well sure." *He rubbed his chin.* "Okay." *And scratched his nose.* "Here's what we'll do. We'll name her* — *of course, this is undoubtedly a moot point, but if this is a girl* — *we'll name her Roberta Gail."*

Roberta Gail? For my beautiful little girl? I wanted a name that would sing, not one that clunked around in my head like a random tune played on a toy piano.

I did the only thing I could think to do.

"Winnie?"

She caught the desperation in my voice across the phone line. "What is it, love?"

"The baby." *I was trying not to cry.* "Trey wants to name him Robert Andrew Torrington the Fourth."

"The Fourth? Well, darling, we'll just have to hope for a girl." *I could hear the smile in Winnie's words.*

"It gets worse." And I told her.

"Oh my. I see your point. But don't despair. We have four months to work on him."

But try as we might, we couldn't budge Trey. I went into labor thinking I was about to bring a Robert the Fourth or a Roberta Gail into the world. It only added to my pain. When at last our baby arrived, Trey was stunned to hear the news.

"It's a girl," someone said.

And in spite of the fact that the father determines the sex of the baby, Trey placed the blame squarely on me. I knew it from the weakness of his smile, from the placing of his kiss on my forehead instead of my lips, from the blue carnations that arrived to my room even before I did. They were removed and replaced with something pink before day's end, but the message was clear. I'd let him down.

"What a beauty." Winnie held her granddaughter as if she were solid gold. "And definitely not a Roberta."

"Oh, Winnie, what do I do?"

"It depends on how brave you are." The twinkle was there in all its glory.

"What do you mean?"

"They'll bring the birth certificate later, and Trey won't be here."

"He won't?"

She shook her head. "You'll have sent him back to work. And because he's Trey, he'll go." She gave her granddaughter's nose a kiss. "Now, this is just my opinion, but any woman who's gone through eleven hours of labor and an episiotomy to boot, after nine months and two weeks of pregnancy, deserves to name her daughter Delilah if she so chooses, or Harry for that matter. What goes on that birth certificate becomes her legal name." She handed the baby back to me after one more kiss, picked up her purse, and gave me one of her famous smiles. "That's just my opinion."

I lay there with my sweet little girl in my arms. My Bailey, the name

I'd secretly called her for weeks. It's who she already was to me. So, in spite of how fiercely my hands trembled as I filled out that certificate, she legally became Bailey Rianne Torrington. The one and only.

This would never have worked if I'd named Robert the Fourth Arnold or Joe, but I do think I'd have given Trey his son to name. In his own way he gave me my girl by not ranting or divorcing me—then. But he was quiet for days and refused to call the baby anything.

Mother, naturally, came to his defense. "What in the world kind of name is Bailey for a girl? Or even a boy, for that matter? It's a surname, Tippy, for crying out loud. You might as well call her Whiteley or Davidson for all the sense it makes."

And when Becca was born it was worse.

"Becca isn't a name," Mother complained, "it's half a name. Besides, Bailey and Becca . . . it's much too confusing. You'll be tripping over your Bs day in and day out. And I, for one, will never get them straight."

"Maybe this will help," Winnie said. "BA equals Bailey, BE equals Becca. A before E, Bailey before Becca. No more confusion."

Mother gave her one of those looks that Bailey has grown so good at.

Oh, Winnie, sweet Winnie. What words would you have for me now? Am I widowed or divorced? Or merely betrayed?

~⁂~

I was so thankful Winnie had loaned me her grit when I needed it. I could use some of it now. Becca thought I worshiped her father, literally, at the closet shrine. She would cut me some slack. But Shawlie was right. I was terrified of showing my room to Bailey and Mother. What was I thinking? I should have sold the house. Then change would have been a natural event, instead of this glaring *look-what-I've-done* approach.

Wednesday of Thanksgiving week arrived, much too soon for

once. I was as nervous as a Beatle in a barber shop. The girls were due by two thirty, and though I was plenty occupied with pecan pies and sweet potato casserole, I couldn't keep my eyes off the digital oven clock.

My remedy for nerves was to clean. Really clean. So once the pies were in the oven, I got busy. Surfaces that already shined got a top coat of something to make them shine even more. Furniture glistened, windows sparkled without a streak, and I could actually make out the start of crow's-feet around my eyes in my stainless-steel double-wide sub-zero. I stopped short of setting the self-cleaning feature of the oven not in use, not wanting to override the smells of cinnamon, cloves, and nutmeg before the girls arrived.

The thought—again—of the girls' arrival sent me on another cycle. Shower doors—oh, how I hate shower doors—that were dried with every single use got a good polishing, as did the brushed nickel faucets. I hung new rolls of toilet paper, folding the end piece to a nice point. I may as well have laid out chocolate mints on the girls' pillows. If I'd had any I would have.

"Mom! We're home."

One fifty, forty minutes early. Bailey must have driven all the way. Perspiration broke out on my upper lip, and it couldn't be fifty degrees outside. I closed the door to my bedroom on my way downstairs. *Coward*, I thought, then quickly agreed with myself, a sure sign I was spending too much time alone.

"Oh, hey." I pasted on a smile as I descended the stairs. "You made good time."

Becca kissed my cheek, while Bailey gave me half a hug on her way upstairs.

"Where . . . where are you going?"

Bailey nodded toward her room. "I just want to make a quick call."

"You just got here."

"I'll be right down."

I watched her till she got to her room and closed the door behind her.

"Mom, it smells so good in here. And I'm starved. Bailey wouldn't stop except for coffee and to pee." She led me to the kitchen.

"Oh, sweetie, it's good to see you." And it was, nerves notwithstanding. "What would you like?"

"A fat turkey sandwich with loads of mayo and dressing. But that'll have to wait till tomorrow. So, peanut butter, I guess. No crust."

I stopped on my way to the pantry and turned. She was smiling her beautiful smile, then broke into a laugh. "Only kidding."

"I cut the crust off your sandwiches till you were twelve."

"Eleven. Bailey was twelve."

"Oh, right."

"Did Gramma cut the crust off your sandwiches?"

I had to think a moment. "No."

"You were a rare kid."

Right.

Becca looked toward the second story of our house. "She's calling Tim."

"Tim?"

"They've been talking, but don't say I told you."

I felt a pang in my stomach. "How long?"

"A few weeks."

"Mother!" Bailey's voice sounded from upstairs.

I dropped the lid to the peanut butter jar and caught Becca's worried frown as we both jumped down from our stools.

"Mother!"

From the landing I saw the door to my bedroom standing wide open.

"What did you do?"

From the look on her face, you'd think she'd found bodies under the carpet. I gave a shrug as weak as the smile I tried to produce. "I just—"

"How could you?" She slapped one fist into the palm of her other hand.

Becca took one step into the room and stopped. She turned and gave me a sadly disappointed look. "Wow." Her tone was not equal to the word. "When did you—?" She turned back to the scene.

I closed my eyes. *Do* not *look in the closet, Becca. Please.*

"I just—" I said again as Bailey swept past me, and winced at the sound of her car keys snatched from the entry table. Then the front door slammed.

"This is"—Becca tried to smile—"nice."

Thirteen

I was three when Aunt Lizzy died, when Mother drew the drapes on her world, so to speak, to keep out the light of all things jubilant. Elizabeth was two years older than Mother, her only sibling and best, *best* friend. By the time I was old enough to understand the loss, I was operating under the mistaken idea that Mother had long since gotten past her sorrow. That shows you how much I know.

Aunt Lizzy was twenty-eight when she noticed the knot just below the crook of the elbow on the fleshy part of her arm. It didn't hurt, she said, but neither did it go away. By the time they did the X-ray, the bone cancer was in too many places to name. The knot was the mother tumor, of course. There were only seven months between the day she discovered it and the day it took her life.

Lizzy was the brightest bulb in Mother's chandelier, but poignant memory will do that. Still, from all accounts, Lizzy was something special. A young and vibrant Winnie is how I've come to imagine her. She was single and childless, which is also tragic because she had so much to offer in the way of love. The photograph that sits on the piano in Mother and Dad's living room is evidence of how grandly she embraced life. It captured her in midlaugh—a laugh that lit up her eyes and drew others in—as she pointed to the object of her humor. I've often wondered what it was that sparked such hilarity, but no one's ever said.

My personal favorite of Lizzy was taken when I was three days old. She's standing in my nursery, arms outstretched like tines on a forklift with me lying across them, a look of mingled terror and awe on her face.

In stark contrast to these is the photo Mother keeps beside her bed. Aunt Lizzy not much older than the piano shot, walking away from the camera, looking back over her shoulder and waving. The good-bye girl.

Oddly, I feel a connection with Lizzy, mostly because she took with her the part of Mother I'd dearly love to know.

Though the circumstances are infinitely different, I now know the pain of losing someone you love. I've come to close each day by pulling off a link in a mental paper chain, moving toward the day when the sorrow will finally be spent. But knowing that Mother's eyes can brim with just the mention of Lizzy's name forty years after her death doesn't lend much hope to my own convoluted mourning experience.

I'm hoping infidelity adds its own healing element to the mix.

After Aunt Lizzy's funeral, Mother found a church to join, one that emphasized the drudgery of the "must-always and must-never" as the door to the stairway of heaven. You must never skip church, not even when Dad suggested a weekend getaway for just the two of them, just because. I was fourteen and thought it the most romantic thing I'd ever heard. He had me arrange to spend the weekend with a friend and went so far as to pack a bag for Mother, all on the sly of course. But weekend was out of the question because weekend meant Sunday.

You must never say no when the Women's Ministries director calls for help with a funeral lunch, even if your daughter is in the volleyball tournament of the century.

You must always wear the proper face when you step through the doors of the church, regardless of how heated the argument you had on the way.

It helps, I think, for Mother to feel she is in control of her own rewards. The one she seeks the most, judging by her efforts, is absolution for continuing to live, while Lizzy died.

Winnie, on the other hand, by her own words, found grace. I didn't understand what that meant for years. I just knew that her form of religion was infinitely more appealing. Yet for the longest time I feared that if and when I embraced that aspect of life, I would follow in my mother's path. Earned absolution seemed the only way to heaven for me. I wasn't Winnie. And I wasn't Lizzy. I was my mother's daughter.

When Mother called to tell me that Bailey would be spending the night with her and Dad, the accusations in her voice were unmistakable: My inexplicably thoughtless actions had hurt someone she loves.

"What's next?" she asked. Shawlie's question, with a much different flavor. "You do realize you aren't the only one who lost Trey? And your daughters are not as ready as you to toss out his memory like an old bedspread."

At least the analogy fit.

❧

"Some pecan pie? I baked an extra." Because it's both girls' favorite. And I'm by no means above bribery, groveling, or both at the same time.

Becca curled into Trey's recliner and shook her head.

"Some tea?"

"I'm good. Thanks."

Okay, no point dancing around the issue. "I was going to show you both the room. Later."

Becca gave a quick nod, looking everywhere but at me. I could see how she fought to hold back tears.

"I've decided not to sell the house." I made my voice as upbeat as possible.

Becca turned to me. "Really?"

I shrugged. "Eventually, but now isn't the time. So that's why . . ." I looked toward the second floor.

Another brief nod.

"I wonder what Bailey wanted, why she went in?"

A guilty look washed over Becca's face. "It's what we do, Bailey and me, whenever we come home. To connect. With Dad."

"To connect." I could have crawled under a rock with the rest of the slugs.

"It's just . . ." She shrugged. "What we do."

Now it was my turn to look at everything in the room except my daughter.

"Did you get rid of" — Becca bit her lip and pulled a throw pillow to her stomach — "everything?"

"No, sweetheart, of course not. Most of his things are upstairs. In his closet." And that's where they would stay. Indefinitely. "You can go there anytime you want."

She gave a weak smile. "Like you?"

Slug, slug, slug. That was me.

"The room. It really is nice," Becca said.

Somehow, an invitation to do a walk-through seemed out of place. "It's just— Oh, honey, he's your father. I know how much you love him, even now, because I know how much I love my own dad. I don't know how much you miss him. I can only imagine—"

"Because you miss him too."

"Yes, I do." That wasn't entirely a lie. "But, Becca, I know this will be hard for you and Bailey to understand, but unless I want to live the rest of my life in the past, I have to get beyond this. Redoing my room seemed the best first step." I reached my hand toward her, stopped short of touching her knee. "I don't want to give up the possibility of having a life again."

Her skin was pale as the November fog. "You mean, with someone else?"

"I only want the option. Doesn't that seem at least a little bit reasonable?"

Becca's eyes glistened as she turned away. "Gramma says some loves are timeless. That they live on even after—" Tears spilled onto her cheeks, dripped onto the pillow. She hiccupped a sob. "I miss him." Her voice was as thin as mountain air.

"I know you do, sweetheart. I wish I could help."

She moved from the chair and sat at my feet, her head resting on my knees. "That's how it was for you and Dad, wasn't it?"

My heart did a sprint, then jarred to a stop. I waited for my breathing to even out. "I wonder if it's ever that way for anyone."

"You two came close." She raised her eyes to me, eyes the color of Trey's. "So close."

Unable to find even the most inadequate words, I simply rubbed her hair.

"That's what I want, Mom, a marriage like yours and Dad's."

"Oh, well, Becca—"

"I worry about Bailey. I don't like that she's seeing Tim again."

My stomach tumbled. "Seeing?"

"Don't tell her I told you, but he drove all the way to San Luis a few weeks ago. Now they talk on the phone every day and her Yahoo inbox is ridiculously full. I liked him before that whole Amy thing but not now. Now he's just scum."

"Scum?"

"For cheating on her."

Ah.

"I can't believe she's taking him back. I mean, why would she do that?"

"How did I not know she was so serious about him?"

"I don't think she was, until Amy. Then, when she thought she might lose him . . ." Becca shrugged, sat back on her tush, and crossed her legs.

When she thought she might lose him. All of a sudden I wondered for the first time if I'd found the sweater and Trey had not died, what would I have done? The thought was as jarring as getting that first ear pierced. I didn't have half the backbone Bailey had, yet here she was, laying herself out like a doormat for Tim McGuire to wipe his dirty feet on. And here was another jarring thought: Was it because Bailey had spent her whole life watching me lay myself out for a dominating husband, regardless of how sugar-coated the dominance?

"And here's the thing," Becca said. "There are plenty of nice guys who'd love to go out with her."

"Well, of course there are. For both of you."

Becca tilted her head and gave me that half smile that never failed to melt my heart. "You say that because you're our mother, but really there are, for Bailey I mean."

"How are things with—" I had to think a moment. "Will. Will Hunter."

She shook her head, gave a little shrug, and turned her green eyes to the fire. "His nose whistles."

I felt my forehead crease. "His—"

"Nose whistles. He has a deviated septum. He can't help it, but it gets horribly annoying after a while." She splayed her hands for emphasis.

"Yes, I can see where it would. How, uh, close do you have to be to hear it?"

"Mom." She smiled a little at that. "Not that close."

And then we shared a real laugh for the first time in weeks. At that moment I'd have given everything I owned to make her two years old again. Her sister too. "I don't want either of you girls to settle. I mean it, Becca. Wait for a man who would cut out his heart for you."

She pulled her knees to her chest in a little hug. "Like Dad."

I swallowed a sigh along with the words I would never say. "Ready for bed?"

Becca stayed in her own room that night and every night after. No more filling the spot where her father used to sleep, no more "connecting." And still I couldn't cry. I lay in my sleigh bed with its new sheets and blanket and pillows and comforter, all traces of Trey "tossed out," as Mother said, fighting against the anger that was taking over my sensibilities.

I looked upward, uncertain if anything bigger than myself existed beyond my newly painted ceiling, but I asked anyway. "If Trey had to die, couldn't it have been before he filed those papers? Before he annihilated every memory of our life together?" *Before I had to know?*

❧

It was the coldest Thanksgiving in recent history, outside and in. Dad took our coats at the door and wrapped Becca and me in a hug, but when I followed my olfactory sense to the kitchen, Mother and Bailey were anything but warm.

I set my sweet potato casserole on the one burner not in use on the stovetop. "It smells like heaven in here."

"Now, how would we know what heaven smells like?" Mother lifted the casserole and slipped it into the warming oven. "How are you?"

"Cold." I produced a shiver to prove it. "It's like a deep freeze outside. How are you two?" I turned my eyes to Bailey.

"Here's the pie," Becca said from behind me. "Hey, Gram."

"Morning, sweet girl." Mother offered her cheek to Becca. "What a beautiful pie."

"Mom, of course."

"But you helped, I'm sure."

"Nope, honest. Everything was done when Bailey and I got home."

Mother gave a sideways look that just missed my eyes. "So I hear."

I moved closer to Bailey. "Happy Thanksgiving."

"Yeah. You, too."

Well, that was something. "What can I do?" I asked.

Mother stopped, as if taking inventory. "Let's see. The glasses are still in the cupboard, and, Becca, you can open the olives."

The dining room table looked, of course, as if Martha Stewart had set it. Each piece of china was precisely where it should be, all the pieces of silverware equidistant apart. I placed the glasses just so, to the top right of each plate, above the knife settings, the frosted leaves facing exactly the same way.

"Everything looks lovely," I said, back in the kitchen.

Mother slid the dressing into the oven and set the timer for forty-five minutes, while Bailey continued peeling potatoes. The menu would be what it always was. A roasted Butterball, mashed potatoes with giblet gravy, a yummy corn concoction, and sweet potato casserole, which was my contribution. The sweet potatoes were whipped with butter, cream, and vanilla, topped with nuts and brown sugar, and baked. There wasn't a marshmallow in sight. Mother had balked the first year I brought it, but it's been a staple every year since. The basics would be rounded out with cranberry chutney, olives, bread and butter pickles, and home-made cloverleaf rolls. I usually made the rolls, but Mother opted this year "to give you more time to recuperate." As if Trey's death were something to be gotten over, like the measles.

We locked hands for our Thanksgiving prayer just as the mantle clock struck one. "Hickory, dickory dock," Dad said, to the same sing-song words playing in my head. Not that I'd ever want to copy her, but how did Mother always manage to begin precisely at whatever hour she was aiming for? As Dad prayed, my thoughts went back to another Thanksgiving, an odd-year one, with Winnie and Robert the Second. It was the year Winnie found grace.

"I think it would be just the loveliest thing," she said, "to go around the table and say what we're thankful for. You know, for Thanksgiving." Her

rust-colored sweater lifted at the shoulders in unison with the edges of her rose-colored lips. Rust and rose. Only Winnie. "Would you start, love?" she said to Robert the Second, whose line of a mouth grew taught and thin at his wife's suggestion. I could see her strategy right off the bat. She wanted to go last.

Robert merely stared, as if the woman beside him had grown a second head.

"Well, then, Trey?"

"Oh, well, um—" He cleared his throat, then his upper management training kicked in. "Well, let's see. I'm thankful for—" He thought a moment longer. "My girls, of course." He smiled in our direction. "A good job, a nice home. For friends and family." He was on a roll. "For a good upbringing and, and, the prospects of a good year to come." The smile said he was pleased with his performance.

"Lovely, Trey, just lovely. Bailey?"

At twelve, Bailey's hormones were knocking around like bumper cars, driving everyone crazy. At any given moment she was impertinent, whining, or on the verge of tears. It was a really bad moment when she was all three at once. Fortunately, today she was only impertinent. "This is way dumb," she said, her braces picking up the light of the candles. I lifted an eyebrow. "Okay," she said with a huff and a roll of her eyes. "I'm thankful for everything Dad said. Except the part about the girls. And the job. And stuff."

"Well," said Winnie, adoring as ever, "that leaves family and friends, and those are truly things to be thankful for. Abbie?"

I don't know why my pulse began to race. After all, three of the people at the table were people I spoke with every day, the ones I was closest to in all the world. I knew exactly what I wanted to say, yet there was a strange disconnect between my brain and my tongue. And everything else. I knocked my wine glass, caught it before it went down, but managed to splatter Winnie's tablecloth. "Oh, Winnie, I'm sorry. I'll just—" I jumped up to run for a towel and caught the hem of the tablecloth in my haste. Down went the tapered candles in their ceramic cornucopias. Trey and Robert the Second put the flames out before they did any damage, but hot wax lay in thick puddles, drying instantly where they tipped. "Oh, Winnie—" I dabbed at the mess with my napkin.

"Not to worry, darling. It's an old cloth." She waved my protests away with a large-knuckled hand.

Yes, it was old. It had been her mother's.

Trey's unsmiling lips were pursed, and splotches the color of cranberry chutney crept up his neck and into both cheeks. No matter what his mother said, the look he wore made me want to crawl to the corner with a dunce cap on my head.

Maybe that's when his affections took a detour, when his eyes began to search out someone with class.

"We'll replace the cloth, of course," he said. As if we could.

"Nonsense." Winnie's hand made another wave. "Ice will take the wax right off. Now where were we?"

Oh, please! Don't come back to me. I willed Winnie to read my thoughts, pleaded with my eyes. Don't come back to me.

"Abbie, darling, you were about to say—?"

In my lap, my hands sought my napkin to keep them busy, but I'd used it to blot up the wax. Instead, I twisted the end of my blouse around my index finger. Yes, I knew what I was thankful for the minute Winnie asked. But how to say it without sounding corny? And in front of everyone? True love. That's what I wanted to say. True and lasting love. "All of you," I said instead, feeling a traitor to my own heart. My eyes blurred. At least there was no candlelight to catch the glistening.

Winnie reached her hand across the table for mine. Her smile was like a balm, and she winked. "Now Becca." She cupped my daughter's face in that same tender hand.

Without hesitation, my eleven-year-old angel said, "Grace." Then she leaned against my arm in the loveliest act of solidarity. "'Cause we all make mistakes."

I could hardly breathe for the pumpkin-sized lump in my throat. Winnie all but glowed.

"Grace indeed," she said. "That's what I'm thankful for too." Then she prayed the first prayer I ever heard her pray. It was only a prayer for our meal, but it seemed as if she were whispering right into the ear of God.

"Mom? Mom." Becca waited to pass the mashed potatoes to me. "You okay?"

I took the bowl, served my plate, and passed them on. "Certainly."

❧

"Mother, the girls and I can finish up the dishes," I said. "You must be dead on your feet."

She loaded the last china plate into the dishwasher. "Now there's a morbid thought."

"Oh, you know what I mean. You've been in this kitchen most of the day. Let me do the pans."

"I already have my sleeves rolled up." It was an expression she'd used all my life to say she might as well finish what she'd started.

But not tonight. I lifted the dish towel draped over her shoulder. "Really. Go sit by the fire with Dad."

"Well." She took the towel and wiped her hands, then squirted some lotion into her palm. "Be sure to wash the silverware first. And rinse them in—"

"*Hot* water. And dry them right away. I know."

"I don't want any spots."

"Here, Gram." Becca poured her a fresh cup of decaf. "And here's one for Grampa."

"We'll finish up and join you," I said.

"All right, then." She took the cups and headed to the living room.

"You mind drying?" I asked Bailey.

"I'll put the linens on to wash," Becca said.

Perfect. If I didn't know better, I'd say she'd read my mind.

"So," I said, when Bailey and I were alone, "are you coming home tonight?"

She shrugged and reached in the sink for a handful of forks. "Ah!" She jerked her hand back.

"Careful, it's hot."

"Scalding's more like it."

"I've got the gloves, let me rinse."

She shook her hand and blew on it. "That's where you get it, you know. From Gramma. I love her, but she's even more anal than you. Hopefully, and I mean hopefully, by the time it filters down to me it will have lost some of its edge."

I smiled and rinsed another pile of silver. "I wouldn't count on it. But about tonight?"

"I have a date," she said.

I tensed in spite of myself, then drew in a relaxing breath. "After?"

"Why?"

"So we can talk."

She opened the lid to the walnut chest and dropped in a stack of forks. After all these years the chest still smelled as fresh as a new-cut tree. "About?"

"Things."

"Oh, well, that helps."

"Bailey."

"All right. But don't wait up. We can talk in the morning."

But I did wait up. Until after one.

"Mother!" Bailey dropped her jacket over the arm of her father's chair and stood with both hands on her slender hips.

"I've got water on. How about some chamomile?"

She closed her eyes and pinched the bridge of her nose. "I don't want any tea. I'm tired. I want to go to bed."

"It'll help you sleep."

"I don't need help. I'm completely exhausted."

"Five minutes," I coaxed. "I deserve that for waiting up."

"Which I told you not to do." She plopped into the chair and draped her legs over the arm without the jacket.

"Was your date with Tim?"

She stiffened, then brought her feet to the floor. "I thought when you said *talk* you meant—" She jabbed a thumb toward my bedroom.

"Honey, what are you doing? Why are you seeing him?"

"Becca is so gonna get it."

"Becca didn't say a word." Not about the date anyway. "She didn't have to."

"What's wrong with Tim?"

"What's wrong—? Bailey, when you left to go back to school we were discussing Amy Brennan's pregnancy."

"You obviously didn't hear. It was all a lie. She was just trying to trap him."

I leaned back into the corner of the sofa. Now I was the one pinching the bridge of my nose. "Well, it's sad to think someone would be that desperate for attention, but, sweetheart, that is not the point."

"She lied, Mother! She wasn't pregnant."

"But, Bailey, she could have been. That's the thing. She could have been. Tim never denied that. He cheated on you. End of story."

She pursed her lips in a perfect imitation of her father, thinking up a reply. "I don't know if it's really cheating if you aren't married."

"Not cheat— Oh, I can just hear what you'd say to Becca right now if you were sitting in my seat having this conversation with her. Of course it's cheating. If a man isn't faithful before marriage, he won't be after."

"And you would know this how?"

All I could see was that sweater and myself dragging Bailey by the hand to Trey's closet. Which, of course, I wouldn't do. "You don't want that kind of pain in your life, Bailey. I know that much."

"If this is about Aunt Shawlie, you've said yourself she's a terrible judge of men."

"This isn't about Shawlie. It's about Tim McGuire. And where do you think that judgment begins? With the first bad choice, which you are making as we speak."

"He said he was sorry. Mom, he actually cried."

Mom? Goose bumps broke out on my arms. How I loved the sound of that word coming from Bailey. I moved to the other end of the sofa, closer to the chair where she sat, and tugged affectionately on the frayed hem of her jeans. "Better his tears than yours, love. Trust me on that."

Fourteen

The week before classes began at American River College I was as nervous as a real college kid going off to university for the first time. I couldn't still the butterflies, couldn't get my mind off them. I was too nervous to eat and too excited to sleep. And all for two classes: American Lit and Fundamentals of Interior Design. This was ridiculous.

And yet, it was about so much more than two classes. I felt as though someone had unstuck me in freeze tag, and I was in the game again, running through the cool grass in my bare feet, without ever having known I'd been frozen.

One trip to the student store brought me right back to reality. I was nothing like the eighteen-year-olds waiting in line for the next available checker with their stacks and stacks of books. I was forty-three and couldn't remember ever having a midriff as worth exposing as they had. Like Bailey and Becca, they were all so perfectly sculpted.

By the time I made my way through the line, which took me

through breakfast and lunch, I wanted a latte, large and decaffein-ated. It was only two o'clock, but I didn't dare consume anything that would keep me awake another night. I located a Starbucks in the same strip mall where Shawlie got her hair done by Jina, with a *J*. I used my fingers to comb through my hair, lifted a lock and checked for split ends, then let it fall to its familiar place exactly halfway between my shoulder and elbow. The length I'd worn it since . . . *forever.*

I paid for my coffee and strolled down the mall in the direc-tion opposite my car, checking my reflection in every window I passed. No way Jina could take a walk-in, I was sure of it. She had a clientele that included a senator's daughter, and even Shawlie made her appointments from one appointment to the next or she'd never get back in the loop.

Still.

"Hi, there." A, uh-hmm, *fellow* with lip gloss stood poised over a large black appointment book, pencil gripped between French-manicured fingers. "Name, please?" His voice rose right along with his enviously shaped eyebrows. If I closed my eyes, I'd have sworn it was Paris Hilton speaking.

"I don't actually have an appointment," I said.

To which he actually giggled.

"I was kind of hoping Jina might just have something—"

"Jina? With a *J*?" He pulled at the pearl button on his black silk shirt. "Oh, sweetie, Jina with a *J* never *just* has anything."

Is that what people really call her? I wondered. Like Joan of Arc or Ivan the Terrible?

"Depending on what you want done"—he gave me a once-over that didn't just wound but assassinated my self-image, then began flipping pages in the appointment book—"we could work you in, say, the third week of April." He was completely serious.

"It's January," I pointed out. No way would my impulse last that long.

"You're lucky. Things simply die right after Easter. But only for a week or two."

"Well, thanks anyway. My friend Shawlie swears by her. I can see why."

"Whoa, whoa. Did you say Shawlie?" A purple-aproned girl with hair to match passed by with a bottle of Evian. She was twisting off the lid and stopped when she heard me say Shawlie's name. "Shawlie Bryson?" she said. "As if there's any other. She's one of my favorite people in the whole world." Her open-mouthed laugh exposed a silver ball-tipped rod that pierced her tongue.

"Mine, too," I said, trying not to gag. "We've been friends forever." It was low of me, I know, to use her name like that, but if it would get me an appointment . . . "I stopped in on the off chance—" I lifted a strand of hair and let it drop, as if I were as disgusted by it as our boy Paris.

"No!" She clutched her chest with a multi-ringed hand capped with short black nails. "You're not . . . you can't be . . . Abbie?"

Well, that was a bit disconcerting.

"Shawlie's told me so much about you! And here you are! Oh, that's weird!"

That's weird? I felt as if I'd walked into Wonderland.

She turned to the keeper of the appointment book. "Stevie, you have to, *have* to work her in." She gave another open-mouthed laugh. "Does Shawlie know you're here? That naughty thing didn't say a word to me!"

"Well, no, I—"

"Jina, there's simply not a blank line for days and days." Stevie riffled a few more pages and sighed dramatically.

"You know, that's okay. I'll just—" *Leave*, I wanted to say.

And never come back. Two minutes in her presence and I was exhausted. I doubted I could stand a whole session. But Jina with a *J* cut me off.

"Nope, nope!" She held up a hand to silence us while she thought. "I've got it. Stevie, call my three o'clock, three thirty, and four. Push them back two hours. I'll work through dinner. It's not as if I couldn't miss a meal."

Right. If today's six was yesterday's four, she had to be a minus two.

"They'll just have to put up with my"—she patted her tummy—"grrrrowling."

"They won't mind? About the time change?" I asked.

To which she and Stevie shared a cozy laugh.

"Come with me," she said.

I followed her to the best station in the shop, my eyes running from her purple hair to the filigree butterfly tattoo between her shoulder blades to the strappy wedges she wore on her perfectly pedicured, size-six feet. I hated myself, but I knew I'd ask where she got them before the day was out.

"Here we are." Jina pointed me to an empty chair beside one occupied by a man who honestly could have been Shawlie's Phillip. I'd met him only a few times, and that was seven years ago, so I couldn't be sure. He gave me a once-over in the mirror, then went back to his *People* magazine, clearly not interested. I was surprised at how that made me feel, like a pear or avocado with a soft spot. "I won't be long," Jina said to me. "We're almost done here." The man, whoever he was, still had foil in his hair.

"Should I look through some style books while I wait?"

"Oh, no, no. I know exactly what I'm going to do with you."

❧

She was a genius. Plain and simple. And Shawlie had apparently learned well from her because Jina did exactly what Shawlie had recommended for my makeover. She cut my hair blunt to the square part of my jaw, the shortest it had been since before I started kindergarten.

"Oh, my gawd! Do you see what this does to you? It's like taking all those layers off the ceiling of the Sixteenth Chapel. You're gorgeous! And Shawlie was right. I'd kill for that neck!"

Her own neck couldn't have been lovelier—unless you took away the dragonfly tattoo. But her point was well taken. The cut alone made me feel reborn. When she added the highlights—gold, not blonde, because it was winter—and the bangs . . . well, I could hardly speak.

"You love it! You love it!"

Yes, I did. I'd gone from frumpy to fabulous in two hours and twenty minutes. Okay, maybe frumpy is a bit extreme, but the contrast was dazzling.

"Next time, two little streaks of red. Here and here."

Of course she didn't mean red at all, she meant plum. She could have meant chartreuse for all I cared. From this day forward, I was hers to do with as she pleased.

I gave her a hefty tip on top of her hefty fee, purchased in jumbo size the shampoo and conditioner she'd used on me, and laughed as I walked past a shiny new Beemer in the parking lot with a license plate that said JINASBB.

Well, if you ask me, that's one baby she earned.

It took five minutes to back out of my parking space. I kept catching my reflection in the rearview mirror and just had to stop to admire the new Abbie. I felt like Maria from *West Side Story*, wondering, *Who could that attractive girl be?*

And then the question came: *Is this what Trey was missing?* I couldn't have been more startled if the air bag had exploded in my face. The dazzle went right out the window. I turned the mirror for a better look, watched my shoulders slump. The woman looking back at me was no more real than if I'd posed for a glamour shot. Tomorrow, when I didn't have Jina to work her magic, I'd just be plain old Abbie again. Plain old Abbie whose dead husband wanted a divorce.

"Hair does not a woman make," I said, right out loud.

And divorce papers don't lie.

"Ah, sweetheart, this is exactly why you don't do things on impulse."

I looked down at my toes, pulling my sticky fingers apart and pressing them back together, over and over again.

Bailey was three, and it was the year of The Little Mermaid *in the Torrington household, the only movie Bailey wanted to watch since getting it for her birthday. From the time she got up it was, "Mommy, I wanna see Ariel." So I'd slip the video into the VCR, and eighty-three minutes later she'd say it again. "Mommy, I wanna see Ariel." When she wasn't sitting in front of the movie, she'd go around the house with her Ariel doll, singing, "Under the sea, under the sea, under the sea, under the sea," the only words she knew to the song.*

At three and two, Bailey and Becca still shared a room, and I thought what fun it would be to turn their room into a scene from the movie. So I found The Little Mermaid *wallpaper border, the perfect paint somewhere between blue and turquoise, and matching bedspreads for their twin beds. The minute Trey left for work I put the girls in front of the little TV in their room, threw a drop cloth over the carpet, and went to work. I measured four feet up from the floor and drew a line from one side of the wall to the other. That's where the top of the six-inch border would go. Then I taped off the baseboard, unscrewed the light switch and plug-in plates, cracked the knuckles of both hands, and started to paint.*

I sang right along with the girls as I worked, not knowing many more of the words than Bailey. But what fun.

"Blue," Bailey said when I'd painted the first section up to my line.

"Bu," Becca repeated.

"Yes," I said, "blue." And it was. Royal Caribbean blue. I stood back and cocked my head, my lips tightly pursed in my concentration. "A bit darker than I expected." I found the roll of wallpaper border and held it close to the painted wall. "But just right." I smiled at both girls and went back to work.

By the time the movie credits were rolling for the first time that day, I'd covered the area below my line in Royal Caribbean blue. Much darker, I mused. "How about a snack," I said to the girls, "before take two?" What I really wanted was for the paint to have a chance to dry and lighten up. Paint always lightens up. I'd heard that on some decorating show.

"Snack," Becca said, clapping her hands. To her, that meant one thing: graham crackers and milk.

"Okay." Bailey pulled herself away from the little TV with her Ariel doll in one hand. But she didn't seem too happy to go.

Fifteen minutes later the paint was as dark as ever. I pulled on the cord and raised the blinds as high as they'd go. "Well, that helps."

"Hep," Becca said from in front of the TV. Bailey was already singing along with the second showing of the movie and forgot I was even in the room.

While the paint continued to dry . . . and lighten? . . . I cut out Ursula, Flounder, Sebastian, the seahorse, and, of course, Ariel from an extra strip of wallpaper. These I would paste to the blue wall beneath the six-inch border for our "under the sea" effect.

This was so much fun.

By one o'clock the beds had been made up in their new sheets and spreads, and the window topper was shirred onto a curtain rod waiting to be hung. Bailey stood by her bed and rubbed her hand over and over the bedspread, pointing out each character by name. Every time she came to Ariel she'd lean over and kiss her.

I decided that nap time would give the wall the extra ninety minutes it needed to be dry enough for the strip of border to really adhere. Becca was always ready for sleep after lunch, and for once I didn't have a moment's trouble getting Bailey down for her nap.

While they slept, I tended to the chores I'd neglected that morning, all the while singing "Kiss the Girl" with all the calypso feeling I could muster. Only I always sang it "kiss de girls," plural, for my girls.

Not surprising, Bailey was the first one up. I heard her little bare feet slapping on the tile floor as she found me in the kitchen. "Mommy, I wanna see Ariel." Her words were lost in a yawn, and her eyes were still puffy from sleep.

"As soon as Becca wakes up. Would you like some juice?"

She nodded, pulled out a kitchen chair, and climbed onto it, never letting go of her Ariel doll. By the time she finished her juice I heard Becca running down the hallway toward the kitchen. I glanced at the microwave clock. I had approximately two and a half hours to get that room put together before Trey got home.

I couldn't wait to show him what I could do.

After Becca had her juice, we went back to their room, where the girls sat down for their third showing of the day. "Under the sea, under the sea, under the sea," Bailey sang, and I hummed along. The Royal Caribbean blue was still really royal, but, hey, it was only one wall and only a portion of the wall at that.

I unwrapped the plastic from the wallpaper border and unrolled a foot or two of the colorful strip. I turned it over, looking for the backing that would pull away to reveal the adhesive side that would stick to the wall. Hmm. I unrolled another foot and checked all the edges, using my fingernail to try to separate the backing from the strip.

"Well," I said and checked the corners carefully for the slightest flap. Then I reached for the directions that had fallen out of the roll when I removed the plastic wrap. My lips moved as I read . . . tub . . . water . . . room temperature . . . glue. What? "No pull-away backing?" I continued to read. Prepare surface . . . smooth. "Smooth?" I ran my fingers over the textured wall as if reading braille.

Could a few bumps make that much difference?

I went and filled a large plastic container with room temperature water and brought it back to the bedroom, glad I still had the drop cloth in place. I measured off the strip from one corner of the wall to the other, held my breath, and made my cut. The instructions said to dunk the whole piece in the water. At one time. "At one time?" I read it again. "Okay."

I held the strip under water until the water become silky with the glue. I counted to sixty since I didn't have my watch on, then lifted one dripping end out of the water. Handling it as if it were a boa constrictor, I matched the straight edge of the strip with the straight edge of the wall and pressed. I held it in place until my fingers cramped. It was imperative, I was sure, to make certain the outer edge was firmly attached to the wall before I continued.

Holding my breath, I let go of the edge and moved my fingers down the strip a few inches and pressed, moved another few inches, pressed, and another . . .

The outer edge began to slither down the wall.

Well, why wouldn't it, as wet as it was? I let go and ran to the hall closet for an old towel. By the time I got back, the strip lay in a bunched heap on the floor. I straightened it out and blotted away some of the gooey moisture. It still felt tacky. Probably just about right.

I lined the edge up with the corner and began again, pressing it hard against the wall. I held it a bit longer than the first time. That and the removal of the excess moisture would surely do the trick.

But no. As soon as I let go, the edge popped away from the wall.

I thought about push pins. Clear ones that you could hardly see. Up in the corner. I finally settled on masking tape, just to hold the strip in place while I worked my way down the wall. I knew by the scene in the movie that I was forty minutes into this. And running out of time.

Vertical strips of tape every six inches held the border in place, but it was clear that in between the tape it was not adhering to the wall.

Surely given enough time the strip would attach as it dried. I moved to the cutout characters, dunked, dabbed, and positioned each one on the Royal Caribbean wall.

"Ariel," Bailey said, coming over for a kiss.

"Oh, sweetie, better wait. She's sticky."

"Sicky," Becca said, following her sister.

I looked at my handiwork. "Yeah," I agreed. "Sicky."

With each character firmly taped to the wall, I went back to check my border. Not only was it not adhering, but now the masking tape was curling.

And that's when Trey appeared. A full hour early.

"Daddy!"

"Daddy!"

Daddy? I turned. Yep, there he was. "I . . . I think the glue must be old. Or . . . or something."

Trey's eyebrows lifted. He picked up the directions and read until I saw his mouth form the word smooth. *He nodded to himself. "Abbie, there are professionals for jobs like this." He spread his arms, taking in my mess from one corner of the wall to the next. The girls took it as an invitation. He scooped them up and kissed the tops of their heads. "How are my girls?" he said, and then, as if extending his scepter of favor, he nodded his head for me to join the circle.*

"Ariel." Bailey leaned over to kiss the little mermaid. Naturally, the cutout stuck to her lips.

"Sicky," Becca said.

Yes, indeed.

I adjusted the rearview mirror until I could see behind me and inched out of my parking space. "Yes, Trey, this is exactly why we don't do things on impulse."

Fifteen

Shawlie would be home tomorrow, having spent the week on a cruise she'd won to Puerto Vallarta and Cabo San Lucas for top sales. But I needed someone today to tell me I hadn't made a ridiculous mistake. I opened my cell phone, scrolled down to my parents' number, and pressed Send.

Let it be Dad, let it be Dad, I thought as I waited for someone to answer.

But no.

"Mother?"

"Tippy. How are you?" It was always the same.

"I know you've probably already had dinner, but how does dessert sound? I could bring—"

"Nonsense. I have a pie."

"Well, then, ice cream? What's pie without—"

"Just bring yourself. I have everything else."

Of course she did.

In spite of the January drizzle, I was actually perspiring as I pulled into their driveway. I made a run for the porch and rang the doorbell, fingers crossed on both hands, hoping Dad would answer. He did.

"Hello, may I help—?" He lifted his glasses to the top of his head. "Abbie?"

"Hi, Dad."

He reached for my arm and pulled me into the light of the entryway. "Abbie," he said again. "You look . . ." He turned me in a full circle. "Positively stunning." I smiled a broad smile as he turned me around again. "It really is you."

"Yes, it's me."

"For a minute I thought—"

"Shawlie, I know. Who'd have known there was such a resemblance?"

He seemed hesitant all of a sudden. "Well, no, that's not what I meant. But here, let's shut the door. We're letting all the heat out."

"You really like it?" Honestly, I felt like an adolescent.

"I do, yes I do. But maybe I'll just"—he pointed toward the living room—"go and prepare your mother."

Prepare?

"Be right back."

"Dad?"

I stood in the entry of my parents' home, like a stranger who had come to sell Avon. I shrugged out of my coat and draped it over the coat rack. I caught myself in the entry mirror, started, and fingered a few strands of bangs back in place. Okay. Maybe not ridiculous. Maybe not at all. In fact, it made me feel as if someone new had taken up residence in the old Abbie. Someone with a future.

"Um, sweetheart?" Dad waved me into the living room,

then turned a tentative eye over his shoulder in the direction of Mother's chair.

I followed him into the room, feeling as though I were crossing a creek on slippery stones. He stepped aside at the last moment, presenting me almost formally to my own flesh and blood.

Mother's breath caught, her eyes widened, her lips went thin.

I attempted a smile. "What do you think?"

She stared up from her chair. Her eyes glistened behind her glasses.

"Mother?"

She brought a hand to her throat. "Just . . . just give me a moment." She reached for a tissue, lifted her glasses, and blotted her eyes. "My. What a change."

"It was a spur of the moment thing. I can't believe I did it."

"No, it looks—" Her eyes filled again.

If Jina wanted weird, this was weird. "Mother, what is it?"

She motioned to the piano, and Dad moved. He came back with the photograph of Aunt Elizabeth. This time it was my breath that caught. It could have been me in the photo. The same jaw line, the same haircut, so much like Lizzy's. Me, so much like Lizzy. A little older, yes, and could I ever remember laughing like that? But Lizzy just the same.

"I never realized how much . . ." Mother placed her glasses on the end table and rubbed her temples. "I think I'll just . . ." She disappeared down the dark hallway. A moment later I heard her bedroom door close.

I took my usual place on the sofa and turned my eyes to the ceiling. "That went well."

Dad came and sat beside me. "It just caught her off guard, sweetheart. The resemblance really is startling."

"Dad, Aunt Lizzy's been gone forty years."

"To your mother, there are days it seems like forty minutes. Not having had a sister or brother, it's hard for you to understand, but your mother and 'Lizabeth were not just siblings, they were best friends. Alice adored 'Lizabeth, looked up to her, wanted to be just like her. Like Becca with Bailey. To this day, whenever something eventful happens, there's sadness in the house because 'Lizabeth isn't here to share it."

"A haircut is eventful?"

Dad gave me a look I didn't often get from him. "It wasn't the haircut, Abbie."

"I know. I'm sorry. It's just that—" I let my head fall back onto the sofa cushion. "She doesn't like me, does she?"

"Abbie, she's your mother. She loves you."

"But she doesn't like me." I held up a hand to stop the rebuttal. "And I'd just like to know why."

He was thoughtful for a minute. "How about some pie?"

"Dad."

"And ice cream."

❧

The phone rang at three ten the next afternoon. Shawlie was home from her cruise.

"How about dinner?" I said after a minute of chitchat. "I have something to show you."

I expected her to argue, to say that she wanted to rest up after a day of travel. But to my surprise she gushed her acceptance. "And I have something to tell you."

Uh-oh, was my immediate thought.

"Shall we meet at—"

"Oh, no, I'll fix something here," I said.

There was a brief span of silence on the line, then I groaned and said what both of us were thinking. "I'm becoming my mother."

"Nip it, Abbie. In. The. Bud."

I hung up the phone and went straight to the fridge. What could I throw together without having to make a trip to the market? Rain had arrived with the afternoon, and now a raucous wind was whipping up a blustery hullabaloo in the heavens, rattling the chimes on my patio for all their worth.

Those chimes were a gift to me from me on the first birthday I celebrated without Trey. Because I love wind chimes. They're the first I've bought since the month we married, when I surprised Trey, just because, with what I thought were the loveliest-sounding chimes I'd ever heard. I hauled out the ladder and hung them myself outside our bedroom window—good thing it was a one-story rancher—where they would play for us on the night breeze.

The lights went out, and from the open window my gift began to present itself. A perfect C at first, resounding all alone. Then, like a conductor tapping its baton, the breeze began to stir and a symphony of chords filled the night.

"Good heavens!" Trey lurched up in bed. "Don't tell me—If the Dawsons think we're going to listen to that all night—" He whipped the sheet back, stuffed his feet into slippers, and marched to the window. He started to close it, saying, "I'll talk to Bud first thing in the—" when he saw the cursed things hanging beyond the screen from his very own eaves.

He turned toward the bed, ghostlike in the light of a near-full moon. "Abbie?" he said.

I switched on the lamp and gave him what must have been a crimped smile. "Surprise."

Trey's forehead creased. He raised his lecture finger to pursed lips and tapped as he sought a response. "For me?" I held my smile as his jaw flexed with each discordant clang. "You really shouldn't have."

He meant it, every word, and he was right. But I hadn't been with Trey long enough to know how structured he liked his world . . . and how unstructured wind chimes were. It was a windy night for September. A long and windy night. I hauled out the ladder again the next morning and brought harmony, muted and bland, back to Trey's universe.

It was selfish of me, I know, to coax Shawlie out in this weather, such a contrast to eight days on the Mexican coastline. But one way or another she'd have to go out, so better one of us than both of us.

Okay. I had eggs, cheese, everything I needed for that breakfast casserole I used to reserve for when Trey was out of town. Everything but the Canadian bacon, but who'd miss it just this once? Besides, after eight days of cruise cuisine, Shawlie would thank me for bringing her back to reality. And breakfast for dinner was sometimes fun. In truth, it had become more frequently fun. Now that I lived alone, dinner was often a bowl of Raisin Bran.

At five o'clock, with the casserole ready to slip into the oven, I headed upstairs to put a fresh touch to makeup and hair. I wanted Shawlie to see the stylish new me at my best. I was still startled every time I passed a mirror, startled and astonished at how radiant I felt.

Then the guilt would whoosh down like a mudslide and carry off the light and easy part of me in its mucky path, purging me of all the good things sprouting up like new growth in the forest, things I shouldn't even want to feel. But why? Trey had been dead nearly a year and a half. If it weren't for the secrets buried all over the house, would I be any less inclined to move on after eighteen months?

Was *she* mourning Trey, Miss Moss Green Sweater of San Diego? The way I should be? Did tears wet her pillow, while mine stayed dry? Did her heart beat with lost love, while mine sat like a paperweight in my chest?

I stared at the stranger staring back in the mirror. "Girl, you are pathetic." I blotted my lipstick to remove the shine and shook up my do. Shawlie didn't have to see me perfect. She'd get the point.

Headlights swept the foyer as she pulled her Jag into the driveway. I unlocked the deadbolt, then hurried to the kitchen and struck a casual pose. She rang once, tried the door, found it unlocked, and hollered as she hung up her coat.

"You are not going to believe the week I had! Think fabulous, luxurious, Epicurean with a capital E." Pleasure punctuated every syllable as she made her way to the kitchen. "I told you you should have— Ah!" Eyes wide as the Canadian bacon our casserole was lacking, Shawlie dropped her bag and let out another shriek. "Abbie? Abbie! Look at you!"

I was grinning like a bobblehead. "Like it?"

"Like it? Even I couldn't have envisioned— Next thing, you'll be wearing the patch."

"What are you talking about? I don't smoke."

"Not *that* patch."

"Shawlie!"

She made a circle with her finger. "Turn around. Let me see the back." I complied only too gladly. "Look at that color, those highlights. Oh, no, do not tell me Jina did this."

"She's everything you said she was, Shawlie, everything."

"You rat. You had this planned all along."

"No, I swear. I just walked in and—"

"No way. You are lying now. No one just walks in and gets Jina."

"I did," I said, and told her the story. She stood with her

mouth open, shaking her head the whole way through. "My own dad didn't recognize me." Instantly, I wished I'd left that subject alone.

"Yeah? What did your mother say?"

"Well, actually she was . . . speechless."

Shawlie hiked an eyebrow. "I'll just bet. Really, what did she say?"

"I'd better check our dinner."

"Abbie." She motioned for me to resume my seat. "Out with it."

I heaved a sigh, disgusted with my own big mouth, when the oven timer went off. Whew. "Make the toast?"

Her eyes narrowed. "We will have this conversation before the night is up."

I got the jump on her the moment we sat down. "Okay, I want to hear all about your cruise."

She didn't even hesitate. She made an O with her lips and fanned her face. "Where to begin? But first, here." Shawlie pulled a box out of her bag. A shoe box. Just my size.

I let out a squeal. "You shouldn't have."

"I would never have heard the end of it if I hadn't." She smirked. "Go on, check 'em out."

I lifted the lid as if there were precious jewels inside, pushed back the tissue paper, and lifted out a sandal. "Oh, Shawlie, how beautiful." And they were. Genuine leather in the most wonderful shade of café latte with bronze, umber, and brick red beadwork, and a one-inch heel.

"Handmade," she said, "from a little village in"—she shrugged—"someplace with an x in the name."

"Ah, well, that narrows it down." I pulled off a sock and slipped my foot in. A perfect Cinderella fit.

"I know you can't wear them till spring, but I couldn't resist. They had your name all over them."

"I love them. The first sunny day . . ." I closed the box. "Now, how was the cruise?"

Shawlie swallowed a bite of egg. "Where's the Canadian bacon?"

Ah, me. "The cruise, Shawlie."

She pointed at me with her fork. "You really should have come."

I'd used the start of school as my excuse not to tag along, but the truth was I didn't know how to justify something so frivolous and fun. Maybe, just maybe I could justify it to myself, but not to anyone else. Not yet. I knew it and Shawlie knew it, but for once in her life she didn't press.

"A cruise is a cruise," she said, showing off arms as gold as graham crackers. "The air was warm as a serape, the water bluer than blue, the food, well—" She puffed out her cheeks like a chipmunk. "And then, then, there was Sven."

"Sven?" Was she kidding? "You fell for the captain?"

"Not the captain, but the next best thing."

"The first mate?"

She huffed out a breath. "Are you going to let me get this out? He was a passenger. Of the first order. In a suite. On a ship! There were fruit and flowers every day, personalized stationery." She paused, as if that were bound to impress. "And . . . a private veranda with a spa."

"A spa? You didn't . . . you know . . ."

"We wore bathing suits, if that's what you mean."

It was. As the closest of friends, there were few issues that Shawlie and I wouldn't broach, but we drew a mutual line when it came to really private matters. So why did I ask? I don't know, but I was glad for her reply. As a woman who'd been married twice and dated when the mood was right, Shawlie's experience was vastly different from mine. Trey is the only man I'd ever slept with, and Shawlie knew that . . . which made her despise him that much more.

"Okay, tell me about—" Was this really right? "Sven."

"Think Cary Grant."

"Oh, well, Cary Grant is good."

"Without the hair."

"Without the hair?"

"You're squinting." The word was drenched in sarcasm, for she'd heard Trey say the same thing to me too many times over the years.

"So are we talking about Cary Grant at forty, or, or . . .?"

She made an "up" motion with her thumb.

"Fifty?"

Up again.

"Fifty-five?" Cary Grant at fifty-five was still good.

But, no, she upped me again.

"Exactly how old is Sven?"

"If he didn't lie on his passport, he's seventy-one. But a young seventy-one. Abbie, you're squinting again."

Well, now I understood the bathing suits.

"Okay, so we can't have it all. But here's the best part. He lives in Nova Scotia."

"Nova Scotia? That's good?"

"Do you know how undemanding a man can be from three thousand miles away? Abbie, it's the perfect relationship. I don't know why I didn't think of it before. And here's the next best part. They changed their flight plans and they're in town till Friday."

"They?" I pushed my unfinished dinner away, not caring one

bit that I was squinting. "What do you mean *they*?"

"He has a brother. A younger brother," she was quick to add.

"I suppose he looks like a hairless Cary Grant too?"

"Not so much, but there is a clear family resemblance."

"To the Grants or the Svens?"

"The Jorgensens, smarty. Their last name is Jorgensen. Sven and Lars Jorgensen."

"Sven and Lars Jorgensen? Are they Swedish or something?"

"Danish," Shawlie said.

"Danes? From Nova Scotia?"

"Something wrong with that?" There was a definite challenge in her voice.

"No, no, I just—"

"They have one or two Danes in Nova Scotia, Abbie."

"Obviously. And they're older than both our dads, maybe combined. No. The answer is absolutely no."

She was frowning in earnest. "I haven't asked the question."

"I took up mind reading in your absence. No. No. No." I punctuated each *no* with a shake of my newly bobbed head.

"It's just dinner, Abbie. Not a date, *per se*. And you, looking so svelte with your new hairdo and all." One thing about Shawlie, she loved her sarcasm.

"Yeah, well, the *per se*'s the kicker, isn't it?" I carried our unfinished plates to the sink.

"Oh, come on. What harm can one dinner do? No one even has to know. We'll go out of town if you want."

"Oh, sure, then I'll really feel underhanded."

"Underhanded?"

I knew instantly I'd gone too far.

"What is underhanded about a divorced widow having dinner with friends a year and a half after her lying, cheating RAT of a husband died in San Diego and not Dallas?"

I sat back in my chair. "It would have been so much easier if he had."

"Had what? Died in Dallas?"

"I mean, if he had to die . . ."

Shawlie sighed away her frustration. "I know I've said it a thousand times, Abbie, but you did not deserve this." She gathered up more dishes and brought them to me.

Twenty minutes later, with the dishwasher swishing away, we returned to the table with mugs of fresh coffee. There was so much of my house I didn't use anymore, like the living room, the den, the formal dining room, and five of the bathrooms, and still I couldn't sell.

"So just one dinner? You mean it?"

Her eyes brightened. "I do. I promise. I pinky swear."

I closed my eyes and shook my head. "All right then." But before the words were out of my mouth I knew I was so going to regret this.

Sixteen

Sleep and I ceased being chums after Trey died. Early on it was the trauma of all that had happened that kept me awake at night. The death, the other woman, the wondering if there'd been more than one, the almost certainty that there had, the anger, the defeat, and the self-doubt that followed on the heels of the whole ugly mess.

Once past the trauma, the empty house kept me awake as I tried to get used to being alone all through the night. A house like ours makes a lot of noise when the sun goes down. Walls creak, pipes crackle, televisions pop, things I'd never paid attention to before. And if the phone rang after midnight, wrong number or not, every nerve went on high alert.

I tossed so much I felt like a salad, but I resisted taking anything with "sleep aid" on the box. If there was one thing I'd learned, it was that I was far more dependent than I'd ever realized. Yeah, there's a big difference between husbands and sleeping pills, but dependence is dependence. Besides, if you ask me, alarm system notwithstanding, a woman alone should be on her guard.

A woman alone. The thought never failed to slice, quick and sharp like a paper cut.

So I'd lay in the dark and call up scenes from our life together, searching for the frames that distorted the big picture, to try to put it all together. But memory let me down. I saw only what I wanted to see, then and now, as easily deceived by myself as I had been by Trey. But it was simpler that way.

And now I had a date. With a sixty-something, hairless Dane from Nova Scotia. My stomach churned every time I thought of it. It's not that I had anything against Danes from Nova Scotia, or even sixty-something, hairless men. Not at all. It was the date thing. I mean, did they even speak English in Nova Scotia? My sleepless eyes went wide. If Shawlie set me up with— No, she wouldn't. She *wouldn't*. I sat up and grabbed for the phone, then I saw the clock. Two seventeen. She'd kill me.

I switched on the light, pulled on my robe, and plodded downstairs to Trey's office. I eased myself into his leather chair and scooted up to the computer. Even now the room smelled like Trey, a blend of coffee and cologne. I closed my eyes and held my breath until the tiny sense of yearning disappeared. Knowing what I knew, why would I ever desire the arms of a man who used them to hold another woman? Loneliness notwithstanding, it was a gross betrayal to myself that I would miss those arms even a little.

I kept my focus strictly on the screen while the computer booted up because more than any other room in the house, this was the one I avoided. It remained just as Trey had left it, with traces of him, and of us, everywhere, right down to the twentieth-anniversary photo he kept on the corner of his desk—the one we'd had taken just weeks before he died. I could never oust him from here, not without hurting my girls. *But when I move . . .* That became my catchphrase, the wish I held on to.

What did he think when he looked at that photo, if he even did? Did he think of the wound he was inflicting before I ever knew the pain? Or did he think of someone else and the wish she held on to? I reached over and turned the frame face-down, the tips of my fingers leaving their mark in the dust on the desktop.

I Googled *Canada, Nova Scotia, language* and read what came up on the screen. English was the predominant language. Well, that was a relief. But back in bed, I spent the next hour looking for ways to cancel. The old mono trick came back to me, and if I'd not been so desperate I'd have laughed out loud, right there alone in my sleigh bed.

With all the strange things swirling through my mind as I finally drifted off to sleep, I woke at eight, having dreamed of a boutonniered Mexican hairless pooch named Lars.

❧

I did not wear the little black dress that Shawlie brought for me, in spite of her nagging. It lay on my bed, draped in its clear plastic bag, while I searched through my closet.

"Abbie, you're a woman," she called from her perch on my bed. "Don't be afraid to look like one, for heaven's sake. You'll look gorgeous in this dress."

"It's January and freezing outside." But I would not wear this man killer of Shawlie's if it were the Fourth of July. Not for Lars. Not for anyone.

"What, you don't have a coat?"

"How about this?" I said, ignoring her. I brought out a pomegranate red sweater and black slacks. Just right for a blind date in January.

"Oh, no. No, no." She jumped off the bed and disappeared into my closet. "You at least have to show off your legs, Abbie. What I wouldn't give to be your height." Shawlie had ceased growing four inches sooner than I, and she'd lamented that forever. "At least your legs. Here, what's wrong with this?" She pulled out the dress I'd worn the last time Trey took me to the theater.

Definitely not.

"You're holding out way too much hope for this evening, Shawlie. Now go and let me get dressed."

"You're really wearing that?"

"You love this sweater."

"Sure, for lunch at the mall."

"Go. Go!"

∞

They picked us up in a limo. A long white limo with dark tinted windows and an RR on the hood ornament. *Well, then.* And though their accents definitely had this Danish-Canadian thing going on, their English was impeccable. As were their manners.

A soft light illuminated the passenger area of the limo, which smelled of fine leather. I sank into what seemed like a sofa, it was so comfortable, and ran my hands over leather soft as a kid glove. Lars leaned across the void between his seat and mine, the light casting a pinkish glow over his lumpy head. He offered me his hand. "Miss Bryson told us so much about you. I'm awfully happy to meet you." He was dressed in a tweed jacket and a dark turtleneck and smelled of something equally tweedy. And pleasant.

Okay, yes, I could see the Cary Grant thing. If I closed my eyes.

Shawlie privately gave me a smirk. I pretended not to see.

They offered champagne, which I declined, accepting a chilled Perrier instead.

"Not being acquainted with your city," Sven said to Shawlie, "we did some research on fine dining in the area. We hope you like our selection."

Shawlie waited with an expectant smile, but Sven missed his cue. We'd have to wait to discover our destination when we got there. But I noted that we were heading away from the city, not toward it, us girls facing backward.

Classical piano on CD offered a backdrop soft as the pink light that tinted our faces. With the smooth motion of the car, and after my long and restless night, I could easily have dozed off. *If that were Trey sitting across from me instead of a complete stranger, I'd snuggle up beside him, rest my head on his shoulder, and float. All the way to dinner.*

My eyes went wide with the thought. I stiffened and took a drink of my Perrier. This was no time for sentiment.

For January, the night was remarkably clear, the air cold as we stepped out of the limo at the entrance of the restaurant. It was an impressive, out-of-the-way place called Vino's. The valet-only parking lot was jammed with expensive-looking cars. Neither Shawlie nor I had been here before. A uniformed doorman held the heavy doors open for us. Each side was rounded and looked like a portion of a huge wine barrel.

We were shown immediately to a table overlooking the south fork of the American River. The swift-moving water was awash in moonlight. A large patio off the lounge would be the ideal place in spring and summer to enjoy a meal with the sounds of the water to serenade. I'd have to remember this place. For the most special occasions, of course.

Our waiter stood in the shadows while Sven and Lars helped

Shawlie and me with our heavy chairs, then he stepped up, took away my white linen napkin before I could touch it, and with a flourish whipped open a black one and draped it across my lap. He did the same for Shawlie, only he draped a white one over the lap of her ivory dress.

Okay, I got it. No white lint on my black slacks. Impressive.

Shawlie leaned over to me and motioned across the room with her eyes. "Isn't that Senator what's-her-name? You know, the one from—"

"Yeah. Wow."

"How did we not know about this place?"

I replied with a tiny, one-shoulder shrug. At the same moment I wondered, *Did Trey? Had he come here with heaven-only-knew who?* I'd become disgustingly suspicious and hated myself for it.

We each took what appeared to be a simple menu, on which were written four entrees in a lovely, gold script, representing fish, chicken, beef, and pasta. There were no prices. Not one.

"Well," Shawlie said, "so many choices."

Sven laughed and held up his water glass to Shawlie as if to say, *Here! Here!* "Such wit" is what he did say.

I looked around the dining room. Every table occupied and lots of smiles. "No one seems to be complaining."

The fish, our waiter said, was trout, newly snagged from the river. Well, that wasn't quite how he worded it, but for me it put a whole new face on "catch of the day." I like my entree fresh, but not haunting. "I'll try the filet mignon."

"Excellent choice," he said, not bothering to write our order down.

"The Chicken Kiev," Shawlie said, to which she received a smile and a nod.

"I can't resist fresh fish." Sven was one syllable ahead of his brother. "And escargot." He made a circular motion with his finger. *For everyone.*

"Well, that's certainly fresh." Shawlie leaned toward me again and, without moving her lips, whispered, "We hope."

I swallowed hard. Snails had never passed my lips, not even that time in Boston when Trey had invited me once to an awards ceremony. He was the top honoree for sales in the nation, first time. I was so proud. The girls were four and five and staying with Mother and Dad. We'd be gone three whole days.

I went shopping for day, evening, and nighttime wear and kept *those* things hidden in my suitcase until I worked up the courage to wear them. The wine would help. A lot. All through the banquet I thought about how undistracted we could be with the girls on the other side of the continent.

And then the snails arrived. In their own six-welled ceramic dish. With their own little two-tined fork.

Trey leaned toward me, gave me a wink. "You can do this," he said.

My dipping heart met my rising stomach just below my underwire bra, right there in the middle of the solar plexus. I wasn't so sure.

Trey picked up his utensil, held it like an instructor for my benefit, and speared one of the creatures. "Just close your eyes and pretend they're little meatballs." He lifted the fork to his mouth, closed his lips over it, and slid it out, empty.

My cheeks puffed out. I tried not to gag, but my revolted stomach was going to win this one, hands down.

I searched out the Restroom sign, looked for the fastest way there. But banquet halls are such difficult things to maneuver. "You can do this, you can do this." Trey's words resounded in my head as I skirted tables of eight, but I was looking for a completely different kind of victory: not throwing up on anyone's tux.

I don't know who was more humiliated, Trey or me, but, bottom line, it wasn't the evening I had hoped for. I applauded his award from the shadows in a far corner of the room, too embarrassed to return to our table. I'm sure he thought I wasn't there. He didn't talk for hours. I left the lingerie in my suitcase and took it back to the store on Monday. Oh well, I couldn't have gotten past the smell of the garlic seeping from Trey's pores anyway.

And now, here they were, delivered to my table, fork and all. Had Trey been right? Could I do it? Pretend they're little meatballs and swallow them whole?

The garlic overwhelmed my senses. Why not just chew a clove and be done with it, for crying out loud, and leave the garden pests to the roses?

I picked up my fork—I would not look down—and fumbled to scoop up one of the six. I found a well. It was . . . empty? I moved my fork to three o'clock. Empty again. This time I ventured a glance and what I saw caused my eyes to glisten. Shawlie talked and talked, keeping our hosts' attention on her lovely face and not her hand, while in the soft candlelight, from behind the bread basket, she speared the remaining four snails, one by one, without the fellows ever noticing. And ate them.

This was going to cost me. Big time.

"You ladies are amazing." Lars dipped his bread in a juicy well and bit off the end. "My wife refuses to eat escargot."

Wife? I heard a *whoosh* in my ears as the blood rushed to my head. I couldn't have been more stunned if I'd been freeze-dried right there on the spot.

Shawlie choked on snail number nine. "Your . . . your wife?"

"Doesn't cruise either." Lars dipped and bit again.

I removed the black napkin from my lap and pushed back the heavy chair. "Excuse me," I said, and there I was, skirting tables again.

Shawlie was right behind me as I pushed open the door to the

women's lounge. I dropped onto a sofa of green brocade. *Green.*
Lately, the color of betrayal. Shawlie dropped down beside me. I
turned and glared.

She moved back a full six inches. "I didn't know! I swear!
Abbie, I wouldn't have— You know I wouldn't have—"

"Cheating men everywhere I turn, only this time I'm the
other woman!"

A gasp sounded from the arched opening between the lounge
and the restroom, and a woman Mother's age lifted her glasses
and squinted at me. "Dear me," I heard her say as she threw me a
second look over her shoulder on her way to the door.

Shawlie pressed her lips together for all she was worth as I
turned to her again.

"Don't you laugh, Shawlie Bryson. Don't you dare laugh."

Well, naturally, that's all it took. Her eyes brimmed with
laughter, with no way to hold it in. It leaked from every pore. She
snorted, choked, then threw back her head and let it out before
it did her in. She'd point to the opening where the woman had
stood, then start all over again, thoroughly enjoying herself.

And me? What is it that makes laughter so contagious? Mad
as I was, I couldn't stop it. It bubbled up from that same spot
in my solar plexus and was just as irrepressible as the nausea so
long ago. I matched Shawlie snort for snort, guffaw for guffaw
until my ribs ached. Once, the door opened and a woman stopped
short, gave us a startled look, then backed out. That sent us over
the edge. Tears annihilated my mascara. I was a mess, with no
way to fix it—there was no room for makeup in my little clutch.
I reached for Kleenex and began to wipe.

By the time we gained control, such as it was, the guys had
to have finished their soup and started on their salads. Maybe the
main course. I'm surprised they hadn't sent someone in after us.

"I swear," Shawlie said, breathless, "I didn't know. A whole week on the ship together, and the word *wife* never came up."

"What about Sven? You think he's married too?"

"Who cares? They're both history."

"Let's call a cab. Just go home."

"That's the least they deserve." Shawlie stood. "Wait, we don't know where we are."

That threatened to start us laughing all over again, but we took deep breaths and gained the upper hand.

"I have it." Shawlie wore such a devious look that I knew whatever she was thinking would be good. "We'll take the limo. Maybe we'll send it back, maybe we won't."

"Thank heaven for coat racks." We'd left nothing at the table. Now all we needed was to execute our escape. Feeling like a bandit, I followed Shawlie to the exit, which was not visible from our hosts' table. We summoned our surprised limo driver, handed him twenty apiece, which he stuffed into his coat pocket with a dip of his cap, and directed him to take us back to my house. Via the nearest McDonald's.

Seventeen

Class began on Tuesday, a cold, soggy January day. I arrived forty minutes early to make sure I found a parking space. The lot closest to the building that housed the English department was for staff only. Just my luck. I parked in lot C, which may or may not prove to be the next best thing, and walked for what seemed a half mile. I located my class with twenty minutes to spare, thankful for the coffee kiosk right outside the building. I ordered a large decaf, added four little tubs of half-and-half—plain, not vanilla—then went back inside where it was warm and waited for the current class to let out.

At five to ten the door opened and kids barely past puberty poured out into the hall, passing me by as though I were a relic not worth noticing, or worse, invisible. My hands were icy cold with nerves and had been since the moment I stepped on campus. I mean, really, what was I doing here? I wasn't qualified for much beyond basic homemaking. Trey had subtly and sufficiently left that mark on my psyche, and with good reason, I'm sure.

Insecure. That described me in a nutshell. A very small nutshell. A pistachio. What did I think I'd do with an education at my age? I didn't have a clue, didn't know how to dream like these kids. Instead, my dream, presented in the fluorescent light of reality, flitted away like an emerging butterfly all too glad to leave its decomposing cocoon.

I started to leave, just get in my car, go home, and bake cookies. But suddenly a poster popped up right in front of my mind's eye. In green neon. It said *Miss San Diego. Bet* she *doesn't bake cookies.* I turned in a full circle, looked for Shawlie, thinking she'd finally managed a way to get inside my head for real. It was more than creepy, but it worked.

I found a seat in the now empty room. I took the middle desk in the middle row, reasoning it might be the place I stuck out the least, a tiny pistil clustered by all the lovely petals that were sure to bloom around me.

I wondered which of the kids who had streamed past me in the hall was the instructor, for only kids had exited the previous class. Reason had it that one of them had to be him. Or her. All I had was a last name, Beckwith, so it was a toss-up. I watched the door with palpitating heart as clusters of kids with tall fuzzy cups filled with designer coffee streamed into the room, bringing the brisk air of youth with them, filling the seats from the rear to the near front.

I was the only one not in jeans. Including the instructor, who turned out to be a man. Not beautiful, but older than me.

My nerves calmed down a notch, but I left my nondesigner, lidless cup right where it was on the floor beside me because I didn't trust my hands not to shake, and I'd die if I dribbled.

The instructor moved to the chalkboard and with a decided back slant wrote *Ian Beckwith* with blue chalk. He came around to the front of the desk, rested his jeans against the edge, and crossed his feet shod in saddle oxfords. I was thinking Bass, or maybe Jos. A. Bank. And that Trey wouldn't be caught dead in shoes like that. And that I could probably think of a better phrase than *caught dead* when it came to Trey. Strange, the kind of chain link in which my mind progressed these days.

Professor Beckwith folded his arms, tilted his head, and looked into the eyes of every person there. No one rustled so much as a sheet of notepaper.

"Words are the DNA of literature," he said in a gravelly, accented, well-used voice. The accent was subtle and belonged somewhere in the British Isles. "As in reproduction, how they are coupled makes all the difference."

A smattering of laughter broke forth, but not from me. I was drawn into the sound of his words from the first syllable.

"We're going to spend the next few months together, dipping our hands into that DNA, right up to the elbow, immersing the sensory part of us into the stuff of life. Or, at least, the stuff that takes us beyond the mundane." He stopped, looked us over again. "Story," he said, the way other men would say *sex*, "is what separates us from pigeons or liverwurst."

There was a bit more laughter.

He reached behind him for a stack of papers and passed a few to the first person in each row. "These are the novels we'll be reading. Not your typical American Literature lineup: *For Whom the Bell Tolls, The Grapes of Wrath*, et cetera. There's nothing wrong with those, of course, but these," he said, indicating the papers we were passing to the classmates behind us, "are books you probably didn't read in high school. And that's the whole point."

A near-perfect specimen of young womanhood in the row to my left raised a manicured hand adorned with six or seven rings.

She wiggled her fingers. "We're going to read all of these?" she asked in a whine that irrevocably shattered the image I had of her.

Professor Beckwith's eyes crinkled in a smile. "You'll get the second page halfway through the semester."

She clamped her lips, glared for a second or two, then gave a *can-you-believe-what-he-just-said-to-me?* look to the two girls in her coterie.

"And for the one or two who won't wait for finals week to begin the semester assignment, here it is." He reached for another stack of papers and handed them out in the same manner. "Claire Ogden Connors was one of America's finest authors, and I mean one of *the* finest."

I gave a little gasp. Claire Ogden Connors was my favorite author of all time. I looked at the paper in my hand, read the assignment, and knew I was in the right place. Just the thought gave me a chill.

"Ms. Connors was born in 1904," Professor Beckwith continued, "and had her first book published in 1936. It was an instant success and was converted to a Broadway play. Eventually several of her books, all *New York Times* best sellers, of course, were made into motion pictures, beginning in the late forties. Her last novel, *Final Storm*, was published in 1951." He picked up a frayed, cloth-bound book. "Anyone read it?"

My hand shot up. "Twice," I said, then realized no one else in the young audience had raised a hand. I lowered mine, cleared my throat, and tried my best to shrink into myself. My cheeks grew hot. This group had the ability to find humor in every little thing.

"Twice. A real fan, I see." Beckwith opened the book to a marked page. "'J. H.: No secrets,'" he read. "'That's your assignment. I want a three-thousand-word essay on what you think this means. Be as creative as you like. There's no wrong answer."

Miss Near-Perfect didn't bother to raise her hand or wiggle her fingers this time. "I thought this was a reading class. We have to write something?"

Oh, the accusation in that one little word, *write*.

The eyes crinkled again. "One of life's little disappointments, I'm afraid."

Chuckles rose from every row but one, followed by another glare, another *can-you-believe?* look. I had a feeling that after this week the trio would adorn some other classroom on Tuesday and Thursday mornings, one where effort was an elective.

Like the one before it, class let out five minutes early. The same clusters of kids that came into the room left in like manner. Two girls, also of the near-perfect variety, passed me on their way to the door, leaving a strong bouquet in their wake. "Don't waste your time," one of them said, looking toward the chalkboard. "He's gay."

Well, I didn't even want to think where that conversation started.

I reached for my bag, having completely forgotten about my coffee. I didn't just dribble it, no, that was too benign. Instead I tipped the cup with my own big foot and watched the liquid spread across the floor like a murky sea at spring tide. "Oh, no," I groaned as my few remaining classmates, who were way too clever to commit such a faux pas, snickered and sidestepped the puddle. I reached in my bag for the only thing I had, a Kleenex.

"This might work better." Professor Beckwith stooped on the shore of my mess and began to sop up the liquid with a roll of stark white paper towels. He'd wad, blot, toss into the wastebasket he'd had the sense to bring along, then start the cycle over again. It took, oh, I don't know, half the roll to get down to the sticky layer the half-and-half left on the linoleum.

I could have died on the spot. "I'm sorry. I'm not usually so clumsy."

"Not to worry. But they have lids now, you know? That you can drink right out of."

Ah, yes, that's what I need, a sippy cup. I felt my face turn candy apple red. I fished a bottle of water out of my bag, twisted the top, broke the seal. Then I poured it over the sticky spot. He tore off more paper towels and blotted, which by now he had down to a science.

Cookies, Abbie, just go home and bake cookies.

He stood, tested the spot with a saddle oxford, and seemed satisfied. "That should do it." He held out his hand. "Ian Beckwith."

"Right," I said, nodding toward the blue chalk.

He hesitated a moment. "And you are . . .?"

"Abigail. Abbie. Torrington."

"Torrington, yes. I saw your name on the roster. You don't by chance know —"

Oh, please don't say Trey. Because if you knew Trey, what else might you know?

"Paul and Nora?"

I let out the breath I was holding. "No."

"Hmm. Not a common name, Torrington. Oh well." He took a step toward the door. "So you're a fan of our Ms. Ogden Connors."

"Since eighth grade when I checked out *Home Body* from the school library. Been hooked ever since. I have all her books. At home."

"Including . . .?" He nodded toward his desk.

"Mm-hmm."

He looked impressed. "Hang on to it. It's a first edition."

How would—? I'd have to check that when I got home.

"Well, see you Thursday."

I smiled, nodded, and walked out into the hall a step ahead of him, though I knew absolutely and positively that he would not see me Thursday. Or any other day. I'd stood all the humiliation I could stand for the rest of my forties.

I did, however, plan a trip to the mall for a new pair of jeans. In case I changed my fickle mind.

༄

I had three messages on my phone when I got home. Shawlie, Shawlie, and— I looked at the name again. "Lars Jorgensen?" I pressed the play button. Shawlie's voice came through the little speaker.

"Hey, girl, your phone's off. Where are you?"

Oh, right. I turned my cell phone off for class and forgot to turn it back on. I deleted the message and waited for the next one.

"Abbie? I've been calling and calling. Are you all right? Listen, the strangest thing . . . Oh, it's a long story. Just call me."

I deleted that one too and picked up the phone to hit speed dial just as message three began to play.

"Ms. Torrington, I'm afraid there's been a dreadful mistake." It was Lars Jorgensen all right. "And I feel just awful. You see, you and I, well, I thought we were just tagalongs. Not, not really a date. My wife would kill me, you see. Sven and Ms. Bryson, they were the date. But Sven wouldn't hear of me staying alone at the

hotel, and Ms. Bryson said she had this wonderful friend who — "
The message stopped abruptly, the memory out of room for even
one more word.

*Dreadful mistake . . . Not really a date . . . This wonderful
friend who . . .* I looked at the phone in my hand. "Who what?
Steals Rolls-Royce limousines?" I was embarrassed beyond words.
Schlemiel. That was me. Schlemiel, schlemiel, schlemiel, jump-
ing smack-dab into assumptions. I mean, who was I to think he
even —

Assumptions? *Assumptions?*

What if . . . I found a chair and crumpled into it. *What if . . . if
I'd been wrong all along? About Trey? That he wasn't . . . That he
hadn't . . .* My heart stopped in midbeat, all the remote possibili-
ties tromping over each other in my head. *Could . . . could Miss
San Diego have been an assumption too? As Lars said, a dreadful
mistake?* My vision began to shrink and I crumpled a little more.
I sucked in a breath, and another, until the lightness in my head
went away. I lay with my head on the back of the chair, my eyes
fixed on a cobweb in the corner of the ceiling. *What if . . .?*

But no. *You have the divorce papers, Abbie. Remember?*

The swell of hope left me like air out of a soufflé. *Yes, I
remember.*

I jumped as the phone in my hand began to trill. I pressed the
On button and brought it to my ear. "Hello?"

"Well, there you are. Where have you been? I've been worried
sick."

"School."

"Oh. School. I completely forgot." I could almost see Shawlie
thumping her forehead. "Did you get a message from Lars?"

"I got half a message from Lars about how his wife would kill
him if he went on a date. I can certainly see her point."

"Abbie? Are you all right?"

"I had an epiphany, Shawlie. I need a latte. With a lid. And a pair of jeans."

"The mall?"

"Ten minutes."

Okay, so it wasn't an epiphany. It just felt like one. But the exhilaration that came with the thought that maybe I'd been wrong about Trey all this time was like a breath of air after nearly drowning. Only to go under one last time.

Yes. I had the divorce papers. Upstairs in my hope chest. End of story.

∾

Shawlie met me at our usual café table, steaming latte in hand. "With a lid?" she said.

"Long story. But I want to hear your long story first."

She pulled two chocolate crescent-shaped biscotti out of a crinkling bag and handed me one. "It's almost funny, really." From the look on her face, we both knew that remained to be seen. "Lars is married. Happily. For forty-seven years."

"Five years longer than we've been alive. Makes me kind of queasy, if you want to know."

Shawlie gave me one of her trademark looks. "He, and you, were—oh, I know this sounds awful—but you were merely tag-alongs on my and Sven's date, which yours wasn't. A date." Funny, Shawlie actually sounded nervous.

"So Lars said." I sat back on my stool, crossed my arms, and tapped my foot in the air, enjoying the upper hand for once.

"They just somehow neglected to get that point across."

"And you found this out *how?*"

"Sven and I had this long conversation on the phone last night, and I told him how upset I was, we were. Are."

"I thought Sven and Lars were history."

"Well, Sven just wanted to clear things up."

"Ah. So, is *he* married?"

She gave me a devastated look, one we used to practice in the mirror together in junior high. "You think I'd go out with a married man after what I've seen you go through?"

She had a point.

"But to answer your question, he was, once. She— oh, well, you're not interested in that."

"Oh, but I am. She what?"

Shawlie took a sip of her drink and ran her tongue over her upper teeth. "It's tragic, really."

I waited.

"She, well, life's different in Canada than it is here." She splayed her hands and looked around the café.

"I'm sure it is."

"A lot different. And she, well, it's fascinating, really."

"Shawlie, you should hear yourself. *Well* this, *really* that. Come on, out with it."

She played with the silver filigree ring on her right index finger, slipping it off and on, twisting it. "Enid was—"

"Enid?" I raised a brow, which Shawlie pretended to ignore.

"—very athletic. She used to participate in these sled races in the north country." Shawlie shrugged. "Wherever that is."

"Sled races? Like with dogs?"

"And here's the amazing thing. She was almost sixty when the accident happened."

"Accident?"

"Abbie, you sound like a mynah bird. Now stop it. She was on the last leg of a race, in third or fourth place—at her age it's just amazing—when she hit this little ravine."

"Ravine?" I held up my hands. "Sorry."

"Actually, more like a dip."

I had to bite my bottom lip to keep from saying the word after her. I wanted to. Really bad.

"And out she went, blankets and all. It was such a fluke, she landed in front of the sled. What are the chances? And got run over."

I looked at her with eyes narrowed and mouth open, and crossed my arms again. "You are making this up."

"I'm not. I swear. Aren't you glad we sent the limo back?"

This time *I* pursed my lips until they hurt.

She glared. "Don't you laugh, Abigail Torrington. Don't you dare laugh."

Eighteen

If the neighbors were taking notice, they'd have seen a light shining from my living room window that night for the first time in months. I turned on both lamps at either end of the sofa, clicked on the fireplace, and went to the bookcase. My finger ran the length of two and a half shelves as I scanned the titles, head bent at an awkward angle, reading the spines. There it was, at eye level on the third row from the top. *Final Storm*, by Claire Ogden Connors. I pulled the book out of its place, leaving a gap in the row like a missing tooth, and blew the dust off the top edge. I really had to get my house back in order, in more ways than one.

I carried the book to the fireplace and shivered while I waited for the temperature to rise enough to kick on the blower. It was nearly as cold in this room as it was outside, if you didn't take into account the breeze blowing in off the Sierras. I could actually see my breath if I worked at it.

The book's smoky blue dust cover looked as pristine as the day I slipped the book out of its floral wrapping paper. Roses probably, in pastel. I know it was floral because the book was a gift from Trey, and Trey always used floral paper for the women in his life. I just didn't know how many that amounted to back then.

I slipped off the dust cover and lay it on the mantle. The cloth binding looked identical to Professor Beckwith's, except that mine wasn't frayed at the edges, didn't bear the marks of a book much read and loved. This gift was one I'd literally never opened till now. Yes, I'd read it twice just as I'd so absurdly blurted in class, and loved it too, but both times from a book checked out at the library. The first time in eighth grade, the second time when I was five months pregnant with Becca.

It was about a woman who— Oh, wow. A woman scorned. Who got even. I think it was time to read it again.

I wiped one hand then the other down the front of my khakis and held the book by the edges, between my palms. With the first two fingers of my left hand I flipped open the cover. There were two blank pages, then a frontispiece with a black-and-white sketch of a cottage, its screen door just a little off-hinge. Wild bougainvillea entwined the posts of the porch and spread along its railing. It had been a lovely place in its day, before the abandonment. You could tell. They didn't make books like this anymore. I'd bet a tall Frappuccino that none of my classmates even knew what a frontispiece was.

The publication date was 1954, and just as Ian Beckwith said, this was a first edition. How could he possibly have known that? But Trey surely did, and told me. How had I forgotten? I ran my hand over the page. The paper was not brittle but held a yellowish hue.

Finally, the fireplace began to blow warm air. I snuggled into a corner of the sofa with my book and a mug of plain old decaf with plain old half-and-half turning it a golden brown. Boring, boring. All I needed now was a cat and an afghan.

Funny, snuggling wasn't something I'd done much of my whole life. Not that I had anything against it in the right context. For example, I didn't mind watching a good movie with Trey's arm around me, dipping into a bowl of popcorn together, my socked foot playing toe tag with his. But when it came to sleeping, I liked my space, didn't want to be touched. At all. It took a while for Trey to learn that.

From the night we were married I drew a line from the head of whatever bed we shared to the foot, just a little left of center. I thought it only right that Trey have the lion's share. I did this in my mind, of course, not with a permanent marker or anything ridiculous like that. But the line was as real to me as if I had. I didn't mind sharing spaces for a while, but when it came time to sleep, the line might as well have been a hedgerow. His space. My space. Simple enough?

But from our first night together Trey acted as though the line didn't exist. He cared nothing about lions' shares or hedgerows. He wanted to touch, and he crossed the line to do it. Every night, as his breathing became slow and even in that place between waking and sleep, as I lay with my back to him, his hand would circle my waist, growing heavier with each deepening breath. It felt like an anvil pinning me to the mattress. I'd scoot a bit toward the edge until his hand slipped off, encroaching, but not touching.

Next, his head would find the crook of my neck, his warm, moist breath tickling my ear. I'd scoot some more and raise the back of my pillow like hackles, a barrier between us. Before long, a leg, hairy and heavy as a tree limb, would wrap itself over mine. I'd disentangle myself, work the sheet between our two append-ages, and scoot as far as I possibly could, clinging to the edge of the bed like a baby opossum to its mother's back.

"Trey? Trey."

His head lifted off the pillow an inch or two, one eye squinting, the other eye closed. Like Popeye. "Abbie? Everything okay, babe?" His words were slurred, sleep-filled.

"Can you maybe just"—I moved a hand's breadth closer to the edge—"turn over?"

"Huh?"

"You know . . ." I made a circle motion with my hand. In the dark. "Other side?"

His head came up another inch. "Ever said what, babe?"

"No, Trey. Other. Side." I made the motion again.

"Sorry." He patted my arm and turned. "I warned you that I snore."

His head hit the pillow and I was sure he'd never remember a moment of this exchange in the morning. But, oh, I had my space. I backed away from the edge, rearranged the covers, fluffed my pillow. I lay there, waiting for sleep in my new and strange surroundings. And then our backsides met, the pads of his feet drawn to mine like magnets.

"Trey? Trey . . ."

I think it comes from being an only child, this sense of extended boundaries, from not having to share a room, a bed, a coconut Mounds, which Dad brought home every Thursday, don't ask me why. I mean, dark chocolate? Not my first choice. In fact, it's the Brazil nut of candies if you ask me. And everyone knows if it weren't for mixed nuts, Brazil nuts wouldn't be much in demand. So who in their right mind would choose dark chocolate over milk chocolate? Yet, to this day, I can't pass up a Mounds bar, especially on Thursdays.

And I can eat every bite of it if I want, dead center in the middle of my sleigh bed, no hedgerow in sight, nothing but room and more room on either side.

A thought hit me then as I continued to hold the book between my palms, careful not to fray or smudge or leave any sign that we'd touched. To leave it just as I'd found it, undisturbed, without transferring any of me on to it. *Is that how I loved the people in my life? Taking pains not to leave any of me on them?*

My heart took a tumble, then righted itself. And I thought of Winnie, who frayed and mussed and left her mark on everyone, inside and out. On purpose. How I missed her.

Then another thought came like a dart between the eyes: *I bet Miss San Diego snuggled.*

The book lay heavy in my hands for I don't know how long before I turned another page. And there was the dedication. "J. H.: No secrets '. . . for there is nothing covered, that shall not be revealed; and hid, that shall not be known' (Matthew 10:26)." *Hmm. The good professor hadn't read that part. Separation and all that, I suppose.*

I took a drink of my coffee, which had cooled considerably, then carried it to the microwave and zapped it until steam rose from the froth. I stopped at the bookcase again on my way back to the sofa, found the burgundy leather Bible Winnie gave me after her conversion, with my name in gold right on the cover. I pulled it out, another gapped tooth on the shelf, another gift left too long unopened.

Matthew wasn't too hard to find once I arrived at the New Testament. But don't ask me to find Jonah or Daniel without a table of contents. I know they're in there somewhere, but when Mrs. Garecht, the third grade Sunday school teacher at the church my mother took me to, said, "Okay, boys and girls, it's time for our Bible quiz," Tommy Jansen would stand and read any obscure verse you could throw at him before I could even get my little white faux-leather Bible unzipped. And he wasn't even the pastor's kid.

Chapter 10 verse 26 in my Bible read, "So do not be afraid of them. There is nothing concealed that will not be disclosed, or hidden that will not be made known." A little different from what the dedication read. I looked at the spine. Ah, of course. NIV. Published in 1954, the verse in Claire Ogden Connors' book was certainly King James. I at least knew that much.

I read the verse again. It didn't stand on its own. That "so" connected it to something. But what? The verse was red, one in nearly a whole chapter of red. I backed up to verse 5, where the red began, knowing these were the words of Christ, and began to read.

"These twelve Jesus sent out . . ." I read the entire chapter and then read it again. I had no idea, really, what it was talking about, other than taking the words at face value. But face value didn't seem to be enough. And I absolutely could not see what the verse had to do with Claire Ogden Connors' *Final Storm*.

At eight forty, with the fire much too warm and my mug long empty, the phone rang. I closed the Bible and smiled at the caller ID as I answered. "Hi, sweetie."

"Hey, Mom, how was class?"

Leave it to Becca to remember. "Class was . . ." I played a brief game of mental ping-pong. "You want the truth?"

"What? Tell me."

I did, and when she laughed, it was a balm to my soul, aromatherapy without the wick.

"I felt ancient, Becca. And I was the only one not in jeans, but I went straight to the mall after class."

"Well, there you go."

"I haven't decided yet if I'll go back."

"Mother—"

Ooh, there was that word, and from Becca. This had to be remedied right away. "What I mean is—"

"What would you tell me," she said, "if I were you and you were me?" She didn't even hesitate. "You'd say, 'Who cares what they think? In the grand scheme of things, what do they amount to? Who are *they* anyway? So you spilled your coffee. Who hasn't done one klutzy thing in their life, including Miss Near-Perfect?' That's what you'd say, and to that I add, at least you got the professor's attention."

"That's a good thing?"

"No, Mom, you have to say it without the question mark, like Martha Stewart. That's a good thing."

"Okay." I squared my shoulders. "That's a good thing." Then slumped. "Why?"

"Mom, do you want to be just one of the masses, or do you want to stand out?"

"Can we add a qualifier to that?"

She laughed again. "Okay, stand out in a good way. So are they cool jeans?"

"Shawlie helped me pick them out."

"All right, then. And just so you know, we'll be a little later than usual on Friday."

"Friday?" What was I forgetting?

"We're coming home, Mom. For your birthday."

Ah, my birthday. Forty-three come Sunday. The crest of the hill and all that. I could see the banner waving in the wind, and then it would be a fast tumble to the bottom, like Jill with her pail, only older, with a bun instead of braids. If the crest was the halfway mark, I was already tumbling and didn't know it. Like Trey, who'd crested at the age of . . . wow, twenty-four. And Aunt

Lizzy who'd crested at fourteen.

Okay, there'd been way too much introspection for one night.

"Mom? Mom? Hell-ooo!"

"Becca. Sorry. What did you say?"

"I said, you think we'd miss it?"

"No. Never."

"Never's right. Well, gotta go. Love you."

"Yeah, me too, sweetie. Say hi to Bailey. And call when you get on the road."

"Will do."

"Oh, Becca—" Too late. A click, and then the dial tone. I looked at the phone in my hand. "You'll be late because . . .?"

❦

By contrast to Ian Beckwith's American Literature class, Fundamentals of Interior Design was tame. And boring. But I had learned the hard way that boring wasn't all that bad. From what I could tell, the class would mostly be a review of things I'd learned about decorating from Shawlie years ago. There are definite advantages to being in real estate, and getting to see the inside of some of the finest homes in the area is at the top of that list. Shawlie would see something unique or intriguing and take me to see it either as her client or her assistant. And I admit I've gone to more than one open house, without even telling Shawlie, when I had no intention of selling my house or buying another one. In fact, it was something Winnie and I loved to do together. She was up for anything, Winnie was. I liked to see the inside of the newer houses that went on the market, with all their professional HGTV decorating styles, while Winnie loved the old, old houses. The ones with plaster walls, engraved cornices over the doors and windows, and hardwood floors smooth as honey hidden under ancient carpet that had long lost its pattern and pile. Winnie was the one to teach me that the good things usually were below the surface.

So if I dropped any class, I'd drop them both.

But I didn't.

It was only because of Claire Ogden Connors. Okay, Claire Connors and Becca. I didn't want to disappoint her. But predominantly Claire. I loved her work and was certain we'd more than examine her writing. We'd learn things about the reclusive author that weren't out there for public consumption. Not that there was a public clamoring for it, not anymore. But her life was draped in mystery, and it had me curious. She lived years after she ceased to write, or at least publish. Why? It was a gamble, this delving into the unknown. I may not like what might be uncovered, which is why I never, ever read biographies about the people I like. But it was a risk I was willing to take in Claire Ogden Connors' case.

I held my breath as I passed the coffee kiosk on the way to class, refusing to be enticed, and patted the Evian in my bag—the tightly lidded bottle, which I'd only break out in case of an emergency, like extreme choking or hiccups.

Ian Beckwith was already there when I entered, a look of alarm mellowing to a smile when he noted my cupless hand. "Morning," he said in that soft, gravelly voice. It startled me so that I tripped, then caught myself, as I realized in an instant that the voice was the absolute real reason I came back. It appealed to my ear like calamine to an itch, soothed a place within me I didn't know was raw.

I took my same seat, noting a dirty heel print on the linoleum where we'd missed a spot on Tuesday.

And, surprise! Miss Near-Perfect and entourage were back.

Today the professor wore moccasins. Moccasins! With blue socks and carpenter jeans, probably American Eagle, and a shirt that somehow tied it all together. On anyone else this would have looked as if he'd dressed from three different closets, but on Ian Beckwith it smacked of academia.

I too was in jeans, which I'd washed three times to rinse out the newness. I smiled and sat up a little straighter when Miss Near-Perfect entered the classroom wearing the same brand.

"Last time," Professor Beckwith said, "we talked about story, the stuff of life. How does an author put words together to draw a person back to those same words for a second look?" His eyes rested on me. "That accumulate the perfect DNA? For you see, there are stories, and there are *stories*." His tongue virtually caressed the word, sending goose bumps up my arms. "Not every accumulation achieves the divine."

I wondered if everyone else within earshot of his voice was as mesmerized as I, but I couldn't break away to look, couldn't take my eyes off the place from which that voice emanated.

"Take, for example, *To Kill a Mockingbird*. Anyone here who hasn't read it?"

I forced my head to turn, saw a few hands inch up, saw the color rise in Miss Near-Perfect's cheek, but no other admission of guilt came from her.

"It's first on your list," Professor Beckwith said.

Miss Near-Perfect raised a finger, which ended with a hot pink, squared-off nail that could have been used for a spade. "I thought you said we weren't going to read the standards."

"My one and only exception," he said, "because it's at the top of my own list. I guarantee you'll devour it like those chocolate-covered caramels you can only buy at See's."

I sat back, forced myself not to ask, *The dark chocolate ones or the milk chocolate?* But I already knew. My mouth watered.

Beckwith picked up a thin book, turned it over in his hand. It was as worn as his first-edition copy of *Final Storm.* "Why would a young white woman from Alabama write a book such as *Mockingbird*?"

Miss Near-Perfect's head shot up. "Woman?"

Ian worked to keep the right corner of his mouth from rising. "Yes, Harper Lee was a woman. And, for you trivia fans, Finch was her mother's maiden name."

Well, I didn't know that.

"Someone from Oregon"—the last syllable was the word *gone* rather than *gun*, the way I always said it—"I can understand." There were a few chuckles. "But Alabama? What makes a writer like Harper Lee put those words together? Form that particular DNA structure?"

"To entertain," someone said. "Naturally."

The professor thought that over for a moment, then shrugged. "There might be those who read *Mockingbird* purely for its entertainment value. Like those who eat carrot cake for its vitamin A."

More chuckles.

"But," he continued, "is the hatred of Mayella Ewell's father entertainment or the injustice of Tom Robinson's life and death?"

"Well, the book wouldn't have done nearly as well if it hadn't been for the movie winning the Academy Award for Best Picture." That came from a young man a few rows behind me.

"So if *Mockingbird* had been published in, say, 1860 rather than 1960, before the emergence of Hollywood, or the Civil War, we wouldn't be having this discussion?"

"No way," the young man said. "Especially if the South had won the war."

More chuckles yet.

"But it didn't," I said.

A puzzled smile crossed Beckwith's face. "No, it didn't."

"Win for Best Picture, I mean. Best Actor, but not Best Picture."

"Ah." His brow crinkled in thought. "Why do you think it didn't win Best Picture, which you're absolutely right about, by the way? Did the judges prefer camels to chifforobes?"

"Camels?" someone said.

"Chifforobes?" Someone else.

"*Lawrence of Arabia*," Ian said, "won the Oscar for Best Picture in 1962."

"I don't know what the judges preferred," a girl who reminded me of Bailey said, "but it's *because* she was young and white and from Alabama that she wrote it. It's how she rebelled against the society in which she grew up. This was an in-your-face diatribe. She was brave, and she deserved her Pulitzer."

Well. Bailey in more ways than one.

"'In your face.' Hmm." Beckwith leaned against his desk, crossed his moccasined feet, tucked the book under his arm, and rested his chin on his fist. The leather tie on one moccasin had come undone.

"I think," I said, my own nervous voice sounding as foreign to me as any I'd ever heard, "she wrote it to create a world that she could control, that presented an ideology she felt needed to be presented."

"So it's a message book after all?"

"All lasting books are, to an extent."

He turned and placed the book on the desk. "No need to qualify, Ms. Torrington. *All* lasting books are. Period. One more question."

One of Miss Near-Perfect's entourage raised her hand to about the height of her ear. "Why do you equate books with food?"

"Because," he said, his blue eyes shining, "there's nothing so delicious as *story*."

I reached for my bottle of Evian, twisted off the lid. And gulped.

Nineteen

"Finally! I was starting to worry." I draped the throw over my shoulders like a shawl and stood to embrace my daughters. Though, truth be known, I'd begun to worry the moment I thought they'd gotten on the road for their long drive home. It had just increased over the past hour.

"I told you we'd be late." Becca draped her jacket over the back of the sofa, stretched like a cat, and kicked off her shoes. "Why didn't you call us?"

"Because," Bailey said, then we all joined in, "a phone that rings after nine sends chills and shivers up the spine."

"That's what Gramma always says," I defended. "I didn't want to startle you while you were driving."

Bailey chuckled, then planted a kiss on my cheek. "It's not like that nowadays. Phones ring at all hours and no one clutches their heart in dread." She acted out the words as she spoke them. "Not anymore."

"You have to admit it's startling any time a phone rings late at night."

"I think we could have handled it," Bailey said.

"So why were you late?"

Bailey dropped her jacket on top of her sister's. "Because Becca joined a cult."

I turned to my last born and raised an eyebrow. "A what?"

Becca rolled her eyes at Bailey. "It's not a cult, and you'd know that if you'd come and check it out."

"Next thing you know she'll be wearing combat boots and a bun."

Combat boots and a gun?

"It's Chi Alpha. A campus club. We do Bible studies and stuff."

"A Bible study? Really?"

"See what I mean?"

"Some of the kids were getting baptized right in the ocean," Becca said.

"Some of the kids, meaning Tate Elliott."

"Bailey, you are such a jerk. Really, Mom, it was so cool."

"In January, in front of God and everyone. A bunch of kooks."

"I'm glad I stayed."

"*We*," Bailey said. "*We* stayed. And that's why we're late." She yawned loudly. "Now, if you'll excuse me, I'm beat," she said and headed for the stairs.

Becca leaned in and whispered, "That means she's going up to call Tim McGuire."

Tim? Still?

"Night," Bailey said.

We watched her climb the stairs and turn toward her room.

"Tate? That's not . . ." I tapped my nose.

Becca shook her head, gave me a kiss. "I'm tired too. We'll

talk in the morning."

I nodded, heard Bailey's door close, then open again. She appeared on the landing, mouth agape, narrow eyes fixed on me.

Oh no, what did I do now?

"Your hair." Bailey descended the stairs like a zombie and tugged at the wrap over my shoulders. "What did you do to your hair?"

My hand went to the clipped ends and pulled.

"Oh. Wow." Becca looked as if she was really seeing me for the first time tonight. "It's" — she swallowed — "cute."

I gave a little shrug. "Wait till you see it in the morning. All fixed."

Bailey crossed her arms. "What did Gramma say?"

"Gramma? Well, she um . . ."

"That's what I thought."

"Bailey, give her a break. If she wants to cut her hair . . ." Becca finished in a thin voice, with a smile that looked more like gas pains. Still, I appreciated the effort.

I continued to tug. "Wait till morning. When it's fixed."

Bailey headed back to her room. "Daddy liked your hair. Long." Her door closed with a sharp click.

Becca backed up the stairs, looking me over as if she might discover something else about me, like, say, an extra nose. "What *did* Gramma say?"

"She was . . . speechless." I was ridiculously upbeat.

"I'll bet. Yeah."

I waved my fingers. "Sleep well."

"Yeah, Mom, you too."

❧

Right.

I watched the hands of the clock circle the blue luminescent face on my nightstand like an orbiting astronaut. Two o'clock, three o'clock, four thirty-five.

Becca's "cult." Tim and Tate. The stricken look on Bailey's face. I had a sinking sensation in the pit of my stomach on all counts and a mind that wouldn't shut down, no matter how heavy my eyes became.

What had happened to my world? I was alienating my girls with every new choice I made. If I had dared to call, Shawlie would have said, "It's time you live your life for you." And I would agree to a point. But my girls are my life, all I have left of it now. And they matter.

Like air and water.

I rose long before anyone else stirred, took a long steaming shower, then worked on my hair till every strand was exactly where I wanted it. Then I sprayed it with the spray Jina used, a tall, cool aerosol can. No spritz for Jina. I had muffins in the oven and a pot of coffee ready to brew when Becca joined me in the kitchen.

"Wow," she said, picking up right where she left off the night before. "It really is cute." She motioned for me to turn. "Who did it?"

"Shawlie's Jina. I walked in and she took me right on the spot."

"No way."

"Of course, that could mean she saw how desperate I was and took pity."

"Oh, Mom. You've always been beautiful, and I loved your hair. But this"—Becca made a full circle around me—"is a whole new you."

"I smell blueberries." Bailey stood in the doorway. She wore red pajama pants with white snowflakes and an army green T-shirt. She had a deep crease across her right cheek from her pillowcase. The sight of her melted my heart.

"I'll start the coffee. The muffins will be ready in four minutes."

Bailey moaned her approval and pulled out a kitchen chair.

"What do you think?" Becca asked her sister. Her smile was huge as she looked in my direction.

Bailey squinted, rubbed her left eye, and squinted some more. "What made you do it?"

As if I'd turned to a life of crime.

"Bailey! Good grief. Mom's been through a lot. If she needs a diversion, well, what's wrong with that?" Psych I. Swell. Now I had both my daughters analyzing me.

I pulled the muffins out of the oven, and when the coffee finished brewing I placed a mug in front of Bailey.

"We lost him too," she said, her voice low.

I turned, but she kept her eyes on her coffee.

"It's different for Mom," Becca said. She took three saucers out of the cupboard and set them next to the muffins. "I mean, she lost like half of who she is, while we have our whole lives ahead of us." She gasped. "Not that you—" She reached out and touched my arm. "You know what I mean."

Yes, I did. Because it was clear that neither Bailey nor Becca thought I should have an identity outside of being the widow of Trey from the day he died until I died too. And that everything I did outside the norm was an expression of my grief at losing him. I should enshroud myself in this tomb of a house like a modern-day Miss Havisham, stop all the clocks at the time of Trey's death, and let the web weavers go to work.

Only I didn't know the time of Trey's death. Not the real time, the time his heart beat its final beat, the time his breath passed over his lips for the last time, the time his eyes closed for good, on another woman's face. No, I can only claim the official time of death, not the intimate one.

I looked into the eyes of my girls, whose pain was so much deeper than mine and was genuine—because in spite of everything else, Trey had loved our daughters and had shown it in all the right ways—and I cursed him. It felt like treason. And like freedom.

"Don't you?" Becca said. "Know what I mean?"

Bailey suddenly lifted her head. "Who's your English professor?" Her eyes were full of suspicion.

"Ian Beckwith." I forced the enticing sound of his voice right out of my head.

She visibly relaxed. "Good." She turned to Becca. "He's gay."

My stomach surged as the high tide of guilt pulled it up and away. I left my muffin on its saucer, unable to swallow a bite. Oh, wouldn't they fall to little bitty pieces if they knew about Lars Jorgensen, these daughters of Robert Andrew Torrington the Third?

❧

The girls worked all afternoon on the cake, the nature of which was a surprise. I had to stay out of the kitchen. I'd never known Bailey to be particularly domestic, and her participation touched me. Usually, she was good for a half-gallon of ice cream. Chocolate chip cookie dough, no matter the type of cake, because it was her favorite. Whatever was left over never made it through the night.

Dinner was at Mother and Dad's and included Shawlie. Nice

to see she and Mother could both sacrifice on my account, but I suspect more than anything Bailey's pull with her grandmother was at play.

Shawlie brought flowers. A big, beautiful bouquet.

"They're from Sven," she whispered. "I've run out of room at the office and my condo. He sends a box every day. Sweet, huh?"

"Every day?"

"And look." Shawlie lifted her left arm to show off a silver watch that was more jewelry than timepiece.

"Wow."

"I tell you, Abbie, this is the perfect relationship. At last."

"Flowers," Mother said. "How nice. You can put them on the dining room table. Next to the others."

Shawlie's lips rose in a false smile. "You can never have too many flowers."

Mother looked at my hair, turned on her heel, and headed back to the kitchen. She had made Swiss steak for dinner, Trey's favorite, but in all fairness I liked it too. Especially the carrots, which were surprisingly missing this time. Instead, there was rutabaga.

I didn't know they made that anymore.

Shawlie poked one with her fork and lifted an eyebrow in my direction.

Ask Sven, the Dane from Nova Scotia, I would tell her later.

"Shall we pray?" Dad said.

We joined hands, and the words that poured out of him about me and for me brought tears to my eyes. I couldn't squeeze them tightly enough to keep the drops from slipping through my lashes and running down the sides of my nose. I let go of Shawlie's hand and wiped them away.

Dad winked when he finished and gave me one of those smiles

that said I would always be his little girl. Even at forty-two. Ooh, make that forty-three. I gave him my own wink in return. Then Mother began to pass the food, clockwise.

◈

I love exchanging gifts, but when I'm the only one receiving them, well, I'd just as soon not. I've never liked that much attention concentrated on me. It makes my head itch. And the last thing I wanted to do was draw attention to my head. Or, more specifically, my hair.

Mother did everything she could not to look at me, while still being as hospitable as it was in her nature to be. At least she didn't go to her room and refuse to come out.

Becca handed me her gift first, an iridescent bag sprouting teal and purple paper shreds, crinkled and festive, that concealed the latest Grisham legal thriller, an oversized mug with pale green stripes and a cat stretched out on a wing chair, and a Starbucks gift card that would get me through the winter.

There was also a bookmark with my name, Abigail, in a swirly gold font. Beneath the name it said, "Gives joy." Beneath that, there was a Scripture. "May the God of hope fill you with all joy and peace as you trust in him, so that you may overflow with hope by the power of the Holy Spirit." It was from Romans 15:13.

"That's what your name means." Becca's smile came straight from the heart. "That's what you do, give joy. And that's my prayer for you." The last she said shyly, with a little shrug of her shoulders.

I could not speak past the lump that I couldn't swallow away. I just opened my arms, which she filled with her goodness. I kissed her cheek, then wiped away the moisture I'd left with my tears.

If she'd given me nothing but that bookmark and her words, I'd have had the best birthday of my life.

"It's going to be one of *those* nights," Bailey said to the group. She handed me a tissue along with her gift. "It won't make you cry. I promise."

The card was one of those rude old lady cards, the one with the cigarette and the cutting words. But it was funny, as it was meant to be. I laughed and passed it around. Then I scooped off the crinkled paper on top of the bag. Inside was a stainless steel travel mug.

Bailey nodded her head toward Becca. "She told me what happened. You can't spill this one. It's safe."

"Safe?" Mother said.

"What haven't you told us?" Shawlie asked.

"Sorry," Bailey said.

"No problem." I held up the mug. "Thank you." To the rest I said, "It's our secret." But Shawlie knew I'd spill the beans—no pun intended—as soon as we were alone. It was the story we'd never gotten around to that day in the mall.

"That's not all, of course." Bailey handed me a box with a Macy's sticker, professionally wrapped, with a bow the size of Rhode Island.

I untaped the edges, like I always did, and slid the box out. Beneath the lid and the tissue paper was a sweater. A moss green sweater.

"Because it goes so well with your . . ." Bailey gave me a sardonic smile.

"Hair," we said together.

She meant, of course, the highlights of burnished bronze that came from my dad's side of the family, the ones that weren't there anymore.

"It'll go perfect with that gold," Shawlie said, giving me a nod of solidarity.

I reached for a strand of hair, which wasn't where it used to be, then reached up higher. "Yes, it will." I winked at Bailey. "Thank you. I love it."

I folded the tissue over the garment and replaced the lid of the box. Moss green. Later I'd have to ask Shawlie if that really was the color, or if my eyes had taken on a jealous hue that I couldn't see beyond. Because if it really was moss green, well, that was just plain weird.

Shawlie's gift was an outrageous pair of long, beaded earrings.

"You'll actually be able to see them now."

I slipped out my little gold rings, the ones I'd worn forever, and draped the silver wires through my ears. I shook my head and listened to the earrings tinkle like tiny wind chimes.

"Sassy," Shawlie said. "Definitely sassy."

If I was trying to keep my hair from being an issue, I was failing miserably.

Mother and Dad gave me a flannel throw, to go with the other two I had draped over chair backs in my living room. In a little psychoanalysis of my own, I deduced Mother was subconsciously highlighting the coldness of our relationship. Or maybe she just wanted me to be warm, now that I had no one to hold me.

Maybe.

This throw was softer than the others, I had to give her that. And it wasn't green.

The cake the girls had worked so hard to produce was a three-layer chocolate raspberry affair they'd seen on the cover of *Martha Stewart Living*, an old copy they'd gotten from Mother. I was really touched by their effort and thanked Bailey for the chocolate chip cookie dough ice cream.

If one had to turn forty-three, this was a fine way to do it.

An opportunity presented itself as Mother was clearing the table of our dessert plates. Dad had slipped off to the restroom, and the girls warmed themselves at the hearth while they discussed their current classes. I motioned for Shawlie to stay seated, then grabbed up the empty coffee cups and followed Mother to the kitchen.

"It was a great birthday dinner. Thank you."

Mother tied her apron behind her back in a perfect bow, adjusted the temperature of the tap water until the steam swirled around her head, then ran a sink full of hot sudsy water. She never added dessert dishes to the dishwasher, even if there was room. Instead, she would wash, dry, and put them away, polish the faucet, then work a dollop of Jergens lotion into her red, wrinkled hands. I wondered how many of my own quirky routines caught the attention of my daughters.

"It was nothing," Mother said.

"I love the throw."

"We're in for a record winter."

"Well, then, I'm set." I pulled a clean dishtowel from the drawer and began to wipe the dishes.

"That's carnival glass. Be careful."

She'd said the same words to me since I was at least ten, regarding these same plates. She had a set of twelve that had belonged to her mother. All twelve dessert plates, cups, and saucers were still on display in her china hutch. All twelve in iridescent marigold.

She had come to own them because Aunt Lizzy died. To Mother, that's where their true value lay, that Aunt Lizzy had sipped tea from the cups and loved them. They'd go straight to Bailey, I was pretty sure.

I drew in a breath, well aware I was losing time, and jumped right in. "So, Mother, why is it you hate my hair?"

"Hate your hair? Did I say that?"

I looked up toward my bangs. "This upsets you. I just wondered why."

Her lips were a firm line as she washed another dish.

"Besides the fact that I look eerily like Aunt Lizzy."

The plate in Mother's hand slipped and fell beneath the soapy water. We gasped in unison and held our breath as Mother fished it out with both hands. Her face had turned as pale as the suds, but the color seeped back into her cheeks when she realized there wasn't so much as a chip. I too was flooded with relief because it would have been my fault.

"Would you like me to finish?" I asked.

She turned and looked me straight in the eye. "No, Tippy, I wouldn't."

Dad was suddenly at my side. "How about if I finish?" He took the towel from my hands. "You're the birthday girl."

❧

The smell of Jergens followed Mother into the living room, where Shawlie, Becca, and I chatted around the fire. Bailey was somewhere else talking on her cell phone, to Tim McGuire no doubt. Mother didn't sit, in anticipation of our leave-taking, which in all honesty I was ready for.

"This was the perfect birthday." I hugged both my parents at once, which was less awkward than hugging them individually, because Dad was so affectionate and Mother was so not. "Thanks for everything."

"Great dinner," Shawlie said. "Thanks for including me."

"See you Easter week, I guess," Becca said to Mother and Dad, her hugs and kisses as guileless as a toddler's. "I'll get Bailey."

"I'm right here," she said, visibly on edge.

She sat alone in the backseat and didn't say two words all the way home.

Twenty

"So what's Chi Alpha exactly, and why does Bailey think it's a cult?"

Becca turned a droll expression my way. "Because she's Bailey."

Okay, point well taken.

Bailey had left the house almost the minute we got home from Mother and Dad's, but Becca and I sat in the den, she in Trey's chair, I in mine, a throw over each of our laps, like two old maids. Only we were far from that, light years from that. I sipped spiced tea from my new mug, while Becca drank a soda from the can.

"It's the neatest group, Mom. We have Bible studies on Thursday nights and prayer circles and mentoring partners. They're even planning a trip to Mexico this spring to work at an orphanage. I'm thinking about going."

"Mexico. Well." I was amazed to see the same glow about her that Winnie walked in after her conversion, her AC life, she called it. After Christ. I thought of it only as After Cancer. The whole awful thing—the chemo, the sickness, the surgery. Winnie's beautiful bald head, which she didn't try to hide. Seemed awfully ungenerous of this God Winnie was so smitten with. Made me not want to get too close, to be honest. "Are you sure it's safe, Becca, this group?"

"Mom, it's not a cult. Really. It's part of an established Christian denomination. I love the church we go to."

"Church too. Boy, you've jumped in with both feet."

"It's the only way, Mom. You can't be lukewarm."

Yes, I remembered something about that from my years in Sunday school. Let your light shine and all that.

"Mom, do you think Dad's in heaven?" Becca's eyes were big as nickels and shiny with the tears she tried so hard to hold back.

Suddenly she was six again.

"Get the sewing kit," Trey said to me, while Becca stood before her dad and wiggled a tooth that was barely hanging on for dear life. Bailey stood close to her sister with her arms crossed, thrilled to be the spectator this time around.

I returned with my round tin box with the painted roses on the lid and handed it to Trey. It was only right that he took charge since he was the one with the guts to pull all those loose teeth. He bent and held the box at knee level, while Becca looked over each colorful spool. Picking the color was the girls' favorite part of the tooth-pulling ritual. That, and the visit from the Tooth Fairy.

"Get the blue one." Bailey hopped up and down. "No, no, the purple. The purple's cool." But Becca just studied the box with the concentration of a chemist.

Finally, she reached in and pulled one out the color of Hubba Bubba bubble gum. She handed it to her dad. Her big green eyes were raised to his, nothing but trust in her gaze.

Trey bit off a twelve-inch length of thread, wrapped it three times around the tooth, which was so loose he could have easily plucked it with his bare fingers. But that wasn't part of the ritual. He held an end of the string in each hand.

"You ready?" he said, his hands in her mouth like a dentist at work.

Unable to answer, she nodded, her eyes still fixed on his.

He winked, as if transferring courage. Then he pulled.

We heard the tooth land on the tile somewhere near the kitchen table. We hit our knees, all four of us, and began to hunt for the treasure, because that little piece of enamel, tucked under her pillow tonight, was worth a fiver at least. It was, after all, her first lost tooth.

"There!" Bailey screeched. "Under my chair!" She pointed until Becca saw it.

She came up with the tiny tooth, cupping it in the palm of her hand as if it really were a treasure. A grin showed off the gap the missing tooth had left, and we laughed and laughed at her new look. The tooth was so ready to come out that it didn't even bleed. The top of the tooth that would replace it had already broken the surface of her gums, like a tiny saw blade, the hard part done.

Her school picture that year was my favorite of all, her gaping hole proudly displayed, the camera capturing my sweet little Becca in transition.

I earnestly hope Trey's life of deceit began sometime after that moment. That everything about our lives up to that point really was magic.

I sighed out a breath. "I don't even know if I believe in heaven." But then I thought of Winnie, and if there was no afterlife place for someone like Winnie to go to, well, then, what were we here for? "I guess I don't really mean that," I said. But I had no idea how to answer her question about Trey, not in my frame of mind. "It's so nice to have you home," I said instead. "It gets so quiet around here."

"What you need is a cat, Mom. Something you can talk to but isn't too much trouble."

I held up my mug. "And thanks to you I have one."

❧

Becca had just gone up to bed and I was rinsing my cup to put it in the dishwasher when Bailey came in. I had expected to get through three or four chapters of my new book before she got home.

"Hey there. You're early. How are things?"

"I'm really tired." Her head was down as she passed me, but I could see her eyes were splotchy, just like mine when I cried.

"Bailey?"

She stopped but didn't turn.

"How about some tea?"

She hesitated, nodded once, and took a seat, while I added water to two mugs and placed them in the microwave. Neither of us spoke again until I set the mugs on the table.

"Everything okay?" I asked. Obviously it wasn't.

She plunked her tea bag in and out of the water, over and over, mindlessly, until I put my hand on hers and lifted out the bag.

"What is it, honey? What's bothering you?"

She huddled over her mug and rocked back and forth in her chair, like she'd done since she was little when something troubled her. "Ever wish you could have a do-over, just once, when it mattered the absolute most?" She answered her own question with a shrug. "Trouble is, we'd probably all save it, never knowing if something more important was just around the corner. And there it would be, like a get-out-of-jail-free card, clutched in our hands unspent as we lay in our casket."

"Ooh, wow, Bailey, that's a bit morbid."

She finally looked up, her red-rimmed eyes piercing me. "But don't you? *Don't* you?"

I let out a breath. "I'd like a whole deck of them, actually. But what would you do over?" My stomach clinched as I waited for her answer, felt like a tooth caught in the grip of Trey's tugging string.

And then her cell phone rang. Bailey gave an apologetic shrug and picked up her mug of tea. "What?" she said into the phone as she exited the kitchen. That's all I heard, but the one word was as tense as her retreating form. She stopped in the doorway, mouthed a good night. A minute later I heard her bedroom door close.

I tried to sigh away my worry, but it wasn't going anywhere. "What would you do over, Bailey?" I whispered, afraid I already knew the answer. Weren't things supposed to get easier once your children were in college?

❧

Sunday morning was all the time I had left with my girls. They'd be on the road by one. Even at that it would be dark by the time they reached San Luis. And I hated that. Two young girls — okay, young women — alone on the highway at night. Especially my young women. I was a worrier, which made me think I must have been adopted, because my mother hadn't worried a day in her life.

Not about me anyway.

And there were things I needed to resolve. Like Becca's cult and Bailey's do-over. Especially Bailey's do-over. But by the time

I went downstairs to mix up a batch of blueberry muffins, straight from the Pillsbury box, Becca had put on the coffee and was adding her signature happy face to the end of a note.

"Becca?"

"Oh, hey, Mom."

"You're dressed. Up."

She wore the cutest slacks and a sweater I hadn't seen before. Not to mention shoes that could have come from Diane Keaton's closet.

She handed me the note. "I was just leaving for church."

My eyebrows hiked up beneath the bangs I still wasn't used to. *Church?* "By yourself?"

She gave me that grin where one side of her mouth goes up and the other goes down. "It's Gramma Winnie's church. I think it's safe. Wanna go?"

"Oh, well, I . . ."

Becca waited while I hemmed and hawed, not giving me the least little help off the hook.

"I was, you know, going to make muffins. And I still need to talk to Bailey."

She strapped her purse over her shoulder. "Good luck. She left an hour ago."

"Left?"

"But a talk would be good."

"Becca, wait. Where did she go?"

"I'm the younger sister, remember? She doesn't tell me anything." Becca planted a kiss on my cheek. "I'll be back in time for lunch."

⊶⊷

The muffins were done and I'd eaten three of them when I finally heard Bailey's key in the door.

"Bailey?" I called from the kitchen.

There was a telltale pause and I could almost hear the sigh that followed it. "Yeah, it's me." Her tone was less than cordial.

"I made muffins." By now I was in the foyer. "And there's coffee." She held a Grande something from Starbucks in her hand. "Oh, well . . ."

"I'm not hungry." She turned and headed for the stairs.

"Bailey." We needed to talk. "Honey." What to say, what to say? "Last night when your phone rang . . . could we finish our conversation?"

A pallor had drained the pink from her cheeks. "I really need to do some laundry."

"I'll help."

She shrugged and I followed her to the laundry room. Once the first load was going, we moved to the kitchen. Just the smell of the muffins made me want to throw up after eating three in a row, but I put one in the microwave for Bailey, gave it twenty seconds, then spread on some butter. It melted into the warm, spongy muffin and dripped onto the saucer. Bailey barely noticed the plate in front of her. She just sat and turned her cup around and around.

"You were talking about do-overs. Last night."

Bailey looked away, out the window at the slate January sky, her cup still at last.

"What would you do over, honey?"

"You first," she finally said.

My breath caught at that. I wasn't expecting to reciprocate. I studied the profile of my firstborn daughter, so different from me in every way, thought about Becca's crooked smile and how much

I loved it, how much I loved my girls. I could hear the ticking of the clock all the way from the foyer in the quiet of the kitchen, could almost hear the beating of my heart. What would I do over?

"Nothing," I said at last, if it meant I wouldn't have one or both of my incredible daughters exactly as they were. "Absolutely nothing."

Bailey turned a solemn face to me. "You're one of the lucky ones."

I thought about that for a minute and nodded. Sometimes life is a trade-off. Bailey and Becca were worth whatever price I'd unknowingly paid. "Your turn."

"It hardly seems fair since you didn't have any do-overs."

"Okay, here's one. I'd take Gramma Winnie to Hawaii. No matter what."

"She never went? But she was so, so . . ." She shrugged. "Tropical."

"Yes, she was. But she never got there."

"Why?"

"It just didn't work out. We always thought there'd be time someday. I really regret not making the time when I had the chance."

Bailey went back to turning her cup. I could tell she was forming in her mind what she wanted to say. So I waited. At last she drew in a breath and slowly let it out. "There are certain things I wanted for myself, things I always told myself I would and wouldn't do. Would go to college." She looked away again. "Wouldn't waste my virginity."

I had tried to steel myself for what I knew was coming, but my breath caught in my throat. I reached for Bailey's hand, ever the mom wanting to fix things, but stopped short. At least I knew to do that.

"That's my do-over. And the really stupid thing is he wasn't worth it."

"Tim?"

She nodded.

I bit my lip and swallowed a host of mean things I wanted to say about young Mr. McGuire and almost every man who'd ever walked the earth. Of course he wasn't worth it. "Can you tell me about it?"

"It was all about that whole thing with Amy Brennan. She would, I wouldn't, so he did. And then he actually comes to my work and tells me she's pregnant. Which, of course, she wasn't. I don't even know if she lied to him or he lied to me. But you were right, he cheated and that should have been that. But to hear him tell it, it was my fault."

"Because you wouldn't."

"Exactly."

My mind was swirling with every nasty name I'd ever heard, ascribing each and every one to Tim. "Are you—?"

"No. But it's not even about that, or about the fact that I could have gotten who knows what from the . . . the tramp." She looked sharply at me. "Can guys be tramps?"

I didn't even hesitate. "I would say yes, Bailey. Most definitely."

"It's that he lied, finagled, and sweet-talked his way into . . . *having* his way, and then he didn't even care. He said we didn't have to worry about being committed to just each other since we were so far away and all. Just as long as I . . . *delivered* every time I came home. That's when I knew. I'd squandered myself on the likes of Tim McGuire. And there are no do-overs." Uncharacteristic for Bailey, her eyes began to well up right in front of me. "It doesn't matter anyway."

"Doesn't matter? Of course it matters."

She shook her head.

"Why?"

Bailey grabbed for a napkin and wiped at her eyes, every action filled with anger—anger that she was crying in front of me, anger that she had a reason to. "It's not like I even want to have a wedding now."

"Oh, Bailey, one mistake doesn't mean you can't have the wedding you've dreamed of."

"It's not that." She looked at me with eyes shining a deep violet blue, the way they turned whenever she cried. "Who would walk me down the aisle?"

Twenty-One

"Here." Bailey handed me a red and white For Sale sign as I helped the girls load the car for their trip back to San Luis. "I picked this up for you yesterday."

I held it, puzzled.

"It's for your car."

"My car?"

"You don't need two, and Dad's Escalade is newer and nicer. Sell the Honda and use Dad's car."

"But, Bailey, my Honda only has fifty thousand miles."

"And Dad's Escalade has, what, seventy-five hundred? It was practically new when he . . . when he . . . Besides, it's paid for."

"So is the Honda."

"Mother, it's seven years old. I went online and found what it would Blue Book for. It's all there on the sticky tab. You can park it in the Wal-Mart parking lot. You won't even have to advertise. I bet it sells in a day."

"Well, that certainly sounds easy."

"Make sure you run any offer by Grampa. He'll know whether it's good or not." She looked at me with eyes as businesslike as Trey's. "It's time, Mom." Then she hugged me, brief and barely touching, but still it was a hug. Sort of.

"Bye, Mom." Becca wrapped her slender arms around me and kissed my cheek. "I guess we'll see you —" She thought for a moment. "Easter?"

I nodded and bit my lip. "Easter." These days I lived for the milestones.

❬❭

Two weeks later when I turned into my driveway after class one afternoon, I pressed the remote to open my part of the garage, parked my seven-year-old Honda in its usual spot, then opened the other door, the one that closed off Trey's Escalade from the wide open world. The door screeched terribly as it rolled up, and I strained to remember the last time it had been opened. Bailey had driven the car somewhere. But when?

My heart thudded as I retrieved Trey's keys from the key rack in the kitchen where they'd hung for a year and a half. They'd come home in his briefcase, which had been shipped FedEx to Trey's office the week after his death. Theo delivered it to the house. "The, um, client sent this," she said, for lack of a better noun, her eyes anywhere but on mine. I could have given her several if she'd only asked.

I didn't look inside the case for weeks, afraid of what I might find, what she, Miss San Diego, might have planted to make her existence known to me. But there was nothing of Trey's other life inside. Only forms, a calculator, breath mints. Trey was a fan of breath mints. BreathSavers, Certs, Altoids, Mentos, Tic

Tacs. They were everywhere. In his pockets, over the visor, in the cup holder of his car, in his desk drawers, by his bed. And always peppermint.

I prefer wintergreen.

"But you see, Ab, you're defeating the purpose," Trey would say. "You don't select breath mints for their taste. You select them for their effectiveness." Effectiveness *was one of Trey's favorite words. "And what could be more effective than peppermint?"*

"It gives me a headache," I would say.

Then Trey would smile that certain smile he reserved for creatures less evolved than he and say, "Ab, it's all in your head." And before I could agree, he'd cover my lips with his lecture finger and move close enough that his pepperminty breath blew warm on my face as he spoke. "See?" he'd say. "Effective."

He had stopped short of finishing with a kiss, and that was how many years ago? I was suspicious of everything now, constantly trying to conjure up the signs.

Trey would never leave a restaurant without taking a peppermint for everyone in his party. In fact, he'd complain to the manager of any restaurant that didn't have peppermints, and only peppermints, to grab on the way out the door. If they had those luscious green and purple mints or, even better, chocolate ones, he'd practically pout all the way home. Every peppermint he gave me went into a little pocket of my purse, where they'd stay till their edges turned soft and white with age. Then I'd find them and toss them out on garbage day so Trey wouldn't see.

I changed toothpaste after Trey died too.

I slid into the driver's seat of Trey's Escalade, the rich upholstery cold even through my clothing. It smelled of new leather. And of Polo. After all this time.

There was a fine layer of dust on the windshield. It had been

a while since the garage had been blown out. There were cob-
webs in the corner, I noticed. Trey would be livid. Once spring
arrived I'd have to hire someone to clean the entire outside of
the house. The eaves, the patio, the pool house, the garage, just
like Trey would do after the final rain of the year. I don't know
how he always knew it was the final rain. He just did.

I reached for the rearview mirror, adjusted it a bit, and ran
my fingers over the padded steering wheel with a touch soft
enough I might have been reading Braille. My throat ached with
tears that still wouldn't come.

"Abbie?"

I started so that I jammed my knee into the console.
"Ahh!"

"Sorry."

"Shawlie, don't do that!"

"Well, for crying out loud, I parked my car in your driveway,
waved all the way up here, did everything but holler, 'Yoo-hoo!'
What are you doing?"

I slid out of the vehicle and gave the door a push. "Believe
me, it's not what you think."

"Believe me, I wouldn't be thinking anything that would
make you say, 'It's not what you think.'"

"Now that we have that straight, come in." I led the way
through the laundry room and into the kitchen. "Coffee?"

Shawlie dropped her bag onto the island and pointed to the
underside of her chin with a French-manicured nail.

I looked to where she pointed, then squinted. "What?"

"There."

I looked again, shook my head. "I don't see anything."

"There," she repeated, as if that would clear things up.

"Shawlie, I don't— Oh, a pimple? You drove all the way

over here to show me a pimple?"

She glared at me a full fifteen seconds. "Not a pimple, Abbie. This." She held up a pair of tweezers so close that it made my eyes cross. I stepped back until I could focus. And shrugged.

"Look." She held the tweezers closer still.

I squinted, stepped back again. "Oh, okay." A single coiled hair, perhaps an inch long if it were pulled straight, protruded from the end of the tweezers. "A hair."

"Yes. A hair." She pointed underneath her chin again.

"You mean . . .?"

"Exactly."

I sat down on my stool, frowned hard, and gnawed my lip to keep from laughing.

"Do you have any idea how long this thing has been growing there? For all the world to see?"

I couldn't help myself. "Awhile."

Shawlie glared again. "You'd think *some*one would have told me."

"I never saw it. Honest."

"Now, on top of everything else, I have to start waxing."

"For one hair?"

She shook the tweezers at me. "You could thread a needle with this."

"And do what?"

"What difference does it make? The fact that it *is* is enough."

"Coffee?" I offered again.

"A quick cup."

When the coffee began to brew I rejoined Shawlie at the island, sliding onto a stool beside her. "Oh, hey," I said, "does this mean you're getting married?"

"Married? What in the world are you talking about?"

"You always said —"

"Funny, Abbie. Very funny."

I reached over and lifted her right arm. The wrist was wreathed with a bracelet of diamonds and gold. "Nice. Have I seen it before?"

Shawlie modeled it for me. "It arrived yesterday, with more flowers. I swear, Sven must own stock in a floral shop."

"And a jewelry store. That's a bit extravagant for just being friends, don't you think?"

"I told you, Abbie, long-distance relationships are the only way to go."

My stomach took a bungee dive. I could feel the color drain from my face. "Well, you could send him a sweater as a thank-you gift. I know just the place to get it."

Shawlie covered her mouth. "I am so sorry. That was thoughtless of me. I only meant —"

"I know." I poured our coffee, added creamer to both mugs, then came back to my roost. "What I don't get is why it still bothers me so much."

"It's because there's been no resolution. The creep hasn't been around to clobber, you haven't been able to get even in court. It's like he got in the last word, and what woman in her right mind can live with that?"

"Some days I feel like I could spontaneously combust, there's so much tension inside me."

"You have too much time on your hands, Abbie, too much time to think. What you need is a job. Come work for me. Wouldn't that be a blast?"

I covered a grimace with my oversized mug. "I think school's enough for now."

"Ah, well, you're probably right. How are classes?"

"The decorating class is interesting, but I think I'll stop with one."

Shawlie waved a hand. "You know way more about decorating than most women anyway. You could probably teach the class." She took a drink of her coffee. "And the history class?"

"American Lit," I said. I took a long drink of coffee. "Bailey says I should sell my car."

Shawlie chewed on that for a minute. "Not a bad idea. You have something in mind?" She looked at her watch. "We could meet for dinner later, then head over to the auto mall. Have you seen the new—"

"She says I should drive the SUV. Trey's Escalade."

Shawlie stopped. "Oh. I get it. You were trying it on for size when I arrived. Well, it is practically new. Leave the windows open for a week or two, hang one of those pine tree thingies on the rearview mirror, and, who knows, you might be able to forget RAT was ever in it."

But RAT wasn't the problem. Not entirely. The real problem was that every time I saw the silver chariot hunkered down in our garage I couldn't help but wonder who else had been using my vanity mirror. "Follow me down the hill to Wal-Mart?"

"Wal-Mart?"

"Bailey says that's the place to park it."

Shawlie stood and reached for her bag. "I know she's your daughter and all, but really, how many cars has she sold?"

I cocked my head at her. "Come on, she's Bailey. What does actual experience have to do with anything?"

"I see your point."

Shawlie followed me back to the garage, where the roll-up door in front of Trey's car was still open. I walked to the Honda, opened the door, and reached inside for the For Sale sign. Then I walked around to the driver's side of Trey's car and slid behind the wheel.

"Hey, what are you . . .?" Shawlie stopped, smiled, winked, laughed. "Good for you, Abbie. Hurray for you."

⹏⹐

Do-overs. I couldn't get Bailey's comment off my mind.

She'd come into this world an old soul, such a serious baby. She didn't giggle and coo and kick her feet like you see on the Pampers commercials. No, from the moment her brand-new eyes could focus she'd study me with a bewildered look as if to say, *Really, I'd expected more.* I'd try to smooth away the crease between her feathery brows with a gentle rub of my fingers while I sang to her "Baby Love." My baby love.

I used to imagine that Bailey was living her life in reverse, from finish to start. That as I traveled toward old age and she back toward infancy there would come one magical moment when we'd connect, like drops of water that converge and then divide to follow their own course again. I'd cherish that convergence for eternity, while the theme from *Rocky* thundered in the universe.

But there was no sign of carefree childhood on the horizon and never had been. Bailey kept to her course, the crease in her brow growing steadily deeper, like the Grand Canyon of creases forged by a river of her own private cares. Mother's genes in me had stealthily surged ahead during Bailey's conception, while my own took a stroll toward that fertilized egg, unaware of the race at hand. *The Tortoise and the Hare* with a new ending.

Bailey was the composite of the two people I struggled with most in my life—one subsurface, the other postmortem. She was opinionated, strong-willed, demanding, insensitive on so many levels, her father's daughter to the utmost degree. But I loved her and I hurt for her. Because I know what she'd done. She'd given something of infinite worth to one infinitely unworthy. She kissed a prince and got a toad, and saw the unlucky exchange the moment it was consummated.

I added Tim McGuire's name to my list of people to curse.

I hadn't been honest with Bailey about my do-over. No, I would not have changed one single step I took with Trey, not if it meant I wouldn't have both my girls exactly as they are. Because I believe our steps are intricately connected like the chains in the afghans Mother crochets. One misstep, one variation, and the pattern is altered from what it was meant to be. There are those who would argue that the final outcome might actually be better because of the misstep. Not me. I like a sure thing.

I picked up the phone. "Bailey. Hi." I forgot at this time of day she might still be in class.

"Mother?" There was a slight hesitation in which I could feel her fear. "Everything all right?"

"Yes. Fine. I just— we didn't really finish our talk the other day. I just want to say that, sweetheart, one wrong choice doesn't have to lead to another. You have a beautiful life ahead of you, Bailey. Don't let it get away from you."

There was no reply, and I thought for a moment I'd lost the call. "Bailey? Hello?"

"I'm here. And thanks. Really."

"Okay then."

"Okay."

So. My do-over would not have been a life without Robert Andrew Torrington the Third. There was too much I couldn't bear to forfeit. It simply would have been not to trust so thoroughly.

Twenty-Two

Ian Beckwith wore rich burgundy Hush Puppies with fringe across the instep, argyle socks, black jeans, a long-sleeved plaid shirt the exact color of his shoes, and a sweater vest that matched his socks. He was big on sweaters. I did my best to overlook that.

Trey would have laughed at the professor's appearance, comparing his own good looks and sex appeal to this bookish man before me, but I thought Ian Beckwith looked just fine. There was nothing stunning about his individual features. His nose was long and sharp, his lips thin, his chin soft for a man. But taken in the whole, and adding the eyes and the voice to the mix, then, yes, he was stunning. Like pistachio pudding made with whole milk, the taste and texture of which never failed to please me. Even the young women in class were drawn like metal shavings to a magnet, but he never seemed to notice.

Our very own To Sir, With Love or Mr. Holland or John Keating.

Or maybe everyone was right; maybe he was gay.

What did it matter? He was just my American Literature professor.

But the clarity of his glacier blue eyes when they sought you out or the way they crinkled when he smiled or, better yet, when he laughed, which was often, well, it made you hold your breath in anticipation. Of what, I couldn't say.

We were finally discussing *Final Storm* and Claire Ogden Connors. I loved that he spoke of the authors we dissected as if he knew them well enough to have sweet tea on their verandas, but I especially loved that he spoke so familiarly of Ms. Connors. I knew next to nothing about her. In truth, I'd never sought out information about her, but now that I did seek, I found there was little to be had. Ms. Connors was your typical literary recluse. Anonymity seemed to come with the nature of the books she wrote, not diminishing but enhancing their popularity.

It never occurred to me before that written pain was more likely than not experienced pain. I don't know how I had missed that all these years. But if deep calls to deep, I'm sure pain calls to pain, and I was now a member of its club. I spoke its language. Fluently. And as I read *Final Storm* for the third time, I heard things in its words I'd never heard before.

This woman knew sorrow, and knew it well.

Ian leaned against his desk, feet crossed in his favorite stance. "Ms. Connors was born in Mississippi, circa Steinbeck, Fitzgerald, and Hemingway. I don't know what it is about the South, but it's bred a good many of our finest authors. Lee, Mitchell, Twain, even Grisham. And those who weren't from the South often wrote about the South. Why do you suppose that is?"

"Who can say?" Miss Near-Perfect rolled her eyes. "Everything there is so sultry."

It was clear the word she really sought was *tawdry*. You could tell by the curl of her lip. Ian kept his own lips in a straight line, but you could see the amusement in the brightness of his eyes.

"Well now," he said, and he took a moment to scratch his chin. "If we eliminated everything east of the Rockies from American literature, what would we be left with?"

"Jack London," someone said.

"Steinbeck." Someone else.

"But we weren't talking about east of the Rockies. We were talking specifically about the South." Miss Near-Perfect again.

"Yes, we were." Ian's voice was raspy and coarse, as if his vocal cords had been used nearly to extinction with all the words he'd delivered with passion over the years. But it pleased the ear, like water over stones. You had to listen. You wanted to. He shrugged. "If we eliminated everything that dealt with the South from American literature, then what?"

"You mean, like playwrights and everything?" This from a young man whose voice faltered as he spoke.

"Sure, playwrights and everything. Maybe it would be easier to ask what we would lose rather than what we'd be left with."

"Tennessee Williams," the same young man said.

"Who, incidentally, was born in Columbus, Mississippi, like our own Claire Ogden Connors."

"Then why's he called Tennessee?"

I didn't see the questioner.

"Why don't you tell us next time?"

There was a smattering of chuckles.

"Edna Ferber," I said. I glanced at the young faces around me and knew by the puzzled looks I'd dated myself again.

Ian cocked his head and looked as if he were debating his reply. "Ms. Ferber was actually born in Kalamazoo, Michigan, and grew up in Wisconsin, but she was a favorite of our Ms.

Connors, as it happens."

"Oh," I said, feeling the heat rise in my cheeks as I scribbled on my notepad a dozen names I could have rightly said. Edna Ferber. What a dolt!

"What's your favorite by Ms. Ferber?" Ian asked.

"*Fanny Herself*," I said, without hesitation.

"Not what I'd have guessed." His smile was as cryptic as his words. He looked at his watch. "But back to *Final Storm*. This was not Ms. Connors' magnum opus. In fact, she didn't have one. If Steinbeck, Mitchell, and Fitzgerald were your champagne and caviar of literary authors, then Claire Ogden Connors was your plain old everyday mashed potatoes."

"There you go with food again." Miss Near-Perfect looked as if the topic was too boring for words.

Ian turned those arcane blue eyes on her, the faintest hint of a smile starting on his lips. "Yes," he said.

And I was suddenly hungry.

⸎

I stopped by Shawlie's office on the off chance she'd be free for a late lunch. I wanted a chicken salad and was tired of eating alone.

Shawlie was at her desk, no client in sight, reading the card on a large vase of Stargazer lilies. She parted the flowers to see who was knocking on her open door.

"Isn't it early for those?" I asked.

"Apparently not in Nova Scotia. This is getting ridiculous." She turned to the credenza behind her, then to the file cabinets. Everything was covered in flowers in various states of bloom, some on the way up, some whose day had come and gone.

I sneezed and took a seat.

"Bless you." Her eyes narrowed. "Or were you being facetious?"

"You know I don't do lilies. Though I must say those are gorgeous."

Shawlie lifted the vase with both hands and pushed it between a basket of multicolored carnations and a dozen near-death, blood red roses on the filing cabinet nearest her desk. "Yeah, well, this isn't the place to be, then." She handed me a tissue. "I swear, I feel like The Undertaker."

My forehead crinkled in a frown. "Trey's dad?"

"Corporately speaking," she said. "So are you ready to sell?"

"Shawlie, honestly, you have a one-track mind."

"It keeps food on the table and fine clothes on my back. It's a great time to list, and I could show you some of the most divine places. I have a new listing on—"

"You know I promised the girls."

She handed me a flyer with a color photo of a house that could certainly be tempting. I read the description, then slid it back across the desk. "When they're out of school—"

"You'll die in that house, Abbie. Mark my words."

"Well, if you're right, we can discuss it then."

Shawlie wagged a finger at me. "I'm going to hold you to that."

"I stopped to see if you want to have lunch. I'm starved." I didn't say a word about Ian Beckwith's *yes* and the crazy effect it had on me. What could I say that would possibly make sense? And besides, wouldn't Shawlie just love to hear it?

"I ate earlier, but I'd love a cup of coffee. What did you have in mind?

"Rosa's Café. Their spicy chicken salad is exactly what I want."

Her eyebrow arched. "Spicy? What's gotten into you?"

I turned toward the door before she could read me. "I love spicy."

"Uh-huh," she said in a way that really meant *since when?* "I'll meet you there."

⤜∾⤛

Shawlie found us a booth while I went to wash my hands. By the time I got to the table she'd ordered for both of us, ever the efficient one. "Spicy chicken salad and iced tea?" she said.

I nodded. "So, any new jewelry to go with the flowers?"

She stuck her leg out the side of the booth and pulled up her slacks. Her ankle was encircled with a fine gold chain from which dangled a heart-shaped charm. She rolled her eyes. "This has gone so over the top. He calls me five times a day, single-handedly keeps Global UPS in business, and has bolstered the entire economy of South America with all! those! flowers!"

"They must not have much to do in Nova Scotia."

"Fine. Sure. Make fun."

"Oh, Shawlie."

"No, no, it isn't your problem." She leaned back as the waiter delivered my salad and poured her another cup of coffee. She turned her cup until the handle was positioned just how she wanted it. She blew, then took a sip.

"You could always send it back, the jewelry, I mean, and tell the florist, 'No More Flowers!'" I speared a strip of chicken with my fork, then savored the flavor. Whew. Hot. I reached for my tea. "And don't answer the phone."

"That's easy for you to say." She toyed with her napkin. "He wants me to come for a visit."

"To Nova Scotia?"

"Honestly, Abbie, you say it like it's the frozen tundra."

"Isn't it?" I took another bite of salad. Whoa. Hoo.

"Sven says there's lots to do."

I couldn't keep my eyebrow down. "I'd skip the sled race if I were you."

"Abbie! That's awful." She took another drink of coffee, gave herself time to lose the scowl. "I went online. The place is absolutely beautiful. Miles and miles of coastline. They call it Canada's ocean playground."

"Must be a ball, playing with all those penguins. And don't forget the arctic seals. But watch the fangs."

Shawlie closed her eyes and shook her head slowly, as if I'd gotten on her final nerve. "Seals don't have fangs, Abbie. They have tusks."

"Tusks?"

"Hel*lo*. Why do you think they call them elephant seals?"

"I had no idea they did."

"Don't you ever watch the National Geographic channel?"

I sat back and crossed my arms. "You and National Geographic? Right. Elephant seals. Ha."

"I'm not making this up." She sat back in a huff. "Besides, we wouldn't go in winter. I was thinking more along the lines of spring break."

Spring break? *We?* When that finally registered, my eyes opened wide. "Oh, no. No, no. No. There's no *we* about it. Not this time."

"Abbie. Come on. I can't go by myself."

I dabbed at my upper lip, where a puddle of perspiration had collected. "Why go at all? Send Sven his trinkets back and—" I broke off with a cough and took another gulp of tea.

Shawlie leaned into the table like an interrogator. "Have you ever *had* Rosa's spicy chicken salad, Abbie? They use cayenne, you know. Lots of it."

Whoo. I pushed the chicken aside and speared a bite of just the green stuff to cool my tongue. I ran my napkin across my forehead.

"You're not going to pass out on me, are you?"

Like she'd care at this point. "I'm not going to Nova Scotia," I choked out. "And neither should you. You don't know a thing about this guy. He could be a serial killer." I pointed my fork at her. "Search *that* out online."

She closed her eyes in a dramatic show and turned her head. "Well, you've certainly been tainted by experience. You are not at all the Abbie I used to know."

"Not the pushover, you mean?" I caught the waiter's eye and lifted my glass. *Please,* I mouthed.

Shawlie wilted. "It's just that— I just don't want to—"

"Throttle the golden goose?"

She sat back again. "Cynical, Abbie, you've become cynical. What I was going to say is that I don't want to carelessly dismiss what could very well turn out to be Mister Right."

"Mister—" I could not believe what I was hearing. "This is all about that whisker, isn't it?"

"For heaven's sake," she hissed, "keep your voice down! And it wasn't a whisker. It was one single hair."

"Mister Right." I jabbed my fork at her again. "You said, not once but a thousand times, that no such creature exists. And I, for one, have learned to believe you. Besides, the girls will be home for spring break, and I have my paper to research and write."

"The girls are all grown up, my friend. They get along

without you every day." Shawlie reached for our tab, but I swooped in and got it.

"This was my invitation," I said.

"Will you at least think about it?"

I gave her one single nod and she smiled. Then I looked at my watch. "I've thought about it. The answer's no."

"You're a snot, Abigail Torrington."

Twenty-Three

I t was odd the things I missed about Trey. Like having a reason to brew a whole pot of coffee instead of one cup at a time, though my new coffee machine made it easy. I simply slipped in a disk, chose coffee, tea, hot chocolate even, and waited for my cup to fill. Voila! Fresh every time. Mother still called it a percolator, though nothing had percolated in my house since, well, ever. She'd continued to use her white and blue filterless CorningWare percolator long after we'd gone to the drip system. She'd mourned for days when the short detachable cord finally sparked, popped, and gave up the ghost, because there wasn't a replacement to be found anywhere in the whole United States. Now, of course, there was eBay and you could find anything. Hmm. Well. Mother's Day was solved. I made a mental note to myself.

I also missed, really missed, having Trey to reconcile the bank statement. He had done it for years because I'd blown my one big chance to show how efficiently I could manage the household budget. Trey had given me the benefit of the doubt along with the checkbook because I'd taken business math in high school. Until he saw my method of reconciliation.

"Abbie. Sweetheart." Trey held up my Flintstones checkbook, pulled his ear, and uttered a chuckle that said, I can't believe what I'm seeing here.

"I love the Flintstones, and the bank had all these great covers to choose from. It was only a little extra."

"Not what I meant," he said. *"How is it possible to write so many checks that are an even amount? I mean, how can that happen?"*

I secured little Bailey into her bouncing swing, wound it up all the way, and waited to make sure she didn't protest. *"Simple,"* I said, turning back to Trey. *"I round up."*

His face lost all expression. *"You . . . you round up?"*

"Or down. Sometimes. But mostly up."

Trey took my arm and led me to the sofa. He sat me down like a two-year-old, then took the cushion beside mine, making sure we faced each other. *"What exactly do you mean by round up? And . . . and down."*

"May I?" I took the checkbook out of his hand. *"For example, I went to the shoe store at the mall yesterday. Not for myself,"* I quickly added. Trey followed my finger as I pointed to Bailey's white strappy sandals. *"Cute, huh? And don't you love that pink polish on her toenails? Anyway, the shoes were . . ."* I glanced at the register, *"approximately eighteen dollars."*

"Approximately? What . . . what do you mean 'approximately'?"

"Well, they were nearly eighteen or just over. If they were nearly, then I rounded up. If they were over, then I rounded down. But" — I thought he'd appreciate this — *"I only round down if it's less than twenty-five cents. Technically you would round down if it's less than forty-nine cents, but this way I almost always cover the service fee and then some. Smart, huh?"* I didn't tell him that I used the extra, because the way I did it there was always extra, as if it were a bonus for something fun, like Bailey's shoes.

"Abbie. Sweetheart." He stopped and rubbed his temples, then eased the

checkbook out of my hand. "Why on earth would you do that?"

"Well, because it's so much easier to subtract. And add. I do the same thing with the deposits."

"No. No."

"Yes. I do." I took the checkbook back. "See here? The check I deposited was technically just under the amount I wrote in. I remember because it was yesterday that I did this, just before the shoe store. So that right there makes up for at least one round down."

"But, Abbie, when you do the bank statement, how do you know which checks have cleared if the amounts in here are different from the amounts on the checks?"

I couldn't help but frown a little. "By the check number, of course."

"And what if you get your checks out of order?"

I shrugged and turned away, presumably to check on Bailey, because, bingo! he was right. Sometimes they did get out of order, and then even I got confused with my system.

"And how do you balance it?"

"Trey, it's not hard. Have you ever balanced —"

"Yes!" he said. "I have."

"Well, then, you just take the amount the bank says, subtract it from the amount the register says, and write it in."

"Write it in."

"On the next line. Then I write OK in red so I know that's where I last balanced."

"You balanced."

My shoulders slumped. "Once in a while, not often, I have to add a little back in. But that's only if there have been too many round downs. Mostly it —"

"Abbie." He pinched the bridge of his nose. "That's the most ridiculous thing I've ever heard. How can you call that balancing?"

"Well, if the bank and I have the same figure —"

Trey raised his lecture finger and pressed it against his lips, then waved it like an overzealous metronome. "You don't have the same figure, Ab. Not even close."

I turned back in the register till I found my last red OK. "We do. See? Right here."

Trey took hold of the checkbook again and closed it with a snap.

He kept it after that. He paid the bills himself and gave me a cash allowance for household purchases. At the end of each month he'd balance the checkbook, now secured in a navy blue cover without even a stripe for decoration, spending an hour finding a penny if it went missing. He used a lot of Wite-Out.

I thought my method was much easier. And I missed my bonuses.

I didn't miss Trey's car. It sold one week after I parked it at Wal-Mart. Bailey was right about the location; no surprise there. By the new owner's willingness to pay cash on the spot, I had a feeling he'd made the better deal, but it was one more thing I didn't have to worry about anymore. It was worth the boasting he undoubtedly spewed after I signed away the pink slip.

"Mother!"

"Bailey? Hi, sweetie."

"Tell me you didn't sell Daddy's Escalade."

I held the phone away and looked at it as if it held a hidden camera. My forehead sprouted drops of perspiration.

"Tell me."

"Well, honey—"

"Mother! How could you?"

"How on earth did you—?"

"Tim told me. He saw Daddy's Escalade with *my* For Sale sign in the window just now and some *man* driving it!"

"The For Sale sign was still in it?" I thought a little humor would help. Wrong.

"Are you purging the house of everything *Daddy*? What is the matter with you? You're acting like . . . like—"

"Bailey. Sweetheart." Egads! Did I really just say that? "What I mean is, I like my Honda. I'm used to it. It seemed more logical to keep it."

"Logical? *Logical*? You keep a ten-year-old rattletrap and get rid of a brand-new, paid-for Cadillac? You call that logical?"

"The Honda's paid for." Even to me it sounded weak. "And it's seven years old, not ten."

"Wait till Becca finds out. She'll cry for a week."

Becca. Oh, Becca. My own eyes stung with tears at the thought of bringing her more pain.

"You could have given it to me, you know."

"The Honda?" Of course not the Honda. I knew it the moment I said it.

"I'm late for class," Bailey said. That was all. No good-bye.

It was two days before Mother called. I groaned as I read the caller ID, because I knew exactly why she was calling. "Hello, Mother."

"Tippy. How are you?"

Her immutable greeting had become like water torture, drip, drip, dripping me toward insanity. One more 'Tippy. How are you?' and I swear I'd slip right over the edge. "Fine, and—"

"So, is it true?"

I thought of several comebacks. *Is what true? . . . Ah, so you talked to Bailey . . . Why don't you like me?* But any one of them would only postpone the inevitable. Might as well get it over with. I inserted a smile into my voice. "I sold one of the cars."

"You sold *Trey's* car, you mean."

"I sold the Escalade, yes."

"Without even discussing this with the girls or asking your father for help. I'm sure you gave it away. Honestly, I don't know what's come over you."

"It's been more than a year and a half since—"

"Since your husband died, Tippy. Died. And without so much as a by-your-leave you sell his car and purge his house of everything to do with him, as if he'd left of his own free will."

A sense of free falling went through me, like it did every time I thought of the divorce papers locked away upstairs in my hope chest. Ha. Wasn't that the mother of twisted humor? "It's my house too." My house *only*, when you got right down to it, but no way would I go that far in spoken words. Not with Mother. "And I haven't purged it." She and Bailey had definitely talked. "Trey is everywhere between these walls. Just not in the garage now."

"Or your bedroom."

There it was again, rearing its head, that thing that had hung between us in the weeks since the makeover. Aside from her bedspread analogy, Mother had not said a word about it. Till now. I wondered if her tongue was sore from biting it all this time. "You haven't seen Trey's closet. He's still there, believe me."

"Death is not a betrayal, Tippy. You have to stop acting like it is."

The free fall ended with my stomach settling somewhere in my toes. "Sorry, Mother, there's my doorbell."

I'd not lied to her outright like that since Shawlie and I cut school our junior year to celebrate the purchase of Shawlie's brand-new bright yellow VW bug. We spent most of the day at Folsom Lake digging our toes in the sand and watching out for the district truant officer. When Mother asked that afternoon how school was, I said, "Fine."

I hated the feeling it left me with then.

Not so much now.

❧

I snatched up my purse and headed to the garage. I needed a book and a latte. The four-car behemoth, larger than most two-bedroom apartments, was so empty now that the clack of my three-inch heels on the smooth concrete floor echoed in the cavernous space. My polemical Honda looked smaller than ever as it sat alone in its usual spot behind door number two, not even a consolation prize if you asked Bailey. I pushed the button, and the door rolled open.

It was another damp, foggy February day in the valley. The sky was the color of ice cubes with an overabundance of minerals in the water. Nothing at all like the clear, perfectly formed half-circle cubes my ice maker plunks out, thanks to my purified water system. Like ice-sculpted mushrooms without the stem.

I shivered as I waited for my heater to blow something other than frigid air out of the vents, switched on the lights even though it was still afternoon, and eased myself up the slope of our driveway. I engaged my left-turn blinker because Trey had instilled in me early on the importance of letting other drivers know my intentions. I braked at the edge of the drive and tried to remember the last time another vehicle had been within sight of my blinker when I emerged onto our quiet street. It was a rare thing if you didn't count workday mornings between seven and eight. But I was seldom on the road at that time.

Ten minutes later I steered my Honda into the Borders parking lot and wound my way up and down the rows until I found a woman in a Mitsubishi Outlander backing out of her space. SUVs were taking over the world. I turned on my blinker—habits die hard—to let others in the market for a parking space know that this one was mine. In a situation like this I always thought of Kathy Bates in *Fried Green Tomatoes* when the snotty brats in the red sporty VW jumped in ahead of her and stole her space. I wondered if I'd have the guts to ram their car like she did, but what I loved most about that scene was her husband's response. He never so much as lifted a lecture finger.

I waved as the woman in the Mitsubishi backed out, and I pulled into the slot she vacated. There would be no testing my mettle today. I can't say I was disappointed. Inside, the store had geared up for Valentine's Day. The display tables were loaded with books on love, romance, seduction, sex, great sex. And love diets? Not my cup of tea these days, not that they ever were, but the covers pulled you right into the pages. *The Celestial Sexpot's Handbook* had me curious about its astrological tips. I mean, *really*? I picked it up and began to thumb through.

"Well, now. I didn't take you for a stargazer."

The gravelly words behind me turned my blood to ice and my cheeks to flaming coals. I turned, hoping, *hoping* someone else had that same textured voice, that same bit of accent. But my luck ran thin these days. Ian Beckwith's powder blue eyes, dancing with humor, fixed on mine. "Hello."

"I was just—" I took a step backward, hands behind me, intent on returning the book as inconspicuously as possible to the stack I'd oh-so-regrettably taken it from. I understood like never before the deadly danger in curiosity. But this wasn't my day. My three-inch heel found the round base of the table, slipped, then twisted. As I reached out to catch myself, I tipped the table. Down I went along with the whole display, which landed beside me with a crash and a clatter. I was thigh deep in salacious material, and a crowd was gathering.

My own mortifying St. Valentine's Day Massacre.

Ian Beckwith stooped down and brushed aside the books. Up close I was surprised to see his saddle oxfords had a scuff on the right toe. "There now. Are you all right?" he asked.

All right? All right?! I was swimming in a sea of books with titles like *A Housewife's Guide to Striptease* and *Yoga for Couples*, complete with illustrations, which I snapped closed, catching his thumb between the pages.

This was more embarrassing than my most embarrassing moment, which had held the record for years. Becca had just started kindergarten, and Trey was being wooed by a start-up insurance company that was soaring its way up the NASDAQ. Trey and I had been invited to join the VP and his wife for Sunday brunch, in Tiburon no less, at the most upscale restaurant in town.

We were escorted to a table on the patio where Mr. and, if memory serves, the third Mrs. Veep awaited our arrival. Honestly, she could have been his daughter — as well as the model for that busty silhouette you see on the mud flaps of a lot of eighteen wheelers rolling down the highway. Her dress was cut beyond low, and if I had trouble keeping my eyes off the mounds, you can imagine what a trial it was for Trey and every other male within eyeshot.

Our waiter handed us leather menus on which was secured one sheet of fine linen paper. Six items were listed in perfect handwritten calligraphy. Six items. No prices. I studied each offering, delighted by the fact that, except for the Omelet Florentine, whatever I selected would be a new experience for me. I chose with care.

"I'm going to have the Eggs Neptune," I whispered to Trey, as the waiter poured coffee into our china cups from a silver urn.

Trey gave his head one quick shake and whispered, "Something else" at the exact moment the Veep said, "Excellent choice."

"I love crab," I whispered back to my husband. And it was settled.

While we waited for our food, the guys made small talk about Wall Street and what a lousy year the San Francisco Giants were having, and it was only the first of May. Shop talk would come later I correctly guessed. Mrs. Veep and I watched the sailboats and exchanged smiles once in a while. Her model-perfect hand rested atop her husband's, precisely where the multicarat diamonds in her wedding set would best throw off their prismatic rainbows from the sunlight. She was careful to keep their hands moving in time to the big star's orbit.

It was one of those days sent from heaven, when the bay sparkled in the sunshine like Blackbeard's treasure and a thousand sailboats frolicked in the wind. It was glorious with a capital G. I sipped my orange juice, which was fresh-squeezed with lots of pulp, just the way I like it. The breakfast rolls were baked right on the premises and were soft as clouds.

There was a lot to be said for being wooed.

Our waiter appeared, hefting a large tray so all four of us could be served at once. He served clockwise, just as he'd taken our orders, beginning with Mrs. Veep. I remember thinking, Mother would be right at home in this place. He moved around the table, setting an exquisitely arranged plate before each of my companions. Then he came to me. I remember I smiled as he lowered the dish. And continued to smile for the full quarter second it took for my brain to register what my eyes were seeing.

In the center of my oblong plate were two English muffin halves, mounded with crabmeat. And when I say mounded, I mean sculpted. The mounds were topped with a pair of perfectly round eggs with perfectly centered yolks, each topped with a perfectly placed mushroom. Of the button variety. The muffins were then laced with creamy white hollandaise sauce.

"Lovely," Mr. Veep said and grinned a wicked grin, while his wife's eyes grew as large as her . . . diamonds. Trey leaned into me, as if retrieving a fallen napkin, and whispered, "Told you."

My face was on fire. As quickly as I could I picked up my fork and gave one of the mushrooms a little flick. It rolled down the mounded slope, right off my plate, and didn't stop until it hit the jam pot. At the same moment, with my free hand I picked up the other mushroom and popped it into my mouth. As if that did anything to lessen the effect.

Fork still in hand I punctured both egg yolks and, in short, did everything I could to disfigure my breakfast. But the image had been indelibly burned on our collective consciousness. To botch a cliché, this bell wasn't about to be unrung. Or, as I liked to think, once the sole's been scuffed there's no returning the shoe.

Neptune indeed. Neptune with a sex change was more like it.

I dropped my napkin and when Trey bent down to retrieve it, I bent down too. "Why didn't you tell me they were delivering a pair of 38 Double Ds on my plate?"

"I tried," he whispered. "Didn't I try?"

"Not hard enough." I took the napkin and straightened it across my lap.

"Pepper?" Mr. Veep said as he offered me the shaker. The man was just plain devilish.

I said, "No, thank you." And so did Trey, to Mr. Veep's job offer. We settled that on the drive home.

"All right?" Ian said again, studying me with a frown.

The only thing that would make this even remotely all right would be if Scotty suddenly materialized and beamed me up. "I think—ouch." My left wrist shot a warning pain up the length of my arm. "Maybe not."

"Move aside. Let me through. Please, people." A scarecrow of a man emerged from the mob. The tag clipped to his shirt pocket read *Arlys W., manager.* He stooped beside Ian, his face one huge frown. I don't know what distressed him more, me or the books. "Let's get her up," he said. They lifted me by the elbows, carefully, as if I'd disintegrate right there in front of them.

I was hoping for nothing less.

"Ah, ah." The groans escaped as they led me, limping, toward the reading circle chair.

"Here. Careful," Arlys said as they lowered me into the worn yellow chintz. "Call 911," he said to an employee.

"No. No! Really, I'm fine."

The girl hesitated, looked from me to her supervisor. He shrugged, conceded. "We'll give it a minute."

The girl nodded, then moved toward my mess. She began to pick up the books and put them back on display as the crowd receded like a human ebb tide.

Ian took my right foot in his hands. I could see blue chalk dust in the tiny lines on his thumb and index finger. My foot was already swollen and dark with bruising. "Doesn't look promising."

"I can move it," I said, and showed him. I did my best not to grimace. It wasn't broken, I was pretty sure. "It just needs ice."

"Is there someone we can call? Your husband? A friend?"

"My husband's . . . gone." I twirled my wedding ring round and round my finger. I hadn't removed it yet. I was still gearing up for the cataclysm I knew it would cause with Bailey and Mother. Except for now, I did my best to ignore it—like Trey had obviously done for who knows how long. "My girls are away at school."

And I'd eat worms, escargot even, before I let Shawlie find me here like this with Ian Beckwith.

"Maybe he's right. We should call for an ambulance."

At that, Arlys raised a lanky arm and waved to another employee.

"No! Really, it's fine. A little ice and it'll be good as new."

"And the wrist?"

"That, too." I rotated it back and forth, surprised it would actually move. "See?"

Ian stood. "Ah, well, you're lucky."

Lucky? I gave what had to be a pained smile. "Aren't I, though?"

"May I at least help you to your car?"

"Thanks, but I'm sure I can—"

"I insist."

I let him help me stand, then I tested my foot. I swallowed. Hard. There was no way I'd make it without help, so I did the only thing I could do. I strapped my purse over my shoulder and took Ian Beckwith's arm.

The going was slow.

"I was looking for biographies," I said as we passed through the theft alarm thingy just inside the doorway. It was a snug fit, side by side as we were.

"Ah," he said, "I think they're down that way." He nodded his head in a direction exactly opposite of where he'd found me. "Looking for our Ms. Connors, were we?"

"Yes. Exactly." I'm sure the thought would have occurred to me eventually.

"You'd do better at the library, or maybe a used bookstore. Anything written about Claire is long out of print."

"Claire?" The way he said her name was somehow intimate. "Did you know her?"

He shrugged the shoulder on his free side. "The way one might know Dickens. Or Michelangelo. Or Job."

"Job?"

"From the Bible."

"Yes, I know. He just doesn't seem to— Ooh, ow."

Ian stopped short. "Sorry. I do apologize. A little slower then?"

I nodded, wishing the Mitsubishi had parked closer. "Thank you."

"The least you should do is call your physician. Have him take a look at you. Or her."

I thought he might be right. "Why Job?"

"Why Job?" Ian chewed on his answer for a moment. "His is a remarkable story that gets right to the heart of a question that plagues us all. Why do the righteous suffer? He opens wide his soul and lets the whole world look inside. Takes guts. Isn't always pretty. You have to admire a man like that."

"Really?" I asked the question as if he might be trying to fool me. "And why Claire? Why is she your favorite?"

Ian unlocked my car door and helped me scoot behind the wheel. "You sure you can drive with that foot?"

I slid the key into the ignition. "I just live a few minutes away."

"Ah." His gaze followed my left hand to the steering wheel. "Gone where?" he said all of a sudden, his head tilted and eyes filled with curiosity, the very thing that had gotten me into such trouble.

"Excuse me?"

"Your husband. You said he's gone."

My hands tightened on the wheel, sending a shock of pain all the way up to my left shoulder. "I should have been more direct," I said. "He died a year and a half ago."

"Ah. Well. My deepest sympathies."

I nodded my thanks and started the Honda. "Why Claire?"

"I have a book I'll bring you next Tuesday. It'll save you a trip to the library." He waved and turned. I watched him disappear back into the store, then I headed home. With no book and no latte.

Twenty-Four

When I turned into my driveway I pushed the button for door number one and parked my Honda right in the middle of Trey's wide open space. That would be a permanent change, I decided then and there. I hobbled into the house, *oh-*ing and *ouch*-ing all the way, pulled a ziplock bag out of a kitchen drawer, and filled it with perfect, half-circle ice cubes from the refrigerator door.

Trey's recliner would have been the perfect place to convalesce, with its kid-soft leather enticing as a hug and extra-padded foot-rest the perfect elevation. For a moment I felt like Goldilocks in the "just right" mode. But not in the mood for a hug from Trey's chair, I went instead to the sofa and propped a pillow behind my back and another underneath my foot. The ice was too cold for comfort, so I hobbled back to the kitchen for a dishtowel. And three extra-strength Tylenol while I was there. I downed the caplets with a full glass of water and limped back to the living room.

On a whim I stopped at the bookcase and pulled my Bible from the shelf, then got myself situated once again on the sofa, this time with the thin terrycloth towel between the ice and my skin. Much better. Yes. With the remote, I clicked on the gas fire and raised the temperature to seventy-two degrees, enough to compensate for the chill I got from the ice. I looked back over my shoulder at the flannel throws draped over my chair and Trey's recliner. Tempting, but I wasn't about to get up again so soon.

I had no idea how much my body hurt until I fully relaxed. My wrist, my arms, my hips, and of course my foot. The swelling was holding steady, but the bruising had turned the outside of my ankle the color of a nice ripe plum. It throbbed with every beat of my heart. Hopefully, the Tylenol would kick in soon. There was an Ace bandage in the upstairs bathroom, a leftover from Bailey's soccer days, which I'd have loved to wrap around my aching wrist. I decided I'd wait until I went upstairs for the night, assuming I made it upstairs at all.

The leather cover of my Bible was cold to the touch. I opened it to the table of contents. I'd heard of Job, of course, but I didn't know his story and had no idea where to find him. Turns out he was just before the Psalms. Winnie loved the Psalms. She said once if the word of God was our spiritual bread, then the Psalms were the croissants. With butter. We could be discussing anything at all and Winnie would be reminded of a psalm. She'd begin to quote one as if it were poetry, because I guess it was, and I'd pause to listen with all my senses. Winnie certainly had her analogy right because the words she'd recite could make my mouth water.

I turned to page 731, Job chapter 1, then rearranged the ice on my foot, which had grown numb with the cold. I should have made a nice hot cup of tea. It would really be good about now.

I debated with myself a minute or more, then blew out a disgruntled breath when I lost. I lay the Bible faceup on the coffee table where the prologue began and doddered once more to the kitchen. I tried hopping, but with all the jarring it caused I might as well have taken a hammer to my ankle and been done with it.

I guess this was another reason to miss Trey. Or at least disdain living alone.

In the kitchen I filled my new favorite mug with water, the one Becca gave me for my birthday, placed it in the middle of the microwave, and set the timer for two minutes and thirty seconds. I was never more glad that I'd gone to keeping my tea bags on the counter to the right of the stove top, which was just under the microwave hood. That decision saved me at least ten steps, since I didn't have to go to the pantry and back. How easily pleased I was these days. I leaned on a stool and counted down the seconds till the timer went off.

On my way to the sofa I grabbed a flannel throw. The one that wasn't green. So the trip to the kitchen served a dual purpose. Trey would have appreciated the efficiency of that.

I paused before settling myself in again. Halfway through that mug of tea my bladder would sound an alarm. I might as well preempt it now. So, groaning with every halting step, I made my way to the powder room underneath the stairs. I did my business then bared my backside to the mirror. Sure enough, the outside half of my right cheek was almost as purple as my ankle.

Why on earth couldn't I have just stayed home and watched Oprah?

Settled again, for the last time of the night I hoped, I picked up the Bible. What was it Ian had said about Job? Something about why the good suffer? Only he didn't say good. He said, he said, what? The word wouldn't come to me. I read the opening two paragraphs, and quite truthfully, they read like an Aesop's fable. *Once upon a time . . . in the land of Uz.*

Dorothy's ruby slippers came immediately to mind.

But I liked this Job guy. Liked how he cared for his children. And what a reputation. I bet there were no green sweaters in his closet. The way my mind worked these days, my thoughts took off like a kitten in a maze with the free end of a ball of yarn. My eyes were on the words, but my imagination was somewhere in San Diego.

A tempest was brewing in the dark night. Rain pelted the plate-glass window like acrylic nails dancing on a keyboard, while wind gusts played the house like a kettledrum, extracting mournful laments with each relentless pounding.

I upped the temperature of the fire two degrees to get it going again and looked longingly inside my empty mug. Much as I wanted more tea, it just wasn't worth the trip to the kitchen. Besides, there was the whole bladder issue to think about. Best do whatever it took to stay off my foot.

I moved the baggie of room-temperature water off my wounded ankle and checked out the bruising, which had gone from plum to a sickly shade of raisin. The swelling had increased in spite of the ice. I should have called the doctor. Yes sir. Urgent care was now my only option, unless you counted staying right where I was, which was far more appealing than braving the storm and the gas pedal.

I was beginning to feel desperate, like I should call someone for backup, just in case. But then I'd have to explain. For that very reason, Shawlie would be the first—and only—one on my to-call list, but even now I could hear her cackling with laughter when she learned I'd taken a dive into a sea of sex manuals in a crowded bookstore, and who knows what I'd broken.

No thank you.

With the exception of her brief forays into marriage, Shawlie had managed to live her grown-up years, thus far, alone. And she was making a pretty good go of it. Here I was whimpering like the runt of the litter crowded out from the last teat, all because of a sprained ankle. At least I hoped it was only sprained.

I hunkered in and read the first chapter of Job. Dumbfounded, I read it again. If you asked me, the whole thing was over-the-top unfair. I mean, God and the Devil in a tug-of-war, with Job as the rope?

In Job's first test—which led me to assume there would be a second—spelled out in detail between verses six and twenty-two, God allowed the Devil to do whatever he wanted with anything that belonged to Job, short of harming the poor man's physical self. Well, Ted Turner the billionaire cattleman had nothing on Job, and Job lost it all in a day! Every last ox, donkey, sheep, and camel. And before he had a chance to catch his breath from that bad news, he was informed that all ten—yes, ten—of his kids had died when the house they were partying in collapsed on them.

I decided if that's favoritism, well, I'd just hide when the Lord came looking for the cream of the crop. Not that he'd ever choose me. I mean, not only am I not the cream, I'm probably not even part of the crop. Because what does that mean anyway?

But poor Job took it in stride. "Naked I came from my mother's womb," he said, "and naked I will depart. The Lord gave and the Lord has taken away; may the name of the Lord be praised."

So that's where that saying came from.

Chapter 2 began with a heading that said "Job's Second Test." I was right. I slipped the burgundy ribbon into the crease of the page and closed the Bible. I mean, the poor man! That's all I could think. Tug, tug, tug, tug. "The Lord gave and the Lord has taken away"? And a second test, after the mother of all first tests? Just give me my F and boot me out the door. I mean, enough is enough. Suddenly I had a picture of God as one of those mean faces carved at the top of a totem pole.

❧

I awoke in a black hole. I blinked to make sure my eyes were really open, but what I saw on either side of my eyelids looked the same. Pitch black. The fire was out and I was cold. In fact, that's what woke me. Outside, the wind howled like a banshee, and a fierce rain pelted the house.

That place in the hollow of my stomach sent a wave of fear through my limbs, like ripples on a pond spreading out from a tossed stone. The house creaked, and I jumped as if I'd been shocked. All because of the dark. I hadn't locked the garage door when I came in, nor had I set the alarm. I'd have much preferred not to recall those facts just then, but the dark had a way of fiddling with my thoughts.

I hadn't slept in the dark since Trey died. I had night-lights in the bathrooms, the hallway, the upstairs landing, the kitchen. I kept porch and patio lights on and called the city if the streetlights went on the blink. Those lights were my security blanket, and, funny, neither Bailey nor Becca complained about them.

I am woman, hear me roar.

Right.

I felt beside me and found the cordless phone, but when the power goes out, it goes with it. I forced myself to take a calming breath. I mean, this was just a storm-induced power outage. We got them all the time. Still, I kept my ears on high alert.

And wouldn't you know it? Even without that much-desired second mug of tea, my bladder begged for relief. Well, darn. I eased my legs over the side of the sofa, stood, tested my bad foot, and got a resounding *No way!* It still wouldn't take my weight. But what could I do? I took a step, grunting and groaning, arms outstretched in front of me. Hobbling was bad enough, but in the dark? Darkness has a density that light doesn't share. You don't walk through it, you wade. And how do you wade on one foot?

I hopped and instantly remembered why I'd opted out of that mode of transportation earlier. The pain that shot up my leg took off in all directions like an exploded grenade once it reached my torso. It zoomed all the way to my fingertips, then pooled in my eyes in the form of hot tears.

Yep, I should have called for backup.

Suddenly, from the foyer my cell phone began to ring a muffled "Bohemian Rhapsody" from deep inside the cavern of my Gucci tote. The ringtone was compliments of Bailey, the purse compliments of me. I've been haunted by Trey's shoe chart since I took it down. I'm trying to rehabilitate my shopping habits.

Without thought, I went for the phone and hooked the little toe of my bad foot on a leg of the coffee table. In agony, I fell into Trey's chair. The words that came out of my mouth were all four-letter. And right there in the darkness, in the midst of my misery, I could hear Mother say, *Tippy. For heaven's sake, don't curse the darkness, light a candle.*

But I wasn't cursing the darkness. I was cursing Trey.

My phone began to ring again. I pushed out of Trey's chair and limped like the pitiful creature I was toward the sound. An eerie glow emanated from inside my purse like something from a sci-fi flick, but I did appreciate the light. Just as I reached for it, the doorbell sounded, sending a fright straight through me. It had to be—I looked at my cell phone—two forty-four a.m. Who in the world—?

"Abbie?" *Knock, knock, knock.* "Are you in there?" *Knock.*

Dad?

"Abbie?"

The doorbell rang again, and so did my cell phone. I answered both at the same time. "Dad?"

"Mom?"

"Becca?"

Dad shone a flashlight through the open doorway into the foyer. "Power's out," he said, as if I didn't know.

"Mom?" Becca said again.

"Sweetheart? What on earth—?"

"Mom, I've been so worried. I've called and called but the house phone just rings and rings. Why haven't you been answering it?"

"The power's out," I said, just like my dad. "Phone's not working." I moved the phone away from my mouth. "Dad, come in. It's freezing out there. And what are you doing— Is . . . is Mother okay?"

"I'm dripping," he said. He didn't budge from where he stood. "She's fine."

"Oh, good. Grampa's finally there."

"Finally?"

"I made him go check on you. I was worried."

"Oh, sweetie, that's nice, but you don't have to worry about me. I'm fine." I kept my weight on my left foot and held the phone in my right hand, and my little toe might be broken now, but otherwise, fine. "Now, you should get some sleep."

"But, Mom, I can't find Bailey."

Twenty-Five

W hat?! "What do you mean you can't find her?"

Dad turned his flashlight straight at me. The shadowy light it threw back at him turned his scowl into something ghoulish. "Can't find who?"

"No one has seen her since yesterday morning," Becca said. The fear in her voice was like a knife to my heart.

"Dad, please, come inside!"

"Well, okay." He took off his hat and gave it a shake, then did the same with his jacket. He left them both on the bench outside the door, then untied his shoes and stepped out of them. "It's awful wet."

Mother had taught him well.

"Becca says she can't find Bailey."

"Bailey?" A deep rut divided his forehead in half from his eyebrows to his hairline, or what used to be his hairline.

"When I couldn't get in touch with you either, well, I just freaked." Becca was near tears. "So I called Grampa to check on you, but I didn't tell him about Bailey. Our whole group is praying."

I instantly had a vision of my totem-pole God. "Oh."

"Oh, Mom, what should we do?"

I hobbled back toward the living room.

"Abbie. Good grief, girl, what happened to you?"

I moved the phone away from my mouth. "I fell. I'm fine."

"You fell? Mom, you fell?"

"I'm fine, sweetie, really."

"You don't look fine." Dad took my arm in his free hand and helped me to the sofa. The glow from his Maglite danced in time with my limp.

"Mom?"

"Hold on, sweetie, just one minute." My cell phone gave two little beeps. "Uh-oh."

"Mom? What?"

"My battery's going." The light from the screen went black, that magical connection with my daughter lost. I groaned. "Make that gone." I flipped the phone closed.

"What's this about Bailey? And what happened to you?"

I gave him the CliffsNotes version of my fall and said even less about Bailey. "No one's seen her since yesterday. That's all I know." I tossed my phone onto the coffee table. "You need a cell phone, Dad. Plain and simple."

"Well, I'd only use it for—" He stopped, and we said it together. "Emergencies."

I nodded.

"How long has the power been out?"

"I fell asleep before midnight. It was on then."

"That storm's not letting up any time soon. We'd better go back to the house and call Becca from there."

"She's having a fit, poor thing, I just know it."

"I'll open the garage door and pull inside so you don't get wet. I think we have some crutches at the house."

"Oh, wait. The power. You can't open the door."

Dad gave me a funny look. "There's a release, Abbie. Trey didn't teach you that?"

If he did, I wasn't paying attention. I gave a weak shrug.

Dad helped me to the garage and got me into my coat. "I'll just be a minute," he said.

And sure as the world, he pulled a little red rope on the garage door and the electric mechanism released. "I'll be."

The wipers were on full speed and still it was difficult to see the lines on the road. Dad gripped the steering wheel with both hands, leaning into it with full concentration. Great gusts of wind challenged the normally smooth ride of the ten-year-old Cadillac, sending us sideways from time to time.

Can't find Bailey. Can't find Bailey. It's all I could think about. Girls her age disappeared all the time, taken and hurt. It was on the news every day. My stomach churned like a stew pot.

"Don't borrow trouble," Dad said, knowing exactly where my mind was.

I swallowed back all my *buts* and *what ifs*. "Is Mother up?"

"She was when I left."

That didn't bring me comfort.

She had water for tea simmering on the stove top when we arrived. She frowned at my limp. "Tippy. What on earth?"

"I fell. Really, it's nothing."

"It's all those new shoes you wear. The soles never have a chance to roughen up. Slick bottoms do not grip the ground."

I nearly reached to rub my backside. Boy, was she wrong about that.

She handed me a cup with a submerged bag of chamomile. I never liked chamomile.

"I'm sure that was it," I said.

She frowned all the harder, undoubtedly doubting my sincerity. I smiled and said thank you.

"Now. Why are we chasing about in the middle of the night? Becca was worried sick when she called here."

"Her power's out," Dad said.

"Becca's?"

"Mine. And she can't find Bailey." Don't ask me why, but I felt as guilty as if I'd misplaced my child, like in one of those dreams new parents always have.

Mother turned an accusing eye my way. "Did you two argue?"

"Not in a while."

"Alice, for heaven's sake, now isn't the time for that. Here, baby, sit down." Dad pulled a chair away from the table and helped me hobble to it.

"Ed, bring an Ace bandage from the hall closet. We'd better wrap that foot."

"First I need to call Becca back. My cell phone died in the middle of our conversation."

"Which is why I'd never own one of those things."

"It was the only phone working when the power went out."

Mother lifted the receiver from her kitchen phone and stretched the cord ten feet to where I sat. "That, Tippy, is because you don't have a single phone connected to a wall."

I took the phone, gazed at the receiver. No speed dial? Lord, and now I had to admit I didn't know my own daughter's number.

Mother brought out her address and phone book, the one

she'd had since I lived at home. The silver letters had long ago worn away, but they'd left an imprint, like a fossil, embedded in the leather. She opened it to the Bs and handed it to me.

The first name on the page was Bailey's, with a listing of all her pertinent numbers, including, I noted, the community number for her dorm. Then came Becca's name, and for a split second I thought of Winnie, with her BA and BE. I found Becca's cell number and dialed it.

"Mom? Oh, gosh, are you okay?" Becca's voice was thick with worry.

"My battery died," I said again, in case she hadn't already figured that out. "I'm at Gramma and Grampa's. Now what's this about Bailey?" I looked on the receiver for the speaker button so we could all hear, but of course there wasn't one.

"I can't find her, Mom. No one's seen her all day. I don't think she went to any of her classes."

My heart began to beat faster. "When did you last see her?"

"Night before last, before I went to Bible study. She was coming in as I was going out."

"And was she okay? Did she seem all right?"

"I don't know. She was . . . she was Bailey." I could envision the shrug that accompanied those words, and I knew exactly what she meant. "She didn't say much. Didn't razz me about Bible study. I said, 'Hey,' and she said, 'See ya later.' It was pretty typical."

"What about her friends? Have you talked to any of them?"

"Everyone I could find. No one's seen her." Her voice cracked. "Not since yesterday morning."

"Yesterday? Meaning Wednesday?!"

"Well, no, Mom, it's technically Friday now. I saw her Wednesday night. Brit saw her yesterday morning. But no one since then, at least that we can find."

Brittany Charles was Bailey's roommate.

"And her car's gone."

Oh, Lord. Oh, Lord. I thought of Bailey flipped over in a ditch somewhere, with no one able to reach me at home, which was the address on Bailey's driver's license and registration. No working phone, no one there to answer the door.

"Mom, I'm so scared." Becca's voice sounded hollow through the phone line.

I swallowed back a sob, waited till I could trust my voice to continue. "Honey, I'm going to call the police, the highway patrol, then I'm coming. I'll be there as soon as I can."

Mother's eyes were wide, her skin pale without its powder. The furrow in Dad's forehead was deeper than ever. "What?" they both said.

I was determined not to panic. "No one's seen her." My voice hiccupped. "Since yesterday morning."

Mother went straight to the drawer the address book came out of and retrieved the phone book. "Tippy. Call information for San Luis police. I'll look up the CHP."

That was Mother, all business, and for once I didn't mind a bit. "But," I said, "don't you have to wait twenty-four hours when someone's missing? That . . . that isn't a child?"

Mother didn't even look up from the phone book. "She's *your* child, isn't she?"

I dialed the number for information.

"City, please," a female voice said.

"San Luis Obispo," I said.

Another voice came on the line, this time a man's. "What listing would you like for San Luis Obispo?"

"The police department."

"Emergency or non?"

"Non?" I didn't know.

"I'll connect you to that number," he said.

"SLO Police Department."

"Yes, hello?"

"How can I help you?"

I swear, the woman on the other end of the line was more calm than I'd ever been in my whole life. "I want to report—" My voice broke off and I hiccupped again. "My daughter's missing."

"Yes, ma'am. How old is your daughter and how long has she been missing?"

"Twenty. She's twenty. And no one's seen her since Thursday morning." My voice rose in pitch with each word I spoke.

"Thursday morning? This Thursday morning?"

I nodded, then remembered I needed to answer. "Yes. I know it hasn't been twenty-four hours but—"

"There's no waiting period in California, ma'am. May I have your daughter's name?"

Thank you, God. I gave her all the pertinent information. Bailey's name, age again, where she lived both here and there, where she went to school, who saw her last—as far as we knew.

"And you say her sister called *you* to report her missing?"

Instead of the police. That's what she implied. "Yes."

"Has she disappeared before?"

"No. Of course not. Never."

"What is the name of your other daughter?"

"Becca, Becca Torrington."

"Rebecca Torrington?"

"No, just, just Becca." I kept my eyes on my shoes, but I could feel Mother give me that tight-lipped glare. *Half a name,* that's what she was thinking. And I bet so was the woman on the other end of the line.

"And is Becca Torrington a student at Cal Poly as well?"

"Yes, she is."

"Okay, Mrs. Torrington. We'll send someone out to talk with Becca and your daughter's roommate."

"Brittany Charles," I said, though I'd already told her that. "Oh, and—" My heart began to pound again. "Bailey's car is gone. She could be hurt." I was trying hard to hold it together.

"If you give me the license plate number I'll check to see if it's been reported in an accident."

"Her license plate. Um, um, it's uh . . ." I threw the question to my parents with my eyes. They both shook their heads.

"You can call back with the information."

"But I don't . . . she could . . ." I drew in a breath to steady myself. "Okay. Okay. I'll call back."

I handed Mother the receiver. She walked across the kitchen to hang it up, then closed the phone book, since I'd need the license number for the CHP as well. "I need her insurance statement. It's at home. If you could take me," I said to Dad, "I'll get it and my car and get on the road." I tried to keep my weight off my right foot as I stood.

"Tippy. You can't drive like that."

I waved off Mother's words. "I have to."

"No, your mother's right," Dad said.

"But, Dad, I—"

"I'll take you." He reached for the hat he'd set on the counter when we came into the kitchen and settled it on his head. "We'd better get going."

I nodded, too grateful to even say thank you. "You have my cell number?" I asked Mother.

"Of course."

Filed under A or T, I wondered. "I'll make sure it's charged."

"I'll call if I hear anything."

"We'll do the same."

∾

I called back with the license plate number as soon as we got underway, but no accident with Bailey's information had been reported. *Reported*, I told myself, still scared to death she was lying unconscious on some remote stretch of coastal highway. *Where are you, Bailey? Oh, God, please. Please.*

I didn't think of a totem pole this time as I sent my thoughts into the rain-soaked heavens. No, this time I thought of Winnie's God. Not my version, but hers. The one whose name was Wonderful, Counselor, Everlasting Father. I don't know what made me remember that, of all things, about Winnie's God, but it made it easier to pray to Him.

I watched the white markers on I-5 whiz by one mile at a time, thinking they'd be whizzing by much faster if I were behind the wheel. Dad, bless his heart, was steady as they come. He didn't need cruise control to keep the speedometer right at sixty-five, never mind that the posted speed limit was seventy on this stretch of the interstate. I'd find myself pushing a phantom gas pedal, only to have my foot scream out in protest. I'd back off, pray to the heavens, watch the white markers, then start all over again.

Bailey. Oh, God. Please, please.

"Better stop for coffee now. There's nothing after this for a good while." Dad pulled off the highway near a crop of fast-food places that had sprung up around Pea Soup Andersen's, a Dutch-style restaurant in the middle of nowhere. "How about McDonald's?"

"That's fine," I said. "I need to use the restroom anyway."

It was still raining, and the bitter wind actually whistled through the open land around us. Dad helped me as far as the door to the ladies' room, then went to order our drinks.

"Lots of cream," I called after him.

I caught my reflection in the mirror as I washed my hands, noted the dark rings under my eyes. I'd slept less than three hours in the past twenty-two, and there wasn't a spot on my body that didn't hurt. Every muscle protested with the slightest movement, and it would only get worse before it got better, considering how hard I'd hit the ground, like being in an accident and not really feeling it for a day or two. But as bad as I looked and felt, it was nothing compared to the ache in my heart and the fear that coursed through my body. It left every nerve feeling electrified.

Where was Trey when I needed him? That was the thought that wouldn't let go.

I hobbled back to the car, my arm hooked through Dad's. "I'm sorry you're having to do this," I said, as he merged back onto I-5.

He gave one slow nod of his head. "I'd have come even if you hadn't hurt your foot."

I swallowed back a sob. "I know." The words came out in a whisper he probably didn't hear.

"You said you fell. What exactly happened?"

The question alone made me blush to the roots. "Well, actually, I lost my footing at the mall, and down I went."

"The mall, huh? The floors can be slick, all right, when they polish that linoleum. Lucky you didn't break something."

It was tile, bone-breaking hard, but I wasn't going to correct him.

"Looking for shoes, were you?"

"Shoes. No, no. A book actually."

"Ah." He took a long drink of his coffee. "'Lizabeth was a reader. Always had a book with her. A fan of mysteries, she was."

"Yeah? Me, too."

"Mm-hmm." He took another drink of coffee.

"You knew her pretty well, then?"

"She and your mother were closer than most sisters. Alice adored her and 'Lizabeth was fine with that. In a healthy way," he added. "She wasn't conceited, not a bit."

"No. I'm sure."

Dad nodded, turned his windshield wipers down. The rain had begun to ease up, though the wind continued to push sideways at the car in frequent gusts.

"I mean, not many high school seniors let their little sister hang around like she was one of the crowd."

I thought of Bailey with Becca. "That's true."

"But 'Lizabeth didn't seem to mind. She was a kind person, 'Lizabeth was."

I looked sideways at my dad, letting the dark shield me as I studied his profile. "Which one did you meet first?" I hoped my voice didn't give away the tangent my thoughts had suddenly taken off on.

"Oh, I met them at the same time, at the McClatchy High School cafeteria. We all had first lunch."

Of course I knew that Mother and Dad had met in high school, that he was a senior and she was a sophomore, but I didn't realize Aunt Lizzy had been right there in the mix. "Did you—" Oh, I did not want this to come out wrong. "Ever ask Aunt Lizzy out? I mean, before Mother?"

Dad put his blinker on, went around a slow-moving semi chugging up the hill, then blinked his way back to the slow lane. "Didn't really think about asking either one of them out. Not right away. We were all just friends. But now, my best pal, Harold, he was smitten with 'Lizabeth, he was."

"Really? Did they go out?"

"He never got up the courage to ask her out, not even when I invited your mother to the winter formal."

I had to ask. "Would you have invited Aunt Lizzy to the winter formal instead, if it hadn't been for Harold?"

Dad gave me a sideways glance, then looked back to the road. "Your mother was a spunky kid, Abbie. A lot like 'Lizabeth back then, lots of fun. Life has a way of tempering people." He nodded once. "It does."

Well, that was certainly the truth. I only hoped I didn't have the life tempered right out of me because of Trey and . . . and everything, to have my girls say to their own children someday, *Gramma Abbie was fun once upon a time. She really was.* Only would they? Even now, would they ever say that? "Why did Aunt Lizzy never marry?"

Dad lifted his shoulder in a shrug. "Couldn't really say. There was a fella she knew in college. Seemed serious for a while, but nothing came of it."

"You think she was sad about it? That she never married? She should have married, a person like her."

"You know, the thing about 'Lizabeth, she was a whole person all on her own, she was. Not many people like that. And remember, she was only twenty-eight when she passed. It's not like her time had come and gone."

I smiled. "That's true. She wasn't exactly an old maid. What a horrible term, *old maid.* Doesn't have quite the same connotation as old bachelor, does it?"

Dad chuckled at that, then turned his wipers all the way off. The rain had stopped for the time being, but if the heavy black clouds that were becoming visible with the break of day were any indication, we were in for another downpour.

"Dad, is Mother disappointed with me because I remind her of Aunt Lizzy on the outside"—which I'd never seen before the haircut—"but I'm nothing like her in reality? Is that what it is?"

"What makes you think you're nothing like 'Lizabeth?"

What he didn't ask was, *What makes you think she's disappointed?* "Fun? Spunky? Come on, Dad."

"Abbie—" Dad broke off, looked out the driver's side window, heaved a sigh, bit the side of his lip, weighing whether or not he'd go on. I knew that, because I knew him. "I think what your mother's disappointed with"—he took another slow breath—"is that you didn't give her a namesake. For 'Lizabeth."

I turned a startled face toward him.

"Two daughters, and not a Lizzy, Izzy, Liza, or Beth between them."

"A namesake?" What could you say to that? It had never occurred to me. My own middle name, Dawn, was Aunt Lizzy's middle name, and if she had died before I was born instead of after, there's no doubt I'd have been Elizabeth and not Abigail, which was my grandmother's name. A double namesake, I was. And I hadn't given my mother the consideration, the solace of so much as even the initial E for the sister she'd never stop grieving. No, I'd given her BA and BE, not at all what she wanted. And half a name.

I opened my mouth, to utter something feeble no doubt, but was stopped when my cell phone rang. I hurried to answer it, not just because someone might have news about Bailey, but also to shut off the noise. Somehow "Bohemian Rhapsody" didn't seem appropriate just then. "Hello? Mother?"

"You can turn around and come home," she said. "Bailey's here."

Twenty-Six

My latest wind chimes would have been like torture to Trey, but one man's torment could be another man's pleasure. Or woman's. Yes indeed. I'd found them at a card and gift shop, of all places, nudged them to make them sing, then kept them singing until a card shopper glared over her shoulder at me. I silenced them with a clang and unhooked them from their hanger, sending another resonating chord throughout the little store as I carried them to the counter. This set, with its longest tube nearly thirty inches, was tuned to the scale of A, according to a card that hung from the paddle. Corinthian Bells, the box said, as the clerk wrapped them up. When I got them home I found a verse from the Bible engraved on the paddle, ending with the words, "the greatest of these is love."

I'd hung them from the arbor over my backyard patio, back far enough from the edge that they didn't get whipped by the wind, but not so far in that they couldn't be caressed by even a little breeze. Their sound was much richer than my first set, which sounded wimpy in comparison, a tinkle to a symphony. Even with my bedroom window closed against the winter cold I could hear the tones, hauntingly melodious in their own dissonant way. Now they drew me from a fitful sleep, made worse because it was the middle of the day.

It took half a second to remember why I was asleep. I sat up and groaned with the physical pain from my fall, then groaned again when I remembered Bailey. She'd said little in the way of explanation when Dad and I got back to his and Mother's house, just that she was tired and wanted to sleep. At home, in her own bed. I was so relieved to see her whole, uninjured by all appearances, that all I could do was nod and will my heart to settle down. Dad asked just one question: "Do we need the police?" Bailey shook her head.

Mother knew the story. I could tell by the way she held her lips, lips that said, *I know far more than I'm telling*, and by the look Bailey gave her when they hugged good-bye. My heart felt squeezed, like it did every time I witnessed that enviable bond between the two of them. I'd seen a painting once at the Crocker Art Museum downtown when I drove for Becca's field trip. It was of an old woman, eyes longing for something she could never have, and it was titled *Desire*. I thought of that painting as I watched the look pass between my daughter and someone other than me. No matter that the someone else was my mother.

The clock beside my bed read one forty-nine. I'd fallen asleep sometime after eight, but only because Bailey slept, and only after I called Becca for the second time to tell her what little I knew. I needed to get up, to empty my bladder and brush my teeth, but I was not eager to put any weight on my foot. Just as I started to push myself up, Bailey appeared at my door, looking only barely awake, hair falling out of a ponytail.

"Where did you get those?"

I followed her eyes to the window. Of course she meant the chimes. "Oh, well, I—"

"They're beautiful."

I sank back on the bed and smiled. "Yes. They are." In fact, they had a sound so pure you'd think it had sifted down through the sieve of heaven.

Bailey climbed onto the other side of my bed and sat cross-legged with one of my pillows pressed to her stomach. She wore flannel pajama bottoms, none I'd ever bought her, a T-shirt, and socks. She pulled the rubber band out of her hair and redid the ponytail. "I suppose you want to know what this is all about." It wasn't a question. "Oh, Mom, your foot. What did you do?"

I couldn't tell if the swelling was better or worse, but the bruise was brown as mincemeat. "I fell," I said, and knew someone would eventually press for the whole sordid account. "But I'm fine."

"It doesn't look fine. Want some ice?"

More ice would probably be good, but I was more interested in why my daughter was here and not at school. "Later," I said. "Right now, let's talk."

Bailey hugged the pillow more tightly to her, looked away, exhaled a slow breath.

"We were really worried, honey. I'm just glad you're okay." I reached out and touched her arm. "You are okay?"

Bailey nodded, then shrugged. "I guess."

"Why don't we start with when you left San Luis, and why."

Bailey focused her eyes on the foot of the bed. Nearly half a minute passed before she spoke. "Yesterday morning. I was on my way to class and Tim called."

Tim McGuire. I might have guessed he had something to do

with this. I literally bit my lip to keep from saying something I'd certainly regret.

"I couldn't believe it at first, what he was saying. I thought, *right*. I wonder what he *really* wants."

That wouldn't be hard to guess. I continued to bite.

"But then I thought, he really means it." Bailey looked away again and shrugged. "He . . . he really loves me."

Loves.

"And I thought, I don't know, I thought maybe I really loved him."

Oh, Lord.

"So" — Bailey turned contrite blue eyes to me, the first I'd seen coming from her since way before the millennium changed — "we went to Reno to get married."

Outside, the chimes caught a gust of wind and resonated in the stillness that fell between us.

Married? "Married?" My eyes went straight to her left hand, which was hidden by the pillow. My heart pounded as brutally as when I thought she was lost. "And that . . . that — " I squeezed my lips together and waited till the urge to call Tim a really bad name passed. "He sent you home to tell us this by yourself?"

She shook her head. "He didn't send me. I left. In his car. And how he manages to get home is his problem. For all I know he's still throwing back drinks at the Stardust and trying to pick up some Daisy Duke wannabe waitress."

"Daisy Duke?" A picture of Sven and Lars came into my head, and of Shawlie and me riding home in their limo. Huh. Maybe one or two of my genes had found their mark after all.

"He was too drunk to realize I might just be offended by that."

"Oh, Bailey." I did my best to sound sorry.

"On our wedding day, Mom." She pounded the pillow for emphasis. "Well, what was supposed to be our wedding day."

"You mean—?"

"You were right. Tim McGuire doesn't deserve me. And I am not throwing any more of myself away on him or anyone like him."

"Sweetheart"—I wrapped my arms around her and winced as my foot twisted into an awkward position—"I am so glad."

"Tim McGuire is history," she said. "I'm holding out for a man like Dad."

❧

Bailey decided to stay till Sunday morning before heading back to San Luis. It would be just the two of us for a day and a half. I'm not sure that had happened since before Becca was born. I loved the prospect.

She helped me get down the stairs to the kitchen for something to eat, but first she made coffee. The smell of it brewing started my stomach to rumbling. I didn't realize I was so hungry.

"Remember how Gramma Winnie used to always make raisin toast for Becca and me? Every time we went over, raisin toast dripping with butter."

"Now that you mention it, yes. We don't have any raisin bread. In fact, I'm not even sure they make it anymore, but we could do cinnamon toast."

"They do, but cinnamon toast is good." Bailey offered a sly smile. "I never liked raisin toast. But I loved Gramma Winnie, so I ate it."

"Bailey, that was brave of you and very kind."

"Yeah, I surprise myself too, sometimes."

"No, no. That isn't what I meant."

She stirred creamer into my coffee and brought both cups to the table. She shrugged a shoulder and gave a half smile that looked just like her father's. "We are who we are." Bailey headed for the pantry.

"The cinnamon and sugar are already mixed. In that white shaker, there by the spices."

She brought it, the bread, and the butter and set to work. "How many pieces?"

"Two. I'm starved. Oh, your coffee is good."

"I use two filters, like Dad. It's never bitter."

"Ah."

When the toast was ready she brought it to the table, then sat across from me. "Okay, here's the deal. You need to have your foot checked out. After we finish our toast we'll get cleaned up and have just enough time to get to your doctor's office before they close."

"Oh, but, Bailey, we can't just walk in. We should call for an appointment."

"Nope. As late as it is, they'll put you off till Monday or, worse, send you to the emergency room. On Friday night we wouldn't get out of there before midnight. You'll hobble in holding on to me, and I guarantee they'll take you right back for an X-ray. That's how things work, Mom. Then, after they do whatever they do, we'll go to dinner. Someplace nice. After all, Sunday is Valentine's Day, and this is my honeymoon weekend." She gave another sly smile, so much like Trey.

"Well, then, I know just the place. At least I know the name. I'll have to Google it for driving directions." *Since I was facing the wrong way in the limo the one time I went.*

"Great."

"So what did you do with Tim's car?"

"Left it at his parents' house and picked up mine."

"Tim's parents?" My eyes narrowed. "Did they know you were planning to elope?"

Bailey shook her head. "They're in Tucson for the winter."

Well, at least there was that. "Speaking of cars." I was taking a risk, I know, of ruining our whole wonderful weekend, but figured I might as well address the elephant in the living room, or rather, the one that was no longer in the garage. "The last thing I want to do is upset you or Becca. You've certainly been through enough, and I'm sorry for that." I reached out and touched her hand, soft as a baby's. "I feel like I'm making my way in the dark with all of this and doing a lousy job. I can't say my choices will always be right, but I have to make them."

"Mom, I think I get it, really. It's just that—" She wrapped her arms around her middle, looked out the window where the wind chimes were sending out their song. "Everything of Dad is slipping away, and I don't want him to be gone."

"He'll never, ever be gone, Bailey. Not only is he in your heart, he's in your smile, your sister's eyes. He left the best of himself in you and Becca." And that was the absolute truth.

She nodded, bit her lip. "I really miss him." She blinked hard, then stood. "I'm going up to take a shower." She stopped at the doorway. "You know that scarf that Gramma knitted for Dad?"

"The mohair one?" I shuddered at the thought of all that itchy yarn.

"Can I have it?"

"Of course you can. It's up—"

"Don't get up. I'll find it."

I limped my way to the sink with our cups and saucers, rinsed them, and placed them in the dishwasher. I emptied the coffee pot, poured in a spoonful of dishwasher powder, added an inch of water, and swooshed the mixture around the inside of the pot. There was nothing like the crystals to keep the glass gleaming. I dried it with paper towels and put it back in its place.

In spite of how bad I felt physically, I hummed. My daughter was safe and having dinner with me tonight, instead of enduring a drunken honeymoon with Tim McGuire. I looked up to say thank you, again with Winnie's God in mind. What I saw was the ceiling, above which was my bedroom. In which sat my hope chest. My heart dipped like a falling star. Oh, no. No. "Bailey! Wait!"

"Mother!"

Oh, Lord.

I made it to the kitchen doorway as Bailey reached the bottom of the stairs. In one hand she held the manila envelope from J. Davis Balfour, attorney-at-law, in the other the papers that had been inside.

"What . . . what is this? What *is* this?" She shook the papers at me, her nostrils flaring with every furious breath she drew in. "You were getting a divorce?" Her voice broke on the last word and she fought to keep the tears out of her eyes. "How could you do such a thing?"

Me? She meant me? "No. Bailey. It wasn't like that."

She shook the papers at me again. "Then what are these?"

"Let's sit down." I hitch-stepped my way to the closest thing with four legs and dropped onto it.

"I don't want to sit down. I want to know what divorce papers are doing in your hope chest. Your *hope* chest, Mother."

Well, at least the irony wasn't wasted on her.

"How did you get into my hope chest?"

"The key is in your jewelry box, where it's been all my life. But that is so not the question."

"Bailey, please sit."

She stood, lips pressed together, hands clenched around the offending papers.

"I'm not going to talk with you standing over me like an executioner." I nudged a chair out with my healthy foot. And waited.

Bailey bristled with the challenge to defy, but as is usually the case, curiosity won out. She tugged the chair another foot away and lowered herself to the edge, her body turned decidedly away from me.

My head pounded now, along with my foot, my hip, my arm. My heart. What in the world could I possibly say that would help? I blew out a breath, forced another one in. "Those papers were as much a surprise to me as they were to you."

Bailey shot me a look. "Right."

"They were, Bailey. Completely unexpected."

"You're saying *Daddy* was divorcing *you*?"

"That's how it appears."

"And you knew nothing about it." It wasn't a question.

"I never had a chance to talk to him about it."

Her eyes narrowed. "Why? When did you get these?"

I hesitated a half second. "Not long after your father died."

But a half second too long. "How long is *not long*? How long, Mother?"

"They were delivered that day."

"That day. You're saying that Daddy died and you were served with divorce papers all on the same day. That's what you're saying?"

The look on my face was answer enough.

Bailey stood and paced, then stopped and turned back to me.

"Well, no wonder."

"No wonder? No wonder what?"

"No wonder you purged the house of everything that had to do with Daddy." She crossed her arms. "And no wonder you haven't even cried."

I felt my spirit wilt like winter jasmine in July. "Oh, Bailey. Honey. I've cried."

"For yourself maybe, but not for him. Not for Daddy." She paced another lap, then shook the papers at me again. "Why was he divorcing you?"

I reached for the papers, but Bailey kept them clutched in her hand. "They say irreconcilable differences, whatever that means." No matter what I had to do, I would not tell her about San Diego.

And what *did* that mean exactly, irreconcilable differences? That we had issues we were unable to settle after trying hard to do so? That we'd given it our best shot and come up short? That we were stubbornly pulling in opposite directions, with one or the other unwilling to turn around?

If that was the case, I certainly wasn't informed.

I thought again about our last night together. Too often I went back to that night, trying to find the clue, the *aha!* that would cause this all to make sense. I could see Trey in his blue plaid boxers, shirtless and tanned from a summer on the lake. Could see the way the cinnamon-colored hair curled on his chest, with a half dozen gray ones mixed in. They hadn't been there in the spring, and they didn't make him happy. I could see his left hand resting on his stomach, and the gleam of his wedding band as the overhead light caught the gold. Even remembered the title of the book he held in his right. Tom Clancy's *Net Force: The Archimedes Effect.*

It was Sunday night and he'd be gone for the week. But he didn't turn off the light, didn't cross my hedgerow for a visit. No, he'd read till I couldn't keep my eyes open any longer.

So there it was. My *aha*.

Later I took notice of the novel, which sat by the lamp on his nightstand, bookmarked at page 121. He hadn't taken it with him on Monday. Another clue?

I nodded toward the chair. "Please?"

Bailey looked away. "I'm going back." She headed upstairs, presumably to get her things.

There wasn't much point in going after her. There was never any doubt when Bailey had made up her mind.

Ten minutes later the doorbell rang, then I heard a key in the lock. Shawlie called my name. "Abbie? Abbie!"

Inwardly I groaned. "In here, Shawlie." What timing.

She hurried into the kitchen, looking as frantic on the outside as I felt on the inside. "Bailey said you need to go to emergency. What happened?"

"Bailey?"

"She called ten minutes ago, said she was leaving and you needed to go to emergency. What's going on?"

I might as well put a sign on my forehead. "I fell. I'm fine."

"Fell? When?"

I shrugged. "What day is it?"

"What day—? It's Friday evening. Are you all right? Did you hit your head?"

"Everything but. And it happened yester— yeah, yesterday afternoon. She knows, Shawlie. About the divorce papers."

Shawlie leaned back on her heels, looked up at me from her stooped position. She blinked, drew in her lips so they disappeared.

I told you. Safe. Deposit. Box. I could practically hear those six little words whizzing around in Shawlie's head, but to her credit she somehow managed to keep them from whizzing out of her mouth.

"What happened?"

Before I had a chance to respond, Bailey was in the kitchen with her bag and jacket. "I'm going back to San Luis," she said to Shawlie. "She probably needs to see a doctor."

"*She* is your mother, Bailey. And she's right here in this room."

"Whatever." The one word wasn't nearly as clipped as it was when she said it to me.

"Bailey." Shawlie waited till she had her attention. "Sit."

She hesitated just long enough to keep her independence before dropping half of one cheek onto the edge of a chair. She kept her body turned away from both Shawlie and me.

"I know this must have come as quite a shock," Shawlie said.

"I suppose *everyone* knows except Becca and me?" This she said to me.

"No one knows. Except Shawlie. And only because she was here." We all knew that wasn't true, that I'd have told Shawlie regardless, but I wanted Bailey to know that the choice had been taken out of my hands. "I can't begin to imagine what's going through your mind."

She closed her eyes as if to say, *I'm not listening.*

"This adds sorrow to sorrow, I know, and I didn't mean for that to happen."

She turned toward me in a flash. "So you lied."

"No. I did not lie. But what was the point of bringing you and Becca into this? It became a moot point the minute your father . . ." I shrugged.

"Died, Mother. He died."

Shawlie shook her head, as if she'd heard enough. "Bailey, your dad was—"

I coughed, and kept it up till Shawlie looked at me. Then without a word, I begged, pleaded for her not to say what she was about to say.

"What?" Bailey said. "Dad was what?"

Shawlie's pause lasted an eon. She turned her eyes from me to Bailey, let out a breath, and in true Shawlie form, said, "A man. Your dad was a man. And no woman I know can figure them out. Not even me. Now, I think I should get your mom to emergency."

Bailey left without a good-bye. There was no point in protesting, no point in asking, begging her not to tell. Though I would have begged to keep her from telling Becca.

Twenty-Seven

Shawlie put her hands on her hips, just like a mother. "This happened yesterday and you haven't seen a doctor? Why? And where exactly are you hurt?"

"My foot. Mostly." I pulled down my sock and showed her.

"Abbie! Good grief! Okay, we're going."

"First I need some tea. The water's hot." I pointed to the stove top, where steam was billowing out the spout of the kettle.

Shawlie obliged, reluctantly. Poured hot water into a mug, dropped in the tea bag. Instantly orange essence sent a burst of fragrance into the room, then settled like so many embers dying on descent. Shawlie left the bag in the mug to steep, something I never did. She set the steaming brew on the table before me, then took the chair to my right.

I pointed to the pot of water. "You don't want—?"

"No."

I dunked the tea bag four times like always, loosing more of its essence, held it up to drip, then placed it on a napkin. I hate strong tea.

"Now," she said, impatient as a teen driver at a red light, "what happened? And why was Bailey even here?"

I held the mug between both hands, drawing from the warmth. "You were right, I should have gotten a safe deposit box. Or, better yet, just thrown the stupid papers away. What did I need to keep them for anyway?"

Shawlie did that thing with her lips again and I could tell she was ready to pop.

"Say it. Go ahead." I lifted the mug to my mouth and waited.

"When have I ever said I told you so?" She looked at me with innocent eyes, then held up a multi-ringed hand, palm out. "When it mattered." She straightened her shoulders and sniffed. "So did Bailey come home just to look in your hope chest? What happened, Abbie?"

"She left school yesterday without telling Becca. Or anyone. To go to Reno. To get married. To Tim McGuire."

Shawlie dropped her head into her hands. I heard a muffled, "Oh, no."

"But . . ."

She looked up, her hands at her lips like a child in prayer.

"She didn't go through with it."

"Well, thank God."

"Believe me, I have."

"So, okay. She didn't get married. What then?"

"Everything was fine. I mean really fine. Bailey was going to stay home for the weekend, we were going to dinner, just the two of us. And then" — my heart jumped, then fell, as if it had tripped over a stump in the road — "she asked about this scarf thing that Mother knitted for Trey a few Christmases ago."

Shawlie made a face. "Not the mohair one?"

I nodded and shuddered again. So did she.

"Bailey went to look for it. I thought surely it's in his closet, probably right there with his sweaters. I didn't know she even knew where the key was."

"You locked his sweater drawer?"

"The hope chest, Shawlie. The key to the hope chest. I don't even know why she would look in there. What would make her do that?"

"What would make her ask for a mohair scarf?"

That was an easy one to answer. "She's afraid Trey is disappearing."

"He already has. Hasn't he?" Shawlie looked around the kitchen as if Trey might suddenly materialize. "That would be just like the RAT to come back and haunt you."

Now there was a ghastly thought. I shivered again. "Bailey was furious. Well, you saw. And hurt. She thought *I'd* filed on Trey."

"You need to set her straight, Abbie, tell her all about —" She jerked her thumb back over her shoulder, in the direction of San Diego.

"Never. I'm not going to."

"You're missing a golden opportunity here, Abbie."

"To do what? Shatter my daughters' image of their father? What on earth would that accomplish?"

Shawlie pushed herself up. "I think I'll have that tea." She looked back at me from the stove. "You wouldn't have anything stronger, would you?"

I rolled my swollen eyes. "The honey's in the pantry."

"Ah, well."

Shawlie fixed her tea, strong the way she liked it, and added some extra hot water to mine. "It smells like an orange grove in here." The way she said it led me to believe she didn't appreciate citrus the way I did. I dunked my tea bag a couple more times, then sipped.

"She was actually going to marry Tim McGuire?" Shawlie's face crinkled in disgust.

"I'm just glad she came to her senses. Before the fact."

"I'll have to give her that."

I stirred my tea absently with the tip of my index finger, then licked off the moisture. "She said she's holding out . . . for a man like her dad."

Shawlie's eyebrows shot up. "Like her dad?" She turned sideways in her chair. "I tell you, Abbie, what that girl needs is a good dose of reality."

"And if it were just Bailey, maybe that's exactly what I'd give her . . . though I doubt it. But it's not just Bailey. This would break Becca's heart. Which is exactly what's going to happen when Bailey tells her about those papers. Oh, Shawlie, why didn't I listen?"

"Don't beat yourself up, sweetie." She looked away and shrugged one shoulder. "I still have my divorce papers from Donald."

"From Donald?" Now, there was a revelation.

❧

When I got up to limp my way to the bathroom, Shawlie decided to take a closer look at my foot. She had me sit back down.

"I really have to go."

"In a minute." She eased off my sock. "Ooh. That looks like it hurts."

"A bit, yes."

"What, did you fall down the stairs?" She pressed lightly on the swollen instep, which sent a shock of pain through my foot. "Sorry." Then she felt all around the bruised ankle and finally checked the range of motion in my foot.

"Aah!" I didn't have any.

"Well, we're off to the emergency room, that's all there is to it."

"Uh, no. No. Just get me some ice. It'll be fine."

"It won't be fine. It's broken."

"What's broken?" I pulled my foot back. "And how do you know?"

"One of the little bone thingies in there. I'm sure of it."

I shook my head. "Friday night in the ER? We'll be there half the night."

She gave me one of her specialty looks. "You have other plans?"

"What, you don't?"

Shawlie gave me her arm to help me out of the chair. "My date broke her foot."

"*Maybe* broke her foot. And shouldn't you be home waiting for flowers or something?"

"Cute. Wait here, I'll get your coat."

"First, the bathroom. Oh, and don't forget my purse," I called toward the foyer. "It's on the—"

"Counter behind you. I got it. Let me help you."

She acted as my crutch and led me to the bathroom. "We'll take your car," she called through the closed door, "since it's in the garage."

"Right," I called back.

It had rained all day and into the night, though the wind had calmed considerably. My chimes had been mostly silent all evening.

Shawlie helped me into the passenger seat of my Honda, then got in behind the wheel and raised the garage door. "Mercy Hospital or Sutter Med Center?"

"I suppose Sutter. It's closer. Not that it'll make a difference. They're probably both swamped."

"Quit whining. If I'm willing to spend my Friday night in the ER, that's the least you can do. Now, tell me how you fell."

"Oh, Shawlie, I don't want to go into it. I just fell, enough said."

"This had something to do with Bailey, didn't it? If that girl—"

"No! Shawlie. Absolutely not. Bailey wasn't anywhere around. In fact, she was in Reno with a drunken Tim McGuire, coming to her senses." I pointed out my window to the intersection we were approaching. "Don't we turn right?"

"The back way's faster, fewer stoplights. If there's one thing I know, it's how to get around town. So how did this happen?"

I turned toward the window again and let out a sigh. No way was I getting out of telling the story. Might as well make it as short and vague as I could. Give her the high points, nothing more. "I was at the mall yesterday—"

"This happened in public?"

"—in the bookstore."

"Oh, Abbie, the humiliation."

"You have no idea. I was looking for something new to read." *And avoiding the telephone.* "The floor was wet or something, my ankle twisted, and down I went." I only told one little lie, about the floor being wet, which it could have been considering the weather.

"What shoes were you wearing?"

"Those red patent leather pumps with the skinny little heels. The new ones."

"Abbie." Shawlie lolled her head my way. "All your shoes are new."

She had a point. "And that's what happened."

Shawlie shifted her eyes from the road to me to the road and back to me again. They stayed on me longer than was safe, considering that she was driving. "You're blushing. In fact, you're red as a rose petal. And trust me, I *know* rose petals."

"I am not blushing. And how could you possibly see? It's dark in here."

"You're lit up like a dashboard. There's more to this story, Abigail. Let's hear it."

"I. Just. Fell."

"Uh-huh."

"Into some books."

"Okay, now you're almost purple."

How did she do this, always get the best of me? "It was a Valentine's Day display. All right?" I let that sink in for a minute.

"A Valentine's display?" Shawlie frowned, then snickered. "I'm beginning to get the picture. And speaking of pictures, were there?"

Shawlie didn't have to tell me my color had shot up another notch. "It just so happened that my English professor witnessed the whole thing. He must think I'm the biggest klutz on the planet."

"Your English professor? And this matters because—?"

"Well, it's just that . . . I mean . . ."

"Abigail Torrington! You like him!"

"Like him? Don't be silly. Of course I don't like him. I mean I *like* him, I just don't *like* him."

"Uh-huh," Shawlie said again. "So why the red face?"

"Well, you make it sound like I'm lusting after the man. And it *was* embarrassing. I mean, *Yoga for Couples*? You know all it's talking about is positions."

"That hardly anyone can get into."

"Exactly."

"So tell me about this guy."

"What, my professor?"

"That is who we're talking about. What's his name?"

"Ian Beckwith," I said, "and he's just a guy."

"Ian Beckwith. Nice name. Does he look anything like it?"

"Like his name? Shawlie, I don't know."

"Come on, what comes to mind when you hear the name"— she thought for a moment— "Richard Gere, for example?"

"I don't know. Tibet?"

"Ah, well, okay, not the best choice. How about Alec Baldwin? Or . . . or Matthew McConaughey."

I looked at her and shrugged.

"I mean, if their names were Howard Box or Dudley Fink, do you think they'd have gotten where they are today? So does he look like his name or not? Is he young, old? Good-looking? Not?"

"He's about what you'd expect in an English professor."

"That's just it, Abbie, I don't know what to expect. I took business courses in college."

I blew out a breath. Sometimes it just wasn't easy to talk to Shawlie. "Okay, I guess if we're doing this name thing, then his should be, I don't know, Dave Smith."

She glanced at me with a frown. "That's awfully plain."

"Mm-hmm."

"And?"

"He's older. But he's not Sven," I was quick to add.

Shawlie gripped the steering wheel a little tighter. "It's not like Sven is ancient, Abbie."

I gave her a look that said, *Oh, really?* which she purposely ignored. She lifted her chin and sniffed. "What, is your professor fifty, sixty?"

"Yeah," I said.

She rolled her eyes at me. "That's not an answer."

I rolled mine back at her. "He's, I don't know, maybe a few years older than Trey." *And he has this voice. . . .* "Oh, and he's gay."

"What?!"

I shrugged again. "That's what they say."

Shawlie chewed on that for a minute, then she laughed. And laughed. "Well, that would certainly be a change from Trey, hmm?"

"Yeah." I looked out the side window. "I suppose it would."

Finally, we turned into the hospital parking lot. I hoped the conversation would now change. The one and only parking space we found was nowhere near the entrance. I groaned; couldn't help it. The place had to be packed.

"I'll get a wheelchair," Shawlie said.

"Absolutely not. I can walk."

"No, no, listen to me. In a wheelchair they'll take you quicker."

⚬≈⚬

Oh yeah? I think they actually thought I was plenty comfortable in their wheelchair, so why hurry?

The waiting room was spilling over with people. I guess I owed Shawlie a thank you for the fact that I had somewhere to sit. She, on the other hand, spent the better part of an hour leaning against the wall before a chair opened up. She wheeled me over and took it before someone else had a chance.

For every patient, and I use the word loosely, there was an average of three and a half supporters. Whole families hung out in the waiting area. Kids playing on the floor, rolling, scooting, picking up who knows how many germs, or what kind, as if they were quite at home.

And I say *loosely* because, well, this was an emergency room and most of the cases weren't. A large woman in Spandex, accompanied by a large man whose beltless jeans sagged relentlessly in the back, was there for an ingrown toenail. I know they're no fun, but honestly, can they hurt enough to willingly spend half the night in the ER?

A twenty-something guy in a black T-shirt, black cargo shorts, and black flip-flops—on a stormy February night—with a dyed black mohawk and more piercings than I could count because he was constantly moving to a beat only he could hear, and I don't mean that he carried an iPod, was there for a headache. A *headache*. Every bit of skin exposed from his neck to his ankles, including his shaved legs, was covered in tattoos. Both second toes had tattoo rings, a matching filigree design that actually wasn't bad, but the rest was—and I know this is completely subjective—hideous.

It had been years since I'd been to an emergency room. Bailey was six and had fallen out of a tree. Now, knowing Bailey for the person she is, I look back and think, *I shouldn't have been the least bit surprised*. But back then it was the most traumatic moment of my life. My little girl was hurt. I was the one in tears. It was Mother's Day, an even year, which meant we'd had brunch with Trey's parents and were spending a bit of the afternoon at my parents' house.

Becca ran inside from the backyard, where the girls had been playing.

She was wailing. "Mommy! Daddy!" I remember thinking, Darn it, Bailey took Becca's Barbie tricycle again. Not to ride it, to hide it. Bailey hated all things pink. "Bailey fell!" Becca cried, pointing outside.

Fell? Oh, Lord. Mother, Dad, Trey, and I jumped up and rushed out of the house. Sure enough, Bailey lay on the grass beneath the huge camphor tree that had been growing since Teddy Roosevelt was a Rough Rider. It was my favorite tree in the whole world, had been all my life . . . till then.

Bailey wasn't moving, but she groaned when she saw our feet. Alive! Thank God, she's alive! Still, my heart pounded like a woodpecker with a deadline.

Trey stooped down beside her. "Where does it hurt, baby?"

Bailey lifted her head to look at Trey, tried to lift her arm, and cried out.

"Uh-oh," Trey said. "It's probably broken."

"Broken?" My voice was nothing but a squeak.

"I've got some bits of plywood in the garage," Dad said. "I'll get something for a splint." He headed off in that direction.

Mother held Becca, whose cheeks were streaked with tears. She sniffled, then lifted the edge of her shirt to wipe her nose. "Bailey?" Her voice sounded as small as she. "Are you okay?"

Bailey lifted her head again and shook it from side to side.

I wiped my own tears as I knelt beside my daughter. "Hold tight, sweetie. Grampa's coming with something for your arm."

"I'll get a towel to cover the plywood," Mother said. She sat Becca beside me, then hurried into the house.

Ten minutes later, Trey, Bailey, and I were on our way to the hospital.

Then, as now, the ER was spilling over with people in varying degrees of emergency. Only the ones with blood oozing from an orifice were taken before Bailey. Her arm was X-rayed, set, and put in a cast, and the whole time, unlike every other child in the emergency room, who was attached to her mother like a baby koala, Bailey wanted her daddy.

Not much had changed.

Three hours and nineteen minutes later, someone called my name. At last. And I mean *last*. No one was left in the waiting area besides Shawlie and me.

"Abigail Torrington." The doctor looked as tired as I felt.

Shawlie pushed me and my chair in his direction, then we followed him through the electronic double doors. He had me step up onto an examining table as I explained, in shorthand, how I'd gotten hurt. He slid my shoe off my foot and studied the bruise around my ankle. "We'll need an X-ray," he said.

"Oh, and my wrist." I extended my left arm. "I hurt it, too."

"Anything else? Besides your pride?"

I smiled at that, 'cause boy was he right. "My hip, but it's only bruised. Mostly it's the foot that hurts."

The doctor nodded. "Someone from radiology will be here for you shortly." He pulled the curtain closed as he left the room.

I glanced at the clock and wondered what *shortly* really meant in a place like this.

"You didn't mention your wrist to me," Shawlie said, "or your hip."

"Well, you know, it was the whole landing thing. My butt took the brunt of it and apparently"—I held up my hand—"I tried to break my fall."

"But instead you probably broke your wrist."

I rotated it in slow motion. "I don't think I could do this if it was broken."

In only twelve and a half minutes a man from radiology came for me. He wheeled the bed with me on it through the halls of the hospital to the radiology department. It took less than five minutes to take the X-rays, then I was back in my cubbyhole, where Shawlie sat waiting. Another fifteen minutes went by before the doctor returned. He held the results in his hand.

"Good news and bad news," he said, not stopping to give me a chance to choose which I preferred to hear first. "The wrist is only sprained. We'll wrap it in an Ace bandage, but be sure to ice it over the weekend. On the other hand, the fourth metatarsal"—he took my foot in his hand again and pointed out the bone—"is fractured. Right about here."

"Ah." I couldn't stop the sigh. "How long before it heals?"

"That depends on how good a patient you are. We'll fit you for a removable cast, but"—he pointed a finger at me—"whenever you're up and about you need to wear it. Except in the shower. Again, ice, ice, ice. It'll help with the swelling, which will help with the healing. No strenuous activity for three to four weeks. Should be good as new." He stopped in the middle of signing a paper secured to a clipboard. "That's a lie, actually." He chuckled. "There's always a chance you'll develop arthritis at the point of an injury like this. A really good chance." He finished signing the paper, then handed it to me. "Hold on another few minutes and we'll get you out of here."

By one a.m. my foot was strapped into the cast, I had my patient orders, and I was ready to go. "Can I drive in this?"

"Sure," the doctor said, "not a problem."

"Well, thanks for everything."

He nodded. "Take care." And then he was gone. Maybe to take a nap.

Shawlie handed me my purse and helped me down from the table. "He wasn't bad-looking. Not a ten, but not a Dave Smith either."

I laughed and shook my head as I plodded my way out of the ER in my removable cast. "Honestly, Shawlie, you're hopeless."

Twenty-Eight

Waiting for Becca to call was like waiting to get that second ear pierced. And if that wasn't enough, I was also waiting for Mother's number to show up on my caller ID because I knew Bailey would tell her even before she told Becca. She was probably on the phone with Mother the minute she backed out of the driveway. So I spent all of Saturday in a state of horrid apprehension, with every muscle taut as a shoe tree.

Not that I used shoe trees. But Trey did. Cedar ones, a pair for each of his dress shoes. Even now, stepping into his closet was like stepping into a forest. All that cedar. All that green.

I was putting my soft cast to the test because no matter how often I mentally repeated the doctor's orders to stay off my foot, I found myself walking the circuit between the kitchen and living room every fifteen minutes at least, unable to sit and rest as directed. Back and forth I'd go, with a mug of tea in my hand, worried till my stomach was in knots over what my girls were thinking about me.

Whatever it was, I deserved it.

I'm a pacer and always have been. I loved to walk my babies to sleep when they were so small I could scarcely feel their weight in my arms. But what I did feel was their tickling breath on my neck, the down of their hair on my cheek. It was like living in another world. I loved breathing in their scent, so pure a fragrance it could only be manufactured in heaven. If ever I get there, I want to go right to the place where they make it.

When the girls got older, if they were late coming home from school or a friend's house, it wouldn't matter what I was doing, there I'd be at the window every minute or two, as if reined in by the cord that continues to connect me to them. I'm not so delusional as to think that cord runs both ways. It's a one-way rope and I know it, the bane of motherhood. A small price to pay, but I'd pay it any day.

I was as watchful with Trey. If he was due in at three or seven or midnight, I'd begin to look for him a few minutes before in hopes he'd be early. If he was late, I was drawn continually to the window, till his car turned into the driveway. Then I could relax.

Shawlie, reigning Miss Independent of the century, says I'm far too wrapped up in the lives of my family. She may be right, but I can't find the end of the tie that binds them to me, and I don't have the desire to pull it loose if I did find it. In truth, I like being connected, like knowing I'm not alone in this world. No matter how alone I feel at times.

One of Winnie's favorite quotes from the Bible, one she recited often, was "Sufficient unto the day is the evil thereof." Meaning, of course, don't borrow trouble. But that Saturday I was borrowing trouble at triple-digit interest. I was a wreck by the time the phone rang at six thirty-nine that evening, so eager to answer, yet so afraid, as if I'd won the cruise of the century . . . to the end of the world.

"Mom?"

"Becca. Hi. How . . . how are you?" Apprehensive as I was, hearing her voice still brought me peace. I resumed my position on the sofa and propped up my aching foot.

"Oh, Mom, I'm so relieved. I mean, can you imagine if Bailey had married that creep? He'd be"—I could almost feel the shudder—"family. She told Brit and me all about it when she got back, even let me come to her room for pizza."

"Wow."

"Yeah, I know. She's not herself at all. This really shook her up. But I'm mainly calling to find out how you are."

How I—? I sat up straight, took my fingernail out of my mouth. "Well, I—"

"Bailey said your foot looks awful."

"My foot? Right. It was just one of those quirky accidents."

"Did you finally go to the doctor? Bailey said she thought you were going to."

"Shawlie took me to the emergency room, and a good thing I guess. One of the small bones in my foot is broken. The fourth something or other."

"Metatarsal."

"Yes, that's right. I'm impressed. So they teach that in Psychology I?" I was rambling on like a dolt.

Becca laughed at my joke only because she's polite. "No. That came from freshman biology. High school freshman biology. Are you in a cast?"

"A soft cast. It comes off when I sleep and shower."

"Oh good. I'm sure that beats the plaster kind."

"To the moon and back," I said. "So, Bailey doesn't quite seem herself?" I crept up on the subject as if it would bite. Because, boy, it could.

"You know how it is. She's been so conflicted about Tim for the longest time. I can't believe she went so far as to go to Reno. I'm just so glad she didn't come back a McGuire."

"Oh, sweetie, me too. So how is"—my heart rate jumped another dozen points—"everything else?" I squeezed my eyes shut and held my breath as I waited for her answer.

"Actually, I wasn't going to say anything, but, okay, now that you ask . . ."

I brought a hand to my mouth and bit the middle knuckle of my index finger. I should have had an answer prepared. After all these months, I should have known what I would say, because how could I think it would never come up, that I'd not be found out? Subconsciously did I know it would? Did I want it to? Want Trey's deception exposed? Now, there was a question for Psych I. But I didn't need a textbook answer because I knew in my heart that the answer was no. I never wanted my girls to know this other side of their dad. And even now, with more than a little of the milk bottle spilled, I'd do what I could to protect them. Even though it meant protecting Trey.

"I want you to be honest, okay, Mom?"

You mean quit with the lie I've been living the past year and a half? That kind of honest? "I'll . . . I'll try."

"Bailey said it would be dumb of me to even ask, but—"

So Bailey did tell and didn't want me to know? Or she did tell and saw no point in letting me into their dialogue?

"You remember me telling you about the missions trip to Mexico?"

Missions trip? To Mexico? Was this a trick question?

"Mom, you there?"

"Yes, sorry, I'm here. And, yes, I remember."

"Well, a few of us are going down over spring break to help nail down a roof on one of the houses at the orphanage."

Nail down a roof?

"Actually, they don't call it an orphanage. That sounds so institutional, you know? They call them children's homes, 'cause that's what they are. There are five of them so far. Each house has a set of parents and eight kids. It's really a neat ministry. But here's the thing. If I go, I won't be home for Easter, 'cause we won't be back till late Saturday night."

My heart sputtered back to life, as if after dipping its toe in the water just to check things out and finding it okay, it decided to venture out a little farther. I rubbed my chest and sighed out a breath.

"I know the whole Easter thing is a bummer, but, well, what do you think?"

What did I think? My daughter, a sophomore in college, was calling for permission not to come home for Easter? She was not calling to ask about the divorce papers still hidden in my hope chest? I thought I'd float away like circus balloons if someone let go of my foot, that's what I thought. But I was still a mom. "How safe is it, Bec? Are any advisers going?"

"They're not called advisers, but, yes, there are three staffers from our church going, along with six students from the college. And, yes, it's safe. The children's home is only an hour or so south of the border and it's in a secured area. It has to be, you know, for the kids."

"Ah. And the roof?"

"It's a single-story building."

"Hmm. You really want to do this? Spend spring break nailing down a roof?"

"I really do, Mom."

"And not because of—?" Why could I never remember that fellow's name? "The one with the nose?"

Becca giggled on her end of the line. "Will? No, this has nothing to do with him. Or any guy. Well, okay, that's not entirely true."

Oh man, I was not up for this. Not after our close call with Tim McGuire.

"There's Rafael."

"Rafael?"

"He's three. You should see his eyes, Mom. They're beautiful. Not sad like they were before the children's home. I saw pictures."

Ah.

"And Jesus."

"Jesus? You . . . you mean like God?"

Becca giggled again. "I mean exactly like God. Nailing down a roof is the least I can do for Him after all He's done for me."

This was Winnie speaking. A younger version for sure, but the words were the same. And the passion, that was the same too. Something in me stirred, a memory, a yearning, something that hurt and yet didn't, that looked, tasted, and smelled like that sweet, crazy woman in a muumuu. A wave of loneliness surged within me. My eyes stung and my throat ached. Between Trey and his mother, Winnie was the one I missed. The one I'd give anything to have one more hour with. Yes, I had questions for Trey that burned in my heart one restless day after the next. But I knew enough to know that the answers he'd feed me would be as satisfying as a spoonful of air.

Not Winnie. A conversation with her was food for the soul.

"Mom?"

"Becca. Sorry."

"If you really don't want me to go I'll—"

"No. No, sweetie. I think it would be good for you to go. If you're sure it's safe."

"It is. And I'll be careful, I promise. We don't leave till the first week of April, but I needed to let them know in order to secure my spot. So, thanks. Really."

"What about money? I'll put a check in the mail."

"That's okay. It's not much and I have it."

"You have it?"

"In my account. I don't spend as much as Bailey. But I will need my passport."

"I'll overnight it."

"Thanks, Mom. So, you sure you're okay with this?"

I nodded even though I wanted to cry. "I'm sure."

"Okay then, I'll turn in my paperwork. It's going to be so much fun."

"Fun? Nailing down a roof?"

"And working with the kids. It'll be a great trip."

❧

How did this happen, this metamorphosis in the heart of my baby girl? Was it a good thing or a bad thing? I mean, what if Bailey was right and this really was a cult, all joking aside? How could I find out? I knew no one to ask. Trey's dad had not been supportive of Winnie's conversion—her metamorphosis—and only went to church on Easter because she cajoled him into it. Since her death, he went only for funerals.

Of course I could call Mother, but I couldn't imagine her having anything positive to say about a church she didn't go to.

She barely had anything positive to say about the one she did.

Becca had told me the name of her church weeks ago, had said it was part of an established denomination, but what did that mean? Cults could be established, couldn't they? I tried to remember the name she told me. Something with God in the title. *Yes, well, that narrows it down.*

The phone book was in the kitchen, and I wasn't. But this was important. I went for it, propped my hip on a bar stool, and turned to churches. One of the first categories sounded familiar. And God was in the title. But then, God was in a lot of the titles. There were dozens of subcategories and pages of listings.

There was nothing I could do but ask Becca again. I speed dialed her number, glad I'd had the foresight to bring the phone with me to the kitchen. I listened to two measures of her ringback tone before she answered.

"Mom? Everything okay?"

"Just had a quick question. The church you go to, what's it called again?"

She told me, then laughed a crystal laugh. "You wouldn't be checking up on me, would you?"

She'd know in a minute if I lied, so I didn't. "You'll understand when you're a mom."

"Love you," she said, and I could hear the smile in her voice.

I was right. It was the denomination I first located in the phone book. But there were at least two dozen churches listed under that category, even a Samoan one. You'd think that many of the same kind of church in the greater Sacramento area had to be safe. But the only place I could think to call just to make sure was the church Winnie had gone to. I trusted Winnie, so I trusted her church.

But I couldn't think of the name of that either. Maybe the

pain medication was getting to me. I went through the phone book once and the alphabet twice, because that usually jogged my memory of whatever elusive thing I was seeking. But not that night. My mind was a jumbled mess of church names and denominations, where nothing and everything sounded right.

Well, the doctor said I could drive.

I got in my car and set out for Winnie's church because I knew exactly where it was located. It was a twenty-five-minute drive to Carmichael, where Winnie and Robert the Second had lived for most of their marriage and all of Trey's life. Amazing that both Trey's parents and mine had been so settled during a time when families were beginning to disintegrate like sand castles at high tide.

I found the church easily enough a few blocks from the Torrington's former home. It was a plain brick edifice with a spire and stained-glass windows. They were dark this Saturday night. I'd hoped, on an off chance, to find a car or two in the parking lot, a light in the office window, but everything was dark and still. I shined my car lights on a sign that rose out of the front lawn and jotted down the name and phone number of the church, as well as the name of the pastor.

That made it easy.

∽

I was tempted to drive back the next morning for the ten o'clock service, but the thought of going into the church alone—and on Valentine's Day at that—was daunting enough without adding to the mix the attention my broken foot would draw.

My plan was to wait till noon and then call the number I'd jotted down for the church office. Maybe someone would answer, maybe even the pastor. But my own phone rang sometime around eleven. Mother's number showed up on my caller ID. Oh, it may have said Edward J. Woodruff on the little screen, but make no mistake, it was Mother. For one thing, Dad seldom used the telephone. For another, the churning in the pit of my stomach left little doubt.

What had Bailey told her? Bailey may have kept her secret from Becca, for now anyway, but from Mother? Not likely.

It was the fourth ring before I made up my mind whether to answer or let the machine pick up. I sat back and listened to Bailey's voice. "You have reached the Torrington residence. Leave a message at the tone and we'll get back to you as soon as we can." *Beep*.

The tone and content were strikingly different from the message on her cell phone. With indistinguishable music blaring in the background, Bailey's far more upbeat voice would say, "Hey, it's me. You know what to do, and if you don't, don't expect me to tell you." *Beep*.

"Tippy?"

Oh, Lord.

"Are you there?"

Pause.

"Well, okay then. Dad and I thought you might want breakfast. We could meet at IHOP if you're up to driving, or we could come up there. There's that place you and Trey took us to for Mother's Day. That last time."

As if Mother's Day didn't count anymore.

"I'm holding a minute to see if you're there. Still holding. Still hold—"

"Mother. Hey. I was, um, in the bathroom." I bit my lip and squinted. Funny. Lying on Sunday seemed more egregious than it did on, say, Tuesday or Friday. I wondered, *Did Trey ever feel that way as he packed his bag every sixth Sunday for his upcoming week in . . . Dallas?*

"Yes, well, with your foot the way it is, Dad and I thought you might want to join us for breakfast instead of fending for yourself. Though, really, now it's brunch."

Her voice sounded normal, not like she was waiting to pounce on me. Still, Mother could be unpredictable when she decided to be.

"Tippy? Are you there?"

"Yes. Sorry." I looked at the half-eaten bagel sitting on the table before me, then out the kitchen window. It wasn't raining, which would make it easy to go out with my cast. "Brunch sounds good. I think I can meet you."

"Good. The one on Madison. Twenty minutes should give you time."

"Okay, I should be able—"

But she was gone. One thing you could say about Mother, she wasn't wasteful. Not of money or words or time. She'd made her point, and that was that.

But this wasn't about brunch. I was sure of that. Bailey had to have told. If only she'd answer my calls.

I backed out of the garage, down the expanse of driveway, and turned onto the road, still uncomfortable driving with the cast, which felt like I had a book between my foot and the gas pedal. I tried driving without it the night before, but the moment I applied pressure to the pedal, the fourth metatarsal let me know it was none too happy about it.

I eased onto I-80 and stayed in the slow lane all the way down the hill. No way I'd make it to IHOP in twenty minutes. Hopefully Mother would allow the hostess to seat them without me before the hordes of Sunday diners got out of church, because then we'd never get a table and it would be my fault. I was assuming we were way ahead of the Valentine's diners. I'd have called my parents' cell phone to urge them to be seated without me, if they had one.

Instead, I tried Bailey's phone again, waited for her voice mail to kick in, and left my fifth or sixth message. I'd lost count. "Bailey, sweetheart, we have to talk. Please, please call." I could understand her anger, how this must look to her. All that time with my secret tucked away upstairs. She had to have been as shocked to find those papers as I was to receive them. The life Trey and I had made for our girls must now seem like nothing but lies.

Because it was.

The parking lot was nearly full when I arrived, only ten minutes late. I parked in the closest spot I could find, which wasn't close at all.

Dad waited in the foyer and smiled a greeting when he saw me. "Mom's got a table." He took my arm and led me to where Mother sat. She offered her cheek, which smelled of Avon pressed powder, the only thing she'd used since long before I was born.

"I ordered hot tea for you," she said.

The picture of efficiency. "Thank you."

Before I had time to adjust my chair, my tea and their coffee arrived. I filled my cup from the little stainless steel pot, which dribbled water onto the table, dunked my tea bag four times, then squeezed in some lemon. I preferred something citrus to black pekoe, but oh well.

"This is nice and spontaneous." At least I hoped. "Thanks for inviting me." I opened my menu, which left my fingers sticky with syrup, and decided an English muffin was all I could stomach if my suspicions were correct.

Dad made observations about how busy the restaurant was, but little else was said till we'd all decided on our order. Then Mother straightened her silverware. "Bailey wants to quit school."

My cup tipped in my hand and dribbled more liquid onto the table. Tippy. Oh, yes, that was me. "She . . . she—?"

"Called Friday night on her way to San Luis."

I set my cup on the table, feeling fourteen instead of forty-three, and steeled myself for what would come next.

"She was quite upset," Mother said. "This ridiculous affair with that interloper has knocked her off course." The sigh that followed came from down deep inside. "You'd think someone would have seen it coming." There was enough emphasis on *someone* that I knew exactly who she meant.

Dad cleared his throat and made a show of opening his menu, his way of saying, *Why not change the subject?*

But we both knew that wasn't going to happen.

"I did all I could to persuade her not to keep seeing Tim, but I couldn't exactly ground her and send her to her room."

"Maybe if you'd done more of that when she was younger—"

"Oh, Alice, we didn't invite Abbie here to badger her." Dad looked over his glasses directly into Mother's eyes. "And if anyone's spoiled the girl, you needn't look farther than your own nose to find the culprit." In spite of his words, the tone of his voice took the edge off the tension that was building.

Mother sniffed. "You've done your share of spoiling, Edward Woodruff."

The waitress returned just then to take our order. She began with Mother and finished with me. "An English muffin," I said. "Well toasted."

Mother arched an eyebrow. "You needn't have driven all this way for an English muffin."

"I ate," I said, thinking of the half bagel sitting on my kitchen counter.

"You might have said."

Dad stirred two packets of pure sugar into his coffee. "It's all right. There's nothing wrong with tea and a muffin."

"Tippy. I just don't think you've handled this whole thing appropriately."

"Mother, I walk a fine line with Bailey. I've tried to be supportive of how she feels and steer her away from Tim McGuire all at the same time. It's not easy."

"I'm not talking about Tim McGuire now."

I sat back and debated whether or not I even wanted to ask. "Then what?" I had to consciously keep from folding my arms across my chest.

"I'm talking about Trey."

"Trey?" My thumbnail found its way to my mouth, clenched between my teeth.

"The girls don't understand—none of us understands—why you seem so indifferent about the death of your husband."

"Alice, you said you wanted to talk to Abbie about Bailey quitting school."

Mother didn't miss a beat. "I realize that people handle grief in different ways, but, Tippy, your way has done nothing but bring more sorrow upon your daughters."

Dad pinched the bridge of his nose. I ran my finger around and around the rim of my cup.

"Your whole countenance these past eighteen months has said a great big *good riddance.*" Mother made a sweeping motion with the back of her hand as if she'd swatted some pesky thing away.

I bit off the end of my nail.

"Good riddance," Mother continued, "to a man like Robert Torrington."

"Those are harsh words, Alice."

"Maybe so, but they need to be said." Mother moved her cup away as the waitress approached with our plates.

There was a full minute of silence between us, and not because we were interested in the food she'd brought. "Why does Bailey want to quit school?"

"She says she's too upset to focus."

"She's going to finish the semester?"

Mother gave a little shrug and cut into a link of sausage. "I'm doing my best to persuade her, but you know Bailey. What you might be asking instead is why she feels she had to come to me with this decision." Mother held her fork and waited for my comeback. She wouldn't have liked any of the ones that came to my mind. "She's an angry young woman, and she doesn't know how to deal with it. I'd say some counseling is in order. For all of you."

My English muffin remained unbuttered. I picked up the stainless steel pot and spilled more water into my cup. "She has to finish the semester."

Mother held my gaze for several moments, then swallowed her reply with a bite of scrambled egg. I suppose she felt she'd dished out a full serving by now.

"I'll talk to her," Dad said. Exactly as Trey would have.

I took a drink of my tepid tea, my eyes squinting against a threat of tears. "Bailey can talk to me anytime about anything." My voice was thick with petulance, and I hated it.

"Tippy. I don't mean to hurt you, but some self-evaluation—"

"Then why do you?" The question was out before I had time to think about it, but in the shattering silence that followed, I decided to forge ahead. "You have no idea what this past year and a half has been like. No idea, Mother. And honestly, I don't think there is an appropriate way to handle grief. It is what it is. It comes out the way it comes out. Containing it is like . . . like . . . trying not to sneeze. People can either deal with me as I am or not. There's nothing I can do but try to get through this with what's left of my family intact." I sighed out my frustration. "I know the girls don't understand all my decisions—"

"You mean like tossing the remains of your husband out of your bedroom and selling his perfectly good car?" Mother was back on her game.

A woman at the table next to us frowned deeply and tried unsuccessfully to keep her eyes off mine. I could tell she had a mental image of me dumping Trey's ashes out the bedroom window.

Mother's mouth was pressed into a thin line with only the smallest bit of a pink V showing in the center of her upper lip, where she'd overdrawn the outline of her mouth with her lipstick. Her nose was pinched and white on the tip, her neck splotchy and red, as if someone had faux-painted a collar around the circumference of it.

Dad kept his eyes on the table and chewed on his lip.

"I mean that I've handled this my way. The girls are getting on with their lives, but me? I have no life. It's like I was married to a pharaoh and now I'm entombed in the equivalent of the great pyramid on the top of Granite Bay. All I want to do is get out, but everyone else wants me buried alive."

Our neighboring diner kept her eyes averted, but there was no question she was leaning toward our table, her ear open wide.

Mother pushed her plate away. "Nobody wants you buried alive. You exaggerate more than anyone I know."

I could have laughed at the hyperbole.

"All I meant was—" Mother expelled a breath through her nostrils and shook her head. "Tippy. You can't continue to think only of yourself. Hard as it must be for you, your daughters need to know that home is still there for them, that it won't be reinvented every time they go back."

Dad swallowed the last of his pancakes. "She's only still there because of the girls."

I nodded. "Exactly."

"The day you leave that house will be a day of deep sadness for Bailey and Becca."

"You'd have me stay there forever?"

"I'd think you'd find comfort in the memories."

That might have been true if Trey had not died in San Diego, if I'd not found that telltale sweater, if that phone call had come from Dallas. I couldn't stop the tears that filled my eyes, but I did keep them from falling. "Everything's changed."

Mother reached across the table and touched my hand. Her own could have doubled as an ice pack to lay over my aching foot. "All the more reason, Tippy, not to add more change."

I inched my hand out of hers and blotted my eyes with my napkin, then stood and put on my jacket. "I love that you gave me a nickname, Mother. I just hate the way you use it."

I was glad, so glad that I'd driven my own car. I climbed in and rested my head against the steering wheel, not quite ready for the trek back up the hill. This should have tasted like a sort of victory, but in truth it felt like coal in my stocking.

One thing was for sure. Bailey had kept my secret.

But why?

Twenty-Nine

Winnie's church wasn't too far away. On a whim I pointed the nose of my car in that direction and made my way through Sunday traffic. There was a mall between me and the church, which meant lots of cars and a long wait at every stoplight.

I didn't expect to find anyone at the church at almost one o'clock on a Sunday afternoon, especially *this* Sunday afternoon, but there were still a half dozen cars disbursed throughout the parking lot when I got there. One, an older model F-150, was parked in one of three spaces marked Pastoral Parking outside the church office. Not a huge perk, but a perk just the same I suppose. I parked a few spaces down, in an area not marked at all, and got out of my car. I was two steps away from the office door when a young man stepped out. He was about to lock the door when he saw me. He stopped and offered a tentative smile. "Can I help you?" he asked.

Really, my plan was to say, *I just have a quick question,* ask it, and leave. What happened instead couldn't have surprised him any more than it did me. An unmistakable sob cut off all hope of me asking him anything, and tears too long contained finally found their release. I couldn't catch my breath, let alone apologize for choosing his doorway to fall apart in.

"Are . . . are you all right?"

Well, obviously no.

He waved to someone I hadn't seen waiting in one of the cars across the parking lot. "I'll catch up," he called. He led me into the office, helped me into a chair, then rummaged around till he found a box of Kleenex.

The tears wouldn't stop flowing, and every time I tried to apologize, my breath caught and my throat constricted. There was nothing to do but wait for this mortifying wave to pass. The young man sat easily in his chair, content to wait it out with me, as if women fell apart in his doorway on a daily basis.

And maybe they did, but if this was the janitor, say, and not the pastor, I was going to die, that's all there was to it.

My eyes were raw and all makeup washed away when I finally felt the flow begin to abate. It was another minute before I trusted my voice. "I am so sorry," I finally said, my voice weak and gritty. "I don't know where that came from."

"I do." He tapped the left side of his chest with his finger.

I sniffed and covered my mouth with the back of my hand.

There are women, particularly in the movies, who actually ooze charm when they cry. I'm not one of them. My lips get puffy and red, as if I've been stung by a bee. Even the little cleft between my upper lip and nose swells until the cleft just disappears, and then I look like a cave woman. Add to it eyes that practically swell shut with a really good cry, and, well, you just want to break out the epinephrine.

Even Trey would avert his eyes whenever I cried. He'd pass me a hankie while looking in the opposite direction or pull me so close to his chest that he didn't have to look at me. Not that I cried a lot in our marriage. But had I known how much there was to cry about . . .

My eyes filled again.

The young man handed me the whole box of Kleenex. "Is . . . is there someone I can call for you?"

I shook my head and soaked up the tears with a new wad of tissues. *There are times you'd like nothing better than to disappear down the nearest darn hole you can find, just dive right down there with the gophers.* This was one of them.

"I know what you mean."

My head jerked up as if on a puppet string. *You know what I . . .?* I'd actually said it? Out loud? Only *darn* wasn't the word I used.

The young man smiled, nodded. "I know exactly what you mean."

"Oh, please, I am so sorry. And so embarrassed."

"Really, it's okay."

"No. No, it's not. I would never talk that way in church. Not ever. Not that I'm in church very often, or that I talk that way very often, but I just never would. Especially in Winnie's church."

"Well, technically, we're not in church. We're in the church office." He looked around the small outer room that had doors leading to three other rooms. "But I suppose you guessed that already. Who's Winnie?"

I hiccupped. "My mother-in-law." I always hiccup after an especially hard cry.

"And she goes here?" He cocked his head and frowned.

"Did," I said and hiccupped again.

"Ah. That explains why the name isn't familiar. Where does she go now?"

I pointed up.

"Oh. I see. My sympathies. For you, not her."

I nodded, sniffed, sucked in a breath, and held it. Not that it ever worked, at least for me, but it was better than sitting there hiccupping.

"They say a spoonful of sugar helps," the young man said. "Sorry that I don't have any."

I let go of the breath I was holding. And hiccupped. "Sugar? Really?"

"They say."

"This is so embarrassing. Really, I don't know what happened. I just had a question and I saw there were cars in the parking lot, so I thought I'd stop, but then I hadn't been here in so long, not since Winnie . . ."

"Ah. So you attended here too?"

"Well, not attended. Just visited. Usually on Easter."

The young man nodded, then produced a warm smile. "If I were going to choose one day a year to go to church, that's the day I'd choose."

"The last time we came here was nine, no, ten years ago. It was an even year."

That caused another little crease to appear between his eyebrows.

I shook my head. "Never mind." My hiccups were getting worse and I could really embarrass myself when I tried to talk with them. "I think I'll just"—I nodded toward the door—"go."

"What about your question?"

"It's not important. Well, it is actually. But I could come back another time. Or maybe call." *Hiccup.*

Suddenly he held up a finger. "Wait here." He disappeared through an open doorway. In just a moment he returned and handed me a packet of sugar. "Break room. I just thought of it. In fact, if you'd like some coffee I could—"

"No, really, I've taken enough of your time. Besides—oh my gosh." I suddenly remembered. "You have someone waiting for you." I jumped up, put too much weight on my foot, and folded back onto the chair.

The young man winced. "I feel your pain. I broke my foot once playing basketball. Made this really awesome jump shot. Then I landed. Not fun. Or dignified."

"No," I said, shuddering with the recall, "it's not." He paused, as if waiting for more, but I'd give up buying shoes before I'd tell him how I broke mine. "I'm keeping you from . . . something, I'm sure."

"Pizza," he said. "Third week in a row. A person can only handle so much Italian sausage. And cheese? Well, it stops me up something awful."

I laughed at his candor. And hiccupped.

He motioned to the packet of sugar. "Just take the whole thing," he said, as if it were a dose of medicine. I did. Just tore the top off the packet, poured the sugar in my mouth, and swallowed. We waited, expectantly, both holding our breath. When it finally seemed safe, I exhaled, and he did too. "Wow. It worked." He was more surprised than I was.

"So it seems. Thank you . . ."

"John. Koslosky."

"*Pastor* Koslosky?" I hoped.

He nodded and I wilted in my relief. Then he said, "Youth pastor."

Youth? Okay, well, it could have been worse. Maybe.

"And you are?"

"Abigail. Torrington."

"Abigail. Nice name."

Nice biblical *name is what he probably meant.* "My mother calls me Tippy." The words were out before I had time to think what made me say them. I'd been teased about my nickname so much in school that, outside of family, only those who'd known me for a very long time, namely Shawlie, even knew about it.

"Tippy. I bet there's a story."

"Yes." But I wasn't going there either.

"So. Now that the hiccups are gone and the . . . um"—he motioned to my eyes—"dam is holding, how about that question?"

"But your pizza."

He shrugged. "If I'm lucky the kids'll save me a slice. If I'm not, they'll save me two." His smile was inviting, and I decided to open up.

"It's about my daughter. Becca. She's in college and she's just darling, and she wants to go to Mexico because of the orphanage, but you have to be so careful about girls these days, and I told her it was okay even though it means she won't be home for Easter, but now I'm just not sure, and Bailey, that's my other daughter, says it's a cult and I guess that's what scares me the most."

John leaned forward in his chair, hands clasped between his knees. He studied me, bottom lip between his teeth, as if I were a specimen, though it looked as if he really was trying to follow me. "Cult? Hmm."

"So you think it could be?" My heart took a tumble, and I had to blink like crazy to keep the dam from springing another leak.

"Would you happen to have any specific information?"

"Yes." I took a calming breath and told him the denominational name of the church Becca attended. "Chi Alpha is the group she's going with."

John smiled, sat back, and relaxed. "I had lots of friends in Chi Alpha when I was in college. There were a few who were crazy—in a fun way," he added. "But, honest, they're okay."

The denomination, it seems, was fine as well.

"So they're going to work at an orphanage?" John asked.

"On the roof of an orphanage, actually."

"Roof. Wow. Good for her."

"So then, you think it's safe to let her go?"

"When you get right down to it, it's not safe going to your local ATM. But when you go in the name of the Lord to do His work, He's promised to be there. I think your daughter will be in good hands." John leaned forward in his seat again. "But if you don't mind me asking, is there something else, besides her trip to Mexico, troubling you? I mean, you were really distraught when you came in here, and it feels like it was about more than this."

All I could say is the man had a gift. I wilted even more, and for the next hour, as we worked our way through a whole pot of coffee, I told him about Trey, San Diego, the divorce papers. Even the sweater.

"And no one knows? Oh, Abbie, that's a lot for one person to carry."

"Well, Shawlie. She knows. And now"—I couldn't keep my lip from quivering—"Bailey. She knows about the divorce papers. She's so angry."

John shook his head thoughtfully. "This is a tough place for you to be. Kids have a tendency to idolize their parents, even when—" He left off, and I couldn't help but think he wasn't talking about Bailey anymore. "I don't pretend to have the answer to such a hard question, but this verse popped into my mind when you were talking. It may be for you." He reached over to the near-est desk, found a scrap of paper, and plucked a pen out of an *I Love Strawberries* mug. I don't think it was his. "John 8:32," he said. "'Then you will know the truth, and the truth will set you free.'" He wrote down the Scripture reference. "Do you have a Bible?"

"At home. Winnie gave it to me."

"I'm sorry I didn't know her." John passed me the paper. "Hard as it is to think about, you may want to find a way to tell your daughters the truth, Abbie. Just tell them like you told me. There was a lot of heart behind your words. They'll feel it. They'll know you love them. And that you loved him."

I reached for more Kleenex, looked out through the smudged glass of the entrance door, and shook my head. "Not ever." I held up the scrap of paper as I stood. "But I'll keep this."

John nodded and looked, I don't know, like he knew a secret. He helped me to my car. "See you on Easter?" he asked. "It's an even year." He smiled though he had no idea what an even year had to do with Easter or anything else.

"Maybe. We'll see."

⁂

The first thing I did when I got home was empty my bladder of two-thirds of a pot of generic coffee. Then I put water on to boil in a pot that didn't dribble, which made me think of brunch, which made me think of Mother. And that phone call from San Diego. How many times in the last year and a half had I thought how different things would be if that phone call had only come from Dallas? Trey would still be dead, yes, and that would still have changed my future, but it would not have rewritten my past.

It would have left intact everything I thought I knew about the man I'd given myself to more than half a lifetime ago. The man who gave me babies.

And a house of cards to raise them in.

But then, there were still the divorce papers.

The kettle began to whistle. I pushed down my thoughts, feeling more and more like an overstuffed suitcase. Eventually the latches weren't going to hold, and what then? What would come spilling out?

"Green sweaters," I said out loud. "Lots and lots of green sweaters." I laughed at such a ridiculous thought and turned off the burner.

The water hit the orange spice tea bag resting in my cup, without a drop wasted, and my kitchen became an orange grove, bursting with essence. The taste buds on the back of my tongue came alive and my mouth watered. My nostrils flared with expectation. I carried the mug to the living room, delaying gratification all the way but knowing when I took that first sip it would not disappoint.

I found what was becoming my favorite spot on the brocade sofa I'd seldom used when Trey was alive, *"because, Ab, our leather chairs are much easier to keep clean."*

As if Trey knew what it was to be clean.

I picked up my Bible, still on the coffee table, and turned to the verse Pastor John Koslosky had written down for me. I backed up to verse 31 and read, "To the Jews who had believed him, Jesus said, 'If you hold to my teaching, you are really my disciples. Then you will know the truth, and the truth will set you free.'"

The thought of freedom from the weight of the emotions my heart lugged around every day, like a suitcase in the form of Trey, was certainly enticing. But it seemed to me the truth was a pretty high price to pay for it.

On a whim I turned to the concordance in the back of the Bible and found the word *truth* in bold caps. Beneath that heading there were two and a half columns of Scripture verses that bore the word *truth* in one form or another. And, honestly, no less than eighty times, Jesus said these words: "I tell you the truth." On another whim I looked up the last verse in which He said it, John 16:23: "I tell you the truth, my Father will give you whatever you ask in my name."

Well, that seemed like a pretty large boast.

Even for Jesus.

Thirty

My plan was to skip both of my classes on Tuesday. For one thing, it was raining again, so I'd have to wear a sock with that clumsy cast to keep my foot dry, and the cast was ugly enough by itself without adding a sock to the mix. And what sock would I wear? Bailey would say the heck with the sock, Becca would wear her green and pink striped one with the toes, and Shawlie would—well, Shawlie would never have allowed herself to fall at a man's feet.

For another thing, it would be humiliating enough to face Ian Beckwith after our last encounter if I looked perfectly normal—which is probably not a word he's ever associated with me—but in a cast? Well, that would just confirm what a lummox I am. Not only can I not keep my coffee cup upright, but I can't even keep myself upright.

That was my plan. But then I could almost hear his sandpaper voice, and I wondered which author he'd talk about in class, what word associations he'd use for *story*, and my stomach began to growl.

The soft cast was royal blue, my jeans stonewashed, my sweater butter yellow. I had trouser socks in a variety of shades, but they'd never keep my foot dry. I rummaged through Becca's sock drawer and found a sock that very nearly matched the color of my sweater. The white toes offset with a gray stripe were an unfortunate feature, but, well, Becca's sock beat anything I had.

Then I went looking for a shoe to tie the whole thing together.

I hobbled into class carrying a tightly lidded latte from the Starbucks knockoff a mile from the campus, glad I had the foresight to stop there because the line at the real Starbucks drive-through, much closer to the campus, was eight cars long. Of course you couldn't tell that, if you had the misfortune to pull in, until you were already in line, and once you were, there was no way out except to wait your turn. I sang the chorus to "It's Too Late" as I passed.

As I shuffled along, oh-so-careful not to let even a drop bubble up through the sippy hole, I kept my eyes on my desk and completely away from the front of the room as the other students poured through the doorway. I made as if I was too busy to even think about chatting with anyone. Not that I ever did. I pulled my notebook out of my bag, opened it to a fresh page, smoothed the paper on both sides of the spiral ring, checked my mechanical pencil for extra lead, pulled off the silver top to inspect—

"Morning."

—the eraser. The gravel of his voice had a smooth/rough tone, like river rocks after years of tumbling in the rush of the water. I still couldn't tell if the bit of accent was English or Irish. I was thinking English.

"Broken?"

"Oh, no, it just needs more lead."

"The foot." His smile was patient, as if talking to a six-year-old.

"Oh." I looked back at my paper, nodded.

"I was afraid of that. I should not have let you drive home."

"Oh, well, I—"

"Surely there was someone you could have called."

My shoulders dropped the tiniest bit. I smoothed my paper again. "It's just one little bone. In the top of the foot."

"Yes, well, glad it wasn't worse."

I may have only imagined the upturn of his mouth as he pivoted to go back to his desk. Still my cheeks flamed humiliation red. Sock or no sock, I should have stayed home. I lifted my cup for something to do, tested the security of the lid, and sipped.

Professor Beckwith took his usual place against his desk. "I realize we're only a fourth of the way through the semester, but for those of you who don't plan to wait till the last forty-eight hours to complete your semester assignment, I have some books here I'm willing to loan. But if you don't bring them back, I will find you." There was a glint in his eyes, but the tone of his voice said he meant every word.

"And," he continued, "for those who really want to impress the teacher, Ms. Connors has a museum down in Chula Vista. Small though it is, a fan"—he shifted his eyes to mine—"would find it worth the drive."

He recrossed his legs at the ankles. He was wearing the burgundy Hush Puppies again, with black jeans and a black-and-white plaid shirt. His hands were in his pockets. I'd have thought the saddle oxfords a better choice, until I saw the sweater draped over the back of his chair. Burgundy, of course. With elbow patches. I could almost see him atop a desk crying, "Carpe diem!"

Then again, maybe not. He was more the *come-let-us-reason-together* type.

"Let's talk about what makes a particular writing endure, what gives it the life of Methuselah."

"Methuselah?" It was Miss Near-Perfect. "You mean like from the Bible?"

Well, I was impressed. I knew who Methuselah was, just barely, but I didn't expect her to.

"Exactly," Ian Beckwith said.

"Okay, well, I don't get it." Her perfectly lined eyes squinted under the weight of all that cogitation. "What does writing a book have to do with being a priest?"

"A priest?" Now the professor's eyes squinted. He let go of a chuckle. "Forgive me, but now I'm the one who doesn't get it."

"A priest," she said again. "He didn't have a mom or something. Or a dad."

That stirred up some murmurings and splatters of laughter. "You've got to have one or the other," someone said.

The professor crossed his arms and smiled. "Actually . . ." He waited till he had everyone's attention. He already had mine. "You might be thinking of Melchizedek, who indeed was a priest."

Miss Near-Perfect shrugged and rolled her eyes. "Whatever."

I clicked my pencil twice and wrote down the name in my tablet.

"Methuselah, though not a priest, lived a very long time." That got a few more chuckles. "Which gets us back to our topic. What makes a classic a classic?"

"A lot of people like it," someone said.

"That makes it a best seller," someone else said, "not a classic."

A third person said, "A lot of people like it for a very long time." He intentionally copied Ian Beckwith's words.

The professor held up a finger and smiled. "That's it. But why? Why should I love the same book that, say, my great-great-grandmother, who lived in a hut in Breconshire County, Wales, loved? What could possibly connect us?"

Ah. Wales. Okay.

"*Story*," a young woman said, and I knew I wasn't the only one affected by our professor's use of that word.

Ian Beckwith laughed. "And what makes story?" He stood there with one eyebrow hiked and waited.

"Characters," someone said.

"Plot." Someone else.

"The perfect combination." Miss Near-Perfect.

Hmm. Well. There actually may be something beyond those blonde roots.

Professor Beckwith raised his finger again and nodded. "What else? Come on. What does every memorable *story* have in common?"

"Desire." The word came from my mouth before I knew it, followed by clusters of snickers and a few woo hoos from the guys. I might as well have said the word *vagina* out loud to a classroom of seventh grade boys. Of course it didn't help that I said it with so much . . . desire. Again my cheeks burned as if lit with a match.

"Desire," Ian Beckwith agreed. He closed his eyes, savored the word. "All lasting literature is about desire. But let's narrow it down. Desire for . . .?"

Voices popped up around the room like kernels of corn in hot oil.

"Courage."

"Justice."

"A whale."

Snickers.

"True love."

More snickers. Probably because the young man who said it had acne and bad posture. The mother in me wanted to hug the boy.

"Freedom."

"Adventure."

"Revenge."

"Truth." The word filled my psyche and poured itself out through my mouth.

"So a writer today hoping to pen something that will still matter tomorrow must do . . . what?"

"Find someone good to plagiarize. Like Hawthorne."

Ian Beckwith chuckled along with his audience. "Better yet, address a timeless desire"—he looked from me to Miss Near-Perfect—"with the perfect combination of characters and plot."

"Being born with a gift doesn't hurt."

I had to agree with the fellow two seats ahead of me and one row to the left. Classic literature doesn't just happen.

⁂

I waited for the class to empty so I could keep my foot out of harm's way before I stood and collected my things. It took less than a minute for everyone to scatter, everyone but Ian Beckwith. I'd hoped he would head for the coffee kiosk right away, as he often did, but today he lingered at his desk.

"Ms. Torrington," he said, as I endeavored to slink out of the room, "I appreciated your comments today. Glad you came. I know it was an effort."

I smiled, gave a single nod, and continued for the door.

"Um."

I stopped, turned my head back.

"There weren't any takers." He indicated the small stack of books he'd brought on Claire Ogden Connors. "But I kept one back for you, just in case."

"For me?"

"It's one I thought you'd like. And the least I thought I could do."

I gave him a half smile. "Why?"

He motioned to my foot. "I think I startled you. At the bookstore."

There was no point in denying it. "I'm not usually so klutzy."

"No. No, I'm sure."

Right.

"Anyway." He picked up a thin book that was not part of the stack and brought it to me. "I will find you," he said, teasing. Sort of. "Now that I know where you hang out."

I couldn't help but laugh as I took the book. "I haven't hung out in years, but if I did it would most likely be in a bookstore. My daughters will love the visual."

"How many?"

"Daughters?"

He nodded.

"Two. Becca and Bailey." *Happy and Grumpy.*

"And they're in college?"

"Cal Poly."

"Both of them? Well. Outstanding."

"Thank you." I held up the book. "For this too."

"My pleasure. Need help to your car?"

"Oh. No. Thanks. I'll just plod my way to the parking lot."

He glanced toward the window that looked out on to a grassy

area where a pair of concrete benches were anchored into the ground. They were sodden. And empty. "At least it looks like the rain has stopped. For now. But watch out for puddles."

❧

I stopped on the way home at a little café known for its soups, all homemade by the owner, a bent, aproned woman in her late seventies. I ordered what I always order, a bowl of split pea, with a slice of fresh-baked multiseeded bread on the side. My mouth watered as I waited, and not just because I was hungry. The blend of all those good things cooking together was to the taste buds what an explosion of color was to the eye. Sensory overload in the best way.

On the booth seat, far away from any possible spills, I opened the book on loan from Ian Beckwith. It was a thin book, 157 pages, published in 1956, five years after Claire Ogden Connors published her final novel, *Final Storm*. Hmm. One hundred fifty-seven pages seemed inadequate for an author who had, in my opinion, contributed a hefty share to the DNA of American literature, to use Ian Beckwith's analogy. Several of her novels had been made into movies, starring big names from yesterday, like Burt Lancaster and Lana Turner, to name a couple of my parents' favorites. Awards had been won by actors, directors, and producers.

I don't know. Maybe more could be said in 157 pages than you'd think at first glance. After all, this was the one Ian set aside, presumably his first choice in authoritative books on the subject of Ms. Connors.

My soup arrived and I tucked the book back in my bag for safekeeping.

Thirty-One

"Okay, so here's what I'm thinking." Shawlie pulled an assortment of steaming boxes out of a white plastic bag that bore the red dragon logo of her favorite Chinese take-out restaurant. She clustered them in the center of my kitchen table, along with packets of soy sauce and a little container of hot mustard. "Plates?" She gave me a look that said, *Your foot may be broken, but so what?*

I took two off the stack in my cupboard, then got spoons and napkins and brought everything to the table. We didn't need forks because Shawlie insisted on chopsticks. "For the experience," she would say. "Chinese without chopsticks is like crepes without suzette."

I knew without looking what we were having for dinner. Shrimp-fried rice, vegetable chow mein, sweet and sour chicken—extra pineapple—and two orders of hot and sour soup because Shawlie wanted one order all to herself. I told her one order was plenty; I'd do fine without the soup. Honest. But

Shawlie seemed unable to comprehend that. We never finished what she brought. And she refused to take the leftovers home. The boxes went into my refrigerator, where they got forgotten and pushed farther and farther back till the noodles were mush and the rice was as hard as it had been before it was cooked. Then I'd finally remember to take them out and dump them. Along with the moldy sour cream, the outdated half gallon of milk, and the celery that had turned a sickly shade of yellow. It was hard to maintain a refrigerator for one.

I dished up my plate, then doused everything with a good dose of soy sauce. "Here's what you're thinking?" I prompted her.

"Oh, right." She spoke around a mouthful of sweet and sour. "I'm thinking we fly to Nova Scotia on the Tuesday morning before Easter. It'll take us all day to get there, so that's just a travel day. Then that'll give us Wednesday, Thursday, Friday, Saturday, Easter Sunday"—she counted each day off on her fingers—"and Monday we come home. What do you think?"

"What do I think?" I held my chopsticks mid-air. "Shawlie, I told you I'm not going to Nova Scotia."

Her face melted into a pout. "But that was before."

"Before what?"

"Before Bailey found those papers. Which, by the way—" She clamped her lips tight to keep from saying *I told you so*. I knew it, knew those words were there, ready to leap off her lips at the first provocation. I'd flung the door wide open, but she kept them inside, teetering on the brink. "And before Becca decided to become Mother Teresa."

"It's a roof, Shawlie. Hardly Mother Teresa."

"At an orphanage? Right?"

"For six days."

"That's how it starts." She pierced a pineapple chunk with one chopstick and stuck it in her mouth. "And it means you're free to go with me for the week."

"Shawlie, I don't want to go to Nova Scotia for Easter."

"What's wrong with Nova Scotia?"

I shrugged. "Maybe nothing."

"See? See? You don't even know."

"And neither do you."

"Then come with me and let's find out. It's been years since we went on an adventure, just you and me."

My mouth turned up involuntarily. "It has, hasn't it?"

The last time was a weekend getaway to the coast on the occasion of the finalizing of Shawlie's first divorce, and in fairness to Shawlie it was a divorce she didn't want. She'd known plenty of men over the years, but Donald is the one man she'd loved. So the weekend wasn't expected to be anything more than a genuine pity party, but it turned out to be memorable on several counts.

Bailey was in fourth grade, Becca in third. And it was the weekend before Bailey's big state report was due. She'd chosen Nebraska for her state. Why Nebraska? Who knew. When I left she had completed her hand-drawn map and a very nice title page for her report. She had several paragraph points for her two-page paper, which she would need to write that weekend. I felt awful leaving Trey with that responsibility. But really, two pages, with all the required information neatly outlined, point by point, in the instruction sheet? Surely Trey could handle that.

And he would have, I'm sure, except that it turned out to be the weekend he broke his nose.

Of course I didn't know that till Sunday night when Shawlie dropped me off—two hours later than anticipated. But an accident on the bridge delayed us. I expected to arrive home, kiss my husband hello, tiptoe into the girls' rooms and kiss their sleeping faces, ooh and aah to Trey over Bailey's report, then tell him all about the seagull with the crushed foot, the full moon over the Pacific, and how hard Shawlie was taking the divorce.

My own perfect little *Brady Bunch*. What I walked in on was more like *The Simpsons*.

"Hi, Mom." *Becca was watching television, an hour and a half past her bedtime, and sucking on a Popsicle. Three pink-stained sticks were stuck to the table beside her chair.*

"Hi, sweetie." *I dropped my bags and looked around.* "Where's your sister and . . . and Daddy?"

Becca pointed to the kitchen. "Bailey's in there. Daddy's . . ." *She thought a moment then shrugged.*

I found Bailey crying at the kitchen table, hunched over a sheet of binder paper with little more than the title of her report at the top. Pushed off to the side were cereal bowls with puddles of warm, colored milk in the bottom. An empty box of Fruit Loops lay face down beside them. Dinner?

"Honey, what . . . what's going on? Where's Daddy?"

She shrugged, sniffed, and wiped her nose on a dish towel. "Upstairs. His nose hurts."

"His"—*I turned her chin toward me with my finger*—"nose hurts? And your paper. Is that all that's done?"

Tears spilled onto her cheeks and she reached for the dish towel again.

"Oh, honey." *I hugged her to my hip.* "Let me find Daddy, then I'll be back."

I left my bags where I'd dropped them and took the stairs two at a time.

"Trey? Trey, are you—?" *I stopped as I turned into our bedroom. Trey was stretched out on top of the bed, one arm draped over his face.* "Trey?"

He lifted his arm and raised his head three inches off the pillow.

"What on earth?"

The bridge of his nose was purple and red, and both nostrils were stuffed with . . . something. Below his eyes were black streaks like athletes wear, so that when you looked at him his face looked like a T in the shade of an Easter egg that's been dunked too long in all the colors. If I'd seen him first I'd have been frantic, wondering how my girls were, thinking car accident, mugging, any number of things. But I knew they were fine, so . . .

"What happened?" I knelt beside the bed, leaned in close to hear his answer.

"Bat," he said.

"Bat? You were bitten by a bat?" My heart thudded so hard it felt like a pinball inside my rib cage. "Where?"

He moved his head slowly in a negative motion. "Not bit, bit."

I leaned in closer. "Hit? You were hit with a bat?"

His head moved up and down the tiniest bit. "Bailey."

I sat back on my heels. "Bailey? Hit you with a bat?"

Trey nodded again. "Teaching her to swing."

Of course. We'd signed her up for summer ball, her first year to play. Her first practice was only days away. "When did this happen?"

"Yesterday afternoon." All his Ns sounded like Ds with his nose packed full of gauze or whatever they used, so everything he said was distorted. And an effort. He kept his words to a minimum. "Spent most of last night in ER."

"And the girls?"

"Mom," he said. Only it sounded like Bob because his Ms sounded like Bs. "Said she'd stay till you got hobe. I said we're fide."

"Oh, Trey, I'm so sorry."

"The report. We didit fidish."

"Yeah, I saw Bailey. I better go —"

Trey nodded.

"I'll be back."

The first thing I did was run a bath for Becca and lay out her pj's. Then I went down to the kitchen, where Bailey was still wiping and sniffing.

"Okay, sweetie, let's get to work."

Bailey looked at me with sad blue eyes. "I didn't mean to hurt Daddy."

She looked so pathetic. "Of course you didn't. It was just one of those things. Now let's get your report finished."

It took less than an hour for me to dictate — I admit it — Bailey's report to her. It was the one and only time I intervened that way in either girl's school work. She got a B minus as I recall. Without my help, under normal circumstances, she'd have aced it. No doubt about it.

Shawlie cracked open her fortune cookie, bringing me back to the present. "It would be such fun."

"Except that it wouldn't be just you and me. It would be you, me, Sven, Lars, and Mrs. Lars." I shook my head. "Not going. Besides, I have other plans."

"Sure you do. You're going to pull up last year's annuals and plant new ones in their place, like you do every April. Gee, I hate to miss it."

Those would have been my plans, and it killed me that she knew it. But that was before class on Tuesday. "The annuals will have to wait. I have real plans."

Shawlie turned an inquisitive eye my way. "Real plans? Like what?"

I hadn't completely formulated them, so I wasn't going to say. But I wouldn't have told her anyway. This would have been one more thing for her to laugh about. Like the annuals. "Homework," I said. "I'm going to work on my paper."

She closed her eyes, shook her head, her face full of pity. "Homework. Those are your real plans?"

"I'm going to have to do it sooner or later. Might as well do it the week of spring break."

"Instead of going to Nova Scotia. I really don't get it. They call it Canada's — "

"Ocean playground. I remember. But, Shawlie? Don't let Sven sign you up for a sled ride."

"Good one, Abbie. You're a regular riot. Here." She handed me her fortune. "This one's for you."

I turned the tiny strip of paper right side up and read, "You are about to embark on a most delightful journey."

⚬⚬⚬

It was nearly two weeks before Bailey returned my phone calls. Because of Becca I knew she was in school and, at least to Becca, she seemed to be doing okay. But, of course, Becca knew nothing about what Bailey had discovered.

The fact that Becca didn't know relieved and disturbed me all at the same time because I didn't know what was going through Bailey's head, how she was processing the information, and what she ultimately planned to do with it. Her phone call one Thursday evening made it abundantly clear.

"That's your nasty little secret," she said. "I'm just sorry I stumbled across it, and if I were you I'd do something with those papers before somebody else gets hurt."

There have been a few times when I should have listened to Shawlie, never more than when she said with all seriousness, "Get a safe deposit box." But no. I kept the papers accessible so I could pull them out at any moment to remind my heart not to mourn Trey's death as deeply as it wanted to. I sat cross-legged on my bed, with Ian Beckwith's borrowed book open on my lap. A white college-ruled legal pad sat off to the right where I could reach it when I wanted to scribble down my notes. I stuffed it inside the book, marking my page, set it aside, and reached for my tea. "I never meant for you to find them."

"Obviously." Her tone was as angry as it had been nearly two weeks before.

"Bailey, can't we talk about this? Civilly?"

"What's there to talk about?"

"The fact that it affected me the same way it affected you."

There was silence on her end of the phone.

"That I was as unsuspecting as you were."

There was a snort. "Really. How is that possible?"

Now it was my turn for silence as I turned that question around in my mind for the thousandth time. "I keep thinking back to our last day together, your dad and me. Keep looking for something that said he wasn't coming home. It just wasn't there, Bailey. Call me naive, call me stupid—"

"You're not stupid," she said, grudgingly maybe, but still it was something. "Why would Daddy leave us?"

"Not *us*, honey. He waited till you and Becca were going off on your own. I'll give him that."

"Well, how fair is that, to leave you at such a rotten time? I know how hard it was for you that Becca and I were both going away. Guys are such . . ." She sighed and left her thought unfinished. "I just thought Daddy was different."

"Nothing's changed about your dad where you girls are concerned. That relationship would never have changed. Not ever."

"That depends." She was quiet for a while, but I sensed she still had more to say. "Mom?"

Just that quick I knew what was coming, what Bailey wanted to ask. I could tell by the tone of her voice, the way it tiptoed up on the subject. I knew her that well. I just couldn't deal with questions from my daughter about another woman in her father's life. At least not today. "Bailey, sweetie, it looks like Grampa's trying to ring through. I'll call you back, okay? Love you." I hung up without giving her time to protest and tossed the phone onto the bed.

Coward. Coward!

She'd know Dad wasn't trying to call. I snatched up the biography of Claire Ogden Connors, opened it to the page I'd been reading, and slapped the notepad onto the bed. "Thanks, Trey, for leaving me with this cruddy mess to clean up. Bailey's right, guys are such—"

The truth will set you free.

The thought brought me up short and wouldn't leave. It swirled around my head and, worse, felt as if it were moving through my soul with the beat of my heart. I found myself writing the word over and over on the notepad. *Truth. Truth. I tell you the truth.* I dropped the pencil as if it had stung me.

"—liars."

Thirty-Two

The redbud tree outside my bedroom window was aflame, and the crepe myrtle trees sprinkled throughout the landscaping exploded like hot pink fireworks that wouldn't fizzle out. Agapanthus blooms in royal blue and purple reached heavenward from the meandering flowerbeds like a profusion of sea anemone. Spring coincided perfectly with Easter, which was less than one week away.

Becca was on her way to Mexico, Bailey was staying on campus to work on her own semester assignments. And me? I was packing. Shawlie had called twice more, bombarding me with her most persuasive sales pitch. Her crazy fortune cookie was right, a delightful journey was just ahead. But Nova Scotia was not my destination. I was heading for Chula Vista.

I didn't tell anyone I was going and wouldn't till I was well on the road. I thought of it as insurance against someone trying to talk me out of what most everyone who'd need to know would certainly consider a nonsensical endeavor. "Why go all that way by yourself," they'd say, "when you could read a book with the same results?"

Because I wanted to. Wanted to do this on my own, without Shawlie, without anyone. Because I never had. Not ever.

Ian Beckwith had looked me square in the eye when he said a fan would find it worth the drive. I took him at his word. On Monday I had my oil changed and tires checked, then went home and MapQuested my route, because those were the things Trey always did before a road trip. On Tuesday morning, five days before Easter, with Shawlie somewhere overhead in the friendly skies, I loaded my Honda and set out for my "most delightful journey." My tank was full, my windows washed, and my CD changer loaded with some of my favorites. By nine I left behind the congested Sacramento traffic and merged onto I-5. I felt as if I was about to be born. I sang along with Celine and pretended my voice did not sound like a chain saw compared to hers.

The weather was exactly what you'd expect for a California day in early April. Cool, breezy, with a blue and white Swiss dot of a sky. It was absolutely gorgeous. I'd gone through Celine's latest CD and had nearly made my way through the sound track for *I Am Sam* when my car began to vibrate to the point that it felt as if I were driving over a Swiss dot highway. The whine coming through the floorboard combined with the vibration to effectively ruin what was proving to be a really great day. With both hands gripping the wheel, I pulled onto the shoulder of the interstate, turned on my hazard lights, and turned off the ignition. My upper lip and underarms became instantly wet and my heart flip-flopped like a fish out of water, a sure sign I was about to enter panic mode.

Tune-up. That was something else Trey always did before a road trip.

Dang.

I hit the steering wheel with both palms.

My little Honda had never let me down, and now it was doing it in a big way. It rocked as if it were shivering every time another vehicle passed, especially the big rigs, which, just then, seemed ridiculously abundant on I-5. I took a few deep breaths and forced myself to relax.

Not fifteen minutes ago I had called Dad to tell him where I was going and when I'd be home. Mother had a standing appointment at the beauty shop every Tuesday morning at nine thirty. I called at nine thirty-five just to be safe. He'd said, "Have a good time and drive safe."

Well, I thought I had been.

I sure didn't want to call him now to come and rescue me.

I asked myself what Trey would do. Or any man for that matter. He wouldn't cry, I knew that much, and I wouldn't either, though it would take a massive dose of self-control to keep from it. What he would do was wait a few minutes and try the engine again. So I slowly counted to sixty three times to keep my mind off my predicament while I waited and to keep from reaching for the ignition too soon. After I was sure three full minutes had passed, I turned the key and gave the accelerator a little push. The whine started out low and increased in pitch and volume with the rising of the RPMs. It died down as they did. I pumped the accelerator three more times with the same disappointing results. And if an engine was supposed to purr like a kitten, I felt like I was inside a cheetah with a chest cold. I knew enough to know you didn't drive a car that vibrated that badly.

I reached for my cell phone and very nearly pressed Send, which would have placed a call to my parents' house again. But I so did not want to be rescued by my dad. For one thing, I really wanted to complete this trip. For another, I could just hear Mother and Bailey chastising me all over again for selling Trey's perfectly good, practically new Escalade and keeping my ten-year-old rattletrap, though it was really only seven, with only—I turned the key and looked at the odometer—sixty-one thousand miles.

This should not be happening.

My thumb hovered over the Send button as I wondered what Trey would do next. And then I knew. I flipped through the card holder in my wallet and stopped when I found my road-side service provider. Thank God I had renewed. I called the 800 number and nearly wept with relief when a real live person answered.

I was on I-5, I explained. Exactly where? I looked around at all the miles of open land. Who knew there was so much of it in California?

"Is there a mileage marker nearby?" the operator asked.

There was. I could just barely make out the shape of the white marker . . . a quarter of a mile up the road. And no, I couldn't read it.

"Should I try to inch my car up to it?" I asked.

"Is your vehicle driveable, ma'am?" That was the question the roadside assistant asked, but what I deciphered by the tone of her voice was, *Then why are you calling us?*

"Um, no," I said.

"Then I wouldn't if I were you."

"Should I walk up to where it is?" I shuddered as another big rig whooshed by.

"I wouldn't do that either."

I was about to just hang up and call Dad regardless of what it cost in the way of humiliation.

"What's the last town you passed through and how long ago

was it?" the woman asked. Finally I detected some compassion in her voice.

"It was Stockton, no Lathrop. Or maybe—"

"Okay, so you're south of Stockton, by how much time?"

I thought for a moment. Rufus Wainwright and I were making our way across the universe when I passed the county hospital on Stockton's south end. That was—I picked up the *I Am Sam* sound track CD cover—four songs ago. But I played "Mother Nature's Son" three times, so technically it was six songs ago. If each song was three minutes long on average, I'd left Stockton . . .

"Twenty minutes." I rounded up. I gave her a complete description of my car, then waited. One hour and twenty-seven minutes. That equated to at least 350 big rigs, not counting SUVs and pickup trucks. When the guy finally pulled up behind me in his big yellow tow truck, I could have kissed his boots.

"Nice day to break down." He looked up at my Swiss dot sky, though now it didn't hold the same appeal for me.

"Nice day?"

He shrugged. "Beats the rain or, worse, the fog."

I was in no mood to be polite, and it showed. But when I saw what he had to go through to get my car ready to tow, I had to concede that it did indeed beat the rain or the fog.

"Okay," he said. He pulled off his leather gloves and stuffed them in a back pocket. "We could go back to Stockton or on over to Modesto." He nodded his head toward the east. "Straight across that way. I'd say either way it's a wash."

It may have been a wash to him, but to me straight across was better than back.

"'Course you could always toss a—"

"Modesto," I said.

He nodded. "Okay then."

He towed me to the nearest Honda dealership and left me in the capable hands of the service center's manager. The name on his shirt was Rick. I managed to catch that as he flashed past me saying, "Be right with you." There were eight cars in two lines waiting to be serviced. It would be a while. I went to my car and retrieved the book I was currently reading.

Four chapters later Rick found me in the waiting room. "Ms. Torrington?" I stood and followed him outside. "What you have is a broken drive shaft. It's part of the transmission," he explained, obviously in response to the way my face crinkled in confusion.

"But you can fix it?"

"Oh yeah. Not a problem."

A good deal of tension left on the sigh of relief I heaved.

"We should have that part here tomorrow about this time. Thursday at the latest."

"Thursday?"

"At the latest."

"Oh no. No. I have to—" I pointed over my shoulder with my thumb to the south. "Can't you possibly get one here today?"

He shook his head sadly. "Sorry, ma'am. We just don't keep parts for cars that old."

"But it's only—"

"You want me to go ahead and order it?"

I nodded. "But please see if they can rush it. I'll be happy to pay whatever."

"See what I can do."

"Hey," I called after him as an idea popped into my head. "Are there any car rental places around?" Maybe I'd just rent a car, something sporty even, leave my traitor of a Honda to be fixed, and pick it up on the way home.

"Several," he said. "Ask the front desk for a phone book."

I walked from the rear of the dealership, where the service center was, to the front, where I knew the main office would be, fully intent on locating a car rental business as close as possible to where I was. But as I passed all those brand-new shiny Hondas, another thought came to mind. I hesitated just long enough at one particular model that a salesman locked in on me and came in for the kill.

"Beauty, huh?" He wore brown wingtips with blue slacks and a maroon tie. His shirt had been white once upon a time, but right now it could use a good dose of Clorox. My eyes went straight to his left hand. No ring. I know that didn't necessarily mean he was single, but that coupled with the dingy shirt, well, I was willing to bet . . .

"Nice, yes." My tone was noncommittal.

"Is there a particular model you're looking for? Something you want to test drive?"

"Oh, I just—" I pointed over my shoulder to the service area, then thought if I really was serious about buying something, it was better not to let him know I was desperate. "Well, actually, I like that."

He smiled when he saw the direction in which my finger was aimed. "Pilot EX. One of our biggest sellers. Good car. Dependable but sporty."

Dependable was good. Sporty was better.

I'd been with Trey a couple of times when he bought a new car, so I knew not to appear eager. "Hmm," I said as if I'd already lost interest. "Do you have one in another color?"

He shifted a marble-sized wad of tobacco to the other side of his bottom gum as if he thought I wouldn't notice. "Same features?"

"Well, yes."

"What did you have in mind?"

"White?" Because we always bought white. Well, Trey always bought white for us.

The salesman shook his head. "White's a popular color, or noncolor as the case may be." He smiled at his observation and rapped his knuckles on the hood of the car. "Not everyone knows that. But, hey, I can make a call, see if I can find one and how long it'll take to get it here."

"Would you? Please?"

"You betcha. Come on in and have a seat." He led me into a glassed-in cubicle inside the main building and pointed to a chair. "Can I get you a cup of coffee?"

"Oh, no, I'm fine."

"Well, I'll just go make that call."

He left me sitting in his office, even though there was a perfectly good telephone sitting on the corner of his desk. He was gone less than five minutes.

"Well now, you're in luck. I located one in Fresno, but it'll be tomorrow afternoon before we can get it here."

"Mmm. Not so lucky after all. I was planning to stay on the coast tonight."

"Well"—he shifted the marble again—"your call."

I looked around at the acres of farmland surrounding the auto dealerships. Trey would know what each crop was, but not me. I couldn't even tell what the fruit trees were. Just that there were lots of them and they were blooming.

I was two hours from home. I could give in and have Dad come get me, have my car towed, then find a new vehicle at the Folsom Auto Mall, where Trey always bought our vehicles. Or I could play farmer in the dell for a night and wait for the white one to come tomorrow, then continue on to Chula Vista. But I didn't want to wait. I didn't want to spend the night listening to the sound of cherries growing. Or whatever they were.

And I didn't want anyone who knew Bailey Rianne Torrington or Mother to ever find out how my Honda let me down.

"You know what? I think I'll take the red one." My palms began to sweat at the thought of driving down the highway in a red car. I could hear Trey. *"They're ticket magnets, Ab. CHP's favorite color. You have to blend in on the highway, and you can do that best in white."* His most persuasive argument was that in the countless miles he put on the road, he'd never gotten a ticket. It wasn't fair because, really, I didn't drive any faster than he did.

The salesman smiled. "Good choice. Can't you just see yourself behind the wheel of that beauty? That baby's got a V6 and 240 pounds of torque. It's fully loaded, seats eight, with leather so rich it smells like the inside of a cow." He stopped and his face crinkled right along with mine. He cleared his throat. "I'll, ah, just go get the sticker off the window."

Trey's voice came to me again. I saw his lecture finger waving before me in an office much like this one. *"You never pay sticker price, Ab. Never. Not that you'd ever go off and buy a car on your own."* He chuckled. *"And you don't take the first offer they come back with."*

That played over and over in my head as I watched the salesman—Lou, his name tag said—walk back to the glass cubicle in which I sat.

"Alrighty then." He rolled his chair up to the desk and pulled out the keyboard for his computer. "We'll just plug us in some numbers and you'll be outta here in no time."

"What numbers?" I asked.

"Oh, well, the VIN number, the price."

"We haven't discussed the price." I was amazed my voice didn't quiver to match my hands, which I hid in my lap.

Lou looked up from the keyboard. "The price is right there on the sticker, Mrs. uh, uh—"

"Well now, Lou, you don't expect me to pay sticker price. No one pays sticker price. Besides, this is a cash transaction." I tried to sound as smooth as Trey would have, but a few of the syllables tripped over my tonsils on the way out. Still, I was holding my ground.

"Cash? Well." His eyebrows did a little dance. "You forgot to mention that." Lou's chuckle sounded just like Trey's. "Plain to see you've done this before. Okay then, we'll just cut to the chase." He lifted his brows and blew out a breath as if he couldn't believe what he was about to say. "I can knock fifteen hundred off that sticker price." He sat back and rocked in his chair, head nodding with the motion of his body. "That's the absolute best I can do." He turned toward the keyboard, his index fingers poised to get to work, just waiting for my say-so.

"I was thinking more like"—I thought for a moment and grabbed a number—"six thousand."

Lou choked on his wad, leaned over the wastebasket, and let it fall. He laughed just short of being rude, then eyed me to see if I was serious. "Six . . . six thousand? Well, Mrs. uh, uh . . ." He waited, sniffed. "Well, that doesn't leave anything for me, and, ma'am, this is how I make my living."

I smiled as if I agreed with every word he said. Then I waited. Just waited, while Lou's fingers hung fixed over the keyboard. Finally they collapsed into his lap. He leaned back and rocked a time or two. "Okay. Okay. I know you're anxious to get out of here and get to the coast. Can't blame you there. So here's what I'll do." He leaned toward me, spoke at a level that meant this offer was for my ears only, even though no ears besides his were anywhere near the vicinity of his cubbyhole. "Twenty. Two.

Hundred. Off sticker price. That's cutting deep enough into my commission to draw blood, but I'm willing to go that far."

Sunlight streamed in through the glass, highlighting the right side of Lou's face. A row of stark white stubble a quarter inch wide ran along the line of his jaw where he'd missed it with his razor. It was nowhere near the color of his chocolate brown hair.

"You know"—I looked out the glass, way beyond him, to the next dealership in the auto mall—"my daughter really likes her Toyota 4Runner. I think I'll look around before I make my decision."

"Toyota 4Run—" He squinted. "You one of them shoppers? 'Cause I heard—"

I stood, strapped my purse over my shoulder. "Thanks for your time."

"Well, hey now, wait a minute. I know you have your heart set on that red beauty out there. Let me . . . let me just talk a minute to my manager. See if I can't get him to come down just—" He held his thumb and forefinger up, about a quarter inch apart. He winked. "I'll be right back."

I sat down but kept to the front edge of the chair with my purse over my shoulder, my body language saying *bring me back an offer I can brag about or I'm outta here*. I wanted to smile. Really smile. Trey would not believe this. Shoot, I didn't believe it.

Lou was gone long enough for me to read each of the Top Salesman certificates on his office wall, which wasn't difficult. They were all identical except for the year and were framed in cheap, brown-rimmed glassless frames. He'd been at this a good while.

Lou nodded as he stepped through the open sliding glass doorway, followed by a man several years younger and thirty pounds lighter. The man held a piece of paper, presumably my laughable offer, and took Lou's chair, leaving him to lean against the wall. "This is Mrs. uh, uh . . ."

I smiled, nodded to the manager.

"So I hear you've got your eye on that dark cherry pearl Pilot EX out there."

"Actually, I wanted white but you don't have one. So I'm willing to settle."

"Settle." He chuckled. "I made a few calls, looking to find a nice used one for you. There just happens to be a two-wheel drive—"

"Oh, no. I always buy new. And I do want four-wheel drive. Otherwise, why have an SUV?"

"That's a good point. Let me just make another call and see if there's not a four-wheel drive on that lot. Might even be a white one."

"So then, you don't want to sell that one to me?" I pointed through the display window to the pearl red beauty.

"Well, sure. I'd love to"—the new guy sat back and cupped his chin in his fist—"if you're ready to talk serious."

I sat back in my chair and crossed one leg over the other.

The manager relaxed a bit. "Lou here showed me your offer." He waved the paper he'd brought in with him. "Now you know we can't go six grand below sticker, but I'll tell you what we can do. Let's walk out and I'll show you a nice little CR-V LX four-wheel drive, five-speed. It comes equipped with a CD player, cloth seats, and a sticker price you'll love." He stood. "Shall we?"

I uncrossed my legs and crossed them again the other way. "I'm not interested in five speeds and cloth seats. What I am interested in is that fully loaded Pilot EX with 240 pounds of torque." *Whatever the heck that is.* "Now, if you don't want to sell it to me, I'm sure I can find a dealer who will." I waited for him to resume his seat. "So what can you do for me?" I sounded confident but kept my arms close to my sides so they wouldn't see the rings forming.

The manager shifted his eyes to Lou then back to me, scratched the inside of his ear. "I think we can knock off another five. That's twenty-seven below sticker. I guarantee you won't find anyone anywhere in this valley who can beat that price."

I leaned forward in my chair. "Take another eight off and we have a deal."

"Eight?" The manager laughed. "You'd be taking food right out of this poor man's mouth." Lou threw out a laugh of his own, nervous as a shirtless chef at a deep fryer, but I knew right then that he did not want to lose this deal.

"Okay." I reached for the paper lying on the desk between us and turned it over. With one of the dealer's very own ballpoint pens that I snatched out of a cup on Lou's desk, I wrote a figure four hundred dollars higher than what I'd just asked for, for a total of thirty-one hundred off the sticker price. "That's what I'll pay." I wrote my cell number below the offer and walked right out of the office. I had no idea where I was going, I just knew this was part of the game. Before I could make up my mind whether to call a cab or my dad, my cell phone rang.

"Mrs. uh, uh—"

"Torrington."

"Did you want keyless entry with that?"

I smiled. "Thank you, Lou. Now, let's talk about my trade-in."

Within an hour I was back on the freeway in my fully loaded dark cherry pearl Honda Pilot EX, with the cruise control set at seventy-two and Michael Bublé coming through a sound system that was no less than studio grade. I high-fived myself in the rearview mirror, proud of the deal I'd made—me, Abigail Torrington, all by myself.

I ran my hand over the leather seats and smiled. As far as I could tell, my new car didn't smell like the inside of a cow, but it smelled awfully nice. Like the inside of a new shoe.

Thirty-Three

I arrived in Chula Vista about eleven p.m., six hours later than I'd originally planned. I found my exit off I-5, then followed the directions I'd downloaded from the Internet right to my hotel. I'd called ahead as soon as I left Modesto to let them know I'd be late so they would hold my room.

The air was cool but balmy as I exited my car. My new car. My new red car. With cruise control—which I aimed to use. I raised the hatch of the rear compartment, lifted out my suitcase, and pulled up on the handle so I could wheel it in. Then I leaned my head inside the car and took another deep breath. Lovely.

My room was perfect, with a queen bed, sofa, chair, desk, refrigerator, microwave, and four-cup coffee maker. The perfect place to work on my research paper once I'd visited the Claire Ogden Connors museum. From my third-floor window I could see the golden shimmer of lights on the black expanse of Pacific Ocean. I slid the window open and listened to the breakers.

I sat on the edge of the bed, slipped off my shoes—the cute

pair of Mexican sandals Shawlie brought me from her cruise in January—and let the events of the day drain away. I was so proud of myself I could barely sit still, for working the deal and for getting all the way down here through L.A. traffic, all on my own. It didn't seem like it for a while, but yes indeed, this was going to be a most delightful journey.

After a shower and one more chapter in the book I was reading, I turned off the bedside light. The window was open enough to let the sounds of the ocean filter in. The next thing I knew it was morning.

The hotel provided a very nice continental breakfast, after which I got back into my brand-new red SUV and followed the easy directions to the museum. Which was closed on Sundays and Wednesdays. I meant to call to check their schedule. I really did. That and the tune-up were the only things I forgot. I think.

Okay, so I had a day to kill. In Chula Vista. There were worse things.

There was a community playhouse, featuring *Ordinary People* this month, but performances were Thursday through Sunday. Darn. There was also an official U.S. Olympic Training Center on the southeast edge of town, hence the rowers I'd seen on the bay throughout the morning and the cyclists tackling the hills around the city. It was that or Knott's Soak City theme park. I decided to go with Team USA for obvious reasons. Besides, the training center was a much farther drive from my hotel than the theme park, a fact that greatly appealed to me since my recent purchase.

The training center was sprawled across a gorgeous 155-acre complex with the San Miguel Mountains as a backdrop. On average, four thousand athletes come every year to train. There were rowers and cyclists as I'd already seen, plus archers, bobsledders, and rugby, soccer, and softball players. Athletes were also there to train for luge, field hockey, skiing, snowboarding, and triathlon events. All of this I learned and/or witnessed on the guided tour.

Later I had an early dinner at the South Bay Fish & Grill, seated at a small table overlooking the marina. Hundreds of boats rocked on the water, their masts reflecting the light of the last dregs of sunshine. Each table in the dining room glowed with candlelight even as the sun dipped in the west, a reminder that it was still early in the season. A diner nearby was indulging in something rich with garlic. I shuddered as visions of escargot rose to tease me. I ordered mustard-crusted salmon, whipped potatoes, and steamed vegetables, savoring every bite, then treated myself to a dessert of bread pudding. The meal was an experience to remember, but eating at a table for one was an experience I still wasn't used to.

By eight thirty, after a walk on the beach and a long, warm shower, I was curled up in bed with my book on my lap and a cup of tea on my bedside table. It was drawing to the end of another fine day.

⚬⚬

The Claire Ogden Connors museum lay within a seagull's cry of the water, though the only thing to identify it as I approached the next morning was a small weathered sign on the west side of the walk leading up to the front door of what appeared to be a forties-era cracker box of a house. My first thought in regard to this being the museum of an American icon was, *You'd think Chula Vista would have a larger tax base.* Winnie could have verified whether or not I was right about the age of the house, coming to within five years of its construction. Little things gave it away, she could have told me, like the type of brick used and how much, along with window styles, but I could never remember the details.

The porch on this particular house stood about five feet off the ground with concrete steps leading up to the wood-plank floor. It was painted gray, or had been at one time. The wide railing that bordered the porch was lined with flower boxes, filled mostly with geraniums, impatiens, and silver blue hydrangeas. The soil was moist and the plants free of brown or dying foliage. Someone cared for them regularly.

The window in the front door had nine panes of glass, each the size of a standard sheet of paper, three across and three down. The painted slats of wood that separated them were blistered and peeling, but the glass was clean. A lace curtain hung on the inside, obscuring the room to which the door opened. I knocked. Then knocked again.

After two full minutes I was on the verge of trying the knob or maybe going back down the steps when I saw movement on the other side of the curtain. A woman opened the door and gave me the friendliest smile, as if she'd been waiting just for me and here I was at last.

"Hello," she said. "No need to knock. When we're open, we're open." She stood aside and waited for me to pass, then closed the door behind us with a light push. The lower curtain edges caught a breeze and rippled with the movement, giving off a scent like dust trapped for a time, before they settled back into place.

The woman was slender and stood maybe three inches taller than me, even with my one-inch heels. Her legs went on forever, and her neck was Audrey Hepburn–beautiful. Her hair was short and spiky and was a blend of more shades of gray than I even knew existed. Streaks of white, like natural highlights, softened just the right places. Her lips were lined and colored in, and her gray eyes were enhanced with just the right amount of makeup. Her perfume reminded me of gardenias. She wore plain white flats, white slacks, and a blue and white striped boat-neck knitted top. She looked sharp as a steak knife. In her day she'd turned plenty of heads, probably still did.

She extended a hand my way. "Lee Baker. I'm the curator here." Then she nodded toward another room. "Come in."

I followed her into a small living room that looked as if it could be the set for a 1940s movie. It suddenly hit me. "Is this where she lived? Where Claire Ogden Connors lived?"

Lee Baker smiled. "Of course. We've converted the home into a museum, as you can see. Most of the furniture pieces are replicas of what Claire actually owned, but that sofa you're sitting on is authentic."

I all but leapt to my feet, turned, and ran my hand over the coarse fabric. "This was hers?"

"It was quite stylish in its day."

"Oh, no, that's not what I meant."

Lee laughed. "I know what you meant. Would you like a tour?"

I nodded. "I came a long way for this." I ran my hand over the mohair again. Ian Beckwith was right. Already I could tell it was worth the hassle to get here.

"The little room you came in through was a closed-in porch at one time, typical for the homes built in the late thirties, which is when Ms. Connors' home was constructed. We use it as a place to display printed materials about our author. You are familiar with her work?"

"Oh, yes, she's been one of my favorite authors since junior high."

"I thought so. You'd be surprised at how many people who

come here have no idea who she was. They just know this is a museum, so they stop in. We try to make the most of that first glance, if you will. Let them know just how accomplished she was right off the bat."

And yet she bypassed all of that with me, took me right into the living room, then took me all through the house. I spent a good deal of time in Claire's office, looking over letters encased in glass that Claire received from her contemporaries, including Thornton Wilder, Marjorie Kinnan Rawlings, and Pearl S. Buck. There was even a typewritten letter from Claire to the Macmillan Company, asking them to consider her manuscript *Home Front* for publication. On the bottom of the letter was a handwritten note from one Edwin Barcliff, acquisitions editor, declining the offer.

"Doubleday went on to publish *Home Front*. It was an instant best seller."

"I wonder how long Mr. Barcliff lasted with the Macmillan Company after that."

"Hmm," Lee said. "One might be able to find out."

The desk where Claire wrote her later novels faced a wall that was more window than wood, which overlooked the bright Pacific.

"Inspiring, yes?" Lee asked.

"I would certainly think so." I ran my hand over the light-colored wood of the desk. "Was this hers?"

"It was. The Remington typewriter too."

"Her family was very generous to donate all of this."

"Actually Claire was the generous one." Lee's eyes lingered on the shimmery scene beyond the windows before she turned back to me. "She didn't have much family to speak of. She left a number of items for a museum in her will."

"Did you know her?" I asked.

"Oh, yes."

Very well from the sound of it.

"I've a pot of coffee downstairs. Would you like to join me?"

"I would. Thank you."

We took the steep, narrow stairway back to the first floor. The pot in the kitchen was exactly like Mother's blue and white CorningWare percolator—the newest-looking item I saw in the entire kitchen other than the cups beside it. Lee removed the lid, lifted out the basket of grounds, then poured the coffee. "I have only milk and sugar, in keeping with the era. No Sweet'N Low, no Coffee-mate."

"Milk's fine."

She withdrew a quart bottle from an old Westinghouse refrigerator that looked to be in mint condition. She held up the bottle and smiled. "Amazing what you can find on the Internet."

"Isn't it?" I took the cup she offered.

"Shall we go out on the porch? It's such a perfect day."

There were two wicker chairs and a table off to one side of the front door on the gray-decked porch. A hummingbird hovered over the impatiens, not the least bit disturbed by our presence.

"You're right. It's perfect."

"The weather was one of the main reasons Claire settled here. That and the ocean, of course. Who wouldn't mind having that in their backyard?"

"She was from—?" I tried to recall what Ian Beckwith had said in class.

"Mississippi. Columbus."

"Right. Right. No, I can't blame her for coming here. It's paradise."

"Or the closest thing to," Lee said.

I smiled, nodded, took a sip of coffee.

"You said you came a long way to be here. Where from?"

"Granite Bay, a little town northeast of Sacramento."

"Ah, yes, I know where that is. Gets quite hot in the summer, if I'm not mistaken."

"You're not."

Her eyes glanced at my left hand. "Did your husband come with you?"

I stiffened and my stomach did that churning thing it did whenever someone mentioned Trey. I shook my head. "I came alone."

Her smile was apologetic. "Not everyone feels the same way about classical literature."

I nodded again, took another sip of coffee, feeling suddenly self-conscious. "Trey and I didn't read the same things." A look passed over her face that said she caught the past tense of my words, but I had the feeling she thought Trey and I were divorced. Then it struck me that by now we would have been. Something seized in the pit of my stomach. "I came because of a class assignment."

"Ah. I see." Her smile made me think maybe she really did.

"It has to do with the dedication in—"

"*Final Storm*." She said it with me. "We're not often asked about that. In fact, you're the first."

"Then how did you—"

"It's the most cryptic dedication in Claire's books. I just assumed."

"There was a Scripture that followed the words *No secrets*."

"'For there is nothing covered, that shall not be revealed; and hid, that shall not be known.'"

"Impressive," I said. A sudden breeze carried the scent of sea life onto the porch where we sat. It felt fresh on my face, my shoulders. I inhaled and held the breath for a moment. "Do you know who"—I had to stop for a minute to think—"J. L. is?"

"J. H. Juditha Hilton."

"Hilton. As in *the* Hiltons?"

"A distant, distant cousin. She did *not* run in the same circles, though she did use the name to her advantage."

"What connection did she have to this story?"

"You've read the book?"

"Three times. It took that many times for me to finally read between the lines. I'm a slow learner, I guess."

Lee fixed her gray eyes on mine. "And what was it you read between the lines?"

"There was a great deal of pain behind this story. And anger. This was personal."

"Woman scorned gets revenge. Hard to get more personal than that."

I nodded, looked into my coffee as if it held its own secrets. "I guess this is a real live example of the pen being mightier than the sword. Ms. Connors crafted her very own perfect 'get even' with her lying, cheating scumbag of a husband, and if she couldn't actually live it herself, she at least had the satisfaction of living it vicariously through her heroine." I kept my eyes on my coffee and off the eyes I could sense were boring into me. I'd exposed way too much of myself just then.

"Revenge isn't all it's cracked up to be." Lee's voice was low and even.

"I wouldn't mind finding that out for myself."

She reached across the wicker table and touched my arm with a freckled hand. "What's your story, Abbie?"

Over the next hour I told her. Everything, as if she were my confessor, disgusted at how agitated I found myself with the telling of it. I'd not gotten one inch beyond my initial response. I was still dumping Trey's underwear and didn't know it, harboring not a suitcase full of green sweaters but a trunk full of vitriol that was burning a huge hole in my gut.

I wanted revenge but had no way to get it.

I took a deep, shuddering breath when I finished the telling and wadded all the napkins I'd gone through into a neat ball. "I don't know where that came from," I said.

"Your heart."

Exactly where Pastor John had indicated.

"And judging by the depth of it, I'd say that was a long time in the making."

I bit my lip and looked away. My eyes were too raw to cry anymore.

"Okay. Now I'll tell you Claire's story. But not here. There's a wonderful coffee shop on the next block where they serve the most poetic sounding drinks in these fabulous ceramic cups with these wonderful sayings. You walk in and you'd think you were in coffee heaven."

"But what about the museum?"

"No one will notice if we close early. We don't get many visitors these days." She nodded toward the front door. "The bathroom's off the kitchen. Go in, wash your face, and we'll walk over when you're ready."

❧

She was right. It smelled exactly like coffee heaven. There were a dozen tables in the café, most of them occupied, and several more outside. We ordered our drinks, then took them out front. As we sat, I thought, *I could honestly become addicted to this breeze.*

"Read your cup," Lee said.

"My cup?" I raised the oversized mug with muted blue and brown inch-wide vertical stripes to eye level, taking care not to spill. "'All the coffee in Colombia won't make me a morning person. Author Unknown.'" I laughed. "Well, isn't that the truth?"

"Mine says, 'Everybody should believe in something. I believe I'll have another coffee.' Same author. My favorite is, 'Chocolate, men, coffee — some things are better rich.'"

"Ooh. Are the mugs for sale?"

"Of course."

"I'm getting that one for Shawlie." I'd told her all about Shawlie.

Lee laughed and so did I. It felt good after an hour of tears. "Have you read any biographies on Claire?" she asked.

I told her about the book my professor had loaned me.

She nodded, as if agreeing it was the one to read. "Claire was a different sort of person, not unlike any number of authors I suppose. She was focused and serious, in spite of the fact that success came at a young age."

"First book a best seller at the age of thirty-two."

"Exactly. She was driven all the more because of it. Life was not a party for Claire. Even after she met and married Derrick Connors, whose life was a party, first and foremost. If there were ever two opposites, it was Claire and Derrick. But she worshipped him."

"And he?" I had a feeling I already knew the answer.

Lee took a long drink of coffee. "Let's not get ahead of our story. Derrick wasn't the least bit opposed to being a kept man. In fact, anything else would have crimped his lifestyle. Claire, for her part, didn't mind it either. It meant they could spend more time together, while she wrote and he reaped the rewards. But with success comes obligation. Travel. More travel. By the third best seller, Derrick was content to keep the home fires burning while Claire flew around the country speaking, which she hated, and signing autographs, which she hated more."

"Why? You'd think she'd have appreciated her fans."

"She did. Immensely. But she was very reserved. Hated crowds." Lee shifted in her chair. "Arthritis in my hip. Hard to stay in one position too long."

"Want to walk?"

"Love to."

"What about the cups?"

"Paid for," she said. "You can get one for your friend on our way back."

We headed west, a straight shot for the beach.

"You've not had lunch I'll bet."

I shook my head and shrugged. "I can wait."

"You won't want to, believe me."

We stopped at a sidewalk kiosk only yards from the pier, where a weathered fellow with a long white ponytail sold "the world's best clam chowder. I swear." Those were Lee's words, not his. One taste and I knew she was right. The potatoes were perfect, not mushy but not too hard, with tender chunks of celery and green peppers mixed in. The clams were big enough to feel on your tongue, and the inevitable few grains of sand sealed the deal.

"They're going to have to pry me loose like a clam from its shell to get me home from this place." Chula Vista. Who knew?

We finished our chowder, then ate every crumb of our bread bowls as we continued our march to the sea. "Your hip okay?"

"Much better, thanks. I sit for too long, I feel like a fossil."

"You certainly don't look like one."

She laughed. "Good genes. Where were we?"

"Claire hated crowds."

"Right. Well, Derrick found more and more reasons not to travel with Claire. The biggest, of course, was that he'd found a mistress. Naturally, he left that off his list of excuses when Claire would ask why he wanted to stay home. He went so far as to take a job as a clothier so he didn't have to keep coming up with new lies."

"Who was the woman?"

She shrugged. "A starlet, naturally. Legs and neck as graceful as a giraffe. A real beauty. As you probably noticed from the photos in the book, even in black-and-white Claire was not."

Well, of course that got me to thinking. Did a man go looking for any reason other than someone younger, prettier, sexier? Even with Jina with a *J* in my repertoire, I felt invisible, aligned with the black-and-white Claire Ogden Connors. Miss San Diego might be saline and collagen, but when the package glittered did a man really care what went into it?

"I hope she bombed," I said.

"The starlet? Her career never got off the ground, but she had Derrick Connors to take care of her, so she at least didn't have to worry about"—Lee lowered her voice and gave me a sideways glance—"the casting couch, if you know what I mean."

I did. "So they both lived off Claire?"

"Well, Derrick did earn a pittance from his job, but, yes, in effect they both lived off Claire."

"None of this was in the book."

"They were discreet, I'll give them that. Today, the paparazzi would be all over this and the tabloids would have a field day. But there was a war on, and the press was far more interested in what was going on in Berlin than in Hollywood. They even managed to keep it from Claire, though I'll never understand how."

My cheeks grew hot as I considered my own dumb ignorance. It wasn't bliss. Not by a long shot.

We had reached the sand, and without hesitation we both slipped off our shoes. My sandals were not made for walking the beach, and neither were Lee's flats. My foot had not long been out of the cast, so I took every step with care.

"Oh, I do love how that feels." Lee wiggled her toes in the warm sand.

It was obviously spring break. The beach was crowded with teens and twentysomethings surfing, swimming, and soaking up the sun. Volleyball nets abounded, interspersed with blankets and beach towels spread out on the sand. The screams, laughter, and music that filled the air nearly drowned out the incessant cry of the gulls that swirled and swooped overhead.

I looked around. "Lord, I hope my girls wear more than this when they go to the beach."

Lee laughed. "There does seem to be a short supply of modesty these days, particularly in beach towns."

"A shortage of fabric too, I'd say."

"Oh, to be that carefree again."

I thought about that for a moment. "I don't think I ever was."

Lee dodged a frisbee. "Whoo."

"Sorry," a boy shouted as he raced by.

"Farther up this way"—Lee pointed north—"the beach gets rockier. Fewer people, easier to talk."

We walked a hundred yards or so, then slipped our shoes back on when the sand became more coarse. Another few yards and a large outcropping of rocks, two stories high, blocked our path. The water crashed and sprayed all around them, leaving foam and seaweed behind to be picked up by the next receding wave in an endless cycle. We found a semiflat, dry place on one of the rocks and sat.

"So," Lee continued, "while the world's eye was on Europe, while Claire's eye was on her typewriter—"

"Derrick's eye was on Juditha Hilton."

"And his baby was in her womb."

Thirty-Four

Baby? The word crashed into my heart as violently as the waves on the rocks, because it was the first time the possibility presented itself. That maybe Trey and Miss San Diego . . . Oh, Lord. I jumped up, had to walk.

"Abbie?" Lee was a dozen paces behind me, her long legs working to catch up. "Abbie!"

I reached the white sand again, and my sandaled feet sank with every step. It took effort to pull them out again, like mired pistons, slowing my pace considerably. My right foot hurt like a toothache.

"Abbie." I felt Lee's hand on my arm. "What's wrong?"

I stopped and we both worked to catch our breath. "They had a baby?"

Realization flashed in her eyes. "Oh, that . . . that doesn't mean— I've said too much, I'm sorry."

"It just never . . . never crossed my mind that—"

"Of course not. Really, I'm sorry."

—that Trey had maybe finally gotten a son. "Did she know? Did Claire know?"

Lee looked as if she'd dangled me over a cliff and now I was asking her to let go of my hands.

"You can't stop now," I said.

She looked off to the west, where the sun was only now beginning its afternoon descent in a sky more white than blue. She shielded her eyes against the intense sparkle of the water as she studied the far-off horizon, then turned back to me with a face full of remorse and compassion. "Shall we get out of the wind?"

I nodded and we walked the few blocks back to the museum. We took our places in the wicker chairs. Another hummingbird, or maybe the same one, darted around the impatiens, then disappeared in the moment it took to blink my eyes.

"You sure you want the rest?"

My heart thudded with such intensity that I touched my chest to quiet it, took a deep breath, and nodded again.

"Well, then." She settled into her chair. "Like I said, they were discreet. Today, after the story made the satellite circuit, no one would give a second thought to a celebrity love triangle and a baby. But back then it would have ruined what little career Juditha had managed to attain, and Derrick would have lost that all-important golden-egg-laying goose, which is all Claire had ever really been to him. I don't know that her career would have been affected, but she certainly didn't deserve the embarrassment this would have caused her.

"So she went on to write two more best sellers and see two others made into award-winning movies, while Derrick kept his little family a secret. If reporters of the time had to generate a good news story, they'd have uncovered it eventually, but this was 1945. Plenty going on to keep them distracted."

"But she did find out," I said. "Otherwise there would have been no *Final Storm*."

Lee gave a simple nod. "Just before Christmas 1948, Derrick's penchant for starlets got the better of him."

"Someone shot him, I hope." I was living vicariously and didn't care.

"He was panting hard after a second one, whose name would eventually land on more than one marquee." Lee raised a sharp eyebrow. "The clothier where Derrick worked was part of a large department store in Hollywood. In that department store there was a fine jewelry store. I don't mean the store was fine, I mean the jewelry was. Extremely. Well, he already had one starlet—unemployed, mind you—and a toddler to support, and Claire was holding the purse strings tight, so Derrick's resources were stretched as thin as the excuses he lived by. But starlet number two was still holding out, and he thought a nice ruby bracelet might stimulate her affections. There happened to be a nice one in the display case of the fine jewelry store, and, well, it *was* Christmas."

"So he took it?"

"Well, he tried, but grand larceny wasn't a skill he'd honed. He was arrested—"

"Please do not tell me Claire bailed him out."

"She was inclined, but only until she realized the bracelet wasn't for her. So Derrick went to prison and Juditha was without a means of support. To her way of thinking she had two choices—well, three, but she refused to go that route. She could go home to Bakersfield"—Lee lifted a "not likely" eyebrow—"or she could try to tap into the golden goose herself."

I leaned toward Lee, my eyes crinkled and creases lining my forehead. I wasn't following her.

"She went directly to Claire, with the child, said she was

entitled to . . . *something*." Lee shrugged. "I'm not sure what."

"And Claire believed her? Without the benefit of DNA testing?"

"Apparently, one look at the child and there was little room for dispute, though Lord knows Derrick tried. He was still hoping Claire would pay for an appeal."

"The jerk."

Lee looked away and sighed. "She refused, of course, on both counts, and went to work on *Final Storm*, a lightly veiled account of Derrick's betrayal. I use the word *lightly*, well, lightly."

I liked this woman.

"And her protagonist got even, as you so aptly stated it."

Really liked her.

"The dedication was obviously a slam. Why was it only to Juditha?" I asked. "I mean, of the two, Derrick was probably more responsible for the affair."

"Because Claire still loved him. It was much easier to place the blame with Juditha. That Claire could still love Derrick after what he had done is a testimony to the depth of her love."

"Or the depth of her foolishness," I said.

Lee's smile was sympathetic.

"But the Scripture. What was that all about?"

Lee recited it again. "'For there is nothing covered, that shall not be revealed; and hid, that shall not be known.'" She shrugged. "Like most of us, Claire liked to think God was on her side."

"He wasn't?"

"That's never the question."

"It isn't?"

"It's whether or not we're on God's side. He's the Team Captain."

I began to sweat in spite of the breeze that forced my arms

close to my sides. This was twice in a short period of time that God had delivered me into the hands of a sermonizer.

Why?

"'For the word of God is living and active. Sharper than any double-edged sword,' so the Bible says. Claire knew that up here." Lee tapped her temple with the flat of her finger. "And she wielded it as if to say, *Better watch out. God's going to get you.*"

I crossed my arms. "And why wouldn't He?" Even I knew enough to know He had a thing or two to say about adultery.

"Because that isn't the kind of sword the Spirit had in mind. God is not willing that any should perish but that all eventually repent. With that in mind, the sword is a scalpel in the hand of God, not a weapon for one man to use against another. Or woman, as the case may be."

"You know a lot of Scripture," I said, not at all sure I liked her response.

"Not nearly enough." Lee studied me for a moment, her face tender. "Well, God did *get* someone, but it wasn't Juditha or Derrick. Claire soon learned hatred is a hard taskmaster."

Lee's story began to taste like an aspirin I couldn't swallow. "She . . . she forgave?"

"Just in time too. Derrick was supposed to serve seven years of a ten-year sentence, but his liver gave out before he was released."

"He died?"

"In prison. Suddenly revenge didn't seem so important anymore. Claire put her desire for that nasty little thing in the Lord's capable hands. It was only after she was no longer bound up in it that she realized she'd enclosed herself in a prison far more binding than Derrick's. She felt freer than she had in a long while."

"What exactly did she do?" Not that I really wanted to know.

"She paid her publisher to pull every unsold copy of *Final Storm* off the shelf. She didn't want that to be the one she was remembered for. Beyond that, nothing for a while. She needed her own period of healing. She'd been ill-used, for sure."

Yes, she had. It was time Someone realized it.

"But after a few years, she got to thinking about that little girl."

"Little girl?"

"Derrick and Juditha's."

Not a boy? That brought some relief.

"By then she was twelve. Juditha had taken her and gone back to Bakersfield after all. Went to work as a hair stylist, eventually owned three salons. Did well for herself. Claire found Juditha with the help of a private detective and met with her. I honestly can't tell you why, but she wanted to be a part of Derrick's child's life." Lee shook her head and so did I. I couldn't imagine that for a minute. "She knew it would cost her, but she was willing to pay. Claire provided for the best schools all the way through college. The girl wanted for nothing. All Claire asked for was a month every summer."

"Excuse me?"

"The girl spent every July right here in this house. All the way through college."

I looked back at the door as if she'd open it any moment and step outside.

"When Claire died, it was as if she lost a favorite aunt." Lee's eyes were shining.

I sat back in my chair as a niggling thought presented itself. "You must be the queen of research."

"It's one of my favorite pastimes, yes, but what I've told you today didn't require much research. Juditha Hilton was my mother. But I suspect you just figured that out."

I stared at her for a full minute, not knowing where to go next. "And Derrick Connors?"

"My father. I think I was two the last time I saw Derrick. I don't remember him at all, just that the two most important women in my life didn't think much of him. And that they both loved him."

"That must have been conflicting. How did you come to care so much for Claire Ogden Connors?"

Lee shivered as a gust of wind swirled around the porch and wrapped us in a chilly hug. "For the first three years I hated when July showed up on the calendar. I begged, cried, demanded that Mother not make me go, but she embraced the idea of Claire's support much sooner than I did. So off I'd go every July first, in the private car Claire would send for me, and make the long drive here to Chula Vista. I was sullen for thirty-one days, homesick to the point of despair, and as unkind to everyone around me as a twelve-year-old can be. Especially to Claire. She did not patronize me, not once. If I didn't eat, that was my problem. If I didn't enjoy the books she provided me, that was my loss. Three years we did this."

"Why? What was the point?"

Lee's eyes began to shine again. "She wanted me to know my father. In a way she feared I wouldn't know from my mother."

I sighed out a breath. "Why do we protect them, these men who tear our hearts out?"

Lee tilted her head and raised an eyebrow. "Is it your husband you're protecting, or your daughters?"

Tears sprang, unwanted. I studied my toenails, especially the places where the polish had chipped, and blinked the tears away. Our little hummingbird, back with a friend, caught my eye. Like windup toys they flitted from geranium to hydrangea and back to the favored impatiens. The flower's name is a derivative of the Latin word for *patience* because their seed pods burst open when touched. That's exactly how I felt sitting there. As if all the stuffing was coming out. "All three," I whispered. I didn't want to cry anymore, but I'd held the tears in for so long.

I walked to the steps and sat where the sun could reach my face, scattering the birds with the transition. Lee joined me. We watched as a pregnant cat, white with black paws, crossed the lawn, lumbering with her burden. She lay down on a green patch beneath the neighbor's lilac tree, licked a paw, stretched, then went to sleep.

"The thing I learned from Claire is that I have no control over what a person does to me, only how I respond to it. She learned to live by that and it made her a contented woman."

"And happy?"

"Contented," Lee said again.

That didn't seem so grand. "She didn't write anymore."

"No. She didn't write anymore. Books, that is. She kept a journal till the day of her death. It reads like a prayer book. Lovely thoughts. Really lovely."

The cat rolled onto her side, and even from twenty feet away I could see the kittens moving in her belly. "Won't be long," I said.

"Very soon, in fact. Her name's Belinda." The cat lifted her head at the mention of her name, sent Lee a lazy look. "We share the house next door."

"You live—"

"Next door. A gift from Claire."

"Shawlie would love it, your house."

"You'll have to bring her next time."

I stood, knowing it was time to leave. "Claire and your mother, did they become friends?"

Lee's smile looked more like a smirk. She thought for a moment before she answered. "We didn't share holidays, if that's what you mean. But they were civil, and I guess that's something. Shortly before Claire died she called my mother, asked her to come over, and gave Mother her own personal copy of *Final Storm*."

"Claire's personal copy?"

Lee nodded. "It was tied up with string. Claire clearly meant for Mother to open it somewhere other than here. So she stopped next door on her way home and asked for a pair of scissors. She cut the string and opened the book to a page where a bookmark protruded, and began to laugh. And laugh. She handed me the book, open to the dedication page. Claire had crossed out the dedication and handwritten a new one. In pencil. Claire only wrote in pencil."

"What did it say?"

"'For in the resurrection they neither marry, nor are given in marriage, but are as the angels of God in heaven. Serves every one of us right.'" Lee broke into laughter and so did I.

"Were you ever married?" I asked.

She pulled a chain from beneath her boat-neck sweater on which hung two gold bands. "Twenty-nine good years. He died six years ago."

"So then it does happen."

She nodded.

"Does that Scripture make you sad?"

"Not in the least. There will be a marriage, and we're all invited. I really hope to see you there."

I frowned, confused.

"First John 1:9. It's sort of like the RSVP."

"I have a lot of reading to do, don't I?"

"It was wonderful to meet you, Abbie." She hugged me, then stood on the porch as I walked to my car. Just as I opened the door, she called, "Be sure to look it up. Oh, and tell Ian I said hello."

Ian?

She winked, waved, and went back inside Claire's museum.

Thirty-Five

That evening was very much like the evening before. Dinner alone, walk on the beach, shower, and into bed with a book. Only this time it was the Gideon Bible I found in the nightstand drawer. Once I realized John and 1 John were not the same, I found the Scripture Lee recited. The RSVP. "If we confess our sins, he is faithful and just to forgive us our sins, and to cleanse us from all unrighteousness."

I had to think about that awhile. I knew I wasn't perfect by any means, but what had I ever done that compared to what Trey had done? Or Derrick Connors? Or any number of people who hurt the ones who loved them? I hadn't named my babies Lizzy, Izzy, Liza, or Beth.

Or forgiven.

Forgiven? Well, that was freaky, that a thought like that should come unbidden. But if I hadn't forgiven, who could blame me? I looked at the Scripture from 1 John again. He forgives? Everything? And because of that, He expects me to?

I just didn't know about that.

I turned off the light and listened to the breakers on the rocks, thinking I'd stew over that concept till sunup. Then, magically, the seagulls were calling and it was a clear shining morning.

I forgot all about Shawlie's mug as I left Chula Vista on my way to . . . Imperial Beach. It had to be easier to forgive someone with a face. Right? And the only connection I had to that face was a sweater shop just a few miles south. It was a long shot. No, it was an impossible shot, but one I had to take. Maybe, just maybe Parker whoever-she-was would remember the person who bought that sweater for Trey in the neighborhood of two years earlier.

Sure, she would.

The Turtle's Neck was a cute shop, the size of an average Starbucks, with decor just as appealing and floor-to-ceiling shelves of nothing but sweaters. And rows of racks with nothing but sweaters. And display blocks with sweaters, and only sweaters. In San Diego County, of all places. It smelled of wool and cotton and an earthy candle that burned on a shelf all by itself. No wool—or anything else—anywhere close to the flame.

A woman my age, give or take two years, turned at the tinkle of the bell, offered a perfunctory smile as I entered, then went back to arranging a rack of turtlenecks according to size. "Let me know if I can help."

She was my kind of clerk—hands off.

There was no one else in the shop, so I took my time as I went from shelf to rack to display block, looking over each and every sweater, checking the pattern, the style, the craftsmanship. To my way of thinking, it was never too early to shop for Christmas. I started then and there with a smoky blue V-neck for Bailey, a mini-cable hoodie in roasted eggplant for Becca, a baby cashmere twin set for Shawlie that was the softest cashmere I'd ever laid my fingers to, and a zippered argyle for Dad. A sweater for Mother was out of the question. It would be too big, too small, too rough, too mauve, too whatever for Mother's taste. And this would be a long way to come to return a gift. Even a certificate was out of the question, for the same reason.

And then I caught myself. What was I doing? Every time I saw that twin set or zippered argyle, I'd think of one thing and one thing only. Trey and Miss San Diego. Okay, that was two.

I wound my way through the shelves again, putting things back as surreptitiously as possible. But I wanted to engage the woman, needed to buy something, so I picked up a plain blue turtleneck sweater without even checking the size.

I deposited my purchase on the counter, and as I waited for the clerk I let my eyes peruse the wall of sweaters behind the cash register, the rack of baby sweaters to its right, the counter on which the cash register sat. Its neatness told me the woman who worked here—most certainly the owner—was more fastidious than Mother, and, well, who could imagine that? This had to be Parker Davis, the woman Shawlie had spoken to.

At the exact moment she entered the clerk's cubby to ring me up, I leaned in to examine a photograph in a sterling frame, five inches by seven. There she was, the clerk, a smile lighting up her entire face, deepening the lines around her eyes, her shoulder-length, honey blonde hair blowing in a coastal breeze. An ocean, blue as cobalt, glistened behind her. And beside her?

I leaned in as far as the counter would allow, my own smile freezing in place. I squinted for a better look, then drew back, eyes and mouth wide. My breath caught on the intake, trapped, as if a valve had stuck closed. I couldn't inhale or exhale. I could only stare.

Beside her. Trey.

She turned winter gray eyes on me, drawing my gaze from the photograph to one half of its subject. In place of that engaging smile was a blend of dread and sympathy. A chunk of silence, thick as an iceberg, hung between us. She was the first to break it.

"It took longer than I expected."

Her voice was smooth and enticing as pulled taffy, but each word required its own span of time to register.

"What?"

"For you to find me."

A squeak made its way past my constricted throat. *Lord, oh, Lord, this was Miss San Diego?*

I took a step back, hoping to somehow undo my last few actions, to not lean in to examine the photo, to not have come into this wretched shop at all. I turned without a word and made my way toward the light flooding in through the glass front, as if it were the doorway to life itself. I felt as if I'd fallen into Wonderland again — only this time the Jefferson Airplane "White Rabbit" version.

"Abbie?"

The single word stopped me cold, as if an icy finger had hooked me by the scruff of the neck and refused to let go. It was all I could do to breathe.

"When you called I knew you'd come. Eventually."

I turned, shook my head, kept my eyes on the deep blue carpet, studied the nap, the circular pattern the burgundy diamonds formed, anything to keep my eyes off this normal-looking woman in whose bed my husband had died. Oh, Lord, it wasn't about lips and boobs after all. And that was infinitely worse. "I didn't call. It was a friend." Finally I looked up, in order to ask my question. "How did— how did you connect that call to me?"

She shrugged shoulders as straight and defined as a master's sculpture. "I put the sweater and the area code together. I knew it had to be you. Or, as you say, someone connected to you. Abbie, I—"

The look I shot her stopped her midsentence. "I'm at a distinct disadvantage here. You obviously know who I am, but oddly enough, Trey never mentioned you."

She looked me square in the eye. "Parker Davis."

"I know that, now."

The bell tinkled and we both turned to look. A pair of women, younger than me, older than Bailey, came through the door.

"Sorry, we're closed," Parker said.

"But the sign says—"

"Emergency. Sorry."

The women backed out, grumbling, and Parker moved past me to lock the door. She turned but made no effort to close the gap between us. "This is awkward."

I looked back at the sweater I'd placed on her counter and nearly laughed at the ridiculous situation I found myself in. But had I laughed, it would have been the laugh of one sliding right over the edge.

"I could make us some—"

"No."

"Or—"

"No."

"Since you're here we should at least talk." She took a step in my direction, smoothed her flawless slacks. Her sweater set, I realized, was the exact one I'd selected for Shawlie. I shook my head and swore under my breath. She obviously thought that was my response to her comment. "I just think it might help."

"I should have gone to Nova Scotia. Taken a ride in a sled."

Only when she looked at me like I just might crack and crumble all over her carpet did I realize I'd verbalized my thought.

She took another step. Her eyes traveled to my hands then back to my face, as if she expected me to pull a gun out of my pocket. "I had practiced what I'd say if this day ever came. Now I can't remember a word."

"You're miles ahead of me." We stood another minute in silence. Because, honestly, what could you say? I decided to come right to the point. "Why?"

She was inching ever closer. When I crossed my arms over my chest, she stopped. "No one ever plans these things," she said.

"Oh, I think they do. I think they lie to their wives on Sunday as they're packing their bags to leave for *Dallas* on Monday."

"Not the first time."

"Ah, well, that's a comfort."

My jab hit its mark, I could see by her face. "Trey didn't think you'd care."

She was right to look for a gun. If my eyes could shoot bullets, she'd be a goner. She clearly recognized that.

"That's . . . that's what he said."

"You believe that?"

"Not anymore." Her perfect shoulders dropped. "Obviously, he lied to both of us."

"Yeah? Well, his lie to me trumps his lie to you, to Cancun and back."

She nodded, looked away, straightened the tag on a striped hoodie.

I looked around the shop. This was not the kind of place Trey would typically hang out in. "How in the world did you two meet?"

"He came in looking for a golf sweater."

"Not the green—"

She nodded.

And I remembered. A weekend trip he took down here to golf in a tournament sponsored by Washington Mutual. He'd asked me to go, but something to do with Becca had kept me from accepting. My insides did a belly flop as I realized . . . possibly . . . I could have prevented this? *No. No!* "I am not accepting the blame for this."

"Excuse me?"

"Did you know he was married?"

"Well, yes." She shrugged again. "He wore a ring."

"And that he had children?"

"He was very proud of his daughters."

"Our daughters." The words came out quick and sharp. "His and mine."

She gave a slight nod.

"Do you have children?" She paused long enough for me to think, *Either you do or you don't, and you should know.* "It's not a trick question."

"I didn't want to bring children into a situation where I wasn't married, and I've never married."

"Seems you didn't have to."

"Abbie, we never meant to hurt you. It's not like we jumped into bed that very first day."

"No, I'm sure you waited a respectable amount of time for that."

Her cheeks flushed and she looked away.

"And, Parker, for the rest of our one and only conversation, call me stupid or anything else of your choosing, but do not call me Abbie, Ab, or Abigail. My name is off-limits to you." My lecture finger was rigid as a flagpole and aimed right at her.

She took an exaggerated breath and let it out. "We're two grown women in the twenty-first century. Can't we be civilized about this? Think about it, A—" She fairly choked holding back my name. "We both lost Robert."

I gave her the most piercing look I could muster. "No. You did not lose *Robert*. He wasn't yours to lose." I hugged my arms, digging fingernails into my flesh.

"If it's any consolation, it was a hard decision for him to make."

"Sleeping with you?"

"The divorce."

There was an apology in her voice, but I couldn't have felt worse if she'd slapped me on both cheeks. "There are a million questions I could ask, but I'll skip to the one that really matters. How did he die?"

The hollows beneath her cheekbones looked as if they'd been swiped with a crimson brush. She closed her eyes, shook her head. "You really don't want to know."

And I thought putting a face to this would help?

I put my very unsculpted shoulders back as far as they'd go, walked to the front of the store. And hit my forehead on the glass when the stupid door wouldn't open. I heard Parker coming with her keys and stepped aside. I kept my eyes straight ahead, clinging to my self-control if not my self-respect. She opened the door. "I'm sorry," she said. "I truly am."

❧

I shivered, even though the inside of my car was as warm as Dad's den in December. I tugged off my wedding band, dropped it in my brand-new ashtray, and without bothering to cancel my reservations for the next two nights, I turned my car toward home. My most delightful journey had gone bad. Very bad.

As I drove up the coast, I replayed my conversation with Parker Davis, out loud, changing what I said to what I would have said had I been able to script the scene. Believe me, my discourse was much tighter the second time around, my sarcasm much more pointed. All the while my grip was tightening on the wheel and my temples pounded to the rhythm of my hammering heart. At the last possible moment, without an ounce of forethought, I took the last Chula Vista exit, as if half of me had taken leave of my senses and the other half went helplessly along for the ride. I parked in front of the coffee shop I'd visited with Lee, got two large coffees in disposable to-go cups. They too were decorated with coffee quips. One said, "Given enough coffee I could rule the world." The other, "Conscience keeps more people awake than coffee." If Trey were here that's the one I'd give to him.

I drove the two blocks to the museum, set the cups on the porch rail, and knocked on the door. I know. It was open. Still I knocked.

Lee smiled through the glass when she saw me and tugged open the door. "Abbie, what a nice sur—" She stopped midsentence. "You okay?"

I nodded to the chairs, handed her a cup, took the other one, and sat.

"What is it?" she asked.

"Why didn't Claire write another book? You said she wrote privately, in journals, but why not another book?"

"I asked her that once." I waited, not sure Lee would go any further. Finally, she set her cup down on the table between us, hiked a foot up under her, and linked her hands around her knee. "She said the wind stopped blowing."

I cast her a curious look, not at all understanding what she meant.

"Like when you have a good wind that fills your sails," she explained, "moving you forward, way beyond the storm clouds. For Claire, it just stopped blowing." She leaned toward me, an intent look on her face. "I know this has rocked your world, Abbie, but there's life after Trey. Betrayal isn't the end-all you feel it is right now. I'm certain of that."

"She's not a starlet," I said. Now Lee was the curious one. "Miss San Diego. She's grown-up, she's intelligent, and apparently she offered something I didn't offer. And I don't know what. That's the really hard part."

"For some men, a different eye color or bra size is enough, Abbie. I barely know you, but I know you well enough to know the flaw was with Trey, not you."

And I knew Trey well enough to know it wasn't eye color that had drawn him away. I could grapple with the why of this for the rest of my life—and probably would—but Lee had struck a chord when she said the flaw was with Trey. She was right. He's the one who wandered, the one who broke his vows. If he'd stopped loving me, it was because he chose to.

"I don't pretend to know what you're going through, but not all men are like him. That much I know."

She was undoubtedly right about that too. "But how do you find them?"

❧

It was midnight when I got home. I'd driven in the rain since the Grapevine and was taut as a tightrope by the time I pulled my new Honda into the garage. I didn't have any wind in my sails either, but I had resolve in my heart. Come Monday there would be a sign in the yard. I had a right to get on with my life, whatever that entailed. I made that decision somewhere around Buttonwillow. Shawlie would be thrilled.

The girls would get used to it. And so would Mother.

On Saturday morning I sat down at the computer in Trey's office and wrote my English paper. No one knew I was home, so I wasn't interrupted. Not that there was anyone to interrupt me. The girls were nowhere near Granite Bay, Shawlie was off somewhere in the frozen tundra, and Mother and Dad rarely dropped by without calling. Besides, they didn't expect me home till Sunday. I was never much for writing, but the words flowed as I wrote as concisely as I could all I'd learned from Lee Baker about the dedication in *Final Storm*. In fact, it was a challenge to keep to the assigned three-thousand-word length.

By four thirty that afternoon, after a full bag of Cheetos, four cups of tea, a half pot of decaf, and numerous trips to the bathroom, I sent the document to the printer. Three thousand words exactly. I had to remove a ton of adverbs and superfluous thought to get there, but I wanted to include everything I could. Ian would certainly be surprised. I'd get an A, no question.

What was their connection, his and Lee's? I'd wondered about that all the way home. If she guessed it was Ian who sent me there, why didn't she say so? Why wait till the moment she was seeing me off? Maybe I'd get a chance to ask him before the semester was over. Maybe one day I'd go back and ask Lee directly.

I read the pages I'd written, one by one as they came out of the printer. When I got to the end, I started back through. Everything about the paper was right. The details, the paragraphs, the punctuation. And yet, everything about it was wrong. Halfway through another cup of tea I realized what it was. This wasn't my story to tell.

Without giving myself time to change my mind, I shredded the pages and deleted the file. Then I started again. This time wasn't nearly so easy as I made up three thousand words of drivel. I came up with a name, Jeremy Highfield, and wove a story about a secret that wasn't, because as the Scripture said, nothing was hidden. Only my format and punctuation were accurate. It was exactly what I might have written if I'd never gone to Chula Vista.

If I'd never gone to Chula Vista.

If I hadn't gone, I'd never have gone to Imperial Beach.

I'd never have had a face or a name or an answer. Or the freedom from my pain even those few things brought with them.

Then I heard it again. *The truth will set you free.*

Would it? Would it really? Because I longed to be free. Of the anger and pain. And the fear of discovery. Of more discovery, that is. Could I live another forty years, more or less, trying to hide that my life wasn't perfect? That Trey wasn't perfect?

The phone interrupted my thoughts.

"Mom?"

"Becca! Hi, sweetie. How are things in Mexico?"

"It was a great week, just incredible. I can't wait to tell you all about it. But we came back yesterday. One of the guys got bit by a spider, and PS—Pastor Steve—thought he should probably see a doctor."

"A spider?" A shiver went through me. "What kind of spider?"

"Not sure. He woke up yesterday morning and it was smooshed to his cheek."

"Smooshed? To his cheek?" My free hand went involuntarily to my own cheek, and I shivered again.

"It was yellow. And fuzzy. His face is swollen, and, well, we had to get him to the emergency room."

Oh, Lord.

"So since we're back, I'm coming home for Easter."

Don't ask me why, but I teared up and got a lump in my throat too big to speak around.

"Mom? Is that okay? I mean, you don't have other plans or anything. Do you?"

"No, no." I hated when my voice squeaked like that. "I'm glad you'll be home."

"And Bailey's coming too. We'll be there by ten."

By the time I regained my control and blew my nose, the phone rang again. This time it was Shawlie.

"I'm home," she said, breathless, as if she'd only just hoisted her suitcase onto her bed.

"Why so early? You weren't due back till Monday night."

"A blizzard is scheduled to come through Halifax tomorrow. It was leave this morning or wait for the thaw."

"They schedule blizzards in Nova Scotia?"

"Don't start with me. I'm tired and hungry."

I laughed. "Hey, come to think of it, I'm hungry too." I eyed the empty bag of Cheetos. "Want to meet somewhere?"

"Pancake Palace."

I knew the one she meant. "Give me twenty minutes."

❧

I got there early and waited in my car till I saw Shawlie's Jag turn into the parking lot. She got out, searched the lot for my Honda, and started to head for the entrance.

That's when I got out of my car. "Shawlie!"

She turned in the direction of my voice, then stopped and stared with her mouth wide open. I'd parked directly under a light for the best effect and stood there beaming like an idiot.

She took giant steps to reach me. "Yours?"

"Mine."

"I don't believe it. You bought a red car?"

"For thirty-one hundred under sticker price."

"No way."

So I told her, and she laughed all the way to our booth. We ordered quickly to get that out of the way so we could talk.

"Well, how was Nova Scotia, Canada's ocean playground?"

Her eyes narrowed. "Why do you say it like that?"

I gave an innocent shrug. "Like what?"

"You know very well like what. And to answer your question, Sven proposed."

It was a full minute before I could think what to say. "Well. Looks like we'll both be selling our homes."

It took a moment for that to sink in. "You're selling?" The look on her face said, *Sure you are.*

"We'll get to my story next. First you have to finish yours." I tried to sound tough, but inside I was melting like the Wicked Witch in a rainstorm. I'd been through enough changes to last a lifetime in the past year and a half. Trey was gone, the girls were mostly gone. Now Shawlie? I figured we'd grow old together, she and I, in matching rocking chairs on a front porch like Claire's. I looked for her left hand but it was in her lap. "So what did you say to him?"

"What do you think? Do I look like I need help with my chin hairs?"

I sat back and let out the breath I'd been holding. The tension I'd carried since meeting Parker Davis began to ebb away. I smiled. She smiled.

And then it hit her. "What were you doing on I-5 in the middle of nowhere when your car died?"

And so I told her that too. Told her all about Chula Vista, about Lee. What I didn't tell her about was Claire. I only said it was worth the drive.

"Okay, and here's the rest." I blew out a breath. "I met her."

"The writer? I thought she was—"

"Miss San Diego."

"The writer was Miss San Diego? In what, 1920?"

"Not Miss San Diego, Shawlie. Miss. San. Diego." I waited for that to sink in.

Finally it did. She covered her gaping mouth, her eyes as big as the pancakes our waitress had just delivered. "No way. How did you . . . where did you . . . find her?"

"Parker Davis."

"She knows her?"

"She is her."

"Parker Davis is Miss San Diego?"

I nodded.

"And you actually stood in the same room with her and had a conversation?"

"I did. *And* I told her *not* to call me Abbie."

Shawlie held her fork poised over her plate, a puzzled look on her face. "Why? What did you tell her to call you?"

"Stupid. Or whatever she—"

"Stupid? You told her to call you stupid?" Shawlie looked at me as if I were.

"Not— I wasn't— You had to be there, Shawlie, okay?"

She held up both hands, palms out. "Okay." She sat back with a thud. "Parker Davis is Miss San Diego. That deceitful little—"

"Exactly."

She jabbed a finger in my direction. "She lied to me." I gave her a minute to realize what an absurd statement that was in light of the big picture. "Of course," she faltered, "that's nothing compared to what she did to you."

"Thank you."

We both began to work on our pancakes.

I squeezed some lemon into my hot tea. "The sweater wasn't a gift."

"How do you know?"

"Trey bought it for himself. That's how they met. And he probably wasn't even trying to hide it. It was just in the bottom of his drawer. And you know what I think?" I stirred my spoon in my cup for no particular reason. "I think it's very likely that she was the first."

A grave look passed over Shawlie's face. "Why do you say that?"

"Just the feeling I got when we were talking. That they really didn't set out to start an affair. That it just happened."

Shawlie set her fork down, pushed her plate aside, and folded her hands on the table. She looked at me as one who was the bearer of bad news. "It didn't just happen."

"I know how you feel about Trey, but this time—"

"Abbie. She wasn't the first. Not by a long shot."

I was chilled, as much by her tone as by the words. My face went slack. "What do you mean?" I asked the question against my better judgment, because I had a sickening feeling I didn't want to know the answer.

"You remember the night Bailey was born?"

"Of course I remember the night Bailey was born." My stomach began to churn.

"After it was all over Trey took me home."

I nodded. "I remember." My voice was barely a whisper.

"He suggested we stop for a drink to celebrate . . . as he ran his fingers down my arm and rested his hand on my thigh."

My heart pounded. I wanted to get out of there, to not hear another word, but I couldn't move. "What did — " My voice broke. I tried again. "What did you say? Do?"

"Since I couldn't very well knee him, you know, with the seat belt and all, I folded his fingers back to the wrist and then I back-handed him. You remember that mood ring I used to wear? It hit the bridge of his nose just right. Oh, what a mess." She smiled. "Then I made him stop the car and let me out. The slug did not deserve you," she said for the millionth time.

"And that's why you felt the way you did all those years?"

She gave me a look that said, *Bingo*.

"Thank you."

"I never should have told you. I wasn't going to, ever. But you need to know, Abbie, it was not the first time. I'd bet everything I own on that."

"No. I mean thank you for the bloody nose."

She shrugged. "It was the least I could do, or maybe the most, under the circumstances. You know what I mean."

I pushed my plate away, not hungry anymore. Honestly, the night Bailey was born? I looked at my ringless left hand and didn't feel even a twinge of guilt. "So what's on the market that you think I'll like?"

She smiled again and her eyes sparkled. "Just wait till you see."

Thirty-Six

I rose early on Easter morning, showered, dressed, and went downstairs to start the coffee. Then I set out baskets I'd put together for my daughters, with fun things like CDs and their favorite perfumes. And Peeps. Because you're never too old for Peeps.

Becca was dressed for church when she came downstairs. I knew she would be.

"What time does the service start?" I asked.

She gave me a questioning smile. "Ten o'clock. Why?"

"I thought I'd go with you. It's Easter, right?"

"Right."

Just then Bailey entered the kitchen, still in her T-shirt and pajama bottoms. She poured a cup of the coffee that had just finished brewing, then picked up the basket that had her name on the card. "Hey, Mom, thanks." She tugged open the bag of Peeps and bit the head off a yellow chick.

Becca looked through her basket and pulled out the little

bottle of Intuition. "I love it. Thank you." Then she handed me a card. "It's from both of us." Inside the Easter card was a gift certificate for Dillards. *No Shoes!* was written at the bottom and underlined. It was clearly in Bailey's handwriting.

She started to sit down at the table with her sister and me. "How long till you're ready?" I asked.

"For?"

"Church. It's Easter, remember?" I nodded toward all the evidence on the table before us.

She started to argue, but she knew we always go to church on Easter. She stuffed the rest of the chick in her mouth. "Thirty minutes."

While we waited, Becca talked about Mexico. In superlatives. "Sweetest little girl." "Saddest brown eyes." "Best trip ever."

"Biggest fuzziest spider," I added.

She laughed. "That, too."

"At least he's okay." Becca had spoken to this PS fellow on the way home from San Luis the night before, so that much was clear. "Do you think you'll go back?" Not that I really wanted her to. I mean, next time it could be her cheek.

"Absolutely," she said. And I knew she meant it.

"So what about you? What did you do this week?" she asked.

"Besides buy a new car." Bailey's hair was still damp, but she looked ready to go. "A new red car."

"My Honda died."

She pointed her lecture finger in my general vicinity while fishing in her purse for her lipstick. "Which is exactly why you should have kept Dad's Escalade."

"Bailey, leave her alone. I think it's beautiful, Mom. Let's drive it to church."

Bailey persisted. "I just think that if she wanted an SUV she should have kept Dad's perfectly good SUV, that's all."

I stood and pulled myself to my full height, which was a good two inches under Bailey's. I hated that at moments like this. "Bailey. I didn't like Dad's SUV. I didn't want Dad's SUV. Suddenly I'm into color. And please don't talk about me like I'm in Honduras or something."

Bailey did a double take. "My, aren't we hormonal this morning."

"There's nothing hormonal about it. But I'm old enough to make my own decisions. You, my darling daughter, have some terribly rough edges that need smoothing. And your people skills, well, quite honestly, they need work."

Becca's eyes grew wide and she sucked her cheeks in to keep from laughing.

Bailey opened her mouth, then closed it. Her nostrils flared once. "I get shotgun," she said, exactly as if she were ten.

❧

The parking lot was almost full when we arrived at what would always be Winnie's church to me. The F-150 I'd seen the last time I was there was in the same designated parking spot. I was really glad to be there, glad Pastor John would know I'd made it for Easter.

We followed the crowd into the sanctuary and found an empty pew a few rows from the back. "This okay?" I asked.

Becca shrugged, distracted, her attention on the stage, where musicians in jeans milled about. Pastor John was one of them. Suddenly he spotted us and waved. I raised my hand and waved back. And realized his wave wasn't meant for me.

"You know him?" I asked Becca.

"Sort of," she said. "You?"

"Sort of."

John put his guitar on its stand and jogged down the aisle to where Becca and I stood. Bailey had already slumped into the pew.

"Abbie, hey, I'm glad you made it." He pointed to me, then Becca. "You two belong together?"

I nodded to where Bailey sat. "We three."

"Ah. Morning."

"Morning," she said, low on enthusiasm.

Just then the musicians began to play. "Well, I'd better—" He pointed a thumb in the direction of the platform. "I'll catch you after." The statement was most definitely directed to Becca.

We took our seats and I turned a cryptic smile on my daughter. "Sort of?"

Her face turned an Eastery shade of pink. "I told you this is the church I come to when I'm home."

"Ah. Well. I can see why."

"Mom." It came out in two syllables.

The musicians played three or four songs in the most contemporary style I'd ever heard in church. I liked it. A lot. Even Bailey stood with the rest of the congregation and moved her lips a little, reading the words off a screen on either side of the platform. An offering was taken, announcements were made, then the main pastor, according to Becca, came to the podium. He assumed a casual stance and leaned an elbow on the Plexiglas structure. I immediately thought of Ian Beckwith. Then he began to talk about the Easter story, but he began with the Christmas story, because, like he said, that's where the whole thing started. "Sort of," he added.

Becca and I exchanged a wink and a smile as the pastor used

the very words we had spoken just a short time before.

"It really began somewhere way back in eternity past, but for our discussion here today, we'll narrow the scope."

Then he went on to talk about Jesus as if He were a close friend he had coffee with every morning. It caught my attention and drew me in. As I listened to the details of the last week of Jesus' life—details I'd heard every Easter for who knows how long—about betrayal, denial, and death, it suddenly became more real than ever before. Because it was this friend of the pastor's who had gone through this. And if the pastor was right in what he said, He had gone through it for me. My eyes blurred and I realized there were tears interfering with my line of vision.

Then I remembered something that had happened years before. On Easter. I couldn't remember if it was an odd or even year, so I don't recall which church we were in, but the girls were small, dressed in matching Easter outfits and white patent leather shoes. With pink bows. My eyes had blurred then too.

Trey leaned over and spoke into my ear. "They're appealing to your emotions, Ab. Don't fall for it." His lecture finger was low and under cover.

So I didn't, because Trey had said not to. When I left church that day, my heart felt like an anvil in my chest. But this time, at the end of the service, as we sang about the stone rolled away, I felt lighter than ever before.

And still my eyes continued to glisten, my nose to run. Pastor John, who was making his way to us, would think I did nothing but cry.

"Good message," I said when he got to where we waited.

"The best." He smiled right into my eyes, gave a nod, and I wasn't so embarrassed anymore. He pointed between Becca and me again. "It's nice to connect the dots."

"My sister, Bailey," Becca said.

"It's great to have all of you with us."

That was followed by an awkward silence, one that Bailey caught onto before me. She reached over and took the keys out of my purse. "Meet you at the car," she said to Becca. "The restroom's that way," she said to me, pointing off to the left. Though who knew if she was right.

Bailey was behind the wheel when I got to the car. "We'll see how it runs," she said.

I could have cheered. Instead I slid into the backseat. "We'll let Becca have shotgun this time. It's only fair."

Five minutes later she slid in and fastened her seat belt.

Bailey came right to the point. "Did he ask for your number?"

"And my e-mail address," Becca said smoothly.

Bailey gave her a cool thumbs-up and lunged into traffic. I reached for my handgrip. And smiled. All the way to Mother and Dad's.

⁂

I smelled the ham before we were halfway to the front door. The ice cubes were beginning to melt in the glasses. "Sorry we're late. We just left church."

"Funny. I didn't see you there," Mother said.

"Happy Easter, ladies." Dad pulled the three of us into a hug.

"We were at Winn— Grace Chapel."

Mother made a sound through her nose that, translated, meant, *I fully expected you to be at our church today, and just what's wrong with it, I'd like to know?*

"Becca's got the hots for one of the pastors at Grace."

"Bailey!" Becca and I said it together.

She shrugged. "Well? Am I wrong?"

"What can I do to help?" I asked Mother.

She untied her apron and hung it over a drawer knob for when it came time to do dishes. "Everything's been ready since twelve thirty. Like always."

We all followed her to the table. We took hands and Dad said grace. Only this time the whole idea of grace meant something entirely new. I felt what was coming to be a familiar sting in my eyes and was glad that Dad's prayer was longer than usual, in honor of the holiday. By the time he finished, I only had to sniff once before I got it together.

"Did you see Mom's new car?" Bailey loved to dive right in.

Mother passed the scalloped potatoes, clockwise of course. "That red thing?"

Bailey speared a deviled egg from the relish tray. "It's kind of cool, actually."

"And I got quite a deal." I told them all about it.

"Hey, that's my girl," Dad said.

"I am kind of proud of myself."

"Pride goes before a fall, Tippy."

"Oh, Alice, give her her moment. I doubt that's what the Good Book meant."

"White would have been Trey's choice. He always bought white cars."

I kept my eyes on Mother until she was forced to look at me. "This isn't Trey's car," I said. "It's mine. I love it." Dad's jaw popped once like it did whenever he chewed, then everything went silent. "And I'd love to take you for a ride when dinner's over."

Mother's back went rigid against the dining room chair. "And who'll do the dishes?"

410 | Sharon K. Souza

"We will," Becca said. "Bailey and me."

Bailey frowned. "Why did I go and start this?"

"You take care to mind my china."

"Of course we will, Gramma. Bailey'll wash."

✄

Throughout the afternoon and the three-layer coconut cake Mother always made for Easter, I thought about the morning's service and about the heaviness that had been lifted from my heart.

It didn't make sense. In light of my encounter with Parker Davis and Shawlie's revelation about Trey, I should have been angry or hurt or both. But whatever it was that had pierced my heart for so long was simply gone, like a festering sliver plucked at last.

Pastor John's words played and replayed in my head. *Then you will know the truth, and the truth will set you free.* I guess they really weren't Pastor John's words, they were Jesus' words. I don't know that my kind of freedom is what He had in mind when He spoke them, but the principle sure seemed to apply. Freedom is what I felt on so many levels. I'd never take Parker Davis to lunch, I was pretty sure of that, which meant I had a long way to go on the forgiveness principle, but I was finally free to go forward with my life. To let the wind blow again.

I wouldn't tell my girls, I was pretty sure of that too. This was my truth. My freedom. This kind of thing was on a need-to-know basis, and I couldn't see that they'd ever need to know that their dad was less than the man they thought he was. I could live with that. Could live very well with that.

But Mother was a different story.

"Ready for that ride?"

Mother sniffed and looked away. "No, Tippy, I'm not. I want to sit here and visit with the girls."

"We'll come," Becca said. She jumped up and reached for her bag.

"No, sweetie, not this time. You're going to stay and keep Grampa company."

"He's asleep," Bailey said, as if I'd somehow overlooked the snoring.

Which was so not the point.

"We'll be back in a bit." I stood and waited for Mother to do the same. She reached for her knitting, as if she hadn't heard, but I knew for a fact that her hearing was as sharp as a tiger's. That was fitting. "Come on."

"Tippy, I really don't—"

"If you behave I'll let you drive on the way back."

Mother pulled her glasses down to the tip of her nose and glared at me over the rim. "If I— What's gotten into you?"

"I just want to take you for a ride in my new car."

"I wouldn't do it," Bailey mumbled, barely moving her lips.

"A short ride," I said.

Mother plunked her knitting back in the canvas tote she stored it in. "I don't suppose there'll be a moment's peace until I go."

"Not a moment's," I said.

"Well, then. Hand me my purse."

"You don't need it. We'll only be—"

"I will if I'm going to drive."

It took great concentration to keep from smiling. "Okay."

We'd barely gotten out of their cul-de-sac when Mother started in. "Trey would turn over in his grave to see you parading around town in a red car."

"Something wrong with red?"

"It's . . . it's—"

"A ticket magnet, I know. Besides that?"

"Besides that, it draws nothing but attention."

"Well, that isn't why I like it, but so what if it does?"

She frowned and asked again, "What's gotten into you? You act as if you've got nothing better to do than throw Trey's good money around and call into question his good reputation."

"How have I done that, Mother?"

"By acting as if you don't care one bit about Trey's memory."

I pulled over to the curb and slid the gear shift into Park.

"I'm not ready to drive," Mother said.

"And I'm not ready for you to. But . . . but—"

"What? You couldn't badger me at home, you had to bring me out here to do it?"

I let out a frustrated breath. "No. I did not bring you out here to badger you. I brought you out here to tell you that— for you to understand that— Trey wasn't perfect, Mother. He wasn't perfect."

She sniffed and kept her eyes forward. "I'm well aware that people have faults."

"That Trey had faults, Mom. Trey."

She turned her head stiffly toward me. "You'd think one thing you'd have learned growing up in my house, Tippy, is not to speak ill of the dead. Now I'd like very much to go home. And I don't wish to drive."

"Trey did not die in Dallas, Mother." I saw her eyes narrow, her nostrils flare with curiosity. "He died in San Diego." I waited a moment for that to register. "Presumably in the arms of a woman named Parker Davis. At least in her bed."

The blood drained from her face and collected in mottled

patches on her neck. "Whoever told you that couldn't possibly have been talking about your Trey, Abbie." Abbie? I couldn't remember the last time she'd used my name. "If he was in San Diego, there was a good reason for it. No need to jump to conclusions."

"An hour after I received the call about Trey's death, I was served divorce papers."

She looked at me, long and hard, to see if I was serious.

"Bailey saw them," I said.

"Bailey saw— you told those girls about this?"

"Bailey found the papers. That's all she knows."

Mother stared past me, then lowered her head and supported it in her hand. "Divorce." The word seemed to strike her like a fist. "I didn't know you were having problems."

"Neither did I."

She checked me again for credibility and saw that I meant it. "I'm . . . I'm sorry."

"I've had some time to get—" *Over it,* I started to say, but that wasn't true. "Used to it."

"This can't have been easy for you."

"No. No, it hasn't. But oddly enough, today I feel sort of removed from it all. As if it were someone else's story." I shrugged. "I can't really explain."

Mother's head dropped lower and her shoulders began to shake. She was crying, holding in the sound, if not the tears.

I reached for her arm but stopped short of actually touching it. "Mom, it's okay. I'm okay. Now."

She shook her head as she wept.

"And the girls won't ever have to know. I'd never hurt them like that."

Again she shook her head, and I realized she was probably crying for Trey and not me at all. She lowered her hands and looked around. *Kleenex. Kleenex. Ah! Yes!* I opened the center console and pulled out some fast-food napkins I'd collected on my trip. I placed a stack of them in her hand. She dabbed at eyes that wouldn't stay dry and blew her nose. Her face was etched with sorrow, but I had no words to alleviate it. I reached for the keys hanging in the ignition, to take us home, away from this awkward place, but she touched my hand before I could start the engine.

"The tumor didn't kill her," she whispered.

My forehead crinkled in a frown, and I shook my head and shrugged. "What?"

"Aunt Lizzy. The tumor didn't kill her." Mother's eyes brimmed again with tears.

I really was at a loss for words now. "Then what?" And why was she telling me this now, of all times?

"I found her," Mother said, with pain as fresh as if it were yesterday. "All alone. And they were all gone. She'd taken them all."

"All gone? Taken—" *Taken?* My eyes went wide. Oh, Lord. "You mean she . . . she . . . Mother?"

She choked back a sob.

It felt as if the air had been sucked out of the vehicle. I turned the key and lowered my window. "Why?"

It was a full minute before Mother could speak again. "It was more than she could bear. The rejection. Just weeks before the wedding."

"Wedding? Are you— are you saying Aunt Lizzy was jilted? And that she—?" I couldn't bring myself to say it. But I knew it just the same, without the words. *Well, no wonder.* That's all I could think, *No wonder.* This explained so much. "Mom, I'm sorry. I'm so, so sorry."

"He broke off the engagement when he learned she was dying. Can you imagine? He couldn't have loved her if he was able to do that. He couldn't have. Not when she needed him the most."

"No," I murmured.

"It was more than Lizzy could bear," she said again, the sorrow as fresh as if it were yesterday. "We never spoke of it. None of us. Ever."

The truth . . . the truth . . .

Had begged for release. Even after all these years.

"If I'd only known. I might have been more . . . less . . ."
What?

"It was my decision, the lie."

"It wasn't a lie, Mom. Not really." *Was it?*

"Whatever it was, it was my choice. So that people remembered Lizzy for who she was, not for what she did. That's what I wanted more than anything, her memory untarnished."

In my mind I saw the photo on Mother's nightstand, the one I called the good-bye girl. Aunt Lizzy so full of life. And I understood. "That's what you gave us, Mother, the real Lizzy, not the desperate one. I'm so glad that's how I know her."

She wiped her eyes again. "Tippy. How did you ever cope with this? With Trey?"

I thought of what I could say, if I could even put it in words, and rejected it all. "I dumped his underwear drawer."

Mother looked at me with startled eyes. And then she smiled. And then she laughed.

"And I tossed him out of my bedroom. And I bought a red car." *And I survived.* "Want to drive?"

❧

On Tuesday I took my paper to class, and at the end of the period I handed it in. Ian Beckwith scanned the first two paragraphs and looked at me with those clear blue eyes, in which I easily read his disappointment.

But I smiled as I walked to my car because on a whim I had handwritten on the bottom of the last page, "Lee says hello." I'd like to have been there when he read it. By the time I located my new red Honda in the parking lot, got in, and started the ignition, my cell phone rang. I smiled again because I'd also written my number on the bottom of the page. I continued to learn from my daughters.

"Hello?"

"Abigail Torrington. Every life is a *story*." If I'd not recognized that gravelly, accented voice, I'd have known it was Ian by the way he used that word, the way it sent shivers up my arms even over a cell phone. "Yours is not a tragedy. Not by a long shot. If you promise to keep it in the cup, I'd love to buy you a latte."

I smiled as Sting sang "Brand New Day" on the radio.

And it was.

etc.

bonus content includes:

- ▶ Reader's Guide

- ▶ An Interview with the Author

- ▶ About the Author

Reader's Guide

1. What would you say is the main theme of *Lying on Sunday*?

2. What was your first thought when you learned that Trey had died *in San Diego*?

3. Did you ever wonder if the conclusion Abbie reached regarding Trey's unfaithfulness was incorrect?

4. Is Shawlie the kind of friend you'd want in a similar situation? Why or why not?

5. Abbie was torn between wanting to protect her daughters on one hand and to respond to Trey's betrayal on the other hand. Should she have been more concerned with her own needs and less concerned with the needs of Bailey and Becca?

6. Abbie's relationship with her mother was severely broken. Was she right in trying to keep the peace at any cost? How would you have dealt with the situation if you were Abbie?

7. In the end, it's Abbie's honesty with her mother that puts them on the road to reconciliation. Could this have occurred much earlier if Abbie had openly addressed their relational issues? Or did the "truth" that made the difference have to be about Trey?

8. Abbie desperately wanted to see Bailey break away from her manipulating boyfriend. Do you think Abbie would have seen things the same way if she'd never discovered how controlled and manipulated she'd been by Trey?

9. What significance do you think "shoes" play in this story?

10. Abbie felt as out of place as terrycloth in a lingerie shop in her college English class. What do you think kept her going back? Have you ever found yourself in a situation where you just didn't fit? How did you deal with it?

11. How important was Abbie's visit to the Claire Ogden Connors museum? To the sweater shop?

12. The "other woman" was nothing like Abbie imagined. Was this a negative or a positive discovery for Abbie?

13. Has a passage of Scripture ever impacted you the way John 8:32 — "Then you will know the truth, and the truth will set you free" — impacted Abbie?

14. Of the five main characters in the book (Abbie, her mother, Shawlie, Bailey, and Becca), to whom do you most relate? Why?

15. Does Ian Beckwith play into the personal growth Abbie experiences? If so, in what way?

16. What do you think attracts Abbie to Ian Beckwith, if indeed there is an attraction?

17. How would you have written the ending for *Lying on Sunday*?

An Interview with the Author

Where did the idea for the story come from?

When I began *Lying on Sunday* I intended to write a story about how a woman deals with and recovers from betrayal. At first my plan was to have Abbie receive divorce papers, then find out that her husband had left her for another woman. But then I thought, so much more conflict could be added to the story if at first she gets word that her husband has died—and then she gets the divorce papers and learns that her husband was leaving her for another woman. She's completely torn between her grief as a widow and her grief at being betrayed. There are absolutely no similarities between the two! So that's how the story was birthed.

Once again, you've written a story with a strong and vital friendship that's central to the story. Was that a coincidence or by design?

Absolutely by design. Other than for a brief period in my mid-twenties, I didn't have a close friend until I was well into my thirties. There were some lonely times during those years when I longed for a close female friend. But I was very quiet, very shy, and wasn't the type to reach out, regardless of how desperate I was. Thankfully, that has changed and I've been blessed with several close friends over the past twenty years. I've learned the importance of friendship and how "good" friends (as opposed to the wrong friends) add to the richness of our lives. So I write about friends for all those who have or desire friends like Abbie and Shawlie.

In *Every Good and Perfect Gift,* your protagonist has a close relationship with her mother. In *Lying on Sunday,* the exact opposite is true. Which is closest to your own reality?

I wish my mother were here to see the fulfillment of my writing dreams, but she passed away in 1997. She was always a great supporter of whatever I did. Whether I was drawing, painting, writing, whatever, Mom lavished her praise on me. We had our issues, as does most every mother/daughter duo, but we were very close. Once I grew up and she mellowed out, we found a comfortable plateau, for which I'm extremely grateful. But when I get to heaven she's the first one I want to apologize to, 'cause I could sure be a brat.

Abbie has an obsession with shoes. Is there something you obsess about to the same degree?

Who, me? Okay, the fact that family will read this Q&A will keep me honest. I'm a neat freak. I'm fighting the urge right now to tidy something up. I've always been very particular about the appearance of my home, I guess because I feel it's a true reflection of who I am. I'm not as bad as I used to be, evidenced by the appearance of my office (which seems to collect clutter these days like iron to a magnet), but I still have my issues. I was visiting my baby sister in Tennessee a few years ago, and throughout the week we played a card game, similar to Canasta, called Hand & Foot, which is played with several decks of Rook cards. I was constantly straightening my rows of cards, and would, on occasion, straighten my sister's cards too. On the last evening we were playing H&F, and I was compulsively straightening my rows, when suddenly Laura reached across the table and messed up all my cards. "I can't stand it anymore!" she said, and we laughed together until it hurt. Now I try not to straighten my cards, until inside I find myself saying, "I can't stand it anymore!"

Writers often pattern their characters after people they know. Is that true of your characters in _Lying on Sunday_?

I plead the Fifth . . . with one exception. Winnie was patterned after my stepdad's mother, Ruth. She came into my life when I was eight years old, and she was always one of my favorite people on the face of the planet. As a teenager, my friends and I would often spend the night at her house because she was so much fun to be around. I never think of Ruth without hearing her laugh. And yes, she loved Don Ho and muumuus. And the Twist.

Have you ever had any embarrassing moments to equal Abbie's moment in the bookstore?

Two come immediately to mind. My first boyfriend was a gorgeous surfer boy named Tom. We were in fifth grade when he asked me to go steady. By seventh grade, alas, he'd moved on to a girl named Amy, but I still always had a crush on Tom. The junior high we went to had inside hallways with linoleum floors where our lockers were located. One rainy day I entered the hallway, and just as I passed Tom's locker my wet shoes met a slick spot on the linoleum and down I went. There were five hundred other lockers I could have fallen at, but no, I had to fall right at the feet of not just Tom, but Tom and Amy. To his credit, Tom didn't laugh—unthinkable of a seventh grade boy. And no, there is no happy ending to this story. But I might write one someday.

But my shining moment came as a married woman. A good friend, Ray, and his new wife, Sharon, stopped in from out of town unexpectedly one day. I was making spaghetti for dinner, which was nice because it was easy to add enough for two more. My kitchen opened up to the family room, so as I was cooking the spaghetti, I would get up to check on its progress from time to time, then return to the family room to continue our visit. I sat down on the sofa where my husband, Rick, and I usually sat. I was close enough that our hips were touching and I was rubbing his leg, just chatting away, when I looked across the room and saw . . . Rick. I jumped up and choked out an apology to Ray whose leg I'd been molesting. Ray's new wife, Sharon, said, "Ray said you all were close . . . I just didn't realize how close." Of course at that we all broke into laughter, and we laughed again and again at the thought of my faux pas. But my face burned bright all evening.

What's the most satisfying thing that's come out of your writing?

I think the fact that people who know me—even those who know me well—are discovering a side of me they didn't know existed. Beyond that, I love hearing from readers who find something to relate to in my stories on a deep and personal level.

What do you hope readers will take away from *Lying on Sunday*?

As always, I want my readers to enjoy the time they spend in the pages of my books. In this story I hope they see that no matter how dark the circumstances they find themselves in, there is *always* light at the end of the tunnel when they yield themselves and their circumstances to the Lord. No one loves us the way He loves us, or did more to prove it.

About the Author

S haron K. Souza, author of *Every Good and Perfect Gift* and *A Heavenly Christmas in Hometown,* has a passion for inspirational fiction. She and her husband, Rick, live in northern California. They have three grown children—one who now resides in heaven—and six grandchildren. Rick travels the world building churches, Bible schools, and orphanages. Sharon travels with him on occasion, but while Rick lives the adventure, Sharon is more than happy to create her own through fiction.

Visit Sharon's website at www.sharonksouza.com.

Escape with a good book from NavPress!

Every Good and Perfect Gift

Sharon K. Souza
ISBN-13: 978-1-60006-175-2
ISBN-10: 1-60006-175-3

After thirty close years, Gabby and DeeDee's lifelong friendship holds no surprises. Except for one: Thirty-eight-year-old DeeDee and her husband have decided to conceive their first child. And while the friends believe they have faced their greatest challenge, an unexpected tragedy will alter their lives and relationship forever.

Havah

Tosca Lee
ISBN-13: 978-1-60006-124-0
ISBN-10: 1-60006-124-9

Why would a perfect woman believe a snake? Eve, exiled to a life outside paradise, nears death. As she waits, she recounts the story of her creation and a cruel existence. Revisit the birth of humankind through the eyes of the first woman ever to live.

A Minute Before Friday

Jo Kadlecek
ISBN-13: 978-1-60006-051-9
ISBN-10: 1-60006-051-X

Just when Jonna thinks she's found good news and a good man, both disappear without a trace, spurring her into detective mode. What happens next will test her faith in ways she's never imagined. Now she will take on the city's greatest power structures and infamous greed, all while confronting her biggest challenge yet: her own heart. The third book in THE LIGHTFOOT TRILOGY.

To order copies, visit your local Christian bookstore, call NavPress at
1-800-366-7788, or log on to www.navpress.com.
To locate a Christian bookstore near you, call 1-800-991-7747.

NAVPRESS